ANGELS & EXORCISTS
THE ROSARY'S REJECTS: BOOK 1

FINNELY RAY

Also by Finnely Ray

"Let Down Your Hair," featured in *Voices of Color*

Demons & Museums: A Rosary's Rejects Novelette

ANGELS & EXORCISTS

Scan one of the QR Codes below to find out.

Spotify

YouTube

Angels & Exorcists contains descriptions of self harm, body mutilation, child and religious abuse, attempted suicide, as well as brief moments of homophobia and transphobia. Reader discretion is advised.

*Dad — This book is gay. Like, *hella* gay. Sorry, but you know how it be.*

Maryam Bishop bobbed her head in time with her raucous music. It was the perfect soundtrack for her hurried attempt to turn her Philosophy 101 homework in on time. The light of her screen glowed like a beacon in the overgrown lot where she sat as she rubbed her drying eyes. Why couldn't these stakeouts ever happen somewhere comfortable, like a well-lit, warm cafe? At least she had finally figured out how use her phone as a Wi-FI hotspot. A mumble caught her ear from beyond her music. She slid her headphones down around her neck, looking up to meet her godfather's dark, stony gaze.

She met his annoyance with a coy smile. "Did you say something, Zack?"

"I told you to turn that down," Zackary Bishop snapped. "You're going to blow out your eardrums and you're distracting me."

Maryam snorted and studied the distant decrepit church surrounded by black vans. A river of people, some in cassocks, others in body armor, had poured out of the vans shortly after Maryam and Zackary had arrived, swarming the place like a dark hive of divine judgement, but the building had been quiet for nearly thirty minutes now. "What exactly am I distracting you from, Zackary? The raid's pretty much done."

Zackary folded his arms and leaned against the lone oak tree they had chosen for their outpost, his dark deep-set eyes glued to the decrepit stone building. "Don't know, but I'd rather not miss it."

Maryam snorted and went back to her assignment. "Try-hard."

Zackary snapped a twig off a low-hanging branch and threw it at her as she typed. "You could have stayed home, you know."

"And leave you to have all the fun?" Maryam untangled the twig from her red curls. "Plus, I want to see the look on those bastards' faces when you tell them, *I told you so.*"

Zackary sighed. "This is about making sure everyone's safe, not my ego."

"That's why you've got me. I'm here for both our egos."

Zackary said nothing. He only readjusted his stance against the tree trunk, but Maryam knew he had rolled his eyes. After knowing someone for twenty one years, it was nearly impossible *not* to know someone that well.

He was right, though. Maryam could have stayed home. Hell, they *both* could have stayed home. The Rosary Order, Zackary's employer, left him behind to hunt dangerous paranormal entities all the time, leaving him to investigate reports of old Catholic ladies seeing Jesus in their oatmeal. Zackary usually bit his tongue about missing the action, but this case had made him panic. At least, he had panicked in the way Maryam knew him to panic, which was to deep clean the apartment, polish every inch of stainless steel in the kitchen, and try to calm himself by drinking chamomile tea by the gallon. Maryam had been about to kick him out when he finally announced he was going to stake out the site. If the Order didn't need him, great. If they did, he would be right there. The plan had brought Maryam her own waive of panic and she had nagged until Zackary had allowed her to come.

She didn't like the idea of Zackary disobeying the Order on his own. They might have employed him, but exorcists didn't take kindly to demons butting into their business.

Maryam shivered in the early October chill. She pulled her coat tighter around her body and cursed herself for not bringing a thicker hat. She had crocheted more than plenty over the last few years. And she should have known better after growing up here in Detroit—she knew how quickly autumn went from comfortably cool to biting cold. She glanced up at Zackary, who had only thrown on a sweater and tied back his shoulder-length platinum hair, exposing his face and neck to the elements.

Maryam snuggled against Zackary's leg, desperate for the slightest trace of warmth. "How are you not cold?"

A small smirk tugged at Zackary's lips. "Hell beasts don't exactly feel the elements like mortals."

Maryam glanced up at him with an eyebrow raised. "I don't think 'hell beasts' have an affinity for herbal tea and podcasts either, so let's ease up on the hyperbole."

She'd heard Zackary call himself all sorts of malicious things over the years: hell beast, defiler, deceiver, just to name a few. Not a single one fit the being she'd grown up knowing as her godfather. The worst Maryam could ever say of him was that he was grumpy. Crotchety even, despite the fact that he seemed frozen in his early thirties. He had never been any of the other nasty things he called himself, even though he had been summoned from Hell. Whoever had given him the name Zaphriel the Treacherous must have been high as fuck, because Maryam couldn't imagine her godfather being anything of the sort.

Zackary fiddled with a loose string on his shirt. "You've read too much of the Bible. Being a demon doesn't mean one must remain uncultured."

Maryam saved her assignment and opened a web browser. "I'm telling Aunt Sarah that you told me to stop reading the Bible."

"Don't go twisting my words."

BANG

Maryam's head snapped up from the screen to see a man stumble out of a back door of the church and sprint across the lot. His fractured, howling voice sent a chill through Maryam too deep to be from the cold. It sounded as if the man were fractured inside—two entities fighting for control of strained, dry vocal cords.

Maryam's stomach churched. She'd prayed for years never to hear a voice like that again.

The command in Zackary's voice brought her back to the presence. "Maryam!"

She submitted the assignment, snapped the laptop shut, and dug out a pile of glass bulbs from her backpack. Inside was holy water, cuts of herbs, flecks of crystals, and small carved stones that Maryam wouldn't be able to decipher even in daylight. She didn't need to, though. She knew the charms would work and that was enough.

The chill died away, replaced by the fiery heat of pumping muscles and laboring lungs as she sprinted after the man. The distance closed quickly thanks to her long legs and athleticism. Her speed was nothing compared to Zackary, though, and he overtook her in seconds, sealing the man's fate. He might not have been a hell beast, but Zackary was still something Maryam would rather not see running full speed at her in the dark, thanks to his towering height and herculean build.

The man shrieked as Zackary tackled him to the ground. Maryam went to work with the charms, dropping them every few feet until she'd completed a wide circle around the two. The man continued to scream until she'd dropped the last charm.

Zackary and the man evaporated before Maryam's eyes as the last orb hit the ground, leaving only scraggly grass, the chilly wind, and the distant hum of I-75. Maryam allowed herself a proud smile at Zackary's handy work—the charms were an invention all his own—then braced herself to enter the cloaked circle.

She took a deep breath and crossed the line. The barrier tickled her skin like static and the screaming began again, providing a descant for Zackary's prayers as he pinned the man with his legs and wrestled a crucifix and flask from his coat pockets.

"Carry our prayers up to God's throne, that the mercy of the Lord may quickly come and lay hold of the beast, the serpent of old, Satan, and his demons—"

"You filthy whore!" screamed the man, clawing up at Zackary's face. Maryam inched closer and saw that his nails were chipped and jagged, his hands and arms streaked dark with dried blood and dirt. "Even Jezebel would call you a slut, you traitor!" He spat a mix of saliva and blood into Zackary's face.

Zackary snarled and splashed the man with holy water from the flask, making him howl.

"Tell me your name and this can end," Zackary growled. The man clawed at Zackary's eyes. He pinned the man to the grass. "I'm not playing with you. Your name. Now."

A wicked, bloody grin spread across the man's face. "It's up your ass, alongside the Church's—"

Zackary pressed the crucifix against the man's forehead, making him scream as skin sizzled. Maryam gagged at the smell of burning flesh.

Zackary pulled away the crucifix. "Something tells me the prayers won't work if I call you '*Up Your Ass,*' so I'll ask one more time. What is your name?"

The man glared up at Zackary with yellowed eyes. "They're going to chain you right next to Judas when you get back down there."

"Wrong answer." Zackary brought the crucifix close again.

"No, no, no!" the man cried. "I am Gall, servant of Beelzebub. He sent us to find Azazel's child. All the lords have sent their messengers, for Hell grows restless for the new dawn."

Shock snuck onto Zackary's face, but disappeared again in a blink. "Tell them that the kid's dead. Has been for years. If they were alive, they would have turned up by now."

Gall sneered. "As if I'll believe the words of the Church's bitch."

Zackary splashed him with holy water again, drawing out more shrieks. "*Hear this prayer, Oh Lord, our God, that your mercy may quickly come and lay hold of the beast, the serpent of old, Satan and his demons, casting him into chains into the abyss. Send the Devil's servant, Gall, back to the realm of darkness and gnashing of teeth.*"

"Don't send me back!" Gall wailed. "They will rip me apart!"

"*And restore this mortal soul to the glory found only in your salvation.*"

"They will turn on you! They will devour you!"

"*I beg of You to hear the prayer of your fallen servant, Zaphriel the Treacherous, once a servant in your court, and count this act amongst my penance, Oh Lord.*"

The man's shrieks grew to an ear-splitting decibel.

"*In the name of the Father, Son, and Holy Spirit, amen.*"

The man gave out one final scream, then went deathly silent. Maryam held her breath.

Zackary pulled a flashlight from his pocket and opened the man's eyes one at a time, then lowered his ear to his chest. He sat up straight and announced, "He's fine." Zackary gathered up his tools and got to his feet. "Well, he'll *be* fine. I don't know anyone who walks away from a demonic possession completely 'fine.'" He turned towards Maryam and began walking her way. "You okay?"

"Yeah. I've discovered that fifty feet is the perfect distance to witness an exorcism without risking any sort of vicarious trauma."

Zackary snorted. "Noted. I'll be sure to tell the research team at headquarters."

Maryam grimaced at the blood speckled across Zackary's face. "He got you good." She dug a crumbled, but clean, fast-food napkin from her pocket. "Here."

"Thank you." Zackary scrubbed his face. "Always with the spitting. Why do they always resort to spitting? Demonic possession doesn't work like the flu."

"Zack?"

"Hm?"

Maryam chewed her bottom lip. "Does it ever get to you? The things they call you."

Zackary paused, then gave Maryam a wry smile. "I hardly even notice anymore. Insults tend to lose their sting after you've suffered torture at the hands of the kings and dukes of Hell."

Maryam continued to frown. "Did he mean what he said about you being tortured again when you go back?"

"Absolutely."

Maryam froze, her heart speeding up in her chest.

Zackary scowled at dirty napkin one final time and shoved it in his pocket. He caught the look on Maryam's face and shifted his expression into a warm smile. He leaned in slightly and placed his hand on Maryam's head. She knew it should annoy her, but it reminded her of a time when the world made sense, even if it had still been filled with exorcisms and demons.

"Don't you worry about Hell," Zackary said. "They'd torture me whether I had been summoned to be your godfather or not. Coming up here to make sure your mother's possession didn't leave a mark on you was a welcome reprieve. Those bastards couldn't use you against me if they wanted to."

"How can you be so calm about it?"

Zackary shrugged and pulled away. "After a few millennia, you learn to make your peace where you can. Besides, maybe I'll get lucky and this exorcism gig will actually save my soul."

Maryam studied Zackary, looking for a crack in his armor, something that told her that he knew what bullshit his words were, at least the part about making peace with being tortured for all eternity by the demons he had betrayed during Heaven's War. She wasn't surprised when she found nothing, though. Twenty-one years and she'd only ever seen Zackary break when her cousin, Matthew, had died in an exorcism gone wrong, but even then, it had been the same grief she had seen in everyone.

The same grief she still saw in herself.

Zackary's dark eyes darted across her face. "Are you sure you're okay?"

"I said I was, wasn't I?"

Zackary folded his arms. "The truth can prick a finger—"

"Or slice an artery." Maryam rolled her eyes. "I know, Confucius. I really am okay." She tucked her shaking hands under her arms, refusing to admit the tremors were from anything other than the cold.

Zackary opened his mouth to chastise her, but his gaze darted past her shoulder. Whatever it was destroyed any sense of ease he had. "Oh, look. The Order is doing their job after all."

Maryam turned to see three figures clad in black running their direction from the abbey, two men and one woman, from the look of it. "Should I keep the charms up and make them work to find us?"

Zackary flashed his goddaughter a stern look. "Don't you dare. Take them down."

Maryam wrinkled her nose. "You're no fun."

"It's not my job to be fun."

Maryam stuck out her tongue, marched over to the nearest charm, then crossed the boarder and waved to the three figures to get their attention. She could now tell that all three of them wore cassocks, both the men and the woman. They did a double take as they spotted her, eyes wide and bewildered as she appeared out of thin air.

The tallest man spoke first. "Maryam? What are you doing out here?"

Maryam racked her brain to place the exorcist's fair features. This was Samuel Davis, a classmate from Maryam's days at St. Mary's Interdenominational Academy. They hadn't been friends, but he'd never bullied her and had always pulled his fair share when they'd had projects together, so she decided to play nice.

Maryam picked up the orb at her foot, bringing down the charmed barrier, revealing Zackary and the man on the ground. "I think we found something of yours."

All three pairs of eyes bulged. Samuel stuttered, trying to find the words to properly respond to the scene before him. Maryam couldn't really blame any of them. Zackary had been performing exorcisms for the Order for nineteen years, but few had the privilege to witness it first hand. She watched them closely as they approached Zackary while she collected the rest of the charms, her muscles taunt in case she had to throw herself between him and the exorcists. It wasn't likely to do much, but at least it would be something.

Zackary finally broke the silence. "He'll be okay. And the demon's already been taken care of. I assume you have medical staff on the way?"

Samuel's mouth flopped a few more times before he managed to reply. "Y-Yeah. Should be here any minute."

"Have all the other victims been accounted for?"

"One more escaped, but we've got a team working on it, and we managed to bag all the cult members."

Zackary nodded. "Do you know which way the other victim went? I could probably help if—"

"Hold up." The other man, a short, stocky brunette Maryam didn't recognize, stepped forward, placing himself between Zackary and Samuel. "You're not a part of this. Neither one of you has authorization to be here." He glared daggers at Zackary. "*Especially* you."

Rage flared in Maryam's chest as she came to Zackary's side, charms gathered in her hands as she placed herself a step ahead of him. "I'm sorry, who are you?"

The man turned on her, his expression still hostile. "Moses Williams. I'm one of the exorcists actually assigned to this operation."

The young woman massaged her temple. "Exorcist in *training*, Mo."

Maryam snorted. "Get a leash for your puppy, Sam. He's going to get hurt."

Moses' expression turned vicious. "And who exactly are *you*?"

Samuel cut in as Maryam opened her mouth. "Enough." He shot Moses a withering look. "Thank you for the help, you two, but Mo's right." He turned back to Zackary. "We have this under control. It's best you two go home before any of the higher-ups notice you." His gaze shifted to the possession victim. "Or you wind up in our report. That's bound to invite questions."

"Indeed, it is." Zackary's gaze darted across Samuel's face. "At least tell me the ritual failed."

Samuel gave him a sympathetic smile. "We caught it in time. The cult only managed to possess a few people with low-ranking demons, like your friend over there." He motioned to the man on the ground. "We broke it up before they could summon Beelzebub."

Tension melted from Zackary's shoulders. "Thank God."

Moses scoffed. Maryam's hands tightened around the charms as she glared at him.

Zackary squeezed her shoulder. "We'll be on our way, then." He pushed her forward and hissed, "March," as he guided her back towards their oak tree. "Always a pleasure, Samuel."

"Have a good night, Zackary. Maryam."

Maryam managed a quick wave as Zackary hauled her away.

"Word of advice, Maryam." He dropped his hand as they neared their post. "If you really want to defend me from the Rosary Order, maybe don't go picking fights with their underlings at the first provocation."

"I wasn't picking a fight," Maryam argued, putting the charms in her backpack. "I was establishing dominance."

Zackary barked a laugh, one of his rare genuine ones. "Is that what that was?"

"Oh, fuck off." Maryam slipped the bag onto her back. "Next time I'm leaving you to the wolves."

Zackary gave her a dry, amused smile as he put on his helmet. "Get on the bike, Maryam." He tossed her the spare.

Maryam caught it with an *oof* as it collided with her gut and glared at Zackary's broad, muscular shoulders, despite her sense of relief. Quips aside, she was glad he was alright. They had been lucky that it had been Samuel who turned them away. Plenty of Order members were waiting for Zackary to step out of line so that they could throw him back to Hell. The thought made her hold him tight as she got on the bike behind him. She savored the warmth that radiated through his jacket, grateful for him, despite how annoying he could be.

The wind grew violent, and the buildings grew tall as Zackary drove them through the heart of Detroit, then into midtown, where locals and Wayne State students roamed and bar hopped in the freedom of a

Friday night. He pulled along the curb beside an early 20th century storefront that bustled inside with happy customers and laughing regulars. The windows glowed with retro incandescent bulbs as a neon sign in the window labeled the place as *Ectoplasm: Coffee and Spirits*.

Zackary steadied the bike and lifted his visor. "Go get ready while I park." He checked his watch. "You're gonna be late as it is. Alex is going to have your head."

"Oh, please." Maryam hopped off the bike and headed for the front door. "After facing down a demon, Alex is nothing."

"Excuse you," Zackary called after her, "*I* was the one facing down the demon."

Maryam turned to shrug, walking backwards. "Eh. Details." She grinned as Zackary shook his head, then turned back around to walk through the front door, back into the warmth of home, the beat of her life, and the lie that her hands weren't still shaking.

Peter plopped on the couch as gently as he could, weary of the mug of tea in one hand and the monstrously thick book in the other, and settled in with a smile on his face. The book store below his apartment was in order, the apartment around him was unpacked, and his sister, Wendy, had gone to bed after complaining about a headache for the better half of an hour. As a result, Peter found himself left to his own devices for the evening. He took a deep breath laced with the scent of hibiscus and old pages as he opened the book. It was the deepest breath he had taken in months, now that he thought about it. He'd been so busy since his aunt had asked him to help with the store that even the act of breathing felt like a luxury sometimes.

He started at the beginning for what must have been the millionth time. He'd reread this old copy of *The Fellowship of the Ring* so many times that the first page was ingrained in him. Visiting the Shire felt like visiting his grandparents' house: safe, bright, joyful, where all you had to do to be considered enough was remember your table manners.

But then his dead father spoke to him fifteen pages in, catching Peter off guard.

In the left hand corner there was an arrow pointed at a crease made over a decade ago. Beneath it, written with the exasperation that laces the notes of all disappointed English teachers, were the words, *We do not dogear books in this family.*

Despite the shock, despite the ache that followed, Peter laughed to himself. The day he'd found that note had been a good one, right in the middle of a family road trip. The argument about what was worse, writing in books or dogearing their pages, had entertained the family across the entire drive home from the Mackinac Bridge.

Peter's throat tightened as he stared at the words. His eyes blurred, preventing him from reading any further. He cursed under his breath as he slammed the book shut, taking his mug of tea with him as he walked to the windows overlooking Detroit's Midtown. He took a seat on the window sill and surveyed his empty apartment.

The contentment he'd felt mere moments ago melted to guilt because how dare he celebrate opening a new chapter in the book store? How dare he not keep his father in the front of his mind when this place had been his? It didn't matter if Aunt Jude had bought the store below. It didn't matter that Adam Bailey had never lived in the apartment above it—this place still belonged to him.

It had to. What else would Peter have of his father if it didn't?

Peter massaged his temple, wishing Wendy was awake or that he could at least call his mother, but odds were that she was elbow-deep in some poor schmuck who had been rushed to the ER. Even if she wasn't, Peter wasn't sure how available she'd be. She hid it well, but Peter knew that Eliza Bailey hadn't taken the death of her husband well. Sometimes Peter wondered if his mother was throwing herself into work not only for the distraction, but as a way to glimpse her husband beyond the vale in the moments when she saved others from death's grasp.

A shriek of laughter drew Peter's attention to the street below. He watched as a group of girls, college students, probably, drunkenly stumbled into a storefront labeled *Ectoplasm: Coffee and Spirits* in green neon. His gaze lingered on the sign. He'd meant to stop by eventually, but moving in and assuring his very frazzled, very pregnant aunt that he could handle the store had taken up most of his time.

He glanced around the empty apartment again. It suddenly felt too small. If Peter didn't get out of the quiet, it would eat him alive. Besides, Wendy was old enough to sleep in the apartment alone.

He chugged his tea, put the mug in the sink and wrote his sister a note before heading out the door with a random, worn paper-back in his hand instead of *The Fellowship.*

Warm, honey light and faint chatter radiated from the bar. Peter was greeted with the interlacing smells of coffee and hops. He flagged down a pink-haired bartender who gave him a skeptical look. Peter noted the "They/Them" pin on their black T-shirt.

"Hey there." He scanned the menu written in chalk. "Anything in particular you recommend? I'm pretty new to the world of micro-brews."

"ID?" the bartender asked a bit tersely.

Peter dug it out of his wallet and handed it over, unsure whether to be complimented or insulted that the bartender studied it with such scrutiny. As they handed it back, their demeanor lightened, and they chuckled.

"That explains it." They pointed to the blue, white and pink enamel pin on Peter's jacket. "You trans guys always have such baby faces."

"Okay, rude." A smile broke over Peter's face as he put away his license. "I've been told my sad attempts at growing a beard only makes it worse."

"First drink is on me if you don't tell my boss I was ready to give you shit."

"Nah, it's fine." Peter leaned on the counter to study the menu again, trying to remember what the hell an IPA was. "I'm still going to need that recommendation, though."

"I got just the thing. Be right back."

Peter took a seat as the bartender walked away and pulled out his phone to study himself in the camera. Did he really look that young? His tawny olive face was rounder than he would have liked, and he couldn't bring himself to cut his thick, dark curls short. Even his recent low fade had been pushing it. He supposed there were worse things than being mistaken for a teenager, though. He couldn't remember the last time someone had called him "Ma'am," at least. He shoved his phone back in his pocket as the bartender came back.

"You seem like a cream ale kind of guy," they said, placing a glass full of amber, fizzing beer in front of him. "And I'm serious." They pointed at him, blue eyes peering over the rim of bright red glasses. "This one's on me."

Peter lifted his hands in surrender. "If you say so." He took a sip of the foam, finding it sweet and earthy. "Don't gotta twist my arm."

The front door flew open, bringing with it a burst of cold air.

The bartender threw up their hands with a scowl towards the door. "Where the hell have you been, loca?" they demanded. They pulled their phone from their apron and checked the screen. "We're supposed to start warming up in, like, three minutes."

"I know, I'm sorry." said a light, feminine voice. "Go ahead and start without me. I'll be right there."

Peter turned to find a towering red-haired woman weaving through the bar, her curls tousled and her face flushed from the cold. She smiled at Peter as she passed, offering a quick greeting that he didn't hear. He was too distracted by the way the light in her green eyes brightened the room. By the time his brain worked properly again, she was halfway up the metal staircase that led to the second story.

He cleared his throat and swiveled back to the bar to find Alex smirking at him.

He shifted in his seat and took a swing of his beer. "What?"

Alex scoffed. "Don't *what* me. I saw the way you looked at her."

Peter dropped his eyes and watched the light catch the amber glow of the beer. "I don't know what you're talking about."

"Mm-hm." Alex untied their black apron and shoved it below the counter. "Her name is Maryam." They glanced up at him through their lashes, one pencil-thin eyebrow raised. "She's single. Unattached. Queer, too, if that helps."

"There's nothing to help."

Alex scoffed as they walked away. "Liar."

Peter watched as they hopped up on the small stage on the opposite side of the bar and sat down behind the drum set. He glanced around the crowded bar, suddenly aware of how very alone he was. He picked up his beer and made a bee-line for an empty armchair near the stage—a spot more popular with their coffee-shop hours patrons, he bet—and cracked open the paperback he had brought. This had been his original plan, after all. Might as well stick to it with the bonus of some live music.

Maryam took well over three minutes to return, but the wait had been worth it. She climbed up on stage in heavy black boots, her legs clad in fishnet stockings beneath torn, frayed shorts and a cropped T-shirt for a band Peter didn't recognize. He wondered if the long, fingerless, fishnet gloves were a callback to the 2000's or just for the hell of it. Either way, they fit her well. As did the large, chunky earrings made of jagged stone.

Alex leaned into their mic from behind the drum set. "Nice of you to join us, Maryam."

Maryam picked up the black electric guitar sitting in its stand, flipped a few switches on the attached amplifier, and threw the shoulder strap over her head. "You could have started without me, Alex."

Alex glowered as Maryam plucked the strings of her guitar and adjusted the tuning pegs. "Oh, yeah. Everyone would have loved a forty-minute drum solo."

Maryam checked her phone. "You've only been up here for twenty. Quit being a crab apple." She looked out over the crowd and shouted, "Good evening, Detroit! How we doing tonight?"

The bar erupted in cheers and hollers.

"We are the Easy Breezy Beautiful Cover Band and we are here to encourage you to buy more booze so we can keep the lights on!"

A door in the far corner of the bar flew open. A man with long platinum-blonde hair popped his head out and called, "I told you to stop opening with that!"

Maryam put her hands in the shape of a heart towards the man with a grin that said she wasn't the least bit sorry. The man glowered and retreated back into the office, leaving the door open.

Maryam gestured to the rest of the stage. "As you can see, we have openings for pretty much any instrument you can think of, so tell your friends—"

Alex launched into a heavy, raucous drum beat, nearly scaring Maryam off the stage and startling Peter bad enough that he nearly dropped his beer.

Peter smiled to himself as he recognized the rhythm as the opening to Judas Priest's *Painkiller*, despite the way his chest tightened. Classic rock had been something he had shared with his father that had been all their own. His mother couldn't stand most of it, saying Peter and Wendy were too young for all that "immoral craziness," and Wendy hadn't developed a taste for it. Judas Priest, AC/DC, The Who, Led Zeppelin, Blondie, Guns n' Roses, The Doors, any and all of it. That music had become a soundtrack that confirmed Peter was his father's son.

Maryam flipped Alex the bird with a wry smile on her face, then came in on guitar.

Easy Breezy could only do so much with just a drummer, a guitarist, and some thrift store electronics, but Peter found Maryam's joy infectious. She brought an energy to the room that seeped into Peter's skin and made him forget his book and the ache of grief all together. She spoke to the crowd like they had all been friends for years, even the newcomers. Something about her wide, welcoming smile and laughter made the bar feel like a celebration of life.

As Easy Breezy's fourth song ended, Maryam's voice cracked against the mic. She placed a hand to her chest, an expression of betrayal on her face.

"I keep telling you to drink more water," Alex chimed in.

"You're not my dad," Maryam fired back. Her mock scowl melted into a grin as the crowd laughed. She waved towards the bar. "Guys, can I get a glass of water?"

"Make it a bottle," Alex added. "The last time you gave her an actual glass, she knocked it off the stage like a cat."

A figure in a dark hood shuffled through the bar towards the stage, catching Peter's eye. He kept his gaze locked on the stranger as a wave of unease settled into his stomach.

Up on stage, Maryam rolled her eyes. "I did not knock it off the stage like a cat." The figure reached the edge of the stage. "I would have had to do it on purpose for that to be the case." Maryam reached down, her gaze still on Alex. The figure reached up and snatched Maryam by her wrist.

Panic poured into Peter's veins as he scrambled to his feet.

Maryam did a double take. "The fuck?" She tried to yank her arm away, but the stranger's fingers dug into her skin. "What is your problem?"

"Where is he?" hissed a weak, raspy voice from beneath the figure's hood.

Peter snatched the stranger by the shirt as several other patrons ran to Maryam's aid. The hood fell away in the struggle, revealing a man with a sheet-white face and a snarl made of gnarled teeth.

"Where is he?" the man barked. "Where is the betrayer who sold himself to the mortals and the light?" He yanked hard on Maryam's arm, nearly bringing her over the edge of the stage.

Maryam snatched the man by his collar. "You have no power here," she snarled in his face.

From the corner of his vision, Peter saw Alex leap from the drum set and dart towards the office. "Zack! We have a situation!"

The man wrestled his free hand into the pocket of his coat. "Who needs power?" His face turned to a nasty grin as he pulled a dirty serrated knife from his coat. "All I want is blood."

Peter scrambled to claw the man's hand from Maryam's wrist as she thrashed in his grip. She jerked back, losing her balance. Her boots slid off the stage and she crashed into Peter, knocking him to the floor. Stars burst behind his eyes as his head collided with something pointed before hitting the ground. Out in the spinning world there were shouts, scrambling, and howls from Maryam's assailant as the platinum blonde man barged through the crowd, grabbed the stranger by his coat, and dragged him towards the back door.

Peter tried to get to his feet, but found a weight still holding him down.

"Oh, my God, are you okay? I am so, so sorry."

The world slowly stopped spinning, revealing the weight to be Maryam.

Peter's mouth dried and he blinked, mouth slightly agape.

"Are you concussed? Do you need an ambulance? We have insurance."

The panic on Maryam's face restarted Peter's brain. "No need for all that. I'm fine."

"Oh, thank God." Maryam's shoulders slumped as she let out a breath and got to her feet, offering Peter her hand.

The room spun as he allowed her to pull him up. He swayed on his feet and winced as the back of his head throbbed.

Maryam frowned. "Are you *sure* you're okay?"

"I am." Peter tried to smile. "I could use some ice, though."

"Of course." Maryam guided Peter to the bar, watching him every step of the way like he might fall over dead. He took a seat and she rounded the counter to scoop ice into a plastic bag. "I didn't get your name."

"Peter."

"I'm Maryam." She wrapped the ice in a clean rag and handed it to him. "Can I get you a drink?"

"Alex got me a cream ale earlier that was really good," Peter dug his wallet from his jacket.

Maryam waved the wallet away. "I'm not about to *charge* you after I just *fell* on you." She walked away before Peter could argue, leaving him to place the bag against his throbbing skull and do his best to ignore all the people he could feel watching him. Maryam returned with a glass of beer and sat it down in front of him. "We don't serve much in the way of food, but our apartment is upstairs, so I could maybe—"

"This is fine. Really." Peter took a long sip. The cold beer aided the ice in easing the pain in his head. He forced a laugh as he caught Maryam watching him, her mouth down turned and her brow knitted with worry. "I'll make it. I promise. My parents have always said I have a hard head." He glanced around the bar, desperate for something else to talk about. "Where'd our unfortunate guest and the bouncer run off to?"

Maryam raised an eyebrow. "You mean my brother?" She jabbed her thumb towards the back door. "He's handling it."

Peter studied Maryam's expression, trying to tease out a hint of what that could mean. "Like 'he's gonna sleep with the fishes' kind of handling it?"

Maryam smirked. "If I told you, I'd have to kill you." She put her thumb to her index and middle finger, putting on a thick, muffled Don Vito Corleone impression. "There's certain things we gotta keep in the family."

Peter snorted. "Yeah, okay." He took another sip of beer. "What's it like working with your sibling? My sister and I would drive each other crazy."

Maryam folded her arms. "It can get annoying, but the fact that he's built like a tank comes in handy."

"No joke. If he had wanted to fight that creep, the dude would have been dead in a single punch." Peter readjusted his ice pack. "What was he going on about, anyway? It sounded like you knew him."

Maryam shrugged. "Never seen him in my life. I was just trying to convince him, *and* me, that I wasn't scared." Maryam did a double-take at her fishnet gloves and frowned. "Son of a *bitch*." She picked at a frayed hole in the pattern that framed a forming bruise. "It took me months to figure out how to make these."

Peter stopped mid-sip. "Wait. You *made* those?"

Maryam nodded as she continued to trace the damage. "Sure did."

"Knit?"

"Crochet."

"Can I see?"

Maryam leaned on the counter, arm extended. Peter did his best to ignore the crackle of energy in his fingertips as he gingerly traced the damage. He hadn't dated in over a year—of course he'd feel some type of way touching another person. That's all it was.

"What about an embroidery patch?" He motioned to the broken stitches that could be pulled together without making the glove any tighter. "You could glue these strands here around the back edges. Hot glue, maybe? Or a few stitches if you have a strong enough needle. Or a sewing machine, maybe? I couldn't tell you which would hold up better."

Maryam pulled her arm back and studied the pattern, eyes calculating as they darted over the stitches. Finally, she smiled. "That could actually work." Peter's heart raced as Maryam studied him. "I think I just may have to keep you around, Peter."

Those words stopped his heart completely. The approach of the towering man who had dragged the creep out of the bar kick-started it again, mostly out of shock, since he moved like a shadow, despite his size.

He was even bigger up close; 6'6", at least, with broad shoulders that could probably block out the sun. His long platinum hair, tied back, made him look all the more formidable, like a soldier from some mystical land. Peter was willing to admit that Maryam made him a bit self-conscious about his height, but this guy made him feel downright tiny. His smile was warm and friendly, though, and a hint of embarrassment softened his appearance.

"I am so very sorry about all this," he said in a clear, gentle customer service voice as he offered Peter his hand. "Zackary Bishop, owner of this establishment. Are you alright?"

Peter shook his hand, the other still holding up the ice pack. "I'm fine, really. Where's our friend?"

Zackary's smile twitched. "Taken care of."

Peter wasn't sure whether to laugh, ask more questions, or leave the bar before he got tangled in what was starting to sound like a crime family.

Maryam started with her *Godfather* impression again. "I already told him that we keep things in the family."

Zackary gave his sister a tired, exasperated look. "I'm sorry she's subjecting you to this. You'd think landing on you like an anvil would have been bad enough."

Maryam stuck out her tongue.

Peter laughed. "It's okay, Mr. Bishop. It's not a bad impression, honestly. I've heard much worse."

Maryam snorted.

Zackary glowered at her, then smiled at Peter, turning his scowl on and off like a switch. "Please, call me Zack. Is there anything I can do to make up for this?" He gestured to the storefront across the street. "Free coffee delivery for a year, maybe?"

Maryam blinked. "Wait,. You work at *Books A'Bailey*?"

"Yeah." Peter sat the ice pack on the counter and flexed his numbing hand. "My aunt owns it, but I handle the day-to-day stuff and live in the apartment above." He felt the spark of a lightbulb turn on in his head. "So, if working with your brother ever gets annoying, feel free to stop by to play Mario Kart or something. I get sick of beating my sister."

Zackary smirked. "Bold of you to assume she's not the annoying one."

"Pfft." Maryam rolled her eyes. "As if. I'm a gift. You're the annoying one." She studied Peter for a moment. "I would like that, though. I'll have to take you up on the offer."

"Yes, we owe you," Zackary said. "Her social skills have been deteriorating over the past few years."

Maryam threw a stir stick at him. "See? *You* are annoying."

Peter chuckled, but it was cut short by the ringing of his phone.

He bit back a groan as he pulled it from his pocket. With his sister staying the weekend, there would be hell to pay if it was their mother and he didn't answer. Sure enough, Eliza Bailey's picture lit up the screen. Peter answered. "Hello?"

"Did you get my messages?" Eliza's voice was demanding and terse. "Where are you?"

Peter did a double take across the street. Sure enough, her car idled in front of the store and she stood on the sidewalk, phone to her ear, braids hanging down the length of her stark-white hospital jacket. Peter scrolled to find unread texts that had been sent in the midst of the creep fiasco.

"Sorry. I'll be there in a second." He hung up and hopped off his bar stool. "I gotta go handle some family stuff. I'll be back."

"If we scared you off, you can say so," Maryam called. "We won't be offended."

Peter gave a wave and jogged across the street to meet his mother shivering in the October cold. Her daughter's backpack dangled from one hand.

"Boy, what are you doing in there when you've got your sister with you?" Eliza demanded. Despite her tone, she pulled Peter into a hug and kissed him on the cheek, bringing with her the familiar smell of tea tree oil and jasmine.

"Mom, she's sixteen. She can sleep unattended while I go out for a drink." Peter squeezed his mother and slung his sister's bag over his shoulder. "Plus, I left her a note." He had half a mind to call his sister and make her come get her own book bag, seeing as this was the third time this month she'd forgotten it, but he decided he'd be a good big brother and take it up to the apartment for her, lest his mother gave him an earful.

"It's not leaving her alone that bothers me. It's that bar in particular I don't like." Eliza eyed the neon planchette, astrological symbols and Illuminati triangles that framed the bar's name with her full lips turned down. "They're just asking for trouble."

"They're normal people, Mom. It's just a gimmick."

Eliza's frown deepened. "Mm-hm. That's how it always seems, at first, 'till you got demons running around and breaking things."

Peter laughed. "You're starting to sound like Granddaddy."

"Your Granddaddy was smart." Eliza's phone pinged. She read the message and sighed. "I'm sorry. I gotta take off again. The hospital's been..." Eliza trailed off.

Peter knew she was planning on saying, "busy," but that wasn't what she really meant. It was her distraction, her safe place as she adjusted to life without her husband. Peter tried not to hold it against her, but times like this—rare moments when he tried to live his own life for five minutes—made it harder than he liked to admit.

Guilt pinched Peter's chest. His job was to protect this family. That's what his father had said. That's what Bailey men did.

And it had taken years for Peter's dad to see him as a man.

Eliza massaged her forehead.

Peter squeezed her hand. "It's okay. I'm holding down the fort."

Eliza forced a smile and kissed her son's temple. "Thank you. I'll pick her up tomorrow night and we'll do dinner or something. Sound good?"

"Sounds perfect. Tell them sick folks I say hi."

Eliza chuckled and circled her car. "I always do."

Peter climbed the steps to his apartment and unlocked the door as the taillights disappeared around the corner. He sighed, more disappointed in himself for getting dragged back here than he cared to admit.

Did he even have a right to be disappointed? Did he have the right to be upset with his mother's demands or his aunt's need for help? He'd *offered* to put his business degree to work for this family and it wasn't like he'd had the greatest job prospects in the months between graduating college and agreeing to his aunt's offer. He'd made his choices himself, but what choices did he really have at the time? He was the oldest. He was Adam Bailey's only son. He'd *fought* to become that son.

He slipped into his sister's room as quietly as the creaky hinges would allow. The carpet felt like eggshells as he tried to avoid disturbing the warped boards underneath. One whined. Peter winced and turned to his sister's bed to find the notoriously light sleeper still motionless and neatly tucked in.

An alarm went off in his head. His sister never slept that neatly—she was normally sprawled out, lanky limbs at odd angles and sheets half-way on the floor. He reached for what should have been her shoulder. The pillow beneath gave way.

"Wendy?" Peter ripped the blankets away. Pillows lay down the length of the bed where his sister should have been. Peter's stomach plummeted.

"Wendy!" Peter's heart hammered faster with every empty room he searched. "Damn it, Wen, if you're playing around..."

But he knew she wasn't. Her laughter would have given her away. She always told on herself like that.

Chills spread across Peter's chest as he called Wendy's number. She didn't answer. Blood roared louder in his ears with each unanswered text message.

His father had charged him with taking care of this family and Peter was failing miserably.

Wendy Bailey knew damn well she had no business being out with these punks she called friends. She should have been at her brother's, preferably studying—at least that was what her mother would say if she knew where she was. But if Eliza Bailey didn't care enough to take a break from her endless shifts at the hospital, why should Wendy care enough to act right all the time? Besides, Peter deserved a break. He'd carried so much since Dad had died. Wendy sneaking out had seemed like a good enough break as anything else.

It had sounded like perfectly logical reasoning in the well-lit cafeteria.

"Seriously, it'll be fine," Alicia had insisted. "I tell my mom I'm spending the night with you at Peter's. You tell him you're going to bed early, then sneak down the fire escape. He'll never know you're gone and we'll each walk away from this bet fifty bucks richer."

It had all sounded so straight-forward—and spitefully satisfying, seeing as Eliza had yet *again* dumped Wendy on Peter's doorstep with little warning—but now, in the dark, on the outskirts of Detroit, Wendy wavered. It was as if the giant abandoned hospital on the other side of the fence was sucking all her confidence away with its black, empty, menacing windows.

David, Alicia's boyfriend, nudged Wendy and asked, "You scared?" with a wicked grin.

Wendy forced a fake laugh. "Of course not. Why would I be scared of a building filled with any number of sharp things that could give us tetanus?"

Alicia giggled as she came up beside her and took hold of the fence. Her pale arm practically glowed in the moonlight compared to Wendy's dark tawny skin. "Why be scared of all that when there's *demons*?"

Wendy studied her best friend. "You don't seriously believe in all that do you?"

Alicia only shrugged. "So long as we don't die and we win this bet, I don't think it matters."

David rolled his eyes. "It's going to be fine." He grunted as he hoisted himself up onto the fence, taking a seat at the top. "We're just gonna take a look around, record some videos, and get out. There's nothing actually here." He offered Alicia a hand. She took it and awkwardly climbed the fence in her lacy black tights and a matching skirt. Wendy had warned her the outfit would get ruined, but Alicia had insisted on matching "the vibe" of the place.

David offered Wendy his hand, but she scaled the fence on her own and leaped to the ground. Scared or not, she'd get in and out herself. Peter would have been proud. At least, he would have been proud if she hadn't snuck out to do some, "whack-ass white people shit," as he liked to call it.

Wendy dusted herself off and looked out across the dry, patchy lawn towards the hospital. "What is this place anyway?"

"It's called St. Damian's Hospital." David leapt to the ground and took a flashlight from his belt, holding it under his chin to cast macabre shadows across his face. "They say that the doctors who worked here were mad scientists. They'd lie to a patient's family, saying that they died, then they would whisk them away to the basement to perform all sorts of terrible experiments on them. A group of nurses found the poor victims and slaughtered the doctors. When they were hanged for murder, they said their deaths would mean they were free to protect patients at the hospital for all eternity. After that, no one wanted to leave their loved ones here, so it eventually shut down."

Wendy slipped her hands into her pockets. "I bet those ghost nurses were pissed."

Alicia jumped from the top of the fence with a squeal, then caught up to the others, latching tight to David's arm. "Apparently, the ghost nurses protect the ghost patients from darker forces since people do all sorts of rituals here."

Wendy stopped short. "Wait, so there could be a bunch of weirdos in there?"

"Nah." David turned the flashlight towards the hospital. "They don't show up 'til midnight. We've still got a few hours." David smirked.

"Why?" He lifted his shoulders and wiggled his fingers, looking like a blonde, teenage Nosferatu. "Are you scaaaared?"

Wendy laughed and pushed him away in an attempt to hide her nerves. "Oh, fuck off, dude." To drive her point home, more for herself than the others, she marched up the entrance steps ahead of the others, but the second her hand touched the door, she froze.

There were no chains. No padlocks. Nothing to stop them from waltzing in, yet Wendy couldn't bring herself to do it. There was a conniving, almost maliciously gleeful aura around St. Damian's. Even if Wendy didn't believe there were ghosts lurking about, there was definitely *something*. Wendy knew her friends felt it too. She could see it in the way Alicia shrunk in on herself, her hands clasped tight to her chest, and David's fake, fractured smile.

Still, fear or not, she needed to do this. Her cut of the bet would cover the rest of the homecoming dress she wanted without her brother's or mother's help. The thought of asking either of them made her cringe. Her brother carried enough as it was. And maybe, if Wendy could show her that she could handle things herself, her mom would actually *talk* to her like an almost-adult rather than a child that needed to be protected from her own family's grief.

Wendy clasped the door and grit her teeth. "Let's go win this bet." She swung the door open, the hinges screaming, and stepped into the dark.

Regret flooded her veins the second she crossed the threshold. A dormant, primal part of her soul told her to run. To claw her way out. To do whatever it took not to wake whatever lurked in the silent dark, but David and Alicia had pushed in, cutting off her exit and forcing her to press on.

Intellectually, she knew it was all just dust and crumbling plaster, but there was something about the rusty wheelchair, the abandoned IV rack, and scattered, deteriorating papers that made it hard to believe. It was as if their owners had merely stepped away for a moment and would be back soon. Wendy didn't want to meet them.

David's voice took Wendy's attention away from the shadows. His face stared back at them from his phone. "All right, Hayden. We're here." He tapped an icon to flip the camera. "Phase one, complete. Now we're on our way to the psychosis ward—"

Wendy snorted. "It's 'psychiatric,' dork."

"Thank you, Surgeon General. *Anyway*, we're on our way to the psyche...the psy...the place where the demon hangs out, or whatever." David flipped the camera back to his face. "See you in a bit...I hope." He stopped the video and slipped the phone back into his pocket.

The stale, dusty second floor revealed more of the same unsettlingly ordinary scene, though with more graffiti. Some people had left art. Others had painted names in colorful, stylized letters. Some had scrawled secrets using swirls of dark sigils, pentagrams, and Latin.

Any sign that the last room at the end of the hall had ever been a psychiatric ward had been lost to time. In a strange, eerie way, the room felt sterile. It had been gutted long ago, leaving nothing but crumbling walls and pillars, making giant canvases for artists and amateur occultists.

Some creative efforts had been ruined by the roof caving in, leaving a heap of broken concrete and plaster with a void of black and stars above.

"The demon's circle is supposed to be black with a bunch of squiggles in it." David scanned the floor until he found marks he considered close enough. "Somebody get a video of this." David took a few deep breaths and held his phone out towards Alicia. "If you stand in it, you're supposed to hear singing or laughing or something."

Alicia clicked her tongue. "I'm not waiting around here for that. Why don't we just have Wendy stand off to the side and whistle?"

David was silent for a moment. "Not a bad idea."

Wendy scoffed and positioned herself by the cave-in, being careful of her footing. The last thing she needed was a trip to the ER. With Wendy's luck, her mother would be out of surgery and spot her daughter being wheeled in.

A curious glint of metal in the roof rubble caught her eye. She pulled it free and dusted it off. It looked to be a coin of some sort, but it couldn't have any monetary value. Not in the last millennia, anyway. Maybe never. Where a face should have been was a blend of squiggles and lines. Wendy could just make out the existence of letters around the worn edges, but they were too faint to read. The coin had two holes on either side, like the coin had been on a bracelet or necklace at some point.

Wendy slipped it in her pocket in case Peter needed some buttering up after her little stunt. He would think it was cool, the nerd.

David cleared his throat and addressed his phone. "Okay, Hayden. I'm here." He glanced around the room. "Here, demon, demon, demon."

"You don't call a demon like you're calling a dog," Alicia snapped.

A car whooshed by outside. A chilly breeze tickled Wendy's neck. She massaged the spot as casually as she could, reminding herself that they were surrounded by broken windows, not ghosts.

"Well, how am I supposed to call it, demon whisperer?" David replied.

"Not like that, that's for sure."

From the depths of the black corridor came a distant, low giggle.

Wendy's heart jumped into her throat.

Alicia whirled towards the sound and took a step back. "Did you hear that?"

David's humor evaporated. "Unfortunately."

Wendy had too. She left her spot and scurried behind David with Alicia, trying to hide from unseen eyes.

"Hello?" David called. Nothing answered. "Hey, we can leave if you want us to. We just came on a bet. We don't want to hang out here. You can have your space back, dude."

The silence that followed was so tense Wendy thought it might snap, shattering the world.

Alicia wrung her hands. "Did you at least get that sound on video, David?"

"Maybe? We'd have to replay the video—"

"Hold on. Listen."

Wendy didn't want to. She wanted to run as fast as she could back to her brother's place, swearing to Black Jesus that she would never sneak out again because the rush of rebellion and fifty dollars wasn't worth all this. She'd pray to the Black Virgin Mary, too. Wendy wasn't Catholic, but extra prayers couldn't hurt.

Chirping came from the inky black depths of the hallway like a canary in a mine shaft. The absurdity of it, a sound so pure and joyful in a place so dark and sinister, turned Wendy's blood to ice.

"We need to leave," Alicia squeaked. "This feels wrong. Not just creepy, but *wrong.*"

David scoffed. "Don't tell me you actually think—"

The chirping stopped.

The darkness hummed, its voice high and sweet like a child's.

"Nope." David grabbed the girls' hands and ran. Wendy's feet hardly touched the floor as they sprinted through the hall and back down the stairs. She nearly cried with relief when they spotted the moonlight pouring from the front door.

Unseen hands tugged on her braids. She shrieked, pushing the others forward and sprinting in a frenzy.

They tumbled out of the door, falling over themselves to flee. Even as St. Damian's shrank behind them, they kept running, propelled by Wendy's scream of terror as if it confirmed that every terrible legend was true. None of them stopped until they were on the other side of the fence.

David nearly slipped and fell as he sprinted for the driver's seat. The girls dove into the back, holding tight to one another as David fumbled with his keys.

"What the fuck was that?" Alicia sobbed. "David, what the fuck was that? Are you and Hayden fucking with us?"

"I swear to God it wasn't me or Hayden," David locked the doors. He ran his fingers through his hair, holding tight to his scalp as if his brain might leak out. He looked at Wendy through the rear-view mirror. "What happened?"

"Something grabbed my hair," Wendy rasped, her throat sore. She gathered her braids over her shoulder.

Alicia glared at her boyfriend. "David, if it's you two messing with us—"

"Ali, I *hate* Hayden Murphy!" A crazed laugh escaped David's lips. "I agreed to this so maybe he'd shut the fuck up about have clairvoyant powers or whatever crazy magic shit he thinks he can do. I never would agreed to *any* of this if I thought he was right about this place!"

"I don't want to think about it anymore." Wendy wrung her hands together as she curled in on herself in her seat. "Can we just go? We got what we needed so you could win this bet. I don't want to be here anymore."

"Same." David turned on the car and peeled down the road, sending up clouds of dirt.

Wendy dared to glance back to look for a sign of life and watched as the dust and dirt settled and swirled into a human figure.

The car careened around the corner before she could do a double take. It had to be a trick of the moonlight. She was frantic and it was dark. Like the voices in the hospital and the tug on her hair. None of it could be real. Wendy repeated it to herself like a mantra.

It couldn't be real. It couldn't be real. *It. Couldn't. Be. Real.*

The only sound in the car was the dinging of Wendy's phone as her brother called, texted, and left voicemails. Wendy read the messages and relayed them to the others, but didn't have the energy, or the right words, to respond.

"In my defense," Alicia said as they pulled up to the bookstore, "The only reason your brother realized you were gone was because you forgot your backpack at home. That's not on me."

David scowled at Alicia in the rearview mirror, signalling that she wasn't helping. Alicia gave him a bewildered look in response.

Wendy sighed, too burnt out to deflect blame. Going along with this stupid plan was on her and it was time to own up to it. "I'll text you guys tomorrow if I still have a phone."

Alicia rolled her eyes. "He can't ground you. That's, like, sibling law."

"Yeah, but he can tell the one person who can."

Both David and Alicia flinched on Wendy's behalf as she got out of the car.

Wendy poked her head back through the door. "We're not telling Hayden Murphy he was right though. David's right—he's annoying as hell. We're leaving this bet with a hundred and fifty dollars and our dignity intact."

"Hell yeah, sister." David reached around for a fist bump as Wendy crawled out the back seat. "Fuck Hayden Murphy."

Wendy gave David an exasperated look as she got out of the car. "You owe me ten dollars of your cut for calling me 'sister.'"

"What? Come on. We almost died tonight," David called. "That should give me a pass!"

"Fifteen dollars!"

David groaned and rolled up the window.

Wendy took her time dragging herself up the stairs, waiting for David's car to disappear around the corner before digging her keys from her pocket. Her brain was so fried from fear that she didn't even bother trying to think of a convincing lie as she let herself in.

Peter whirled on her as he stood with his phone to his ear. His dark eyes shifted from panic to anger at the sight of her. "What on God's green earth is wrong with you?" he demanded. "Do you *want* Mom to lock you in the basement? I was just about to call her."

A hint of weight eased up from Wendy's shoulders. Peter hadn't called Mom yet.

Wendy's heart twisted as she watched a range of emotions play across her brother's face. He looked so much like their dad.

"Where were you?" Peter demanded. His inflections were a perfect mimic of their father's and they twisted Wendy's heart so hard that she couldn't find the energy to lie. She was too busy massaging her temple in an attempt to keep herself distracted to she wouldn't start crying.

If Dad was still there, none of them would be like this—not Wendy, not Peter, and certainly not their mother.

"Alicia, David, and I snuck into St. Damian's hospital on a dare."

Peter slicked back his curls and let out a puff of breath. "Those crazy white kids are gonna get you killed. I keep telling you."

Wendy sucked on her teeth with a glare. "Like you didn't do equally stupid shit when you were my age. And you don't exactly run with the Black Panthers, neither."

Peter glowered.

"'Aight, listen. We can work this out." She slipped the coin from her pocket and held it up to the light. "For starters, I brought you a present."

Maryam woke up grumpy and irritable. That damn demon had given her nightmares—she had been twelve years old again and a demon was torturing her cousin, Matthew. The more Maryam begged for it to stop, the worse it tortured him, demanding Maryam answer riddles she didn't understand.

The demon who had wandered into Ectoplasm hadn't been that powerful. Zackary informed Maryam after the fact that it had been a hellion—an underling that demons built from the scorched soil of Hell and the blood of sinners. They were mainly used to carry messages and spy on each other, but every once and awhile the lords, princes, and kings of Hell sent them to Earth for small missions. Exorcising it had been easy and a few Order members had been willing to swing by to pick the man up and take him to St. Francis' Hospital, which was attached to the Order's headquarters.

Coffee helped Maryam's mood, especially with a touch of whiskey and whipped cream. She slumped down the stairs after double-checking her class schedule and leaned in the doorway of Zackary's office. He stopped typing, removed his glasses with a huff, and massaged his temple instead of greeting her.

"Uh, oh." Maryam took a sip of coffee. "What happened?"

Zackary set his glasses on the desk. "Kelly heard about you being attacked and quit."

Maryam rolled her eyes. "I was not *attacked.* I was hardly even manhandled. Still, that's unfortunate. I liked Kelly. She was a cutie."

"Alex told me they can cover a few of her shifts, but the rest of them are when you have class..." Zackary massaged the bridge of his nose. "I should have left this place a pipe dream and stuck to what I'm good at."

Maryam scoffed into her mug. "Of course. How could you possibly want more out of life than telling people that their toaster has *not,* in fact, burned an image of Jesus into their breakfast?"

Zackary cracked a smile. "You make it sound so dignified."

"What can I say?" Maryam shrugged. "'Dignified' is my middle name."

"It most certainly is not." Zackary slipped his glasses back on.

"Okay, yeah, technically it's Grace, but they're practically the same thing."

"Keep telling yourself that."

Maryam flicked a paperclip at him. "Rude."

Zackary pressed a few keys, then tipped back in his chair to take a stack of papers from the printer. "Don't hate me but—" Maryam's shoulders tensed. "—I need you to run this report over to the Order." Zackary slipped the papers into a manila envelope, fastened it shut and handed it to Maryam.

She took it with a groan and dramatically slumped against the desk.

"Oh, knock it off. I haven't asked you to take anything to them in months and I have to look for Kelly's replacement." Zackary began typing again. "I'm emailing your aunt that you're on your way, so don't even think about ditching that report in a dumpster."

Maryam groaned louder, chugged her coffee, and headed for the door with the envelope in hand. "You're positively the worst."

"I'm a demon," he reminded her with a smirk. "It's sort of my M.O."

Maryam put her thumb and first two fingers together and took on a deep, raspy Italian mobster accent. "What if I made you an offer you can't refuse?" She darted for the door with a yelp as Zackary chucked a stress ball at her.

Ectoplasm was close to a bus route that would take her to St. Mary's Interdenominational Congregation, where the Order hid in plain sight. Not that it hid particularly well. Between the church, schools, and hospital, the St. Mary's collective stuck out against the cityscape like a Rembrandt in a Jackson Pollock gallery.

The bus dropped Maryam off a block away from the church, giving her time to brace herself for whatever bullshit the Order felt like handing her, because the incident last night would absolutely result in some sort of bullshit—either it would be Maryam's fault that a helion had showed up at Ectoplasm (because of course it was) or Zackary hadn't handled the situation quite right (because of course he hadn't), or some surprise third thing. Maryam honestly wondered why she wasn't more used to it by now. Zackary was a demon and Maryam was demon-kissed—a child born of a demon-possessed mother. They would never do right in the Order's eyes, no matter how hard they tried.

Well, *Zackary* tried. Maryam was content with being a problem.

As Maryam walked through the sanctuary of St. Mary's, her agitation eased a bit She felt small and inconsequential against the vast silence and the vaulted ceiling painted to mimic Heaven, and that was an improvement, in her opinion.

No one beat up on children who were small and inconsequential. They went unseen. Invisible.

You couldn't strike the invisible for the sin of existance.

The sanctuary was built like the churches of the Old World. Thick carved stone pillars supported a ceiling decorated with portraits of saints and angels, framed in the soft blue and whites of bright, crisp mornings. Small chapels lined the main aisle, hosting small wooden benches for parishioners to take a moment with martyrs and saints framed in intricate gold leafing. The Mother of God hovered at the front altar, carved in white marble with streaks of sunlight radiating from her crown thanks to the window behind her. Unnamed shepherds bowed in awe of the Christ Child in her arms. There were other routes to the Order's lobby, but this way had always been Maryam's favorite, because she knew full well that this was the closest she'd ever get to Heaven.

She made her way around the altar to a small room off to the side with an exceptionally plain elevator. A security camera blinked above a nearby keypad as Maryam punched in the code. The elevator dinged open, then carried Maryam down, deep below the earth. It dinged again and released her into a bleached, stark-white copy of the church above. The walls and pillars were practically blinding without any artwork to ease their glow and where the church had chapels, the Order's lobby had corridors that seemed to go on forever, each with a department name listed above: *Residential Hauntings, Psychic and Telepathic Communications, Extraterrestrial Phenomena, Cryptozoology, Demonology, Exorcisms.* And this was just the first floor. Maryam wasn't sure just how far down the structure went.

A blonde young woman sat behind a sleep black desk in the center of the stark chamber. Her blue dress with red polka-dots was the only pop of color against the rest of the space filled with men and women in cassocks and suits. The occasional scholar from the depth of the archives or eccentric from the research department occasionally crossed the space, but even their aged tweed jackets and loose cotton clothes seemed muted in the chamber's harsh artificial light.

Maryam walked up to the desk and leaned in with a disarming smile. "Ellie McDonald. How are you doing today?"

Ellie did a double take and beamed before leaping up and pulling Maryam into a hug. "Hey, stranger! It's been too long."

"Well, you know. School keeps me busy." Maryam pulled away and ran a hand through her curls, trying her best to pretend to have swagger. She caught the eyes of several other people from her school days and winked. They either flashed her dirty looks or looked away as if they hadn't seen her.

Just because she hated being at the Order didn't mean she couldn't get something out of it. Attempting to flirt with Ellie McDonald, the gorgeous former Rosary Academy prom queen, always seemed to be the easiest.

It was her classmates' doing, really. Maryam had never figured out who started the rumor that she was trying to turn all the girls in her class into lesbians, but she had certainly had fun with it over the years.

Maryam sat the report on the desk. "Zack needed me to bring this to my aunt. I know she's pretty busy, so would you mind...?"

"You're in luck, actually." Ellie's genuine smile grew. "She just got back from an investigation. I saw her walk towards her office about five minutes ago."

Maryam grimaced. "Lucky me." She drummed her fingers on the desk, racking her brain for an excuse to stay put. Finding none, she dropped her hands. "Later, El."

"Bye, Maryam. And come around more!"

Maryam waved, then shook her head as she walked away. This place didn't deserve Ellie McDonald.

The corridors of the Order reminded Maryam of the endless halls in *The Shining*. Her aunt's office had been in the same place for years, yet Maryam still had to read each name plate to find it. *Sarah Bishop, Ordained Exorcist, Certified Demonologist*, caught her eye. She knocked and sincerely prayed to the crucifix hanging on the door that no one would answer.

Instead, Maryam heard a faint, "Come in." She glared at Jesus as he hung on his cross—Because, really? This prayer was too much for the guy who walked on water?—and let herself in.

Sarah Bishop sat with a phone clutched between her slender jaw and narrow shoulder as she took notes. "Yes...Of course...Yes, naturally." Her eyes fell on Maryam and lit up. "Okay. I'll talk to you soon." She hung up, got to her feet, and rounded the desk with open arms, practically running to greet her towering niece. "Maryam! Good heavens, are you alright?"

Maryam forced a smile as her aunt hugged her tight. It felt like Sarah was trying to pick her up, despite only coming up to Maryam's chest. Maryam's grip around her aunt was gentle. Even when she hadn't towered over the woman, she had worried she might break Sarah, with her short stature and dainty frame.

Their differences made Maryam wonder if the two of them really were related sometimes. Sarah's pin-straight blonde hair, and delicate features were so radically different from Maryam's imposing height, broad build, and bright red hair. The fact that she hadn't ever seen a picture of her parents didn't help. She could have easily been left on the church's doorstep for all she knew. Weirder things happened at St. Mary's on a daily basis.

"I don't see or hear from you for *months*, until you get attacked by a demon?" Sarah pulled away, looked Maryam over, and frowned. "This is why I didn't want you out on your own."

"It was just a hellion, Auntie. And I wasn't *attacked.*" Maryam wiggled out of Sarah's grip and handed over the report.

Sarah took the envelope, but didn't pay it much attention. She was still too busy studying her niece. "There's no such thing as 'just a hellion.' And there wouldn't be anything to handle if you were home safe."

Maryam snorted. Home? Safe? That was rich. But it wasn't as if Sarah knew any better—she and Maryam's mother had grown up in the orphanage run by the Order, St. Bishop's. The Order had trained Sarah and given her a job; albeit a strange one. The Order was her everything.

Maryam didn't know much about her mother's relationship with the Order before she died but, given how unwilling anyone was to talk about Mary Bishop, she imagined it hadn't been great. Like mother, like daughter, she supposed.

"I'm really okay, Auntie. Zack handled it like a pro." A smug smirk crept onto Maryam's face. "It's almost as if these self-righteous pricks should use the demon in their arsenal."

Sarah sighed. "Don't start. You know how that conversation is going to go." She gently slapped Maryam in the arm with the envelope. "And don't swear. You're in a church."

"Technically I'm *below* a church."

Sarah shot her niece a shrewd look.

"Either way, I'm right."

Sarah sighed again. "Maryam—"

"If Zack was going to sabotage the Order on behalf of Hell, he would have done it already, Aunt Sarah. He's had twenty-one years." She folded her arms. "What about when Claude keels over? He's gotta be pushing a hundred by now, right? Then again, if he's drinking the blood of orphans, like I think he is, we'll probably never be rid of him."

Sarah's look sharpened as she hissed, "*Maryam Grace.*"

A firm knock at the door cut Sarah off before she could begin a proper scolding. She craned her neck and smiled at whoever had either the authority, or the audacity, to let themselves in. "Morning, Father." Sarah gestured to Maryam. "Look who paid us a visit."

A low, calm chuckle grated against Maryam's skin. "Well, if it isn't our prodigal daughter." The cold, level voice rooted her to the carpet and dumped ice in her veins.

She should have known better. She'd spoken of the Devil and now he had appeared.

Maryam braced herself and faced Father Jonathan Claude, senior exorcist of the department, member of the Head Authority Board, and Maryam's former headmaster.

"How are you, child?" the priest asked. "We were starting to think you'd forgotten how to get here. How long has it been?"

"A few months, maybe?" Maryam placed a plastic grin on her face with her lips pursed and her arms folded.

Father Claude sized Maryam up with icy blue eyes atop a vulture-like neck. His pencil-thin lips twitched into something resembling a smile. "I hear you stay rather busy between school and your entrepreneurial endeavors, so I suppose it's understandable." The priest folded his hands and stood stiff. "Last night's little episode doesn't seem to have slowed you down at all."

Maryam pretended to inspect her nails. "Oh, I'd hardly even call it an episode, given how fast Zackary took care of it." She glanced down at Claude—having a few inches on the old priest felt like a small win. "How could we have avoided this little mishap, though, I wonder?"

"*Maryam.*"

Maryam's gaze darted to her aunt, her heart cracking a bit at the sight of Sarah inching towards Father Claude. Did Sarah know that she gravitated towards the old priest, and away from her niece, when the two were in a room together?

Father Claude rolled his shoulders, brushing off Maryam's slight like a fleck of dandruff. "We'll review Zackary's report and see where we can improve."

"Hm. You do that." Maryam checked her phone. "I should head out. I'll tell Zack you say hi, Auntie." She made it a point to hardly give Father Claude a passing glance as she headed for the door.

"Don't forget Matthew's birthday dinner on Friday."

Maryam froze in the doorway. How had she forgotten? As if seeing Claude wasn't bad enough, Sarah had to go and drop that bomb on her. She kept her eyes locked forward as she muttered, "Yeah. I'll be there," and walked away.

Maryam slipped into the elevator without a good-bye to Ellie and walked to the bus stop with her hands clenched tight in her pockets. She dropped on the bench and allowed her head to hit the glass backing with a loud *thump*, garnering several startled looks from other waiting bus riders. She debated giving a few glares to get the eyes off her but ignored them instead. It wasn't their fault her mood was spoiled.

Maryam took her seat, popped in her earbuds, rolled up her sleeve, and began tracing the long slender scar beneath the longsword tattooed against her inner arm. Tracing one way, she took a deep breath. Tracing the other, she let it out. She repeated the ritual three times on her left arm, then three times on her right where an identical tattoo covered an identical scar. The anxiety eased, but was replaced with a sense of disgust deep in Maryam's gut. All these years, and that old vulture still got under her skin just by breathing too close. The bastard.

Then again, maybe it wasn't his fault. Maryam knew she was a problem. Maybe she was a coward, too.

She tried to shake the gloom as the bus reached her stop. There was no point in dwelling. He would always hate her. Matthew had been his star pupil, the Order's golden boy, and his death was Maryam's fault for daring to draw breath as a demon-kissed child. If she had just died before being born, the demon that had possessed her mother would never have hunted her Matthew wouldn't have wound up in the crossfire. Her aunt and uncle wouldn't have lost their only child and wouldn't have been stuck with Maryam instead—a walking disaster that grew up accidentally summon demons and getting drunk off stolen communion wine.

This is what unholy things do...

Maryam shook away the thought and got off the bus. She ordered an iced coffee to ease her frayed nerves and made her way upstairs to study. As she fished a bottle of Kahlua from the fridge, Zackary emerged from his room dressed head to toe in black leather with his motorcycle helmet in hand.

"Where are you off to?" Maryam took a sip of her coffee.

"Got a call about an open-and-shut case up near New Haven." Zackary grabbed his keys from the coffee table. "Tools going missing from a surveying sight, personal items ending up in trees. Typical faerie nonsense. The little assholes'll get offended if a cryptozoologist showed up with nets and whatnot, so they're sending me. Should be quick."

"They seriously expect you to just drop everything?" Maryam frowned. "New Haven's like an hour away."

Zackary shrugged. "It's not like I'm paying for the gas. Besides, I haven't gone for a proper ride in awhile. I could use the fresh air. Try not to burn the place down while I'm gone."

The weight on Maryam's chest made her let the remark slide. "Zack?"

He paused and looked at her over his shoulder.

Maryam bit her lip. "It's Matthew's birthday on Friday."

Zackary tensed.

"Did you want to come to dinner?"

"I work that night."

"But—"

He slammed the door, ending the discussion.

Maryam sighed, added another splash of booze to her coffee, then pulled out her books.

Zaphriel the Treacherous had been summoned to Earth hundreds of times in the eons after he'd been damned to Hell. He hadn't flown during any of them. He was too cowardly to risk opening himself up to the memories intertwined with the sensation of riding the wind and defying gravity. Besides, who was he to enjoy the thrill of freedom and power like that? He didn't deserve it. He didn't deserve any of the blessings that had come his way.

Motorcycles proved to be a decent substitute, at least. The flecks of autumn colors and the puffs of chilly breeze that slipped into his jacket woke him up inside and pushed away the heavy, painful reminder that Maryam had handed him.

Zackary cut his engine on the edge of a gravel road, slipped off his helmet, and closed his eyes. Taking a deep breath, he soaked up the icy air on his warm face and listened to the syncopation of bird songs and rustling leaves. He savored it all, a glutton for every detail that would keep him going when he was thrown back into Hell, because good things never lasted forever.

The crunch and crackle of gravel distracted him. He opened his eyes to watch an old red truck meandered down the road. A stout middle-aged man climbed out with a kind smile. Zackary had met enough mortals over the centuries to recognize a good one on sight. It was all in the eyes. John Porter's eyes said that he was a decent man. Naïve and simple maybe, but good-hearted. Faeries had no business giving a man like him a hard time.

Mr. Porter offered Zackary his hand. "Mr. Bishop, I take it? You look younger than you sounded on the phone."

Zackary grinned and took Porter's warm, calloused hand. "Blessed with good genes, I suppose, Mr. Porter."

Mr. Porter took off his raggedy ball cap and used the brim to scratch his forehead. "Hope they're blessed enough to solve my problem. C'mon, I'll show you the house." He slipped his cap back on and began down a path overgrown with ferns.

Zackary sensed nothing out of the ordinary. No unexplainable buzz of energy on his skin, no sudden cold spots, no strange smells or sounds. Nothing paranormal had come this way for awhile, as far as Zackary could tell.

The forest gave way to a meadow that framed a rotting cabin so decrepit that Zackary wondered if it would disintegrate before his eyes. No wonder Mr. Porter was tearing it down.

The man hooked his thumbs through his belt loops. "My granddad always said his parents were God-fearin' folk. Even found an old cross over the doorway, but tools and materials still keep disappearing and winding up in trees or missing all together. And last night..." Mr. Porter massaged the back of his neck.

Zackary raised an eyebrow. "What happened last night?"

Mr. Porter glanced around like a child about to repeat curse words. "Mr. Bishop, you believe the people you help, right? You don't think we're crazy?"

Zackary flashed a disarming grin. "I wouldn't be in this line of work if I thought people who encountered the supernatural were crazy, Mr. Porter."

The man took a deep breath. "Well, last night around dusk I came out here to check on the place. Tryin' to see if it was troublemakers or something. Didn't want to waste your time."

Zackary noted a shift in the wind and a sudden fresh floral smell in the air. If he strained hard enough, he swore he could hear laughter.

"There were lights. Low down to the ground and swinging like lanterns. There was music, too. Flutes and bagpipes like at one of them renaissance fairs."

"Did you feel threatened? In any danger at all?"

Mr. Porter shook his head. "I felt drawn to it. Felt this sort of giddiness, like a kid going to a carnival. Didn't find nothing, though. I followed the sound, followed the lights, but ended up back at my truck."

Zackary knelt to the ground, took a pinch of dirt, and breathed deep. There was something wild intertwined with the scent of soil. Something earthy and rich like forgotten wine and rotting leaves. New grass. Rain. Smoke. The clean, fresh scent that marked lands claimed by the Christian God had been washed away. Folk born of older ways had claimed this place. By the smell, they were peaceful. There was no iron tinge of blood, thankfully. He'd hate to have anything come to blows—he'd just bought this outfit.

Zackary scattered the dirt and got to his feet. "You were right to contact the church, Mr. Porter. There is definitely something here. Nothing dangerous, mind you. Just playful."

Mr. Porter shifted from foot to foot. "Can I ask what it is?"

Zackary chose his words carefully, well aware that they were being watched. "I believe they like to be called the good folk, or the little people."

"You don't mean faeries, do you?" Mr. Porter whispered. "Faeries aren't real."

Zackary bit back a groan, hoping no one listening would take offense and make his job harder for it. "Come now, Mr. Porter. You were ready to believe it was a demon when we spoke on the phone. Why not the little people?"

The man tripped over his words for a moment. "Well, I mean, they're *pagan*. Pagan stuff ain't real."

Zackary stifled a long sigh behind a taunt smile. Human arrogance never ceased to baffle him. The Order had given him a job to do, though, so he gave Mr. Porter his best customer service smile. "I'm afraid things are a bit more complicated than that."

Mr. Porter only scrunched his brow in response.

Before the mortal man could have an existential crisis, Zackary reached into his pocket and drew out a stack of business cards. "Why don't you go about your day? I'll get to work and call you once I'm done. If there's no activity for seven days, give the number on this card a call and let them know all is well."

Mr. Porter took the card and adjusted his hat. "You be careful, Mr. Bishop."

"Of course." Zackary nodded, then watched as the man walked towards the tree line. Once he was gone, Zackary turned towards the condemned cabin. "Come on out," he called gently. "It's just us. You have nothing to fear. You'll have no judgment from me."

Only the wind in the trees answered.

He pulled a small bell from his pants pocket and gave it a ring. Nothing. From his other pocket, he drew a plastic bag. The sunlight caught the glimmer of honey that soaked the cornbread inside—leftovers from several nights ago. Maryam always made the bread too sweet for Zackary's taste, but it would be perfect for whatever imp, brownie, or sprite was causing trouble for Mr. Porter.

"I brought you a treat," he said, waving the bag. "A peace offering."

Footsteps skittered in the tall grass, but he spun to find nothing. Scampering footfalls on dry wood drew his attention to the rotting porch. He inched forward, giving the bell another ring. Whispers replied.

Zackary crept closer, crouching to shrink himself. "Come now, friends. Surely there's somewhere you'd rather live than this decrepit old place."

The grass rustled again. Before he could turn, a hefty weight slammed into him, sending him face-first into the dirt. Zackary's panic spiked as he scrambled for control. Whatever this was, it wasn't something he'd prepared for.

He managed to flip his assailant on their back, pinning a pair of slender wrists with one hand and holding a knife to the attacker's throat with the other. Shock registered in a pair of deep azure eyes as they scanned over Zackary. The eyes turned mischievous. Hungry. The smirk that spread across that handsome face was downright sinful.

"Tell me," the faerie purred. "Did it hurt when you fell from Heaven, my demon lovely?"

"Save it, *pixie*." Zackary spat the word like a curse. At second glance, however, he wondered if he'd identified the faerie correctly. Pixies didn't normally have ram-like horns that curled to fine tips around their pointed ears, like ancient trees emerging from a sea of wavy blue-black hair. Zackary's heart hammered as he wondered if that hair felt like silk. He shook off the question and tried to keep his attention on more pressing issues.

Horns like that were usually a sign of nobility within the Hemlock court, the faerie court nearest Detroit. Offending a faerie with those sorts of ties was one of the quickest ways to invite trouble, but court faeries typically had human-like skin tones, not leaf green. And they certainly didn't roll around in the grass in undone department-store button-ups, exposing finely toned muscles all the way down to the low-riding waistband of their tight jeans.

Zackary swallowed hard. The Order's entire dispatch team was fucking dead when he delivered this report. This was not what he'd signed up for today.

The pixie bit his bottom lip as he drank Zackary in. "Oh, but don't you want to have some fun?" He craned his neck so his lips nearly brushed Zackary's. "Demons like fun, don't they?"

Zackary's body went rigid at the intoxicating scent of red wine and roses. "Drop the enchantment, pixie," he snapped. "You can't magic your way out of this."

"I'm not working any enchantments." The pixie tilted his head with a coy grin. "You have only yourself to blame for the dirty thoughts in your head, demon."

Zackary glared down at the pixie. What a time for his lack of sexual preference and centuries of loneliness to bite him in the ass. "What are you doing hanging around human lands?" he demanded.

The pixie raised an eyebrow and leaned back. "*Human* lands? That family hasn't bothered with this place for decades. One of them feels like playing historian and suddenly I lose my home?"

"It's not yours if someone has laid claim already."

The pixie snorted. "Next you'll tell me I should respect a tree when a dog pisses on it."

"We can do this the easy way or the hard way, pixie. Your call."

"My call would be that you forget the human and play with me."

Zackary tightened his grip on the pixie's wrists. "I don't have time for games."

The faerie writhed and took a sharp hiss of breath with a devious grin. "I'm sure I can convince you to make time."

"*Pixie—*"

The air stilled, then snapped with static energy. The pixie's smile grew fragile and fake as if he hid a row of razor teeth behind his lips. "Say that word with malice one more time and I'll make you wish for the horrors of Hell, *demon*."

There was so much sickly-sweet poison in his voice that Zackary...well...he wasn't *afraid*, but he still loosened his grip. He'd come prepared for harmless forest folk, not someone with real power behind their words.

He licked his lips, tasting the earthy tinge of magic in the air. "Then, I suppose I'll need your name, stranger."

The faerie's gaze softened. "Emrys." He said the word slowly, as if he needed practice with it himself. "My name is Emrys."

Zachary lowered his voice as if he were trying not to spook a deer. "Well, Emrys, hostility is clearly getting us nowhere. If I let you up, can I trust you to be reasonable?"

Emrys scoffed. "I can promise not to turn your mind to rot, but not much more than that."

"I'll take it." Zackary sheathed his knife, got to his feet, and offered Emrys his hand.

Emrys stood on his own and dusted himself off. He studied the bagged cornbread for a moment—Zackary hadn't even noticed him snatch it—then tossed it into the bushes. The branches rustled and small voices squabbled.

Zackary took his turn sizing Emrys up. Mischief had returned to those azure eyes and a wry smile sat on Emrys' lips that spelled trouble. Zackary hated how beautiful he was. *Hated* it.

Zackary pulled his gaze away from Emrys and surveyed the surrounding meadow. "I apologize for starting off on the wrong foot," he said. "I should know better because I know what it's like to lose your home." Zackary ran a hand through his hair, self-conscious of the way Emrys watched him. "But you can't stay here. I have a job to do and bills to pay."

Emrys gave a dry laugh and crossed his arms. "Demons have bills?"

Zackary hesitated, but decided a little vulnerability on his part wouldn't hurt. "They do when they have a charge to look after."

Emrys' thin brows pulled together. "Charge? You're a guardian angel? Well, guardian demon?"

"Of sorts."

Emrys gave a whistle of awe. "Aren't you something?" He folded his arms again and began pacing. "What a shame. We could have had fun, but I don't like kids."

He bolted for the cabin.

Zackary snatched at him only to catch the slice of a crystal dagger across his palm. He hissed and dug in his jacket, flinging a fine mist of salt at Emrys, ignoring the way it burned his skin. Emrys thrashed and cursed as the salt made contact. Zackary seized the moment of distraction and tackled him onto the porch.

"What the hell was that?" Emrys exclaimed.

"Blessed salt. Stings like a bitch, doesn't it?" Zackary wrestled the iron crucifix from beneath his shirt and over his head. The image of the cross would do nothing, but the burn of iron had a way of helping faeries see reason.

"Wait," Emrys pleaded. He jerked away from the metal, his muscles taut and face pale as he hissed. "Wait, wait, wait. We can bargain, demon."

"And why would I do that?"

"Because you're one of the good ones."

Zackary paused.

"You are, aren't you?" Emrys' eyes darted across Zackary's face. "You're out here defending humans against what they can't fight themselves. You're caring for another," Emrys rambled. "This isn't the first home I've lost. Not by a long shot. Help me find a place I can stay for good, and I'll leave. I'll get the others to leave too."

Zackary weighed his options. He could drag Emrys off the property and charm the place so he and his friends could never step foot on the land again, but that didn't feel like the right choice—the choice that would prove that he and his brothers could be redeemed.

The demon released the pixie and stood up. "Fine." He sighed and massaged his temple. God, he'd gone soft. "Once a week, for one hour and one hour only, I'll help you search for somewhere you can stay permanently. In the meantime, you and your friends clear out. I hear Porter's still having trouble and the deal's off. Understand?"

Emrys stood upright, massaging his wrists. "Sounds fair to me. This hangover has me swearing off partying for a while anyway. That's the only reason you caught me."

Zackary rolled his eyes.

Emrys kept his gaze locked on him for a quiet moment, his body still. He extended his hand. That smirk Zackary couldn't trust was back on his face. "An hour a week, you help me look for a home and the lot of us never come back here. Deal?"

The demon took his hand, the slice across his palm already scabbed over. "Deal."

Emrys' smile widened at the touch of dried blood and the spark of magical heat between their hands, promising that if either of them backed out, there would be nasty consequences to pay. Fine by Zackary—he'd been in enough magical pacts over the years to know the rules.

A slight smirk tugged at Emrys' face. "Why do I get the feeling that, even with a proper deal in place, you still don't trust me?"

Zackary scowled and pulled his hand away. "I would be a fool to trust you. A deal doesn't mean you're bound to act right outside its confines."

"Fair enough, I suppose." Emrys wiped the flakes of blood on his already dirt-stained pants. "So, where do you reside? It would probably be easier if we did this at your place, for obvious reasons."

"Detroit. I have a place in Midtown called *Ectoplasm*. If you take this road back to I-75—"

Emrys held up a hand to stop him. "I'll find you, I'm sure."

Zackary studied the pixie, weighing his words. When he noticed the way Emrys seemed to revel in the attention, he glared, then began back towards the path to the road. "See you soon, I suppose?"

"Naturally."

The word sent a chill of dread down Zackary's spine and hung over his head like an omen. With a tired sigh, he hopped on his bike and began to think of ways to explain to Maryam that they'd have a pixie hanging out once a week. An hour wasn't much, but faeries were infamous for taking miles upon miles if you gave them an inch and Maryam was a born trouble-magnet.

By the time he got home, he had something resembling a plan that let him keep his part of the deal and made sure Emrys couldn't influence Maryam for the worse. He found her behind the bar cleaning the espresso machine. She did a double take at the sight of his dirt-streaked clothes.

"What happened to you?"

"Dispatch didn't do their job," Zackary grumbled. He took a napkin from the bar counter and scrubbed at the blood still on his hand. "Those bastards owe me hazard pay."

Maryam laughed and began making Zackary a cup of tea. "Doesn't everything they pay you count as hazard pay? Exorcism isn't exactly a desk job. Ginger hibiscus?"

"Please."

He set his helmet on the seat next to him and massaged his temple as the racket of Alex's drums grated against his already frayed nerves.

Wait. Why was Alex playing? The place was empty and Easy Breezy never played this time of day. And who on earth had Maryam allowed to touch Matthew's guitar?

Zackary faced the stage to find Alex gleefully hammering out the even, steady rhythm of *Seven Nation Army* while a stranger played a rendition of the guitar solo that Zackary hadn't heard before. He didn't recognize the stranger, not that he had much to go off of with the man's back turned as he head-banged with Alex, but he must have been a regular for the drummer to be that comfortable.

Zackary had known Alex for years and was still lucky to get a smirk out of them every other week. "Who's Alex's friend?"

Maryam frowned as she handed him his tea. "He told us he was *your* friend."

Zackary's stomach plummeted. "What do you mean?"

Maryam blinked. "What do *you* mean? He came in here about thirty minutes ago and said you two were working together on some sort of project and..." Maryam's face paled. "Shit."

Zackary's heart stopped. "What?"

Maryam took a step back. "Don't be mad, okay?"

"Maryam—"

"We were just talking, and he mentioned he needed somewhere to stay and I jokingly said all we had available was our front closet, and then he saw Matthew's guitar and tried to talk music theory. I know jack fuck about music theory. He said he'd teach me if we let him sleep in the front closet and I said that we had a deal if he proved he could play. I thought we were messing around. He said he was waiting for you."

Zackary closed his eyes, took the deepest breath of his life, and pinched the bridge of his nose. "Did you shake on it?"

Maryam muttered a tiny, "...Maybe."

Zackary took an even deeper breath, eyes squeezed shut.

"Did I sell my soul to some sort of ancient evil?"

"It's not as bad as all that," Zackary grumbled. "You just got us a faerie roommate."

Maryam wrung her hands. "He said he'd pick up Kelly's shifts, if that helps," she muttered.

"It might," Zackary replied. "Just give me a minute." The song ended and he whirled on the stage with a glare.

Alex whooped with excitement and the stranger laughed as he turned to place Matthew's guitar back on its stand. His azure eyes fell on Zackary, and sparkled. Fair skin and dark brown hair had replaced leaf green and deep midnight blue, but that damn smirk gave Emrys away like a neon sign.

And that neon sign told Zackary he was diving head-first into trouble.

Peter rolled Wendy's "present" between his fingers as he sat at the bookstore register, eyes glued to the book in his lap. Yes, he was technically on the clock, but the store was empty and inventory was done. On the clock, off the clock, it didn't matter. He wanted answers about whatever the hell Wendy had brought back from her little adventure to St. Damien's.

The symbols on it were occult, of that he was sure, but it had taken an obsessive amount of internet sleuthing to find real explanation for what he was looking at. He knew full well that his time could be better spent on reading more useful things—like job listings with upward mobility—but he hadn't felt this alert and alive since he'd left college. More specifically, since he'd left his electives.

Latin, Ancient Near-Eastern Archeology, and Introduction to Religious Anthropology had lit a passion in him that his finance and business classes hadn't. If anything, those classes often felt like they were sucking his soul out through his eyeballs. But he didn't have the stomach for medicine like his mother, engineering made his brain hurt, and any sort of impractical field had been out of the question if he wanted financial help from his parents, so here he was with a degree in Finance with a minor in Management Information Systems like the dutiful son he was.

At least he had been able to order a worn copy of *The Dark Pope's Grimoire* from the internet to light that spark again. The pages were brittle, and the binding threatened to dissolve if Peter even dared to sneeze, but it was the closest thing to an answer that Peter had found.

The sigils contained in the book's "Index of the Dark Court" proved to be the most useful part. The coin's years of wear didn't help his attempts to decipher its symbols, but at least Peter felt like himself for the first in the seven months since his dad died.

The front bell jingled.

Peter lifted his head to find Maryam sauntering in with a book in her hand, her shoulders back, and an easy smile on her face.

All she said was, "Hey."

Peter froze, then scrambled to shove the coin and the book beneath the counter. "Hey. What's good?"

Maryam smirked as she watched him. "Don't worry." She gave him a wink. "I'm no snitch. Slack all you want."

Peter tried to laugh as naturally as possible and massaged the back of his neck. "Thanks." He eyed the book in her hand. "What brings you in?"

Maryam set the book on the counter—the one Peter had brought with him the night Maryam had fallen off the stage. "You left this at our place. It took a few days to figure out who it belonged to, which was pretty silly on our part, considering you're the only person we know that runs a bookshop."

Peter picked up the book and turned it over in his hands. "Thank you. I appreciate you bringing it back."

Maryam shrugged. "I also need a book to review for my English 101 class. Figured I'd come pick one out while I'm waiting for the bus."

"Where are you off to?"

"I'm meeting a client downtown."

Peter leaned on the counter. "Client?"

Maryam studied the gifts and knick-knacks on the counter. "I do web design as a side gig on occasion."

"Got any room in your schedule for yours truly?" Peter grabbed his phone and pulled up the website his father had built for the bookstore around the fall of MySpace.

Maryam took one look at the screen and pulled her lips between her teeth. When that didn't keep the laughter at bay, she hid her mouth behind a fist. "Oh, wow."

"Yeah."

"That's uh..."

"I know."

"I mean...neon Papyrus on black was considered edgy at one time."

"He did that for Halloween one year and never changed it back."

"I'm sure it looks better on a desktop."

Peter slipped his phone back in his pocket. "It doesn't."

Maryam laughed and Peter's heart grew light.

"I'll make you a deal," she said. "Find me the shortest book possible for my class and I'll give you a discount."

"How much do you care about this project?"

"Macro-econ is kicking my ass, so not much. I just need the easy A."

"I got just the thing." Peter rounded the counter and headed back to the classics section.

He refused to use the stool to reach the higher shelves out of pride, but he suddenly wondered if straining on his tiptoes did more damage to his image.

Not that he needed to care about his image. He and Maryam were just acquaintances, at best.

Peter slid a worn, yellowed copy of *The Great Gatsby* from the shelf and handed it to Maryam "It's a quick read, chock full of symbolism and metaphors—all the stuff teachers love—and it's about how the promise of new money and the American dream are bitter, gilded jokes. You seem cynical enough to enjoy it."

Maryam scoffed as scanned the cover "I don't know whether to be flattered that you put that much energy into reading me or insulted."

Peter watched her scan the back of the book, more eager for her approval than he cared to admit.

His stomach flipped as a wry smile came to her lips.

"A story about a man trying to steal another man's wife in an age dedicated to freedom, dancing, and drinking?" Maryam chuckled and flipped the book over in her hands. "That explains why every high school but us read it—this was definitely banned at St. Mary's."

Peter leaned against the shelf, scrubbing at his face to hide a growing grin. "So, did I just earn myself a new loyal customer?"

"We'll see how I like it first. I'll still give you that discount on the website, though. Mostly because I've helped grandmas set up blogs about knitting and fruit cake recipes that look better."

Peter laughed and headed towards the front. "I don't know whether to be grateful that you're showing me mercy or insulted."

"If you take it as an insult, it'll only stoke the fire of our budding Mario Kart rivalry, so all offense intended."

Peter decided his father would have loved this girl.

Maryam added a bag of black licorice to her purchase at the counter, claiming that three dollars for the book wasn't enough to spend at a local store. As Peter rang her up, he silently built up the courage to voice the question on the tip of his tongue.

"My sister's probably coming over Friday night." He handed her the purchase. "She's also a fiend at Mario Kart. If you don't mind more company, wanna join us?"

Maryam's eyes lit up. "I'd love to, but..." She wrinkled her face with a sympathetic smile as she took the bag. "I have a family dinner that night."

"No problem. Swing by afterwards?"

Maryam nodded with a grin. "I'll do that. Thanks. I'll text you when I'm on my way." She felt around for her phone. "Now that I think about it, I don't have your number."

Peter was faster on the draw, pulling up a new contact window on his phone and handing it over. "I'll text you."

"Sounds good." Maryam typed in her information, then did a small double take at the time in the corner of his screen. She looked over her shoulder to find a bus pulling up to the sidewalk. "Shit. I gotta go."

She handed Peter back his phone and headed for the door. "See you Friday."

Peter's heart fluttered and he cursed himself a total dork. "See you Friday." He looked down at the phone screen and swore to himself—he'd agreed to pick Wendy up from a boutique in Corktown at five and it was 4:50. He locked up the store, shot his aunt a text, and jumped in the car.

A shadow in the rear-view mirror caught his eye as he pulled onto the road. He glanced up, ready to curse at a tailgater under his breath, but he found nothing. He dropped his eyes to the street again.

Darkness shifted in his peripherals. This time, in the back seat. He whirled to find nothing.

He turned back to the flash of taillights and slammed on his brakes. As his heart hammered in his chest and his knuckles gripped the steering wheel, Peter decided that maybe it was time to take a break from researching the occult.

He turned off the AC. It felt like icy breath snaking across his skin. He opened the windows and cranked up the radio in an attempt to feel less alone. Peter found himself counting down the minutes until the car was occupied—it felt like the longest fifteen minutes of his life.

He pulled up to the boutique's curb to find it empty and texted his sister.

C'mon, now. I gotta get Alicia home.

She typed back, *Calm your surgically removed tits. We're on our way.*

Peter replied with a middle finger emoji. Wendy did likewise. Three minutes later—Peter counted—the girl emerged from the store, playfully shoving each other and giggling.

"Ready for homecoming?" Peter asked as they slid in.

Alicia buckled her belt, only to wriggle and stretch so that she could poke her head between the siblings. "Absolutely. Everything's going to be perfect, thanks to this one hot cashier. We would never have found the accessories to match Wendy's dress without him."

Wendy contorted her arm to smack at Alicia. "Shut *up.*"

Peter side-eyed his sister. "Seems awfully friendly. How old was he?"

Wendy folded her arms. "Twenty maybe? He said he was going to cosmetology school."

"Did he give the other sixteen-year-old customers that much attention?" Peter could hear his father's inflection his voice.

Wendy massaged her temple. "Shit, Pete, he was just being helpful. It's his job. It ain't that deep."

"How do you know?"

"He was gay!"

"Watch your tone. I could still tell Mom about the other night."

"Don't be a dick. We already made a deal about that. Don't hold it over my head."

"I'm looking out for you, seeing as you've proven you can't do that yourself." Peter flashed Alicia a pointed look in the rear-view mirror.

She gave a stiff, toothy smile in return. "Yeah...sorry about that, Peter."

"I don't need you to look out for me like this," Wendy snapped. "You're not Dad."

You're not Dad. You're not anything.

Peter slammed the door on that particularly dark corner of his mind.

Strange. That voice hadn't crept up on him in a long time.

Silence fell in the car. Wendy changed the radio to something more upbeat, but the tension still lingered under the music. Alicia tapped Wendy to show her something on her phone. Both girls giggled, painting a layer of normalcy over the uneasy air of the car. Peter flexed his hands and rolled his shoulders, trying to force away the feelings winding tight around his core like a taut rubber band. He hated it when he got like this—tense and protective like a weak imitation of his father. Once they reached Alicia's house, he waited for her to get inside and then tried to find something, *anything* to say to his sister.

Wendy played with this strings of her hoodie. "You don't have to prove anything to me, you know," She pulled the hood tighter around her face. "I know who you are. Mom knows who you are. Dad knew who you were by the end."

He had, and it had cost him nearly everything. Peter and Wendy's paternal grandmother, aunts and uncles hadn't spoken to them since Adam Bailey announced that he was standing by his son and Adam Bailey's childhood church refused to open their doors to the family unless they stopped, "enabling this distortion of God's design." Peter couldn't decide if all his father had lost had been worth it, given how spectacularly Peter was failing as a brother and a son.

"Bailey men take care of our people. You take care of them."

"And I really am sorry about the other night," Wendy added, cutting through Peter's stormy thoughts.

Peter sighed and slicked back his curls. "Yeah, I know." He dropped his hand back to the steering wheel and drummed his fingers against the leather. "I'm sorry I got snippy. I didn't have an older brother to learn from. I had Dad. And, well..." Peter shrugged. "You know how high-strung he could get."

Wendy nodded, then broke out into giggles. "Remember when you came home with your first fade and that fake gold chain you spent your entire first paycheck on?"

A smile tugged at Peter's mouth. "Dad dropped his favorite coffee mug."

"Mom chewed your ass out pretty bad for buying that stupid thing."

"Then I made the mistake of telling her I was trying to embrace my 'roots.'"

Wendy's laughter grew. "She made your dumbass *read* Roots."

"Dad tried to 'bond' with me by reading it too." Peter leaned back against the headrest. "It was all a cover so he could try and find out if I was a lesbian."

Wendy's laughter turned into a cackle. "And when you lied and said yes, he started grilling every girl you had over."

Peter turned to study his sister, brow furrowed. "You remember all that?"

Wendy folded her arms. "I was nine, not a *baby*."

"Close enough." Peter reached for Wendy's head.

She snatched his wrist before he could reach the braids their aunt had spent six hours weaving the day before. "Hey! Not the hair." She wrestled Peter's hand away from her head and held tight to him after he gave up, studying the lines of his palm. "You're enough as you are. You know that right? You don't have to be Dad. You don't have to be..." She shrugged. "I don't know. Whatever it is super light-skinned folks like us are supposed to be, because I know that bothers you sometimes too. We never really got good instructions on that."

Peter snorted and pulled his hand back. "Thanks." He put the car in reverse. "Though, I'm the only super light-skinned person in the car. You're run-of-the-mill light-skinned."

Wendy punched in the arm. "Asshole."

"Act right. I'm driving."

Wendy flipped him the bird. Peter let it slide. Peace and quiet were hard to come by on the weekends with his sister, which was most weekends.

Back at the store, Wendy hopped out of the car before Peter had even put it in park. Before he could scold her, she studied *Ectoplasm* across the street and said, "How was that place, anyway?"

Peter grabbed his things and got out of the car. "Pretty cool. They have a band that plays. It's only two people, but they're pretty good."

"Did you make any friends?"

Peter raised an eyebrow. "Since when do you care if I'm making friends?"

Wendy scoffed. "C'mon, Pete. Don't think I don't notice how little you go out."

Peter dropped his eyes to his keys to find the one to the store. "Don't worry about it, alright? You and Mom come first."

Wendy folded her arms. "What are you going to do once I'm off at college?"

"Follow you, obviously."

Wendy dismissively clicked her tongue and headed up the stairs to the apartment. "Mom gave me money for takeout. What do you want me to order?"

Peter slipped the key into the store lock. "Anything without seafood."

"Shrimp stir fry for days. Got it."

Peter ignored the quip, mostly because he wasn't in range to throw anything at Wendy for it.

He did a sweep of the store, making sure everything was just as he left it, books where they needed to be and the shelves dusted. He paused when he found a shelf dusty enough to leave a streak with his finger and pulled his phone out to text Wendy to come downstairs. Putting in a little elbow grease into the family store would be good for her.

Foot steps raced towards him from behind.

Peter whirled and found nothing. It was the floorboards. Only the floorboards. He was having an off day. That was all it was. Everyone had them.

He just needed to stop reading occult manuscripts, his mind would settle, and this would all go away.

Maryam added a splash of Bailey's to her coffee and took a sip. It wasn't strong enough. She added a long, healthy pour and tasted it again. Still not enough. Not for the evening ahead of her.

Emrys watched from the peninsula counter as Maryam continued to mix her drink. "Is it now customary among mortals to inebriate oneself before a deceased loved one's birthday celebration?"

"I'm aiming for a nice healthy buzz, thank you very much." Maryam took another swig. "I only got completely inebriated for one of Matthew's birthdays." She absently gestured her sword tattoos. "Trust me, once was enough." She considered adding more alcohol, but Zackary emerged from his room with a scowl, distracting her.

"That's what you're wearing?" He looked her over with his nose upturned.

Maryam straightened her forest green blazer and flexed the leather elbow patches. "It stays. It was Matthew's. I think Aunt Sarah and Uncle Hiro be happy to see it out of the closet." She fastened the buttons at the wrists. "Probably the only thing Auntie'll ever be glad came out of a closet in this family."

"Oh, stop it," Zackary chided. "You don't mean that."

Maryam pursed her lips and added more Bailey's instead of arguing.

Zackary turned to Emrys and scowled. "And what are you doing for the rest of the evening?"

"Working, of course," the pixie cooed. His voice was like a ray of sunshine against Zackary's icy demeanor. "You turned down my other suggestions to pay my part of the rent."

"Your other suggestions equated to maybe forty dollars."

Maryam choked on her coffee.

Emrys cackled. "Ouch. You're particularly moody tonight. Sounds like you could use some of those suggestions."

Zackary's eyes narrowed to murderous slits.

Maryam coughed to cover her laughter in a vain attempt to maintain her neutrality. The squabbling was amusing, but she still felt bad that Zackary had to pay the price for her oversight. At least, he acted like he was paying a price. The way he carried on, one would think Maryam had given Emrys her first-born child, not a part-time job and a cot in the front closet.

"Come down when Maryam leaves," Zackary ordered. "I don't trust you up here by yourself."

Emrys scoffed. "I'm not a house pet. It's not like I'm going to rip up the sofa. Though you're more than welcome to put a nice collar on me."

Zackary slammed the door in response.

Maryam laughed openly. "He'd probably warm up to you more if you didn't prod him so much."

"Maybe, but where's the fun in that?"

"Wouldn't it be more fun if he didn't, oh, I don't know, despise you?"

Emrys smirked. "That demon doesn't despise me. Of that, I can assure you." He grabbed the Baileys bottle and slid it toward his own mug. "Though, he certainly isn't what one would expect. I thought demons would sleep with just about anything. That's how we got the Nephilim, then the faeries, and all sorts of creatures and monsters. Isn't that what got them in trouble with God in the first place?"

Maryam shrugged. "Zackary never talks about his part in all that. My cousin, Matthew, mentioned that he had kids once upon a time, but he also said that Zack doesn't like talking about them, so I've never asked." She took a sip of her coffee. "And in the demons' defense, the Nephilim issue has been handled. They all got wiped out in Noah's flood, I think. That's how the story goes, anyway."

Emrys frowned. "So, Zackary isn't interested in sex at all?"

"I have no idea. He gets flustered and annoyed whenever I ask him about his love life and usually ends up lecturing me on privacy, so I'd just say he's stick-up-his-ass-sexual." Maryam lifted her mug to her lips.

"Really? He struck me as a top."

Coffee sprayed across the table as Maryam choked from an attempt to laugh with coffee in her mouth. Emrys jumped out of the way with a satisfied grin on his face. Maryam coughed as coffee dribbled down her face and she grabbed a handful of paper towels.

"Fuck you, Emrys. You did that on purpose." Maryam mopped up the counter, trying her best not to let Emrys see her smile. "If I get coffee on this blazer, I'm gonna murder you."

Emrys winked. "Don't threaten me with a good time."

The front door creaked open. "Maryam, where did you put that..." Zackary studied them both. "What happened?"

"Nothing." Maryam threw away the evidence. "What were you looking for?"

Zackary eyed the two suspiciously. "The new shipment of merlot."

"It's that box under the cash register."

"Thank you." Zackary looked at his watch. "You should head out soon if you want to get to the cemetery before everyone else."

Maryam checked her phone. "You're right. I'll tell everyone you say hi." Once Zackary had left, she inspected her blazer, then jabbed a finger at Emrys. "You're a brat." He blew her a kiss as she grabbed her purse, pausing at the door. "Go easy on him tonight. Matthew's birthday is a hard day for him."

Emrys gave her a sympathetic smile. "I promise to play nice."

"Thank you."

Maryam walked out into the late afternoon and slipped on her headphones. On the bus, she closed her eyes and told herself that Matthew's ghost lived in the vibrations, shielding her from the world for a bit. She ran a thumb over the scar beneath the tattoo on her right forearm.

She hadn't done well with her shield gone. Better, now that she was away from the Order, but not well. She wondered if she'd ever really be well, or if there ever had been a time when she was.

Maryam snorted to herself. Of course not. She was demon-kissed—a child born of a woman in the midsts of demonic possession. And even if the demon had left her mother's body, leaving nothing but a corpse, and Maryam had supposedly been born healthy, something had always felt...off. Why wouldn't it? Evil like that left stains on a soul. Everyone knew that. That evil had even come back and killed Matthew, for Christ's sake. With him gone, it felt like a matter of time before those stains consumed her.

They almost had once before.

The bus lurched to a halt. Maryam opened her eyes to find her stop. She hopped off the bus and popped into a flower shop to pick up a bouquet of black-eyed Susans and a package of peanut butter cups.

They'd buried Matthew in the far corner of the cemetery where the Order had been placing their dead for generations. Some tombstones were too worn to read, showing just how long the Order had protected this corner of the world from the dark.

"Happy birthday, Matty." Maryam placed the flowers in the vase built into the headstone and plopped down beside it, unwrapping the candy. "We got a new roommate. He's a faerie, of all things." She paused to listen with her imagination. "I don't know. He said something about reclaiming the term the other night." She placed Matthew's candy on top of his headstone and popped hers into her mouth. "Holy shit, you should see him and Zack go at it. This dude is totally smitten but Zack acts like he hates him. He seems to think Zack is secretly obsessed with him, but I don't see it. You know Zack, though. He's hard to read."

She unplugged the headset from her phone and turned up the volume. "I brought your playlist." She stretched out on the cool grass and watched the cotton-candy glow of evening bleed across the sky, snuggling into the lush lawn as if the grass could hold her like Matthew had when she was young.

It was the closest she'd ever get to him again. Stained people like her didn't get into heaven. Jesus could have been crucified three times over and it wouldn't have been enough blood to save her. Not when she'd had a demon in her blood before she'd even drawn her first breath. And Maryam couldn't shake the feeling that, if the demon couldn't have her in life, it would gladly wait for her in death.

A familiar, irate voice spoke in the darkness. "Maryam Grace, honestly."

Maryam opened her eyes and sat up to find Sarah dressed in a black ensemble, as if she were repeating the funeral. Her Uncle Hiro, also in black, extended a hand to his niece with a soft smile that crinkled the corners of his eyes more than Maryam remembered. His black hair, while neat, was longer than Maryam remembered. She couldn't believe Sarah hadn't nagged him into shaving the faint patch of beard shadowing his face. And how long had his hair been peppered with gray? Had it been like that the last time she saw him? The only unchanged thing was the purple band on his wrist with a coin engraved with Zackary's sigil. A crescent scar arched above the band, marking the day Zackary had tasted human blood, rooting him in the mortal world with the unholy fabrication of a mortal body.

Hiro opened his arms for a hug once his niece was on her feet. "How are you, cupcake?"

"I'm okay." Maryam beamed, savoring her uncle's warmth and his cedar scent as she squeezed him back. She lightly hugged Sarah and managed to smile. "Like the suit?" she asked, turning around for them to see.

Sarah's nose wrinkled, but the ghost of a smile tugged at her mouth. "It's still hideous, but it's good to see it."

Hiro studied the suit with a grin. "I think it looks good on her."

Maryam smirked. "Thank you. It's nice to know *one* of my guardians encourages my creative side."

Sarah rolled her eyes and stepped onto the grass towards her son's grave. "If your 'creative side' hadn't broken so many vases and statues at church, I might be more inclined."

Maryam shrugged. "God works in mysterious ways."

Hiro chuckled as he followed his wife.

Maryam moseyed to the paved path to give Sarah and Hiro some time with their son.

Aunt Sarah didn't cry at the grave anymore. She hadn't for a few years, now that Maryam thought about it. She mostly looked worn, as if the grief had beaten her and she had made peace with that. Hiro pulled her close, allowing her to put her head on his shoulder. He turned in search of Maryam, offering her his free arm when he spotted her. Maryam shook her head and took a few steps back for emphasis.

She never joined them in their mourning. She was an intruder in this family now that Matthew was gone—now that Maryam's presence had stolen him away. They had to try their hardest to convince her that the demon that had possessed him was not the one who had possessed her mother, but there was something in its eyes, something in the way that it smiled up at her from Matthew's broken, bloody mouth when they had found him that had told Maryam that it knew her.

Little one of our blood. A throne of mortal bones awaits you. Human blood shall be your wine.

It didn't matter how many times her guardians claimed the demon was lying, Maryam had woken up screaming for months with images of Matthew's dead body chained to that radiator in his apartment, animated by a spirit not his own. Hell, she still had those nightmares.

Sarah let out a deep sigh and placed her hand against Matthew's headstone. She hung her head in silent prayer for a moment, then turned to Maryam with a sad smile. "Ready for dinner?"

Maryam nodded, inching towards her guardians like a dog waiting to be struck. They didn't have to blame her for what had happened—she knew, even if she hadn't been the one to stop Matthew's heart. She tensed as Sarah gave her a side squeeze and looked towards the exit, desperate to get somewhere she could numb the night with a few beers. The alcohol in her coffee hadn't helped the way she had hoped it would.

Maryam turned with her aunt and uncle towards the parking lot and found Father Claude walking right towards them.

She bristled and pulled away from her aunt. "What the hell is he doing here?"

Sarah winced at the barbs in Maryam's voice. "He asked about today after you left the office the other day and, well..."

Hiro's gaze darted between Maryam and his wife. "You didn't tell Maryam that he was coming?"

Maryam snorted and folded her arms. "The second she told you, 'I'm putting Claude and Maryam in the same room,' you should have known something was wrong." Hiro shot Maryam a wounded look. Maryam ignored it. He'd forgive her.

Maryam watched as the priest came closer and whispered to her aunt, "Tell him we canceled," she hissed. "Tell him something came up and we have to reschedule. Tell him to fuck right off for all I care."

"*Maryam Grace.*"

"I'll tell him, if you want. It would be an honor."

"You will do no such thing."

"This night is for Matthew's family."

"The Order *was* Matthew's family. It is still the beginning and end of *this* family. When are you going to grow up and accept that?"

Maryam recoiled.

Hiro wrapped an arm around his niece and squeezed as he called out, "Evening, Father. Didn't expect to see you so soon." He gave his wife a pointed look. "Sarah said you were meeting us at the restaurant."

Sarah glowered back.

Father Claude gave a sheepish smile. "Yes, I owe you an apology. I certainly meant to meet you two there, but I seem to have lost the address." He reached in his pocket and displayed his simple flip phone. "And you know how I am with technology."

Father Claude's smile towards Maryam was a muscle twitch away from a sneer. "And I get to see Maryam twice in one month? What a blessing."

"I actually have an early class tomorrow," Maryam lied. She wriggled away from Hiro with her eyes down. "I'm just gonna go."

She skittered around the priest, walking in the grass to give him the widest berth possible. Hiro called for her. She slipped on her headphones. Rapid footfalls followed. She stifled a groan and turned to find her uncle slowing from a jog, bent over and panting. She'd crossed more distance than she'd thought. She lowered her headphones to let him speak.

"Maryam, don't go," Hiro huffed. "I'll talk to Sarah. I'll figure something out."

No, he wouldn't. Not with the Order watching.

Maryam forced a smile. "It's really okay. We just lost a barista, so I had to open this morning. I'm exhausted. It's probably best if I turn in early."

"Maryam, please." Hiro had to reach up slightly to squeeze her shoulders—when had she gotten taller than him? "I haven't seen you in over a month. Stay? For Matt?"

Anger pricked Maryam's chest. "Matt's dead," she blurted. "Having pizza with that bastard won't change that."

Hiro flinched, but held tight to his niece. "Sweetheart, you can't keep this grudge up forever. I know you have it in you to be the bigger person—"

Maryam jerked away. "Letting someone punch down on you isn't being the bigger person."

"But—"

Maryam jabbed a finger at him. "Don't you dare try to tell me that's not what he does to me. What the *entire* Order does to me."

Hiro's mouth hung open as he searched for words. He gave up with a sigh. "I'm sorry. I know they do." He lifted his gaze to his niece, brow tense and eyes pleading. "But there's some things you can't fight. Not with this world the way it is."

"And who decides the way this world is going to be, Uncle Hiro?"

Hiro's eyes darted across Maryam's face, his lips tight together as they held back a lifetime of secrets. "Forces beyond our control, sweetheart. Beyond Father Claude's control."

Maryam snorted and shook her head. "Well then, I guess I'm sorry too." She slipped her headphones back on. "Bye, Uncle Hiro. I'll try to text more."

With that, she walked away.

She rode the bus home in silence, using angry, blaring music as a buffer against the world rather than a celebration of what Matthew had left behind. She didn't feel like celebrating anymore. She felt like drinking obscene amounts of alcohol and pretending everything was fine, because if she had built a life away from the Order, why shouldn't she be fine?

Maryam massaged her temple as the bus arrived at her stop. She considered canceling on Peter as she hauled herself to her feet—she wouldn't be much company in her current mood.

The universe, however, seemed to have other plans.

"Hey, stranger."

Maryam paused, closed her eyes, and took a deep breath before turning to find Peter across the street, straining against the nearly-bursting grocery bag in the crux of his elbow. He flashed her a smile and managed a waive, despite the bags. She internally groaned, looked both ways, and crossed the street. So much for sneaking away to drink herself stupid.

"What's up?" he asked. He looked her up and down with a grin. "Nice suit. Heading to dinner?"

Maryam fiddled with the hem of her jacket to avoid his eyes. "I actually sort of skipped out on dinner."

Peter paused. "Did something happen? Are you okay?"

The worry in his voice threatened to break her.

"I'm fine. It's just, um..." Maryam bounced her gaze from building to building. To the changing streetlight. Anything but Peter's face. "This dinner was supposed to be for my cousin's birthday, but someone I can't be around showed up and, um..."

And her aunt had defended him and her uncle was powerless, and now Maryam was alone, because being alone meant being safe, no matter how much it sucked. Her throat closed and her vision blurred. She palmed at her burning eyes and tried to slow her shaking breath.

"Oh, shit. Hey." Peter set his bags down and reached for Maryam, then paused, letting his hands close as he waited for some sign that he was allowed to touch her.

Maryam didn't even know the answer. She just wanted to disappear.

"Whose ass do I need to kick?" Peter asked. "I know how to hide a body."

A punch of laughter escaped Maryam. She sniffed and covered her mouth, trying to hold back her giggles. The sound was almost as embarrassing as crying in front of a near stranger. "Please don't. I'd hate for them to put a black bag over your head and make you disappear."

Peter smirked and folded his arms. "They'd have to catch me first. Besides, I'm not proud. If I ask for your brother's help, I'm sure we could take 'em."

"Heh." Maryam wiped her eyes, equally amused by the mental image and the fact that the story about Zackary being her brother stuck so well—now that she was grown, they looked too close in age to tell people he was her godfather without people asking questions. She took a deep breath and her vision started to clear. "I'm sorry."

"Don't be sorry."

Maryam could have melted into the softness of that voice, which, she decided, was stupid. She cleared her throat and shoved her hands in her pockets. "I mean I'm sorry that I had to ruin the illusion that I'm a cold-hearted badass."

Peter snorted and picked up his bags. "Please. I never thought you were a cold-hearted badass."

"Of course you did. Everyone thinks I am."

"Yeah, okay." Peter readjusted his bags. "Cold-hearted badasses don't include the Indigo Girls in their throwback sets."

Maryam gave a mock gasp of offense. "How dare you. My gay foremothers are totally badass."

"Badass? Yes. Cold-hearted, absolutely not." He looked Maryam over again, more at ease and less worried.

The door to the apartment above his store opened. "Peter, what the hell? Did you get lost?" A teenage girl leaned over the railing looking strikingly like Peter, though her face was splashed with more freckles.

"You really need to cut back on that swearing." Peter called back.

The girl ignored him and grinned. "You're Maryam, right? Hi, I'm Wendy."

Maryam smiled back. "Hi, Wendy." She played back the siblings' names in her head. "Aw, Peter and Wendy, like *Peter Pan*. That's cute."

"Thanks," Peter smirked. "I planned it that way."

Wendy rolled her eyes and Maryam blinked with a blank smile, not quite understanding the joke. "You busy, Maryam?"

She tensed. "I was going to come over later. I don't want to intrude if you two have plans."

Peter shook his head and headed for the stares. "It's fine. Come on up if you're cool with frozen pizza for dinner. Maybe if you're here, my sister will behave."

Wendy stuck her tongue out at her brother.

Peter flashed Maryam a mischievous that sent a flash of energy down her spine. "Besides, I'm curious about what other artists you consider cold-hearted badasses."

God, he was handsome. And fun. It was stupid to care, and yet she followed him up the stairs anyway.

Her nerves turned to dread on the threshold as the scent hit her like a bullet train, knotting her stomach and freezing her blood. It hid under the rose-scented air freshener, like a stain on the air. The smell of rot, decay, and brimstone.

She'd smelled it the day they found Matthew dead and possessed.

It was the smell of a demon.

8

Maryam forced a smile as she slipped off her jacket. "Cute place."

Peter set down his bags and threw open the freezer. "Thanks. My aunt didn't feel right charging me rent, seeing as I'm pretty much running the store for her right now. That, and it was my dad's place."

"Sounds like a good set up." Maryam glanced around the living room, looking for anything out of the ordinary. All she found was leftover college furniture and surprisingly healthy plants.

A picture on the TV stand caught her eye. In it, a much younger Wendy, dressed as a pirate, grinned as she sat on the knee of a curly-haired white man in a skeleton costume. Their beaming smiles matched, as did their deep brown eyes. An older girl with two puffy pony-tails and a princess dress, dangled over the man's shoulder. Maryam recognized those dark eyes and realized it wasn't a girl at all.

"Is this your dad?" she asked, picking up the picture. "You both look like him." She pointed to the kid with pigtails in the picture. "You make a cute princess, Peter."

Wendy froze, her expression stormy and her body tense.

Peter only smirked as he punched numbers into the oven display. "Thanks." He pulled out a baking sheet.

Maryam went back to studying the display. Her eyes fell on one featuring Peter and Wendy a few years older. Wendy clung to their father while Peter stood in front of a woman in a graduation gown, her dark tawny arms tight around his shoulders and her cap atop a crown of locked hair decorated with golden beads. "Is this your mother? She's beautiful."

Wendy stood a bit taller, one eyebrow ticked up in curiosity. "My brother being trans doesn't bother you?

"Why would it bother me?" Maryam studied Peter as he continued to flit about the kitchen. He didn't look her way, but the tension in his movements told her he was listening. "His name is what really threw me off, honestly." she answered. "Trans guys always pick dramatic fantasy names like Alastor and shit."

The siblings exchanged looks—Peter's a scowl and Wendy's a gleeful grin—before Wendy began to cackle.

Peter threw a dish towel at her. "Shut your ass up."

"Oh, I like her." Wendy wiped the tears of laughter from her eyes. She turned to Maryam beaming. "We're definitely keeping you."

Maryam felt a genuine smile tug at her mouth. "Did I hit too close to home?"

"Of course not."

"Don't lie, *Apollo*."

Maryam pinched her lips between her teeth. "Peter, tell me you didn't."

"My name's Peter, so obviously not."

"Yeah, because Mom threatened to write you out of the will."

"Why you gotta put our business out there like that?"

"I'm the little sister—it's my job."

"Keep it up and I might make it my job to tell Maryam how long you slept with a nightlight."

Wendy's expression melted into dread. "You wouldn't."

Maryam laughed, preparing to apologize for tearing a family apart, but a shadow in the corner of her eye brought her joy to a screeching halt. She turned to face the small hallway where she had seen the shadow to find nothing. The chill across her skin told her there had been something there, though.

"Mind if I use the bathroom?" she asked.

Peter motioned to Wendy with the frozen pizza box in his hand. "Show her where it is, will you?"

Wendy got up from the old recliner and led her down the hall to the small baby blue restroom. Maryam's smile dropped the second she shut the door. She glared into the mirror above the sink as if her reflection was in league with whatever haunted the apartment.

"All right, you bastard," she hissed. "What do you want?"

No answer. Not even a creak in the walls.

Maryam listened to the siblings in the living room. She slowly turned the doorknob so that the old metal wouldn't creak, then slipped into the room on her right.

Judging by the tidiness, it was Peter's. Just like the living room, nothing looked out of place. The adjacent bedroom looked like a typical teenage girl's room with its flowery comforter on the bed, celebrities on the wall—Maryam mouthed, *"Nice,"* at Wendy's Jimmy Hendrix poster—and a desk buried under school work. Maybe she had a deck of tarot cards that hadn't been properly cleansed or a spirit board tucked away?

She nearly jumped out of her skin as Wendy called, "Maryam, do you want pepperoni pizza or veggie?"

"Hold that thought," Wendy said. "I forgot my phone charger in the car."

Peter clicked his tongue. "You oughta staple that charger to your forehead."

There was a soft *thump* as a pillow collided with her older brother. "Boy, shut up."

Maryam's heart settled back into her chest as the front door clicked shut. She darted back into the bathroom and ran a hand over her hair, eased her breathing, then looked back to the mirror that still held no clues. "I know you're here."

She dug in her pocket and pulled out a small vial of holy water. Zackary had started giving her little religious trinkets after Matthew's death to comfort her, but this was the first time she'd ever had to use one.

Maryam uncorked the vial and began sprinkling the room. "Let's see how you like this, asshole."

Once she felt confident that the sprinkled water would do its job, she closed the vial and left the bathroom. She slapped the fake smile back on her face just as Wendy asked again which kind of pizza she wanted.

"I'll honestly eat whatever you have, so long as it has cheese and grease." She eyed Peter, who sat on the couch with a video game controller in his hand. "Trying to get a head start?"

He smirked as he clicked around the screen. "I'm just getting it set up. I like to win fair and square." He offered her a controller. "Don't pick Peach. Wendy'll throw you out the window."

Wendy took her place back on the recliner. "Oh, hush. I will not. Though I do expect you to honor the rule of dibs and I already called her."

Maryam eased herself onto the sofa. "That's fine. I like Daisy better anyway." She stifled a squeak as the broken frame made her tumble into Peter. Like an awe-struck doofus, she sat frozen, noting how warm he felt, how good his earthy cologne smelled, and just how good it felt to be this close to someone that made her feel safe.

"Sorry. I should have warned you," Peter chuckled, his voice low and kind.

Maryam's heart fluttered. She could listen to that voice all night.

Wendy dragged her back to reality. "Ya'll gonna start making out or can we play?"

Peter hurled a pillow at her. "You're such a brat."

Wendy laughed as it collided with her shoulder. "Then let's go!" She pressed a button and the screen shifted to three separate panels.

"No fair! You chose the course when we weren't looking."

"It's not my fault your head isn't in the game."

Maryam inched away to sit on the couch properly and elbowed Peter as she sent her kart zooming down the road. "I say we gang up on her for that."

Peter smirked, sending her heart fluttering again. "I like the way you think."

Maryam told herself that she would give the demon an hour. To her surprise, she didn't even have to fake having fun while the time passed. The siblings were ruthless, Peter with his gameplay and Wendy with her distracting smart-ass remarks.

But then the apartment shook. It was small enough that nothing fell from the shelves, but pronounced enough that both siblings went still and sat up straight.

Peter paused the game and looked at the girls. "Did you feel that?"

Wendy craned her neck to look down at the road below. "I did. Did a semi go by?"

"That didn't feel like a semi."

Maryam followed Peter to the glass. The nearest light was red, meaning if it had been a truck, it would be sitting on the street below. The road was clear and none of the pedestrians seemed to have noticed anything out of the ordinary.

Maryam inched away. "Will you excuse me for a second?"

Wendy shrugged. "Okay, but that means you forfeit the next round."

Maryam heard the last of the decorative pillows hit Wendy as she shut the bathroom door and looked in the mirror. She closed her eyes and took a deep breath. Maybe she'd been lucky and gotten rid of the spirit all on her own. Before she could gloat at the thought, she gagged on the smell of sulfur.

She opened her eyes and her blood ran cold.

Her expression in the mirror stood still, whites and irises alike now narrow bottomless ink-black pits. "Hello there, child," the reflection said in a deep, suave voice with Maryam's mouth. "So observant. You knew I was here the second you walked in. I felt it in the beating of your heart. It takes someone special to do that."

Maryam swallowed hard and controlled her breathing. The effort proved a good distraction from the phantom ragged breath in her ear. Matthew's bloodshot eyes seeped in from her memory. "Get out," she hissed.

"Why?" Her reflection scoffed, raising a hand to its right earlobe. "Especially now that I have you to play with."

She felt a pinch on her ear and writhed away. "Get the fuck off me," she snarled.

The reflection cackled. "Now, there's some fire." It leaned forward, eyes burning through Maryam's soul as its head tilted further to the left than should have been possible. "What are you, young one?" The reflection closed its eyes and inhaled deep. Maryam didn't like the glee on its face when it opened its eyes. "You smell like mortal rot, yet your blood burns like ours and your soul tastes like a faerie's. I recognize it from their reveries."

"You're probably smelling my roommates, you freak," Maryam snapped. "And if you don't leave Peter and Wendy alone, I'll call both the faerie *and* the demon so they can kick your ass."

The reflection giggled. "You honestly think they could do anything to me? You've clipped your demon's wings and that pixie might as well be a lamb." It looked Maryam up and down, its expression quizzical. "But you're not the one who clipped that demon's wings, are you? You don't carry his seal, nor are you marked as his master, yet he serves you. Why?"

Zackary served *her*? In any other context, the idea would make her laugh. Instead, she racked her brain for a Bible verse.

"For by grace you have been saved through faith—"

The reflection growled and clenched its hand into a fist.

Maryam choked, gasping for air, and clawing at her throat, doubling over as she wheezed. The invisible grip hauled her upright, forcing her to meet the reflection's eyes. The invisible nails dug deeper into her skin.

A twisted, nasty smile spread across her reflection's face. "You think it's that easy, young blood? You think because one of us does your bidding, you have power?" The reflection's eyes narrowed and pulled Maryam closer. "Although...maybe you do..."

"Piss off, you bastard." Maryam rasped.

The reflection dismissively clicked its tongue. "You're not the least bit curious about what I sense crawling underneath your skin?"

"I'm curious why you think choking the life out of me is going to make me believe a word you say. You didn't even buy me dinner first."

A knock at the door drew the reflection's attention.

"Maryam, you okay?" Wendy asked.

The reflection released Maryam, leaving her coughing and choking down air. "I don't need the girl, you know."

Maryam's gasps stopped short.

The reflection's expression turned into smug victory. "Get out. Tell either of the siblings what you know, and I'll rip out her throat before they can even call you crazy." It shoved her towards the door.

Wendy knocked again. "Maryam? I don't want to be rude, but it's an emergency..."

Maryam flung the door open. "Sorry. I'm not feeling good."

Peter's brow furrowed as he got to his feet. "What's wrong?"

"Nothing. I just need to rest. Again, I'm really sorry. Rain check?"

"Of course, but Maryam...?"

She paused and watched the calculation in his beautiful eyes.

"You can talk to me," he said, his voice gentle. "You're safe here."

Maryam's chest fluttered. She didn't know what that was like—to be safe with someone. The only thing that had ever felt safe was running. That and squabbling with Zackary.

Yet, somehow, she believed him.

While Maryam might be safe with him, Peter wasn't safe so long as that demon lurked about. She shrugged on her jacket, gave one last wave, then bound down the stairs and across the street. Zackary caught sight of her through the glass. Her fear must have shown through, because he was there to meet her at the door, arms outstretched to hold her up, thank God. She wasn't sure she would have been able to stay standing with how violently she shook. Emrys followed close behind.

Zackary gently pushed aside her hair and traced the red marks on her neck. "Who did this?" he snarled. "Was it Peter? I'll kill him."

Maryam shook her head and wrung her hands, her throat threatening to close. Fuck, why did she always freeze up like this when her words actually mattered?

"It wasn't Peter," she choked out. "There's a demon. It's after him."

Emrys Hemlock liked weird. The good kind of weird. "A wild party turns into an even wilder orgy" weird. He mentioned as much to Zackary on his break as they scrolled through nearby state parks to get in their weekly twenty minutes of house-hunting.

The demon seemed no closer to cracking, but Emly noted the way he rolled the mouse scroll wheel with more force than necessary.

Zackary massaged his temple, eyes still glued to the screen. "You're sharing this wildly inappropriate information with your new boss because...?"

"You seem shy," Emrys answered, popping a fry in his mouth. He'd opened a tab the second Zackary had given up protesting and let him work at the bar. "I just want you to know that, whatever you're into, you can't scare me away. I'll try pretty much anything once."

"Have you considered the possibility that I'm just not attracted to you?"

Emrys dust his food with a packet of salt. "If you only fancy women, just say so. Nothing a little magical glamor and alcohol can't fix."

"My preference isn't the issue here. It's you."

Emrys continued to eat as he mulled the idea over. "Not possible," he concluded around a mouth full of chicken tender. "I'm a delight."

Zackary glared, but only for a moment. His expression turned to concern as he glanced out the window. Emrys turned to spot Maryam and her bright red hair as she sprinted across the road. Zackary jumped to his feet and ran to meet her, Emrys following on his heels. Maryam stumbled into the bar with panic scrawled across his face as Zackary caught her.

He held her as if she were fragile.

"There's a demon." She sounded like she might hyperventilate. "It's after Peter."

Zack's eyebrows pulled together. "Are you sure?"

Maryam nodded "Absolutely. I smelled it when I walked in. It smelled like..." She swallowed hard. "It smelled like Matthew's place the day we found him."

Zackary's expression turned stormy. "Did you get a name?"

"No, but..." Maryam shifted her gaze to Emrys. "It said, *your soul tastes like a faerie's. I recognize it from their reveries.* Know any demon party crashers?"

Emrys eyebrows shot up. "None come to mind." An idea struck him and he smirked. "Looks like I'm going to have to crash a party of my own."

Zackary frowned. "You can't just contact a few friends and ask around like a normal person?"

Emrys shifted his hands to his hips. "Faeries don't do normal. Also, parties are the best time to get folks to spill all kinds of juicy secrets."

Maryam stood up a little straighter, a little less afraid. "So, we're going to go party with faeries to save Peter?"

Zackary shook his head. "Emrys and I will put together a plan to go *talk* to faeries. You will stay put."

"No. I want to go."

Zackary squared his shoulders. "Absolutely not."

Maryam folded her arms. "Zack, *please*. I can't let Peter get hurt."

"It's too dangerous."

Maryam groaned. "Seriously? You're always telling me how I *'can't run from my demons.'*" She added the most mocking air quotes Emrys had ever seen. "Now that there's an actual demon across the street, I can't help?"

Zackary frowned. "You just barely avoided a panic attack, Maryam."

"I'm not going to have a panic attack over faeries, Zackary."

Before Emrys could inform her that faeries could give her far worse than a panic attack, Alex inched into the group, gaze nervous and their posture slouched. "Sorry to interrupt, but can one of you handle the asshole at the end of the bar? He won't stop asking for my number or joking about spiking drinks. It's giving me yikes-vibes."

Zackary's gaze darted to the man in question—blonde, pompous, cocky. He narrowed his eyes into a fierce scowl meaner than anything he ever flashed at Emrys. "It would be my pleasure."

Emrys held up a hand to stop him. "Easy there, He-Man. I'll handle it."

Maryam cracked something close to a smile at that. Emrys gave her a reassuring wink and walked away.

His ease dissipated the second he studied the man Alex had motioned to. He knew the wrong kind of trouble when he saw it. The man scanned the crowd with a smug aura of entitlement that made Emrys' blood boil. He looked every woman up and down, his free hand itching to touch what he thought was rightfully his, and scoffed at most of the men. It was as if Emrys was staring at a human version of the crown prince of the Hemlock court—a spoiled, arrogant snake whom Emrys loathed to call his half-brother.

He hated the stranger instantly, but still forced himself to smile. "Excuse me, sir."

The man stopped watching the bar and glared at Emrys.

"Seems like you've been bothering my coworker." Emrys leaned in close on the bar and lowered his voice. "I'd hate to have to ruin your evening by asking you to leave."

"I haven't done anything wrong," the man snapped. "Just been sitting here drinking."

"And harassing dear Alex for their phone number—"

"It's illegal to try and get a girl's number now?" The man sneered.

"No, but it is exceptionally rude to keep asking, especially since they aren't a girl and you clearly don't respect that fact."

The man rolled his eyes. "She's one of *those* freaks?"

Emrys' hands tensed to fists. "In addition to being impolite, you were apparently talking about spiking drinks?"

"You're kicking me out because that goth bitch can't take a joke?"

Emrys snatched the man by the collar as something within him snapped. "You're done."

The stranger's fist collided with Emry's mouth. His vision exploded into stars as he hit the ground. Movement shot across his blurred vision. Zackary had leapt over the bar, wrestling the man from his stool.

Maryam knelt at Emrys' side, easing him to his feet as the world spun. Zackary hauled the man toward the front door, deadly silent and still as the man fought back in vain. Emrys followed in a stumble, ignoring Maryam's order to sit down and watched from the doorway as Zackary launched the man onto the pavement.

The man skidded on the sidewalk with an *oof* and picked himself up off the ground with a wheeze. "What the hell, man? I'm a paying customer."

Zackary towered over him, his expression dark and stormy. "Not anymore. I see you within a block of my place again and you'll have more than a few scrapes to be worried about. Are we clear?"

The man glared at Zackary. "That faggot put his hands on me first."

A switch in the universe flipped.

Maryam froze.

The air ignited with static energy and Zackary's hands turned to trembling fists as he took a towards the man. His eyes melted into deep vats of pitch and his features hollowed as his skin faded to marble white.

Terror etched itself into the stranger's face, bringing a bloodthirsty grin to Zackary's thin, twisted mouth. "Insult one of my people again. Please. I insist. It's been so long since I disemboweled a man with his own bones." His voice was dark and ancient, like a quiet roar from a forgotten beast on the edge of waking.

Emrys didn't recognize it. Any of it. Not that voice, not that face, not even Zackary's posture. The pixie's stomach plummeted as he remembered that demons weren't born—that title was earned through blood, betrayal, torture, and hellfire.

"Zackary" was a farce. The thing in front of Emrys was vengeance and rage incarnate.

He could feel Maryam trembling behind him. Her grip tightened on his arms until it hurt as bad as the tightening in his chest.

"Em, get back," she whispered. She sounded as different as Zackary looked—small, shaking, and powerless. Emrys looked at the way she cowered with a new sort of fear—she was afraid of him. Terrified. The center of Zackary's whole world was so scared she'd shrunken down to the size of a child.

Emrys knew what that sort of fear felt like.

He shook Maryam off, marched across the sidewalk, and grabbed Zackary by the forearm. "That's enough." He dug his nails into Zackary's marble skin.

The look Zackary gave Emrys could have cracked bedrock. Sharpened predator teeth flashed from behind his lips as he growled low in his chest. "Get. Off."

Maryam tugged on Emrys' shirt. "Em, listen to him."

Emrys gently pushed her back, refusing to take his eyes off Zackary. "This isn't right. This isn't you."

Zackary let out a chuckle like a tremor. "And what do you know of me, pixie?"

"I know this isn't who you want to be."

Zackary loomed over him. "I could turn you to ash."

"You won't hurt me." Emrys' grip tightened. "Not like this." He swallowed hard and stood on his toes until his mouth brushed Zackary's, sharp teeth and all. His pulse hammered in his ears, whether from the danger or the thrill, he couldn't say. "Not when you could put me on my knees and make me choke on you instead."

Chilly autumn snapped back into place.

A disgusted scoff broke from Zackary's lips. "Why are you like this?"

Emrys' gaze darted to Zackary's eyes and found the deep, near-black brown gaze he'd come to expect. The color was like a comforting cup of coffee on a cold day. Like warmth and safety that Emrys wanted to melt into.

Emrys leaned back and shrugged off his relief—because it wasn't like he *cared*. He just would have missed out on one hell of a notch in his belt if Zackary incinerated a human in public. He didn't know much about the Rosary Order, but they most certainly wouldn't like that. "If it got your attention, what does it say about you?" He ran a finger up Zackary's chest. "And that was a genuine invitation, by the way."

Maryam pointed down the road before Zackary could snap at him. "He's getting away."

Zackary glanced over his shoulder to watch the man sprint down the road with a scoff. "Degenerate," he grumbled. "Let him go. Pretty sure he'll think twice about throwing around slurs and generally being an asshole in public now."

Maryam pulled her blazer tighter around herself and shivered in the cold. "You didn't need to go turbo-mode, Zack. I could have taken him."

Emrys chuckled. "Oh, please, you two. I've been called far worse."

"So, what?" Zackary whirled on Emrys. "He might not have deserved to be *incinerated* for what he said, but he at least deserved a good beating, especially after hitting you."

"Honestly, Zack. It's fine. Again, I've dealt with worse." Emrys chuckled and pulled at a loose thread on his sweater, unwilling to meet Zackary's eyes again. He'd almost prefer to face him down as a demon again—at least he had a course of action for that.

This...this, he didn't know how to handle.

His heart skipped a beat as Zackary caught his chin and lifted his face, those brown eyes deep and serious.

"Well, you don't deal with it anymore." Zackary's thumb brushed the split in Emrys' lip from the punch. "Not in my house, you don't."

There was a pinch of pain, then the warm tingle of skin knitting itself back together and a lightness in Emrys' chest that he decided he didn't care for. He traced his healed lip with his tongue, then smirked. "If it's your house, can I call you daddy?"

Zackary sighed and dropped his hand. "You're unbelievable."

"I believe the term you're looking for is 'bratty.'"

"Keep it up and I'll deck you myself." Zackary headed for the bar. "C'mon. I gotta do damage control and figure out what to do about Peter's demon problem."

Emrys hung back, deciding that he needed the cold night air to clear whatever weirdness had settled over him out of his head.

Beside him, Maryam let out a long, exasperated sigh, doubling over as if fear had been the only thing holding her up. "What the *fuck* have you seen in life that you can flirt with him seconds after seeing his turbo-mode?"

"The queen of the Hemlock court, for starters," Emrys answered bitterly. He watched Zackary through the glass. "Is that a frequent occurrence?"

Maryam shook her head, pulling her hair from her face. "I haven't seen him get like that in years. The last time was when I, uh...got really sick and had to go to the hospital. Zack would hardly let anyone near me." She studied Emrys for a moment. "It took my uncle hours to do what you just did in ten seconds. He almost had to lock him in the basement."

Emrys raised an eyebrow. "I'm just that irresistible, I guess."

Maryam scoffed. "Yeah, how could anyone resist someone as humble as you?" She gently touched Emrys' elbow as she walked back towards the bar. "C'mon. Zack's right. We need to get cracking on this demon situation."

Emrys followed, but not without a long look at the windows above the bookstore across the street. As a car drove by, Emrys could have sworn the headlights caught a tall, looming figure in one of the dark windows. He rubbed his eyes, and looked again. Another car passed. Nothing. Just a trick of the light. No demon would be that obvious.

Still, Emrys couldn't help but wonder what exactly they were up against if it didn't fear the power Zackary had almost unleashed.

10

Peter got a call from his mother an hour after Maryam left.

"Can you take Wendy back to the house tomorrow after the store closes? Something came up at the hospital."

Peter sighed and massaged the bridge of his nose, drawing Wendy's attention from the sofa. "Yeah, sure."

Eliza's tone sharpened. "What's with the attitude? I gotta work."

Funny. She hadn't had to work this much before their dad had died.

Peter wanted to live another day, though, so instead he said, "I don't have an attitude." He dug a fifth of Jack and the ice tray from the freezer. This conversation always required booze. "Wendy was just looking forward to us all having dinner tomorrow."

"We'll do it next weekend, baby. I promise."

"That's what you said *last* weekend, Mom."

"Baby, I know, but I'm the only one who can cover. I said I'm sorry."

Was she *really* the only person who could cover, or did thinking that give her yet another excuse to feel in control when the death of her husband had left her, and her children, feeling incredibly *out* of control?

Peter took a drink instead of asking.

Wendy draped herself over the arm of the sofa. "I could just take the bus home if Mom can't get me. Then you can have Maryam over and make out, but I won't have to see it."

Peter took an ice cube from the tray and whipped it at her. "Smart ass. And you don't gotta take the bus. I can take you."

"If you'd just take me car shopping...I almost got the money saved up from baby sitting and lawns and shit."

"Don't swear. And I can only handle one argument at once, thanks."

Eliza came back on the line. "Who said we arguing? You wanna argue, we can argue."

Peter threw back his glass. Sipping the liquor wasn't going to cut it. "Can we not do this? I already said I can take Wendy home."

There was no point in fighting. Peter knew that. Eliza Bailey couldn't be told much of anything. If she wanted to work herself to death at the hospital, that's exactly what she was going to do, woe to anyone—*especially* her children—who tried to stop her.

Eliza paused. The chatter and calls over the PA system were like white noise in the background. "I'm sorry, Peter. I'm serious, we'll all hang out next week."

"'Aight, Mom. Tell all those sick folks I say hi."

His mother chuckled. "Okay, baby. Tell Wendy I'm sorry. I love you both."

"Will do. Love you too."

Peter hung up, and poured himself another drink, ignoring the concerned way his sister watched him.

"I really can get home on my own if you want some time to yourself. I can pull the bus schedule up on my phone. I won't get lost. You should try to spend time with Maryam again. She's cool. And I think she likes you. I *know* you like her."

Peter shrugged. "I don't mind hanging out with you."

Wendy turned so that she hung off the sofa upside down, her braids dangling to the floor. "I know you don't. That's why you're cooler than most older brothers."

Peter snorted.

"But that's just it, Pete—you're my *brother*. Not Dad. You need your own space to do your own thing, preferably with Maryam. I want a sister."

"Don't get crazy. We're not even dating."

"Do you want to date her, though?"

"I'm too busy."

"Oh, yeah. This old bookstore really keeps you on your toes."

Peter shot Wendy a dirty look. "Fuck off, Wen."

"Now who's swearing?"

Peter whipped another ice cube at her. Wendy squealed and hid behind her hands, then scrambled to catch herself before she fell off the couch and landed on her head.

"I'm not really feeling Mario Kart anymore," Peter sighed. "Wanna just stream something instead? I want to run downstairs and make sure the shop's okay."

Wendy grunted as she hoisted herself up. "You checked it three times already."

"Let me humor myself."

Wendy grumbled something about Peter being old, which he let slide, and headed towards her room while he meandered down the stairs.

Peter didn't like the store at night. The uncanniness of it, the lived-in sensation, despite the emptiness. The old-book smell, the lingering warmth, the tattered posters. It all felt at odds with the stale air of emptiness, especially the emptiness his father left behind. It hit him hardest at times like this. His conversation with his mother and sister didn't help. He knew he used the store the same way his mother used the hospital. What he didn't know was how to stop.

He still wondered if applying for jobs outside of Detroit would help. Someone would hire him eventually and he could put some distance between himself and the grief. Here, there was no way around it. The fact that he was a disappointment brought its own sort of grief, making moments in the darkness like this all the worse.

The store had been his dad's project—his own slice of peace after his military career had ended. It wasn't meant to be generational, but Adam Bailey had died and Eliza's sister bought the place. Then Peter hadn't been able to find a job that paid enough to move out after graduation. And so, here he was: barely afloat, lost, and amounting to nothing at a neck-breaking speed.

Peter's internal dialogue screeched to a stop as he rounded the corner and found a pile of books on the ground, their shelf stark and empty.

He darted to the front door, blood like fire and ice as he panicked. The windows were pristine, unbroken, and the front door gave a locked, metallic rattle when he tried to jerk it open. Somehow, that made it worse. A break-in he understood. There was a course of action for it. What was he supposed to do with books flying off their shelves of their own accord?

That couldn't have been what happened, though. That was impossible. He tried in vain to slow his ragged breath, his hands shaking as he dialed Wendy's number.

"You lock yourself in, nerd?" Wendy asked on the other line.

"This shit isn't funny, Wendy. I told you the shop is off limits for pranks."

"Peter, what the heck are you talking about?" Wendy slowly replied. "I've been up here all night."

Peter studied the books closer as his sister spoke and realized it had only been the titles focused on the fringes of organized religion: books about witchcraft, and other marginal spiritualities and philosophies. *Cunningham's Book of Shadows*, *The Collected Works of Aleister Crowley*, and *The Satanic Bible*, were just the first ones that caught his eye. Someone, something, had been looking for a particular book.

A black paper-back flipped upside down caught Peter's eye due to its distance from the others, causing him to do a double take when he realized it was his copy of The Dark Pope's Grimoire.

He picked it up gingerly as though it might bite him. His nerves were so frayed that he jumped when a pile of torn paper fell out and fluttered to the floor. He set the book on the counter to study the damage. Most of the text had been shredded. Peter could only make out the words one or two at a time and had no idea where to even start putting it all back together.

One entire page survived.

Peter squinted in the dim light to make out the words: *Anzuri—The Third Duke of the Western Hell-Lands. He is a proud lord that has clung to his name from the First Days and will instruct his summoner in all the magics of the time before the Flood, if the summoner vows to help him ascend back to Heaven.*

A metallic glint on the floor caught his eye. The coin, talisman, whatever it was that Wendy had brought from St. Damien's, had fallen to the floor. He picked it up and looked it over, studying the worn surface.

His heart stopped.

What if...?

He turned on his phone's flashlight and shined it on the page. Below Anzuri's paragraph was a printed version of a collection of hand-drawn symbols.

One that matched, if Peter looked closely, the symbols on the coin.

Wendy's voice tensed on the other line. "Pete, you're freaking me out. What's going on?"

Peter couldn't answer. His brain couldn't fire the synapses needed to understand what he was seeing and his mouth had gone desert dry.

"Peter, answer me or I'm coming down there with a baseball bat," Wendy snapped.

"Swear on Dad's grave you haven't messed with the store today."

"Jesus, Peter, what the fuck—"

"Wendy, please."

Wendy was quiet for a long moment. "I swear on our father's grave that I haven't set foot in the store today, to mess with it or otherwise. Now, tell me what's going on. You're scaring me."

Peter swallowed hard against his dry throat. The truth was bound to scare her even more, but this wasn't something he was about to tackle alone, with or without his dad's wishes. When Adam had said that Bailey men took care of their people, there was no way in hell that this was what he had in mind.

"Wen, I need you to come down here," Peter finally said. He looked down at the coin, strangely cold in his hot, sweaty palm. "I think you brought more back from St. Damien's than you bargained for."

11

Maryam groaned as Zackary emerged from his bedroom dressed to the nines. "Are you *absolutely sure* I can't go with you guys to the Hemlock court?"

"I absolutely am." Zackary's face pinched as he concentrated on his cufflinks. Between the white button-up and high-waist slacks, Maryam had to admit that he cleaned up nice. "We're going for information, not to party."

"You have to look like you're partying though, which means you have to look like you're having fun. History has shown that you hardly look like you're having fun when you *are* having fun."

Zackary flashed her a dirty look. "The last thing we need is someone feeding you faerie-made food while our backs are turned, or whisking you away to dance for a hundred years."

Maryam glowered as she propped her feet up on the coffee table and scrolled down the "Detroit's Most Haunted" website on her phone. "At least let me check out St. Damian's. It's the only one that checks off all our boxes."

"I said no."

"But researching other hauntings is a waste of time! I can handle it." Maryam leaned over the back of the sofa. "I go in, find the demon's name, and get out. Worst case scenario is I don't find anything. Plus, think of your health—you'll have to be nice to Emrys for more than five minutes. You might give yourself an aneurysm."

Zackary snorted. "Thanks for your consideration, but the answer's still no."

"So, you're really going to let me sit here and stew in anxiety?"

"Sure am."

Maryam drooped against the back of the sofa with a long, dramatic groan. While she didn't expect the theatrics to accomplish anything, they certainly made her feel better. It at least felt like doing something.

A heavy palm gently dropped onto her head.

"Hey."

She craned her neck to look up at Zackary with a pout.

Zackary gave her a soft smile—one of the rare ones that reached his dark eyes. "I know you're scared, but I need you safe. Peter and Wendy are going to be fine. I promise. This isn't like what happened to Matthew."

Maryam looked away. "I didn't say it was."

Zackary ruffled her hair.

The click of heels on the wood floor drew Maryam's attention as Emrys joined them from the bathroom. His trousers hung low and tight on his hips while glass beads shimmered in the light against his loose black silk shirt.

"Don't worry, Maryam May." Emrys used the pitch-black window as a mirror to adjust a twinkling earring. "I'll take you to one of the more subdued revels another time." He gave his disheveled hair an additional tussle. The dashing rogue look fit him well. Maryam made a mental note to have him teach her how to do her eyeliner like that before he moved out. It looked sharp enough to cut a man.

Judging by the way Zackary studied him—his gaze lingering on those tight pants—he approved of the outfit, too. Emrys caught his gaze in the window and smirked.

Zackary busied himself with his cuff links again. "You're not taking her anywhere."

Emrys batted his eyelashes over his shoulder. "You don't trust me, demon lovely?"

Zackary glowered in response as he grabbed his keys and the bike helmets. "C'mon. We've got a job to do."

Emrys gasped, his eyes alight. "We're taking your bike?"

"The Hemlock court isn't exactly inside city limits." Zackary paused at the door to jab his finger at Emrys. "Don't go reading anything into it."

The pixie's smirk turned wicked. "Me? Read something into an intimate motorcycle ride? Never."

"Oh, shut up," Zackary grumbled.

Emrys winked at Maryam on his way out the door. Then, she was alone.

Painfully alone, with only her reeling mind for company. It circled around and around once central thought: If she didn't do something,

Peter could die and Wendy would grow up just like her and if she sat by and did nothing when she had options, this tragedy would be on her hands.

Just like Matthew.

This is what unholy things do...

Maryam studied her sword tattoos, wondering when and how Wendy's pain might manifest if her brother died. She wondered if she'd survive.

Maryam snatched her keys and phone from the coffee table. She'd be fast—in and out of St. Damian's before Zackary and Emrys even made it to the Hemlock court. She'd take a ride-share instead of the bus to save time.

Once she ordered a ride, she made her way downstairs with an old tote filled with salt, holy water, a crucifix, and a Bible. She'd be fine.

She'd be fine.

There wasn't a GPS in Detroit, or anywhere, that would register St. Damian's as a viable destination, so Maryam had her driver drop her at a bar two blocks down. He gave her a skeptical look at her lie about a girls' night, given the sketchy state of the bar, but he shrugged, let her out, and drove into the night.

St. Damian's proved to be less creepy than Maryam had expected. Shifting shadows couldn't whisper dark, cryptic half-truths like Peter's demon. Artifacts scattered across the dusty floor couldn't dig their fingers into her neck. The racoon that scurried across the hall *could* bite, but it seemed content to mind its own business.

According to every urban legend, the largest concentration of paranormal activity came from the psychiatric ward on the second story. She skipped up the stairs, whistling to keep her nerves at bay, hoping to signal to whatever lurked in the dark that she wasn't afraid, even if that was a lie.

Despite her confidence that the demon was more interested in Peter than its former decrepit home, Maryam couldn't help but notice the shift in the air as she stepped into the psych ward. It was abrupt enough that it made her stop short and knotted her stomach. The last hint of autumn's heat dissipated. The distant sound of cars had hushed to silence. It didn't even feel like the air moved, despite the broken windows. Maryam swallowed down as much fear as she could and tipped-toed through the room with her eyes locked on the shadows.

The graffiti had gotten worse since the last photo had been uploaded online, making it harder to find anything that looked like a demon's sigil. She never thought she'd be happy to have a childhood littered with copies of ancient occult manuscripts and demonology textbooks, but here she was.

She eventually found what looked to be a circle with worn away letters and distinct lines too stark and calculated for tagging. She snapped a picture and sent it to Hiro.

Any idea who this belongs to? Maryam typed as she began making her escape.

Her gaze flitted between her phone and the exit until Hiro texted back, *That's Anzuri, a Duke of Hell and one of the original Watchers. Where are you? Call me.*

Maryam halted to a stop. A member of the Dark Court and one of the angels who first descended to Earth. Great. Two for two.

She began jogging just in time to hit something painfully solid. Energy burst forth from nowhere, sending her flying through the air. The room spun as her head hit concrete and her feeble attempt to get back to her feet threatened to bring up the Pop-Tarts she'd wolfed down for dinner.

Maryam searched for an alternative way out as the world slowed down, but the clack of footsteps stopped her cold. A figure emerged from the darkness.

"Leaving so soon, child?" asked a deep, playful, too-familiar voice.

The demon clicked his tongue as he stepped into the moonlight. His eyes caught the pale glow, setting them alight and otherworldly with their deep purple hue. Maryam couldn't decide if it was her possible concussion or those strange eyes seated above such a sinister smile that made her nauseous.

She swallowed hard. How much energy had he already siphoned from Peter? She had always thought that demons needed a summoner to grant them a material body, like what Hiro had done for Zackary, but the creature before her looked like flesh and blood. Or did he start out with more power than most? If that was the case, Peter was in more trouble than they had initially realized.

And so was Maryam.

She slipped her trembling hands into her pockets. "Well, what can I say?" Maryam faked a smirk. The second this bastard knew she was scared, this was all over. "You're a bad host, *Anzuri*. I'll come back on a day when your place isn't a shit hole."

The demon chortled and motioned towards the ruins around them. "No point in cleaning up if I'm in the middle of moving, is there?"

"I'll warn you once. Leave Peter—" Maryam's phone buzzed with a call. Her eyes darted down. It was only for half a second, but even that was too much.

Anzuri lunged in a blur. Maryam dove out of range. She drew the crucifix and swung.

Anzuri avoided the arch of her arm as if she'd been moving in slow motion. "Rude." He slicked back a black lock that had fallen from behind his ear. "Didn't your pet demon teach you any manners?"

"He taught me how to recognize a little bitch when I see one, if that counts."

Anzuri launched himself again.

Maryam pried the holy water open. With a flick of her wrist, it splashed across his face. The water hissed as he roared in pain and clawed at his eyes, leaving Maryam to scramble for her Bible. No sooner did she reach the Psalms did it fling itself from her grip as if yanked by an invisible hand. Anzuri lifted his palm and Maryam sprawled towards him as if gravity itself was dragging her towards his clawed grasp.

She gagged as he tightened his grip on her windpipe.

"You're trying my patience." He pulled her closer. "I don't want to waste energy killing you and, despite your poor life choices, I'm assuming you want to live, so I'll give you one more chance to walk away."

"Chance this, asshole."

Maryam's knee slammed into his diaphragm. Anzuri wheezed as he went down, but not without grabbing Maryam by her ankle and yanking her to the ground. He came down on top of her, heavy and solid. She spat in his face, earning a blow from the back of his hand.

As her head spun, his voice rang in her mind, even though it was little more than a whisper. "I'll make you a deal: tell me what you are and maybe I'll find you a place in my new world," he whispered, his breath hot and his lips warm against her ear. "You must sense it—that you're different."

Maryam writhed and snarled as his body pressed into hers. "What I am is pissed off."

"Fine. I'll find the answer myself." The demon's mouth eased over her cheek as he pulled back, making Maryam's skin crawl as his dark purple eyes locked with hers, his lips only a hair's width from hers. "I wonder if your mind is as pretty as the rest of you."

Maryam writhed. Anzuri snatched her jaw, his pointed nails digging into her skin.

"Oh, don't be like that," he cooed. "I'm doing you a favor."

"Go to Hell," Maryam snarled.

The demon placed his forehead to Maryam's and breathed deep, his eyes closed. They snapped back open. Maryam stared back into her own green gaze.

"Lead the way, my dear."

Maryam opened her mouth to scream.

Then...nothing. No sound, no movement of air. She was static before the lighting strike.

Either seconds or hours later, she smelled cheap floor polish and rubber.

Maryam opened her eyes to find a high ceiling crisscrossed with support beams and industrial fluorescent lights, currently off. She sat up with a groan, too sore to be panicked, and massaged her neck as she tried to figure out where she was.

Thick plastic bleachers lined concrete walls decorated with championship banners. At the far end was a stage hidden in rich purple curtains. Above the stage was a relief of the Virgin Mother. Framing her were the words: St Mary's Academy.

Maryam's blood turned to ice. How the hell had Anzuri gotten her here? He couldn't have possessed her and walked her body across town—that took time and the wearing down of a victim. Even at his full strength, Anzuri wouldn't have been able to gain control and puppet her body across Detroit that easily.

Maryam forced down a few deep breaths. She could handle this. She could do this.

What had that bastard said right before it all went dark? *I wonder if your mind is as pretty as the rest of you.*

Maryam studied the curtains again.

An iceberg solidified in her stomach. They'd replaced the purple curtains with a royal blue set when she was in 7th grade, meaning Anzuri hadn't brought her to St. Mary's—he had brought her inside her memories.

She felt like the iceberg might hurl itself up through her throat. She knew exactly what memory it was.

She has to find Anzuri and get him out of her brain.

Maryam sprinted for the exit and launched herself through the door, into the dark, familiar hallway of the academy. The squeak of her sneakers echoed as she passed empty class room after empty classroom.

She skidded to a halt in the main lobby. "Anzuri," she called through a wheeze. "Anzuri, you bastard, where are you hiding?" She stilled her ragged breath to listen.

From the opposite hallway came the faint clicking sound of metal on metal. Maryam crouched and softened her footsteps as she followed it.

She glanced up above the room it came from. Her mouth went dry as she read the words, "Music Room A."

She raised herself up just high enough to peek through the window. Sure enough, there was Anzuri, but Maryam hadn't expected him to be picking a lock on an old worn chest she'd never seen before. Maryam could make out a sigil branded into the wood, but it wasn't Anzuri's.

It didn't matter. A random wooden chest hadn't hijacked Maryam's mind. Anzuri had.

Maryam slipped her hand through the cracked door and wrapped her fingers around a music stand, praying that the element of surprise would do more damage than the cheap metal itself.

On the silent count of three, she hurled herself into the room.

Anzuri whirled with a sickening look of glee, catching the music stand in one hand and Maryam's collar in the other. With only a small shove, Maryam was airborne one second and slamming into the blackboard the next. She landed face-first on the dirty classroom floor, wheezing and coughing, unsure whether clearing her vision or getting air in her lungs was the priority.

"I didn't want to do this the hard way, you know." Anzuri tossed the music stand aside and knelt in front of the chest again. "The more force used to explore a mind, the more damage is done to the host." He took hold of the lid with one hand, bracing the other against the box, grinning at Maryam like a child opening a Christmas present.

"But something tells me you can take it," Anzuri's grip tightened, "My little ankida'shi."

The lock tore like wrapping paper. Maryam collapsed to the ground as she burst into flames, shrieking, and writhing against the burning and snapping underneath her skin as if her skeleton was rearranging itself. Her back spasmed against the weight of new limbs that tore free from her skin and spine as she craned her neck over her shoulder. Her pained scream morphed into horror.

Wings arched from her back to the sky, soaked red with her own blood.

Finally, the pain took mercy on Maryam, giving over into sweet, numb darkness.

Zaphriel wasn't in Michigan anymore. Not really. Even the outskirts of the Hemlock Court made him feel overwhelmingly mundane.

The whine of strings, the whistle of flutes, and the rumble of drums pulled the woods onto another plane of existence. The night air felt crisp like cider and smelled like dried leaves laced with a hint of smoke and cloves. Pinpricks of light fluttered just outside of Zackary's vision and voices whispered long-forgotten secrets in ancient tongues in time with the wind. A towering man with a deer head and hooves straightened his suit of leaves and vines and sized Zackary up as he walked beside Emrys. A woman in a dress equal parts silk and glistening, dewy spiderwebs giggled nearby as her dragonfly wings shimmered in the torchlight. A child ran between Zack and Emrys, her leaf-green hands and mouth stained red with berry juice and her eyes deep pools of blue from corner to corner.

Between the curve of his horns and the swaying grace of his steps, Emrys blended in here. He came alive here. "Stay close." One hand brushed Zackary's sleeve. "I don't want to lose you to revelry for a hundred years."

Zackary scoffed. "I don't think you have the same effect on demons as you do humans."

"Don't be so sure. Everybody has their price." Emrys ran a finger up Zackary's arm. "Their vices."

Zackary ignored the heat that lingered on his skin and scowled. "I don't need a refresher on vices, thank you very much."

Emrys swiped a pair of crystal glasses from a table and took a sip of one as he handed the other to Zackary. "Your loss, as always." He took a longer sip, closing his eyes as a moan echoed off the sides of his glass. Lowering the drink, he motioned to the other guests. "Nothing in life is free, lovely, especially in Faerieland. If we want information, we'll have to give everyone we talk to something."

Zackary raised an eyebrow. "Such as...?"

"A good time, for starters, so at least *try* to act like you don't find the very idea of fun deplorable." Emrys took another deep gulp of wine. Licking it from his grin, he locked arms with Zackary and dragged him into the fray. "Let's go."

Zackary lifted his glass and cautiously let a trickle of the tart wine leak into his mouth. When the world didn't tilt, he dared to drink a bit more as Emrys greeted a pair of faerie women whose eyes lit up with recognition.

"It's been a while, Emrys," said the first, sizing him up with eyes like stars. "We've missed you."

Her friend did the same to Zackary, twirling a dark curl as her maroon butterfly wings fluttered. "Who's your friend?"

Emrys beamed, gesturing to his partner in crime with his empty glass. "Ladies, this is Zackary Bishop, a dear demonic friend of mine."

The butterfly's eyes grew hungry as she set her glass on the tray of a passing waiter. "Well, isn't that something? What brings you to the Hemlock court on the arm of our favorite prince?"

Zackary choked on his wine. "Prince?" he rasped, turning to Emrys.

The beat and timbre picked up. Emrys let go of Zackary and handed his glass to a stranger. "Oh, I love this song." He opened his hands to the faerie women. "Ladies, would you do us the honor?"

The woman with eyes like stars took Emrys hand with a bow. "Of course, Your Highness."

The butterfly woman took Zackary's before he could protest. Her grin revealed sharp canines. "I've been told I'm quite a good teacher. I don't even bite."

Zackary swallowed hard. "That's very kind of you, but Emrys—"

Emrys winked at him as his dance partner led him atop a hill ringed with mushrooms. "Don't tell me you finally want me around the minute a lovely woman takes interest. It might give me the wrong idea. Besides..." He looked from Zackary to the butterfly woman, then back. "I'm sure you two have so much to talk about."

With that, he disappeared into the reeling crowd.

Zackary let the butterfly woman lead him up the hill and set her free hand against his chest. He tried not to tense, remembering what Emrys had said about exchanging fun for information. Next to damnation, a little dancing and flirtation wasn't a large price to pay.

"You seem close to Emrys." Zackary held the woman tight around the waist. "He hasn't told me much about his life here."

"It's a bit of a sore spot," the woman sighed forlornly. "Seeing as the queen still wants him dead."

The chill of the night air turned sharp in Zack's lungs. "His mother wants him dead?"

The woman giggled. "She's not his mother, silly. The queen's a royal. She's as pure-blooded as they come. Prince Emrys' mother was a pixie maid too beautiful for the king to resist. The queen would have likely turned a blind eye if it hadn't been for those handsome horns of his."

"They give him away as the king's son," Zackary concluded.

"Oh, it's far more than that. They mark him as a potential heir. Only two of his half-siblings carry them. The queen didn't like the idea of competition, so she tortured his mother when she hid him. The poor woman held on just long enough for him to escape. Her majesty grew bored of looking for him eventually, so as long as he stays out of sight, she doesn't bother with him. I don't even know if she remembers his name."

Zackary's blood went cold. He cursed himself for being so cruel. He'd hissed the word "pixie" at Emrys like it was dirty. That had been his murdered mother he had been talking about.

It's fine, Emrys had said. *I'm used to worse.*

Zackary's heart sank. God, he was an idiot.

The butterfly woman lifted her hand to Zackary's face. "Oh, don't be so sad. It's a tragic thing to see one so handsome looking so forlorn.

There's hardly a soul in court that doesn't adore Prince Emrys. We'd never turn him in."

Seizing his chance, Zackary took her hand and lightly kissed the back. He gazed at her through his lashes over her wrist with a sly smile. "Woe be it to me to disobey the words of a fine teacher such as yourself."

Color rose in the woman's cheeks. "I can't take all the credit." She looked away with a cough and stole a glass from another dancer who seemed too drunk to care. She took a long sip, then handed the rest to Zackary. "You're quite the student."

Three more glasses of wine, four songs, and countless flirtations later, Zackary dared to ask for what he really needed, though the hill had begun to spin in such a blur that it was hard to remember who he was supposed to talk to.

"We're looking for a demon who used to frequent these parties." Why did it feel like he was yelling over the music? "It would have been decades ago, but we don't know much more than that."

"Demons and their summoners come and go." The butterfly woman shrugged. "Do you at least remember the name of the human who summoned him?"

Zackary shook his head, nearly toppling over.

As they twirled, the woman stood on her toes and whispered in his ear, "You weren't by chance being so lovely just to find an old flame, were you? That would be so cruel."

Zackary held tight to her shoulder, lest she fly away into the spinning world. "Never. A young man's life is in danger and I need that demon's name."

The woman clicked her tongue and dropped to her feet. "You tell the truth when you could have lied. Lies turn a person's scent sour. We might not be able to tell them, but we can smell them."

Zackary wasn't sure he would have understood that sentence even if he was sober.

"You were lovely company and a good dancer," the woman said. "I don't have any information but let me try to find someone who might." She spun Zackary away into the hands of another faerie and was gone in a blur before he could protest.

He was lost in a sea of wings, owl eyes, shrill laughter, deer antlers, silken finery and crude leather. Stunning beauty and the macabre swirled around him like a storm. The music echoed inside his skull, shoving out why he had come and how long he had been there. The closest thing to a coherent thought was a name.

Emrys. *Prince* Emrys.

Zackary tried to escape the dance, only to be shoved, jostled, and yanked back into the fray until he couldn't remember where he was trying to go. The world finally paused when a pair of hands steadied him, and a familiar slurred voice spoke.

"Drank a bit too much faerie wine, did we?"

Zackary looked down to find Emrys with his hair and shirt more disheveled than when they had arrived, his smile lopsided, and his eyes unfocused.

"Haven't it in two hundred years," Zackary mumbled. "Forgot how strong it is."

Emrys cackled, clinging to Zackary to stay upright. "You're such an old buzzard."

"Oh, shut up. You're not so young yourself."

"Younger than you, cradle robber." Emrys laughed so hard that he lost his balance.

Zackary couldn't catch him. He couldn't even catch himself.

The two fell through the crowd and tumbled down the hill, collecting dried grass and dirt as they went. The world stopped spinning with a jolt as Zackary put his hands out to stop himself. When he opened his eyes, he found Emrys beneath him, eyes wide and mouth agape in confusion. It was the first expression Zackary had seen from him without any hint of smugness or arrogance.

For some reason, that made it hilarious. Zackary tried and failed to keep from laughing. Emrys joined in until they both had tears in their eyes, sore stomachs, and residual giggles neither one of them could suppress. Zackary couldn't remember the last time he had laughed that hard.

He froze as Emrys tucked a lock of hair behind his ear.

"You have a lovely laugh. You should use it more often."

Zackary shivered. Emrys' voice had never been laced with sultry smoke like that before. His deep blue eyes were serious for once, and his brow scrunched as he studied Zackary's face. He traced a line from Zackary's ear to his jaw, then leaned closer. Zackary pulled away.

Emrys caught his chin and pulled him back. A hint of trouble came back to his smirk. "What is it about me that frightens a big scary demon like you?"

Zackary swallowed. His mouth went dry. "You don't frighten me."

Emrys' words brushed against Zackary's mouth, tinging the air between them with notes of wine. "The most treacherous thing about you is that lying tongue of yours, demon."

That word didn't sting so much when Emrys said it.

"Nothing about you frightens me."

The faerie prince smiled against the demon's lips. "Prove it."

The demon silenced him with a kiss.

It was supposed to be a single kiss. One kiss and he'd finally get some peace and they could get back to their damn mission, but then Emrys' hand slipped from Zackary's chin to the nape of his neck. His other hand glided under Zackary's shirt and traced his spine with teasing, feather-light touches.

Zackary forgot his own name as Emrys' tongue slid along the roof of his mouth. He forgot everything else as he bit Emrys' bottom lip and made him moan. There was nothing in the world besides Emrys' hands tangled in his hair and on his skin like blooms of heat in the cold dark.

Emrys slipped his leg between Zackary's thighs and rubbed against him.

Zackary dug his nails into the cold earth for fear he might snap right there in the grass. He could leave Emrys breathless, spent and begging—

A throat cleared nearby, hitting Zackary like a pail of ice.

He scrambled to his feet, listening as Emrys followed suit. Zackary couldn't bring himself to look at him.

A woman met his gaze, despite his height, thanks to a pair of intimidating heels. Her sharp eyes narrowed at Zackary, looking as if she was calculating just how easily she could destroy him. No earthly force could, but Zackary got the feeling she could give God Himself a run for His money. Long blonde curls framed her pale, angular face. Her dress was all angles too, made of dead twigs and ragged cuts of dark velvet up to her plunging neckline. Jagged chunks of obsidian hung from her ears.

Ram-like horns twisted above her head, erasing her need for a crown.

"Emrys, when a friend tells me you are in need of my assistance, I expect you to be a bit more presentable than this," she said, raising an eyebrow. She didn't look a day past twenty-five, but the smoky honey tone of her voice told Zackary she was likely centuries older than her brother.

Emrys dusted himself off and straightened his shirt. "Sorry. Didn't know anyone had gone to find you."

Zackary choked back laughter as he listened to Emrys do his best not to slur.

"You carry our horns. You have an image to uphold." The woman looked Zackary over.

The usual swagger slipped into Emrys' voice. "Of course. Next time I'll be sure to keep my sexcapades in the broom closet right next to the war room at Hemlock Keep."

The woman choked on a chuckle, tried to regain her composure, but failed, bursting into a fit of giggles. "You heard about that?"

Emrys joined in with laughter of his own. "Maeve, *everyone* heard about that."

The woman wiped a tear from her eye. "We shouldn't be laughing. Poor Aisling hasn't left her room since she realized how thin those walls were."

Zackary looked from Emrys, to the woman, and back, feeling a bit lost and confused.

The woman opened her arms to Emrys, who squeezed her tight. She squealed with delight as Emrys leaned back, nearly lifting her off the ground.

"I'm sorry, Zack." Emrys put the woman down. "This is my eldest sister, Maeve, second in line for the throne of the Hemlock court." He grimaced. "The only sister that wouldn't give her mother my head on a platter, though Aisling sounds like she might be loosening up just a bit."

Maeve scowled. "Hardly. She's still a little tart." She extended her hand to Zackary.

He took it, forcing himself to meet her eyes when he would rather go find a hill to hide under. "Zackary Bishop."

Maeve held tight to his hand as he tried to pull away, her gaze darting across his face in calculation. They shot wide as she gasped. "Emrys Bowen Hemlock," she exclaimed, whirling on Emrys with a smirk Zackary had seen on the bastard prince's face a hundred times. "You're bedding a *demon*?"

Zackary ripped his hand away. "No one's bedding anyone!" Heat flooded his face. "It was the wine."

"It was an appetizer," Emrys cooed.

Zackary had wanted to apologize to Emrys for that damn kiss, but now he just wanted to throttle him.

Maeve snorted and folded her arms. "You Abrahamic types never change." She looked back to her brother. "I heard you need help finding a name."

Zackary cleared his throat, trying to focus. "Yes. A friend of ours is being haunted and we need the name of the demon to cast it out."

"He often frequented our realm apparently," Emrys added. "Would have been a good long while ago. The human did his casting at St. Damian's Hospital."

Maeve stroked her chin as she thought it over, then snapped her fingers. "I remember him." Her face turned from pride at her efforts to concern. "His name was Anzuri. He was a poised, articulate fellow, but..." Maeve wrung her hands. "Unnerving. There was something about those purple eyes none of us liked. We always gave him a wide berth."

Zackary had stopped listening at the sound of the name. The world had all but fallen out from under him.

Anzuri. The Blood of Heaven. One of the original, most vengeful members of the first Fallen. A member of the dark court with twenty legions of demons at his command—that's who was hunting Peter, sinking his claws deeper into the human man every minute.

Zackary had seen how deep those teeth could sink into a soul.

If Anzuri got too close and found the truth about Maryam...

Zackary whipped out his phone and dialed her number. No answer. He tried again. Nothing.

"We have to go. Maryam's in trouble."

Emrys furrowed his brow. "How do you know?"

"Because I know her. Something isn't right." He stood still for a moment, trying to get a sense of how well he stood on his own two feet. Still wobbly. Still tipsy. He wasn't about to sabotage himself by driving his motorcycle drunk, especially with Emrys. He knew what would clear his head, though.

"Are you afraid of heights?"

Emrys shrugged. "I've never been high enough to know, honestly." He snorted and folded his arms. "Well, not *physically*, anyway."

Zackary ignored the joke and winced at the strain of unused muscles as he unfurled his wings and brought down the power he used that hid them. Their massive shape engulfed the siblings, drawing wide-eyed looks of wonder. He avoided their eyes, focusing instead on the sky. He hated when people looked at him like that, like he was still worthy of such admiration—as if he were still an angel.

Emrys shut his gaping mouth. "You expect me to be afraid of heights when you're the one carrying me?" He threw himself into Zackary's arms.

Zackary scrambled to catch him before he fell on his ass. "This is serious, Emrys."

Emrys wrapped his arms around Zackary's neck and whispered in his ear, "So am I."

"Zackary Bishop." Maeve stepped forward and placed a hand on Emrys' shoulder.. "I don't care what my mother says or whatever lovers' quarrel you two need to work out. He's my baby brother." She leaned in close with a tight, stiff smile. "Hurt him, and I'll make you wish your humans would send you back to Hell."

Zackary hadn't thought it possible to fear anything more than Hell's dark court roaming the earth. Maeve Hemlock proved him wrong.

Emrys awkwardly chuckled and gently pushed Maeve away. "Okay, sister dear, he gets the point. We must be off now. Lovely to see you, as always."

She stepped back, eyes still locked on Zackary.

Zackary tightened his grip around Emrys. "Hold on tight."

He hadn't flown in centuries maybe longer, but his body remembered every movement. The bend of his knees, the spring in his ankles, the pump of his wings. It came as easily as breathing the crisp thin air of the clouds.

Emrys squeezed tight, burning his face in Zackary's neck. "Oh, no. It's so high. I'm so scared."

Zackary could hear the coy smirk on Emrys' face. He took a deep, centering breath to fight back the temptation to drop him. "Get your phone out and get me directions to St. Damian's Hospital to distract yourself, if you're scared."

Emrys clicked his tongue and muttered, "Chivalry is dead," as he dug out his phone.

Zackary brought them down on the inside of the fence around the hospital. He could practically taste the hospital's insidious darkness. It was metallic and sickly sweet with rot. His muscles tensed and his stomach churned. He turned to Emrys and placed his hands on his shoulders as he met his eyes.

"Promise you won't follow me."

Emrys' brow knitted together with genuine concern. "You and Maryam are going to be okay, right? You're just grabbing her, yelling at her, and dragging her out."

Zackary couldn't answer. "Promise me, Em."

Emrys gulped. "I promise."

The cold air had burned off Zackary's buzz, yet he still found himself dying to pull Emrys in for another kiss—for good luck, for courage, he didn't know. He just wanted him close for reasons he didn't want to understand. Instead, he released him, then paused to listen.

Music. Somewhere in the night, someone was playing music.

It sounded like it was coming from high above. The roof, maybe? How had Maryam gotten up there? Zackary took to the sky and scanned the building.

The sight below nearly made him drop to the ground like a stone.

It was Maryam. The sight of long red hair told Zackary as much, but nothing else about her was right. A pair of wings caked with blood hung limp from her back as she stood on the roof's edge. She stood with her phone in one hand, the other hand in her pocket, looking more like she was waiting for the bus than standing above the entire human world with her wings on full display.

Zackary landed hard. "Maryam!"

She stood up a little taller and paused the music.

"What the hell are you doing?" Zackary growled. "I told you to stay home. And how did you—"

Zackary froze as Maryam faced him.

She was an impressionist's palette of yellow, purple, and red—not an inch left unbruised or free of sores. When she smiled, blood seeped from her gums and her lips split as if she hadn't touched water in days. Her eyes were onyx pits, filled with cruelty and malice where a soul should have been.

Her eyebrows shot up. "Zaphriel?"

Zackary's heart sank like a stone. He knew that voice—it had taunted him thousands of times within the depths of Hell's prison. Maybe millions.

And its owner had broken Maryam's powers free.

"You look well," Anzuri said through Maryam's mouth. "Better than a traitor like you deserves, honestly. Though I have to thank you for finding the time to make a new ankida'shi." Those mangled lips smiled wider. "She's just what I need to take back this world."

13

Zackary watched in horror as Anzuri looked down at his arm—Maryam's arm—and flexed the fingers, stretching and straining like shie was a suit that didn't fit right.

"I never imagined you of all people would have the balls to make another one." Anzuri studied the back of Maryam's hand. "You took what happened to the others pretty hard."

Zackary jabbed a finger at him. "Keep any mention of my children out of your goddamn mouth," he snarled through his teeth.

The corners of Maryam's mouth twitched. "Still a touchy subject, I see. Was this one's mother a better lay at least? The last one was pretty boring, from what I heard. Never let you get creative."

"Keep it up and I'll rip out your teeth one by one after I snatch you out of that body." Zackary's fists trembled as red seeped into his vision.

"And Maryam's not my child. Not by blood." He swallowed hards, his next words heavy in his throat. "Her father is Azazel."

Maryam's eyes went wide. Her head lurched back as Anzuri cackled. "Oh, that is too rich." He wiped a tear from Maryam's eye. "You're seriously up here playing wet nurse to the spawn of the demon who locked you away in Hell's prison?" He broke into another fit of giggles. "That is sad, even for you, Zaphriel. Imagine the revenge you could take with her." He slid Maryam's hand along the curve of her breast, the other sliding across her hips. "Imagine the fun."

Zackary popped his knuckles—it was either that or snap Anzuri's neck, which, unfortunately, wasn't actually his. "I am going to make sure you burn in the core of Hell's hottest fires."

Anzuri rolled Maryam's shoulders with a smirk. Her wings shuttered as they stretched. "You couldn't touch me in Hell and you can't now."

"I don't see any bars keeping me from throttling you." Zackary slowed his breath, readying to throw off the human facade that fit like a second skin.

Anzuri must have noticed the shift, because the air began to crackle with energy, the night suddenly hot. His ink-black eyes widened and he stretched the smile on Maryam's face until it was big for her face with too many teeth. He raised her hands, fingers spread and strained, as if the light that began to glow between them weighed as much as the universe.

The bruises and the sores on Maryam's body worsened.

"Physically no, there are no bars." Anzuri sneered. "But a human still holds your leash while I'm running loose." With a sharp jerk of his hand, a glistening sword of sparkling flame erupted into existence, the blade bluish silver and the hilt void-dark with pinpricks of light like stars.

"You'll have to thank little Maryam for me when you get back to Hell. She'll be in the cell right next to yours."

Zack glared. "You're bluffing."

Anzuri shrugged. "I don't know, brother. It's pretty quiet in here."

Zackary's heart froze. A deep, nearly-forgotten part of himself snapped.

With a sharp exhale, he burst into light. Eyes like stars, his hair like wisps of the sun's corona, and his body, now truly towering, like the pillar of a nuclear explosion.

If the sword Anzuri summoned was a comet, Zackary's was a supernova: all colors and light, energy, and awe.

Hiro might ultimately hold his leash, but it was a long one.

"Give her back," Zackary ordered. He didn't yell, didn't demand, yet the crumbling concrete beneath trembled.

As did Anzuri. He contorted Maryam's face into an animal's snarl. "You gave up your right to make demands. I broke you in Hell and I'll break you again."

The demon charged.

His blade met Zackary's and the clang of their blades sounded like the splitting of bedrock.

"Maryam!" Zackary shouted, teeth gritted as he pushed Anzuri back. "Maryam, I know you're in there. You've got to fight him!"

"See, this is what made you weak, Zaphriel," Anzuri hissed. "You always fought for the wrong people and the wrong reasons."

Zackary parried another blow, pushing Anzuri onto the defensive. "I fight for the only reasons that matter."

Everything hurt as Maryam came to. From the tip of her heavy, alien wings to every cell in her limp body pressed into the charred wooden floor. She couldn't remember what had happened before the world burst into flames.

A hallway in her mind. A malicious face. A locked chest. The music room.

Through the fog and the aching, she heard Zackary's voice. Quiet at first, then louder and urgent.

Maryam, you've got to wake up.

Moving made her joints feel like sandpaper, but she gritted her teeth and forced herself to her knees. The weight of her wings threatened to pull her backwards to the floor. She used the door frame to get to her feet. Once she was up, her legs threatened to give out and her stomach rolled violently, catapulting her toward the nearby locker room.

Black bile came up as she burst through the door, hot and sticky like putrid tar. Her eyes watered as her body strained, spewing filth onto the floor. With nothing left to vomit, she forced herself upright and stumbled to the line of sinks. If she could wash her face and her mouth out, maybe things could start making sense, but then she saw her face.

Or, at least what had once been her face.

Her eyes were still green, but now a bright electric shade and her pupils had morphed into goat-like slits. The teeth in her agape mouth were now sharp, her canines long. She pressed her tongue hard against one. A small point of piercing pain and the coppery taste of blood convincing her it was all real. Her ears stuck out long and pointed, even more so than Emrys'.

Her blood boiled into seething foam.

All those years...

Claude beating her down. Sarah and Hiro's secrets and their fear of the Order. This *thing* hiding beneath her skin was the reason for all of it. What they all hated. She'd almost beat it—the self-loathing, the hatred, the scorn, the fear, all of it. Almost, but now Anzuri had ruined it all.

The porcelain sink cracked in Maryam's grip.

That bastard was going to pay.

It didn't matter how strong Anzuri was or how many demons he commanded in Hell. He inhabited a body that had never flown, so Zackary took to the skies. Anzuri chased after him, a snarl on Maryam's face and his blade poised to run Zackary through. Zackary's advantage in the air didn't mean he could be sloppy. For the first time in his service to the Bishop family, Zackary faced a force that could destroy his mortal body if he wasn't careful.

"You're an embarrassment. Did you know that?" Anzuri's blade met Zackary's with an ear-splitting crash. "Being humanity's bitch, doing their bidding, pleading for our pardon in your prayers like a child afraid of being whipped. I can't wait to skin you alive back in Hell once I take over everything above it."

Zackary slid his sword against Anzuri's, sending him dropping like a stone to dodge the tip of his blade. "Don't you bastards ever learn? We *lost*."

Anzuri snarled, straining to beat Maryam's inexperienced wings. "This time will be different. We won't be burdened with dead weight like you." He swung again, faster and more desperate. Zackary noted how he panted for air. "It's almost a shame I have to steal Maryam away like this. She'd understand."

Zackary parried and lunged, nicking Maryam's shoulder. He cringed in silent apology. "Show's what you know about humans."

"She's not human."

"She has their heart."

Anzuri recoiled, grasping the wound Zackary had dealt, paling slightly. "She would be welcomed in Hell as a princess—the realm's future queen." He wiped Maryam's blood against her jeans. She was gonna be *pissed* when she got back and saw that. "The first of her kind born in millennia—"

Anzuri gagged and clutched his chest, doubling over in the air as if Zackary had run him through, black eyes wide in terror.

Zackary hadn't touched him, though. The attack must have come from the inside.

Zackary smirked. "Unfortunately for you, she's not the 'princess' type."

Maryam stumbled through the maze of her mind, still dizzy and nauseous. She shivered at the way her wings dragged against the steps. It felt like someone forcing her nails across a chalkboard, but it strained her back to keep them up.

The halls of the academy had shifted. Somehow, despite the eleven and a half years she'd spent within them, she couldn't find her way back to that damn music room. It was as if the halls had become a labyrinth with shifting passageways.

"Anzuri!" she shouted, voice raspy and shrill. "Anzuri, you bastard, you want my body? Fight for it fair and square!" She stilled and listened for something, anything, that might help.

Down the hall to her left, light as a whisper, she could make fragments of voices.

Don't you bastards learn? That was Zackary.

She would be welcomed as a princess. Rage pricked in Maryam's chest. Definitely Anzuri.

She eased herself down the hall, following the voices just on the other side of whatever veil kept her trapped. She scanned the classrooms as she went, hoping for something, anything that could be a weapon.

Maryam paused. Why the hell was she *hoping*? This was *her* mind.

She closed her eyes and thought. Where would a weapon be in the school? The cafeteria was too far away and the church, full of relics perfect for inducing blunt-force trauma, was on the other side of the Order's campus.

This was the school as it had been when she was eight. That meant Matthew had been eighteen—the year he took biology and dissected a frog. Maryam remembered because she'd been inconsolable after the fact when he'd told her. She opened her eyes. Across the hall now stood a classroom where lockers had been.

A plastic skeleton grinned at her from inside.

Maryam threw the door open and yanked open drawer after drawer until a pair of scalpels rolled out from under a crumpled sheet of paper. She slipped one in each back pocket and prayed she could get the jump on Anzuri before he put her on her ass.

She slipped back out and began again towards the voices.

Finally, after what felt like hours, Music Room A emerged from the shadows. Maryam pressed herself as flat against the wall as her wings would allow—which wasn't much—and she craned her neck to peek inside.

Anzuri sat on the floor with his legs crossed, back straight, and his head tilted down, looking nothing like a demon as he sat in a ring of glowing candles. He looked like any pious human in prayer, peaceful and confident, sure that his god would meet him where he sat in the dark. Gripping both scalpels, Maryam decided to send him to talk to God face to face.

She counted to three and launched herself, aiming for his throat. Anzuri's eyes snapped open. He snatched both of Maryam's wrists tight enough that she heard something pop. She gritted her teeth as she pushed against him, refusing to blink or wince, losing ground as he uncrossed his legs and stumbled to his feet. An elated grin spread across his face as he towered over her.

"Impressive," he said through his teeth. "Annoying, but impressive."

Maryam spit in his face. Anzuri slammed his forehead into the bridge of her nose.

Black spots and stars filled Maryam's vision as red-hot pain bloomed across her face. Anzuri's grip disappeared, then the scalpels.

Maryam's vision cleared just in time for Anzuri to plunge them both into her right thigh.

She screamed as blinding pain dug deep into her leg. A swift kick to the back of her knees and she went down, landing among the candles. She gulped down air, one hand trembled around the hilts of the blades. Brand new curses poured from her mouth as she gripped. She refused to whimper. She yanked them both free with a cry and let them clatter to the floor, biting her lip as she pressed her hand to the open wounds.

"You're strong for one raised among such weak things." Anzuri circled Maryam like a raptor.

She lifted her gaze to him with a snarl. "Get bent, you son of a bitch."

Anzuri tsked as he shook his head. "Is that anyway to thank me? I *freed* you, child. I gave you back your power."

"You showed me what a mistake I am."

Anzuri spoke in an all too familiar voice. "*Are* you a mistake, Maryam? Or is that what *they* think you are?"

Maryam's stomach threatened to hurl itself up through her throat at the sound of that icy, condescending voice. Father Claude's voice.

"If you don't stop fucking with me, you bastard, I swear I'll—" Maryam came up short as she whirled to find the old priest staring down at her.

Just like he had the day she'd summoned that demon. Just like he had before he struck her across the face and grabbed her hard enough to bruise her little arm and shook her hard enough that pain shot down her neck, screaming at her about how *dare* she and how he would *beat* the Devil out of her if it meant the Order would be safe from things like her.

Claude crouched beside her, balancing on the balls of his feet with a serpentine smirk on his face.

Maryam fought against the urge to shrink away.

"You are the breath of God and the lifeblood of His Creation draped in the skin of that he loved most—the child of our great general, Azazel." He reached out and lifted her chin. "You are the pinnacle of creation." His grip tightened as his smile widened. "*Embrace* it, Maryam. And if you can't, burn the humans' hatred and fear as fuel until you can step into your power."

Maryam's gaze finally met Claude's. Where there should have been frosty blue, there was royal purple.

"Don't fucking tell me what to do." She strained to grab the nearest candle, the melting wax burning her hand. "Only Zack gets to do that."

Anzuri's smug expression faltered.

Maryam plunged the burning candle into his eye.

Anzuri howled, dropping her and clawing at his face. "You ungrateful bitch!" he shrieked.

Maryam dove, knocking him back and pinned him to the floor, though her leg screamed in protest. "I've been called worse." She took a deep breath, steadying herself and trying to remember a single verse that worked on all demons. Matthew had mentioned 1 Samuel before hadn't he? Something about appearances being misleading.

Something about the Lord looking at the heart, despite what people saw.

The verse clicked into place as Anzuri pried the candle from his eye socket.

Maryam bellowed for her godfather. "Zackary, 1 Samuel 16:7!"

Maryam's voice, her real, honest-to-God voice, was like music from Heaven.

"Zackary, 1 Samuel 16:7!"

Anzuri clasped Maryam's hands over her mouth as if he had belched.

Zackary could have cried at the sound of that voice. With Maryam distracting Anzuri from the inside, Zackary swung his sword again, keeping his brother on the defensive, slow and stumbling.

Anzuri swiped at Zackary. Zackary jabbed. Anzuri swung again, this time too low. The twist of Zackary's parry sent his blade tumbling to the roof below. It shattered into a million points of light.

Zackary snatched Anzuri by the throat, Maryam's wings beating like a frantic frightened bird. His brother clawed at his hand and gasped for breath.

"What's your plan now, Zaphriel?" Anzuri hissed. "Her power can not be put back in Pandora's box. She'll never be the same, but there's still room for her in my world. I'll let her go."

Zackary shrugged. "Maryam's a tough girl. We'll figure it out." He lowered his voice as he began, *"But the Lord said to Samuel, 'Do not consider his appearance or his height, for I have rejected him.'"*

Anzuri shrieked and clawed at Maryam's ears. "Stop it! Stop it, stop it, stop it!"

"The Lord does not look at the things people look at. People look at the outward appearance, but the Lord looks at the heart."

Anzuri thrashed violently beneath Maryam. "Where will you hide when they see the truth?" His spit speckled her face as he screamed. "And they *will* see it. You can hide no longer, child." Anzuri's voice turned rabid and wild the tighter Maryam held him—a dying animal still fighting. "They'll destroy you!"

"Anzuri, in the name of the Father, the Son, and the Holy Spirit—"

His screeches sent a tremor through Maryam's skull.

She raised her voice to a roar. *"In the name of the Father, the Son, and the Holy Spirit, I command you to return to Hell!"*

The room trembled, faded, and then existed no more.

Panic seized Zackary's chest as Maryam's eyes closed and her body went limp. He caught her under her arms, holding tight as he eased her down to the roof.

Maryam groaned and winced as she tried to turn her head. "Zack?"

Zackary scooped her up before she could crumble to the ground. "I'm here, sweetheart. I've got you. It's okay."

Maryam strained to open her eyes as a tired smile tugged at her mouth. "We both know it's not." Her head lulled against Zackary's chest. "When were you going to tell me the truth?"

Zackary's heart sank.

"Zack!" Emrys' voice came over the side of the building. "Zack! We need to go!"

Zackary looked out over the night. Sirens cut through the breeze as three sets flashing lights sped down the road towards the hospital.

Shit. This was going to be a lot of paperwork.

Zackary rushed to the edge of the roof and spotted Emrys down below. "Can you get home alright on your own?"

"Yes, but..." Emrys squinted up at him. "Is that *Maryam?*"

"It's a long story. Meet me at home."

"Can you two stop yelling?" Maryam murmured, nuzzling her head against Zackary's chest. "My head hurts so much."

Zackary squeezed Maryam close and shot into the air, masking them both so that they blended with the night sky—they had clearly acquired more than enough witnesses.

Maryam shivered in the wind, burrowing against Zackary as best she could. "There's no way to make this okay, is there?"

"We'll find a way. I know we will."

Zackary cursed himself—here was the truth, bleeding in his arms after all these years, and yet he still had the audacity to lie.

The clock read two a.m. when Peter's bed shook with added weight. Sleep held him tightly enough that he thought Wendy, still a child in his half-dream haze, had crawled into his bed, frightened by a nightmare. He opened his eyes and couldn't breathe. Couldn't even tremble.

The nightmare had come to him.

An inky, smoky shape clawed its way up his body. The sight replaced every fiber of his soul with frozen terror. As its ice-cold claws dug into his legs, all he could do was stare. A spindly hand blotted out his vision with black.

Needle-sharp pain splintered through his head. Every sense was consumed with white-hot pain as a darkness deeper than space swallowed him. His eyes watered at the stench of sulfur and heat seared his skin.

Hell. He was in Hell.

His father's gaunt face emerged from the dark, his features twisted in rage. "You couldn't do it." The face snarled. "I knew you couldn't do it."

"Dad, I'm trying."

"You can't protect this family. You can't be the man of this family."

"Dad, please—"

"We were all better off when you were a girl."

"Stop it!" Peter reached to cover the mouth.

It sank its rotting, mangled teeth into his hand.

Peter bolted up in bed screaming and thrashing, his body covered in cold sweat. His slowing breath trembled in his chest even worse than his hands. He looked at his clock. 02:02. A nightmare. It had been a nightmare.

Movement in the corner of his eye drew his gaze towards the doorway. His blood turned to ice as a black mass slinked into the hall.

Peter swallowed hard, forcing his fear down until pressure melted it into fury. He grabbed the metal bat from beneath his bed and sprang to his feet, chasing after the figure. He would *not* be terrified in his own home. His father's sanctuary.

He would be the man his father needed him to be.

He found only silence. Nothing in the hallway, nothing in the living room, kitchen, or Wendy's room. Nothing in the bathroom except his ashen reflection with wide eyes and creases in his forehead he thought might be permanent. His gaze dropped to his bare chest. He did a double-take at the sight of angry red marks rising against his skin. He leaned closer, tracing just outside the tender flesh. It looked almost like a burn.

Worse, it looked like a brand.

Peter recognized the pattern, Anzuri's sigil, and his stomach knotted. He lurched for the toilet, hurling up what little was there. When the nausea settled, he got to his feet, hands trembling, and washed out his mouth. Then, he did the only thing he had ever done in a crisis: He called his mother.

Eliza's voice was groggy and dazed. "Peter? What's wrong, baby?"

Peter swallowed hard, not knowing where to start. "Mom, something's wrong."

"What do you mean?"

Peter could hear the shuffling of sheets as Eliza sat up. "Mom, I..." Peter licked his dry lips and lifted his eyes to the burn on his skin. "Mom, I think something's in the house with me. Something bad."

"Baby, I need you to call 911 and—"

"It's not a person, Mom." Peter's stomach rolled as he realized telling the truth was nearly as scary as the haunting itself. "I think it's a demon."

The only reply he got was silence.

"D-Don't blame *Ectoplasm.* It wasn't them, I just..." Peter ran a hand over his head. "Fuck, Mom, I don't know."

"Peter," Eliza said softly. "What did Grand Daddy always say about praying?"

Peter came up short. That's what she wanted him to do? Pray?

"Mom, this thing *physically* attacked me. It's a little late for that."

Panic spiked in Eliza's voice. "What do you mean it physically attacked you?"

"It *burned* me, Mom. I...I'm not sure what happened, but I was asleep and it felt like my chest was on fire. It was painful enough to wake me up."

Eliza was quiet. "Honey, are you sure it wasn't a dream?"

"Maybe. It felt so real, Mom. It felt *evil.*"

"Do you want me to talk to Pastor Marcus? See if he'll see you?"

Peter bristled. "When hell freezes over, maybe."

Stupid. He should have seen this coming.

"Peter, if it wasn't a dream, what else do you actually expect me to do? Who else am I supposed to call?"

"Someone who won't dead name me the whole time, preferably," Peter snapped. "Someone who doesn't kick out a family that's been members of the congregation for generations because they stood up for their trans kid."

Eliza went still. "You're right, Pete. I'm sorry. I just...what do you want me to do?"

Peter's jaw clenched. There was nothing she could do. Nothing his father's childhood church could do. Not since Dad had taken them out and never looked back.

Adam Bailey had lost three generations of community when Peter came out and for what?

We were all better off when you were a girl.

Peter flinched and studied the brand in the mirror. Maybe it was better if his mother didn't help. If she saw how real it was, all hell would break loose until Eliza figured out what had happened to her son. She wouldn't let him out of his sight until she got to the bottom of whatever this was and she could get hurt. *Wendy* could get hurt.

Peter couldn't live with himself if anything happened to either of them. He couldn't live with the idea of what Adam Bailey would think.

"Maybe I just slept wrong." Peter pushed the fear and fire from his voice. "It gave me weird dreams, and freaked me out. I'm sorry I made you worry."

"Peter..." Eliza trailed off. "You think you might be spending too much time at the store?"

Rage flared in Peter's chest, white-hot and foreign. "You want to talk to me about working too much?"

"What is that supposed to mean?" Eliza snapped back.

"You know exactly what it means," Peter fired back. "Ever since dad died you've been hiding out at the hospital."

"Peter David Bailey, you know damn well I'm working to take care of your sister on my own now."

"What do you mean *now?* You've always been the breadwinner. That hasn't changed. You can't spend time with us because that would mean facing the fact that Dad's gone." Peter couldn't believe the words spilling out of his mouth, or the angry fire behind them. He'd never even *considered* speaking to his mother this way, let alone following through with it.

It felt good, though. Good in a way that made him feel guilty.

Eliza's voice iced over. "You don't get to throw that in my face. Not when you decided to hide out in that store instead of going to grad school when he died."

Peter froze. Red dotted his vision and he bit the inside of his cheek until he tasted blood. It was either that or say things he would regret for the rest of his life. Things he'd never even consider saying if he were truly himself.

He took three deep breaths before speaking. "I'm sorry I brought it up. This isn't a good time. We should probably go back to bed," he said, voice trembling.

"Good idea," Eliza replied coolly. "Good night, Peter."

The line went dead.

Peter's shaking grip was so tight that he feared his phone might crack. He closed his eyes and forced deep breaths into his lungs. Slowly, the fury faded enough for him to think clearer. He took one more breath, dropped his phone into his sweats pocket, and walked straight to the freezer. The sharp, sweet taste of whiskey cleared his head even further as he threw back the bottle.

This wasn't him. He *never* spoke to his mother like that. Never got so angry he thought he might lash out.

It was the demon. Anzuri.

Peter's gaze shot to the kitchen island where he'd kept the talisman. He couldn't pinpoint why, but keeping it in clear view made him feel better. Comforted. Bottle still in hand, he picked it up and looked it over.

He took another swig, put the bottle down, and took out his phone to text Wendy, "You need to stay at Auntie's place on the weekend until I get this sorted out." Hopefully, he could figure it out before she insisted she had to help and found her way over to the apartment.

He had to. He didn't have a choice. Not if he was going prove that Adam Bailey hadn't lost it all for nothing.

The gates of Hell clawed at Anzuri. Hands like shadows. Hands like flames. Hands like mist and hands made of whispers. They snatched and scratched his skin, his very soul, yanking him violently back into darkness.

You won't take me you won't take me you won't take me.

The mantra was all Anzuri had to hold on to. The mantra and the boy at the other end of the tether.

He'd sunk his claws in deep—deeper than he'd meant too, gorging himself on the shadows haunting Peter like he'd found an oasis in the desert.

Human blood. Human pain. It was the only thing that could keep him rooted on Earth. And this earth was *his*. He wouldn't be cast out. Not again.

He needed to hurry and take Heaven. He needed the Song of Enoch. If he could take Heaven, he could take the cosmos. He would have the power to bend every knee, but he would refrain, because he would truly be merciful and generous, unlike the One they all called God.

Anzuri reached out for a dark corner to hide in for a while. A sting cut through his chest. Zaphriel, damn him, must have cleansed the hospital after he got Maryam back, thinking it would get rid of him for good.

Zaphriel, of all bastards, had bested him with that half-breed brat, all because he had a proper mortal body for the mortal realm. He was tied to the Earth. Anzuri was holding on by a thread.

He drank Peter's pain in deeply.

It hadn't been his intent to wake him. In Anzuri's panic, he'd poured more energy into manifesting than he meant to, but he savored the sickly sweet taste of Peter's terror. He plunged into the depth of Peter's mind and soul, like a savory sauce atop a raw, bloody steak made of everything the boy tried to hide. Every fear. Every insecurity and wicked, shameful thought washed over his tongue, thick and satisfying like blood. In Hell it was too easy. Here, humans writhed and squirmed when you bled them dry. And, oh, how they screamed.

Anzuri forced himself to pull back. He couldn't break Peter. Not yet. He'd fall apart and all would be lost.

Once he felt strong enough to pull free from the gates of Hell, Anzuri slithered away, leaving Peter screaming and terrified in his bed.

The cool night air on the roof blew away the rotting stink of Hell. Anzuri gulped it down the way he had gulped down Peter's darkness, savoring the smell of asphalt and car exhaust as if they were perfume. And it was quiet. Oh so very quiet without the shrieks of the damned, the cackles of those who tormented them, the orders and arguments of his demon brethren, fighting to defend their scorched little corner of eternity.

The night was so still he could hear the beat of wings across the street.

He was too weak to make himself be seen, even if he wanted to. Still, he made himself as small as he could in the corner of the roof and peaked over the edge to watch Zaphriel land with Maryam in his arms. Whether she was unconscious or too beaten to move, Anzuri couldn't tell, but her wings hung limp from her shoulders either way.

The bastard banished Hemlock prince panted as he appeared from the fire escape. "Alex is pissed that they haven't been able to find either of you all night. What do we do?"

"Tell them it was a family emergency and Maryam's sick," Zaphriel answered. "I'll be down as soon as she's settled to smooth things over. The place isn't a mess, is it?"

"No more than it usually is."

Zaphriel glowered at the prince, who snickered.

"The bar's fine, Zack."

The demon scoffed and began towards the door. "Glad to see you still have jokes."

"Got to keep sane somehow, seeing as someone's been keeping secrets."

"Says a prince of the Hemlock court." Zaphriel towered over him as he stood above the fire escape with Maryam in his arms. The Hemlock prince met his eyes, shoulders square and chin out, unafraid of the once-heavenly being who could incinerate him with a thought. As much as Anzuri hated him on principle, he had to admit his courage was impressive.

"When all of this blows over, we're having a little chat about how long you were going to keep that little tidbit of information from me," Zaphriel hissed.

The pixie stood on his toes to get closer, a smug smirk forming across his mouth. "Only if you tell me how long you've wanted to try out that trick with your tongue."

Zaphriel grumbled something Anzuri couldn't hear, then began down the stairs, leaving his little play thing to follow behind.

Hell was going to have a field day with that little bit of gossip once they finished storming the gates of Heaven. Maybe they'd have a little fun tearing the faerie apart while Zaphriel was forced to watch.

First thing first, Anzuri had to find a way to get that blasted book. Peter's store proved useless and, until the boy finally gave into despair, he was stuck lingering like a tethered storm cloud. Zaphriel and Maryam would be watching. He had to work fast.

If a contracted demon was roaming the area, that damned Rosary Order had to be close . They were bound to have a copy of the Song of Enoch—that would get him into Heaven. All he had to do was break down his human host a little more and the universe would finally belong to him, his brothers, and, if she finally came to her senses, his little ankida'shi.

After all, what king didn't want a pretty little thing on his arm?

15

Emrys had seen some shit in the last 150 years, but this was...Fuck, he didn't know what this was.

He hovered beside Zackary as he maneuvered Maryam into the apartment and onto the sofa where she lay limp, her eyes heavy-lidded and distant.

"Stay with her," Zackary said. "I'm going to strengthen the wards around the building and handle things with Alex."

Emrys eyed Zackary's shirt. "Covered in blood?"

Zackary looked down at the streaks of crimson and dull rust-brown. "Fair point."

Before Emrys could make a quip, Zackary's shirt was off, flipped inside out, put back on, and he was out the front door.

If Emrys hadn't been able to think of a flirty comment at the sight of Zackary shirtless, things really were fucked.

Maryam stirred on the sofa, thankfully providing a sign of life. She pulled herself forward, planting her elbows on her knees, back slumped with the weight of her wings and her tangled mane of hair hiding her face. "Em, help me to the shower." Her voice was flat and monotone, nearly dead.

"Should...should we wait for Zack?"

Maryam turned to him, her goat-like green eyes narrowed in simmering rage. "Help me to the shower, or I'll crawl."

The look sent a chill down Emrys' spine. It had been decades since he had seen someone so Other, even with all his time in Faerieland. He had no point of reference for what had happened at the hospital, what she was, or what it all meant.

All he knew was that she was hurting.

He sighed and moved to help. "Okay. C'mon." He bent down and gingerly wrapped one arm around Maryam's waist, looping her arm around his neck.

Maryam shivered as Emrys' arm brushed below her wings.

"Sorry."

Maryam only clenched her jaw in response. She shuffled across the apartment, moving like an elderly matron. Emrys leaned Maryam against the sink as he got the shower running, then turned to find her struggling to get her jeans from around her ankles.

"Do...do you want help?"

"If you don't mind." Maryam worked her foot out of its pant leg.

Emrys eyed a bruise above the elastic of her boxer-cut underwear. "Are you comfortable with me seeing you naked?"

Maryam snorted as she kicked off her shoe and the pant leg at the same time. "I get the feeling you've seen tits before."

"Fair enough." Emys took the hem of her shirt and helped her wiggle her head and arms out. Her wings were a special challenge, seeing as they could barely fit in the small bathroom as it was. In the end, Emrys had to finish what the new appendages had started and tear the clothing off her.

Maryam eased herself into the shower and fell to her knees. Her eyes closed, face scrunched, she lowered herself to the shower floor with a groan, her head on the porcelain and hands clenched into fists.

Emrys scrambled to take down the shower-head and kneel beside her, stroking her hair as the hot water ran pink over her raw, broken body. "Maryam? What do you need, lovely?"

"I don't know." Maryam peaked through her hair, somehow looking a decade younger. "Just...be here?"

Emrys gave her a gentle smile, tucking her hair behind her ears. "That I can do."

Emrys scrubbed the blood from Maryam's wings as gently as he could, only accidentally yanking out a single feather. Once they were white again, he moved onto the rest of her, gingerly washing her torn-up arms and back, grateful that the bruises and sores had already started to fade. He lifted her gently to her knees to wash her hair. She held tight to the sides of the tub, eyes shut tight and mouth scrunched as though she had to concentrate on staying upright.

The silence grew to be too much as Emrys rinsed her scalp. "You know Zackary won't let anything happen to you, right?" He hung up the shower head, grabbed a nearby towel, and began to ring out Maryam's hair.

"He can't save me if the Order yeets him back to Hell," Maryam muttered.

"None of that talk." Emrys got to his feet to hunt for a comb and a ponytail holder, then knelt again and began working at Maryam's hair before she could collapse in on herself. "It won't come to that. I won't let it."

Maryam shook her head. "You can't stop the Order, Em. No one can."

Emrys rapped the comb against her head. "Don't move. I'm working. And he's not going anywhere until I get what I want. I dare the Order to get in my way." He placed the comb between his teeth and began pleating her hair. "I'll cross Hell or high water," he said around it. "Literally."

That pulled a hint of a smile to Maryam's face. "How'd you learn to braid?"

"My mother." Emrys took the comb back out, using it as a third hand to weave Maryam's hair together in an intricate pattern. He hadn't braided in years, but could still do the pattern with his eyes closed. "When I was small, she styled my hair in all sorts of ways to hide my horns. No one realized I was a boy until I was nearly twelve."

"You're a boy?"

Emrys rapped her with the comb again. "Glad to see that demon didn't traumatize the smart mouth off you."

With her hair braided, and patted dry, Emrys bundled Maryam up in the towel and got her to her feet. "Any shirt in particular I can rip to shreds?"

"Don't bother. There should be some string halters in the top drawer of my dresser. The sweats on my floor are clean."

"Any preference from what I grab from your underwear drawer?"

Maryam gave Emrys an exasperated look. "I really don't care, Em. Just don't bother bringing a bra."

"A respectable choice." Emrys excuse himself from the bathroom.

Emrys took a detour to put the kettle on before returning to help Maryam dress. By the time he had her curled up on the couch, the kettle began to whistle. Just as he busied himself making them both tea, Zackary slipped back into the apartment, bringing a sense of tension that rolled through the apartment like a fog.

Maryam got to her feet, eyes sharp as she gripped the sofa and hobbled around it towards her godfather.

Emrys' grip tightened on the kettle. "M-Maybe we should—"

Maryam pointed at Zackary. "You owe me a goddamn explanation."

Zackary's lips pursed. "When you're feeling better."

Maryam's mouth morphed into a snarl as she dared to take an unsupported step. "No. *Now.*"

"Calm down so that I can—"

Maryam stood against Zackary's chest, nearly meeting his height in her new body. "Don't you fucking tell me to calm down, *Zaphriel the Treacherous*."

Zackary jabbed Maryam in the shoulder, stretching taller and wider to tower over her. "Don't you *dare* throw that name in my face. *Ever*."

"Enough, both of you!" Emrys wriggled between them, trying in vain to push them apart.

Zackary gently took Emrys by the arm to pull him out of the line of fire. "This doesn't concern you."

Emrys smacked his hand away. "The hell it doesn't."

Zackary glowered.

Emrys glared back. "You don't scare me, you broody old gargoyle." He whirled on Maryam, pointing in her face. "And you, missy. Put those teeth away and put some damn respect in your mouth. You don't get to take this out on him."

Maryam's rage fizzled out, replaced with confusion and exhaustion. Apparently, she didn't have the energy to be mad at more than one of them.

Emrys looked from one to the other. "I don't know what kind of Abrahamic clusterfuck this is, but I know you're on the same side. More importantly, you're family. I've seen enough to know that means something in this house, so sit down and act like it."

Emrys held his ground, eyes glued to the two as they exchanged barbarous looks but made no more moves to jump at one another. Maryam made her way back to the sofa and Zackary began to pace the length of the coffee table, running a hand through his hair. Convinced the fragile peace would hold, Emrys excused himself back to kitchen, made three mugs of chamomile tea, and brought all three successfully back to the living room with only his two hands. With the tea distributed, he tucked his feet underneath himself on the other end of the couch and watched Maryam watching Zackary, who focused entirely too hard on his mug.

"The sooner you spit it out, the sooner we can fix this," Emrys said.

Zackary shook his head. "There is no fixing this."

"What even is *this*?" Maryam refused to blink. "Tell me what I am, Zack."

Zackary faced her, jaw clenched, eyes pleading. He opened his mouth and let it hang open as if the words weighed heavy. He sighed and tried again. "We had our own word for you in the First Days.

We called you *ankida'shi*. It meant..." Zackary's face scrunched as he shifted through thousands of years of language and memories. "It loosely translated to, *'the breath, the bridge, of Heaven and Earth.'*"

Maryam raised an eyebrow. "What is that? Akkadian? Sumerian?"

"Older. It was a purely oral language. Humanity hadn't started writing things down yet. I guess you could say it was Proto-Sumerian, if you really need a name for it." His mouth tensed, as if he was tasting something sour. "In time, humanity came to call you the Nephilim."

Maryam's face blanched. "No." She shook her head. "No, they're all dead. They've *been* dead. They died in Noah's flood, if they ever existed at all. My mother was possessed by a demon."

"No, she wasn't." Zackary massaged the back of his neck. "Your mother...when she left the Order at eighteen...she fell in with a dangerous crowd."

A tired laugh escaped Maryam's lips. "Dangerous enough to resurrect a race of blood thirsty giants?"

Zackary's jaw clenched. "Your cousins were nothing of the sort. Tall compared to humans at the time? Yes. Powerful? Yes, but never bloodthirsty. Not until the angels came after us."

"So, who were these friends of my mother that wanted to bring back the Nephilim?"

"Ankida'shi," Zackary corrected. "And the group call themselves the Sons of Enoch. They want to return the world to the way it was before the war with Heaven—fallen angels roaming free, teaching humans everything from science, to astronomy, to magic, building a society alongside them. They believed the ankida'shi were the key—ambassadors between the cosmic and the human so that the centuries of bad blood could be healed, and the universe could experience true freedom."

Maryam's expression shifted to disgust. "So, a cult."

Zackary nodded. "Their leader, Solomon Lynch, claimed to be a messenger of the High King of Hell. He said that the Devil himself ordered the creation of a new generation of ankida'shi, one spawned from Lucifer and his most powerful generals. The thought was that these children would one day have the power to free all the demons in Hell, ushering in a new era of advancement and education."

"And my mother thought this sounded like a good idea?" She scoffed and took a sip of tea. "No wonder no one talks about her. She sounds like a whack job."

Zackary frowned. "It's not wrong to want a better world. I can understand where she was coming from. It's just..." He scrubbed at his chin. "When my brothers and I came to Earth, we didn't mean for things to get so twisted. We wanted the world that the Sons of Enoch still believe in, but..." Zackary's eyes grew distant as he watched the steam from his mug.

"But it's going to take more than a bunch of supernatural one night stands to make things better," Maryam finished.

A wry smile came to Zachary's face. "That's one way to put it. The Sons of Enoch knew that Heaven wouldn't stand for it. That it would result in war. They didn't care, but your mother did. She ran when she learned the truth—she wanted to bring Heaven to Earth, but not at the cost of bloodshed." He drained his mug and got to his feet. "I need something stronger."

"Same." Maryam massaged her temple. "Vodka cranberry?"

"You read my mind. Emrys?"

Emrys jolted upright, surprised that they had remembered he was there. "Just tea for me, thanks."

"Did my mom at least tell the Order where the Sons of Enoch were hiding?" Maryam asked.

Zackary shook his head, then took a heavy shot before mixing a pair of drinks. "A lot happened all at once." He took the ice tray from the freezer. "She went into labor during her escape. You started crowning as she banged on Sarah and Hiro's door, apparently." He gave Maryam a tired smirk. "Not even properly on Earth yet and you were already a pain in the ass."

Maryam looked too exhausted to rise to the quip. She watched the steam float up from her tea, her face somber and eyes dull. "And destined to end it, apparently."

Zackary's expression dropped as he carried the two drinks back to the living room. "The only dreams that determine your destiny are your own, Maryam. Not the Order's, not your aunt and uncle's, and certainly not those of the Sons of Enoch." He handed Maryam a glass, clinked his against it, and sat across from her on the coffee table. "That's why Hiro summoned me to lock away your powers—he and Sarah wanted you to have the chance to be normal." He shrugged and took a sip of his drink. "Well, as close to normal as a child can be in the Order."

Maryam took a deep gulp, scowling against the blend of tart juice and vodka. "They did a bang-up job."

"You can't blame them. Not for everything." Zackary swirled his drink. "Your aunt and uncle tried their best to figure out what to do, but your mother wasn't...well. She wouldn't stop bleeding."

Maryam tensed.

"Eventually, they decided they needed to assume some risks. Hiro rushed her to the nearest emergency room, but..."

"I get it," Maryam snapped. She faced the dark window, avoiding Zackary's face, her chin perched in her hand as her knee bounced. "Skip that part. Just...what happened next?"

Zackary sighed. "The Order showed up. They must have eyes in every hospital in Boston in case any possible possessions came in, because it wasn't ten minutes between Hiro warning Sarah and Claude banging on the door with five other exorcists in tow. He nearly lost a hand when he tried to take you from me, which he obviously did not take well." The ghost of a smile touched his lips. "Hiro was nearly excommunicated for summoning me to protect you. Probably would have been if I had actually ripped that old bastard apart."

"Is that how you ended up my godfather?" Maryam asked. "How did Uncle Hiro get the Order to go along with it? Something tells me they weren't thrilled."

"That's a story for another day. I'm surprised Jonathan Claude didn't die of a hernia when he found out, though."

Maryam rolled her eyes. "Naturally." She swirled her glass. "Why is that? What is his deal?"

Zackary took a sip of his drink. "That is something I'm not qualified to explain. From what I understand, Claude was the one who found Sarah and Mary on the Order's doorstep as infants. Apparently, they were both quite ill, but Claude spent a great deal of time looking after them to make sure they made it. The three of them always had some sort of bond after that. It was Claude who recognized Sarah's aptitude for spiritual work and recommended she join the Order as an exorcist."

Maryam snorted into her glass. "Yeah, okay, a priest paying a pair of orphaned children extra attention. *That* doesn't set off any alarm bells."

Zackary had been poised to take another drink, but stopped at Maryam's words with a scowl on his face. "I know we're not on the best terms with the man, Maryam, but honestly."

Maryam rolled her eyes. "Oh, please. We both know he's a snake. He couldn't surprise me if actually had a forked tongue."

Zackary glowered.

Maryam ignored him and grabbed a coaster for her drink. "Anyway, what happened after you nearly beat Claude with his own arm?"

Zackary ran a hand over his hair. "You and I were essentially put on house arrest while Hiro, Sarah, and Matthew had to stay at the Order's headquarters. After about a week of debate, an agreement was reached: You live, and I get a reprieve from Hell so long as your powers stay locked away and you don't learn what you are."

A near-crazed laugh escaped Maryam's mouth. "Cool. So, I've killed us both."

"Not if we lie our asses off," Zackary argued. "I'd bet good money that the Order has already been alerted that something unusual happened at that hospital, but it'll take them at least until morning to put together enough of the pieces to form a plan, which gives us an edge. Can you get me one of your crochet pieces? Something that won't draw attention?"

Maryam got to her feet and disappeared into her room, hobbling like an old woman and appearing moments later with a woven black choker with a single moon charm in the center. "Will this work?" She handed it to Zackary, letting it pool in his palm.

"Perfect." Zackary looked it over, shifting so that the beads caught the light. "Emrys and I are going to fashion you a glamor so we can throw them off our scent."

Emrys lifted an eyebrow. "We are?"

Maryam's brow furrowed. "What's a glamor?"

"It's a spell woven to create an illusion. They can be tied to items to create charms" Emrys explained. "Pretty basic magic."

Zackary met his eyes. "For you, maybe. We demons are used to using glamor on ourselves, but the magic associated with making a physical object hold one is a tad more finicky. I'm out of practice and we can't mess this up."

"And you expect me to help for...free?"

Zackary glared down at Emrys.

Emrys leaned forward and gave him a playful shove. "Lighten up. I'm kidding."

"What do you need me to do?" Maryam chimed in.

"For now, you need to rest," Zackary said. "You look dead where you sit."

Maryam shrugged. "I'm feeling better. Besides, it's nothing I didn't do to myself."

"Don't think like that. Not about this." Zackary pulled her close and kissed her forehead. Holding her face a bit tighter, he met her eyes. "I promised your mother I wouldn't let anything happen to you. I'm keeping that promise if it kills me. Now, go get some sleep."

Maryam sighed, gently taking hold of Zackary's hands, and dropping her head against his chest. "You'll come get me if the Order shows up with a warrant, right?"

"If the Order shows up, you run." Zackary lifted Maryam's face. "I mean it. You don't fight. You don't argue with me. You run and you take Emrys with you."

Emrys snorted. "I'm well aware of how little dignity I have, but we both know I'm not about to leave you to face the Order alone."

"He's right. We're in this together now," Maryam argued. "All three of us."

Zackary stayed silent, his eyes searching Maryam's face for something—anything that would tell him that she'd do what he told her, just this once. Emrys watched, wondering for the first time in a long time what it felt like to be that known—that loved.

He immediately scoffed at himself and finished his tea. He was a lot of things—sentimental was not about to be one of them.

Zackary gave up, shoulders slumped, and let her go. "Go to bed, Maryam."

Maryam slipped away, her hand lingering in Zackary's as long as possible before letting it drop to her side. The second her door clicked shut, Zackary dropped to the sofa, his head in his hands.

Emrys folded his arms. "On a scale of one to fucked, how much trouble are we in?"

"*Extremely* fucked," Zackary answered, voice muffled.

"Not as bad as I expected, honestly."

Silence sat in the room like a fallen guillotine blade.

Zackary got to his feet, taking both his and Maryam's glasses to the kitchen.

Emrys watched as he kept his gaze down. "There's something you're not saying."

Zackary poured himself another shot and threw it back. With the glass back on the table, eyes on the counter, he said, "After we build the charm, you need to leave."

"Excuse me?" Emrys shot to his feet. "You're going to ask for my help and then kick me out? But, what..." Panic threatened to close Emrys' throat. "What did I do wrong?"

"Nothing."

"Then why—"

"This 'Abrahamic clusterfuck' is not your fight. I won't let you get hurt on account of us."

"But the deal—"

"Fuck the deal." Zackary finally raised his gaze to Emrys, his dark eyes sharp. "Go back to Porter's land if you want. We're about to have much bigger issues on our plate than issuing a refund."

Emrys sputtered a nervous laugh and folded his arms as if to hide the way his chest was caving in. "You and your world don't scare me. I keep trying to show you, but you won't let me."

Zackary's eyes narrowed. "This isn't the time for your little game, Emrys."

Emrys glared back. "Do I look like I'm playing, Zackary?"

"If this goes south and the Order finds out you're helping us, they'll come after you. The demons that will want Maryam's power will be after you. You will be *tortured*."

"You can't scare me with torture." A scream tore through Emrys' memory. Blood pooled in his mind and bone flashed white before he could lock it all back where it belonged. He shook his head to clear it. "I watched the Hemlock Queen rip my mother apart."

Zackary paled.

Once the words were out, Emrys couldn't stop them.

"My mother hid my horns for years. She wanted me, but the queen wouldn't stand for a pixie bastard running around with a legitimate claim to the throne. I honestly don't know if my father gave a shit one way or another. Probably not.

"Eventually, they got too big to hide. She kept me in the kitchens and washrooms, but someone snitched. My mother hid me while she gathered food so we could run. The queen cornered my mother with a pair of her knights—she'd come to see to my death herself. She thought my mother had stuffed me away somewhere else in the keep and to get her to talk, she..." Emrys wrapped his arms around his waist to keep his growing nausea at bay.

He shook his head again. "When I say I'm not scared of you, or the Order, or anything else that comes looking for Maryam, know that I mean it." He locked eyes with Zackary. "I've never been to Hell, but I've gotten pretty goddamn close. And I'll tell you another thing, Zackary Bishop." Emrys pointed to Maryam's door. "That girl was born with a violent, bloody title that she did not ask for, just like me. I will not be a coward and abandon her the way my father abandoned my mother, so you better be ready to hex the ever-loving *fuck* out of this place if you really want to get rid of me."

Zackary stared at Emrys in silence, his eyes darting across his face for a long moment with more sincerity than Emrys cared for.

He cleared his throat. "Besides, you *both* made deals with me, so unless you want magically prolapsed assholes from the rebounded spell, I suggest you keep me around."

Zackary choked on a laugh. When he failed to keep it down, he laughed in earnest, one hand covering the ridiculous grin spreading across his face, eyes squeezed shut. "I'm sorry. It's been a stressful night and I wasn't expecting that." He opened his eyes, now rimmed red in laughter-tears, and offered Emrys Maryam's choker. "Here."

Emrys crossed the living room and let Zackary drop it into his hand. "Don't know why you're laughing." He traced the twisting of the stitches, calculating how to weave magic and illusion between them. "Magically prolapsed assholes are no joke."

Zackary snorted, then cleared his throat in an attempt to clear the amusement off his face. "Will you stop saying that?"

Emrys hid a smirk by keeping his gaze down on the choker. A chill skittered across his skin in the new silence. He looked up to find Zackary watching him, the shadow of a smile on his mouth and his eyes calculating, but also gentle.

Emrys' stomach seized. He didn't know what to do with gentleness. He never had. "What?"

"I owe you an apology, Emrys."

Emrys ticked up an eyebrow.

Zackary placed his hands on the kitchen peninsula, studying the backs of them. "The day we met I threw the word pixie in your face like it was a curse. I don't even know why I did it."

"Abrahamic complex, maybe?" Emrys went back to studying the necklace. "You lot always act like you're better than us wild folk, with your books and your fancy robes and your thirst for conquest."

Zackary chuckled. "We really are a self-absorbed lot, aren't we?" He stood quiet again for a moment. "Whatever the reason, I was wrong. I'm sorry. And I'm sorry I've been a bit of a jackass ever since."

Emrys started counting the beads to avoid Zackary's eyes as his heart hammered in his chest. When he couldn't take the sound of his own pulse in his ears anymore, he smirked up at Zackary through his lashes. "How badly do you want to make it up to me?"

Zackary sighed. "You really can't let us have one nice thing, can you?"

Emrys shrugged. "Can't blame me for trying."

"Do you *ever* give up?"

Emrys smirked. "Why would I do that after the way you kissed me tonight?"

Zackary's face reddened and he busied himself with washing the glasses. "That was the faerie wine talking."

"Keep telling yourself that." Emrys went back to studying the beads, stealing glances at Zackary's strong shoulders as he worked, remembering how safe he felt in those arms.

Emrys shook the thought away. "Your shirt is still inside out, by the way."

Zackary tugged at his collar and chuckled. "Thanks."

Emrys watched as Zackary stripped off his shirt, this time eyeing the way his broad chest tapered to a narrow waist that framed a toned set of abs, savoring the familiar way lust warmed his blood and quickened his breath. This feeling was known. This feeling he had a pattern to it—chase, fuck, leave. Anything else would be asking for trouble.

Or worse, death.

16

Every bone, muscle, and ligament ached when Maryam awoke, yet her mind felt curiously numb. She began to roll onto her back, which bent her wing at an uncomfortable angle. She rolled onto her stomach instead, burying her face in the pillow with a groan. Fuck, that was right. She had *wings* now.

The sound of voices, clanking cookware, and sizzling food seeped through the door. Maryam didn't understand how. It felt like the world should have stopped last night, at least until she processed all of this. She placed her chin on her pillow and studied her palms.

Was she crazy, or were her hands a bit further away than they were supposed to be? And were her fingers...longer? She couldn't shake the uncanny feeling that she was taking up more room in her bed than usual. It was like a pebble rubbing her brain raw.

"Maryam?" Zackary called. "Are you up yet?"

"Working on it," she replied, her voice course and dry. Maryam dragged herself out of bed, popping nearly every joint in her body as she stood and stretched. Digging in her drawers, she found a long-forgotten halter top that tied around her neck and behind her back so she wouldn't have to cut up any clothes and wrangle her wings into silts. A semi-clean pair of jeans lay on the floor nearby. Sure enough, the hems sat a few inches above her ankles. She scowled down at her feet. Great. As if she hadn't already felt like a giant.

Her height was the least of her problems. The eyes that stared back at her in the full-length mirror could haunt nightmares. Maryam searched for herself in the long pupils against vibrant green irises. She saw herself more in the wrinkled brow and tense mouth than in those inhuman eyes.

Maryam avoided her reflection as she raked a brush through her hair and threw it up in a ponytail. She dug a clunky pair of sunglasses from her junk drawer and put them on her face. Did she feel stupid? A little, but angels had giant white wings and faeries had long pointed ears. Those things linked her to creatures that weren't so bad. Nothing good in the supernatural world had the eyes of a goat.

She emerged to find Zackary standing over the stove and Emrys slicing apples at the counter. Watching them work without any tension or bickering felt even more alien than her new body.

Still, it brought a smile to her face. "I can't remember the last time you made breakfast."

Zackary turned to her with a grin that melted instantly. "Maryam, take those off."

Maryam adjusted the glasses. "Why? I can see just fine."

"That's not the point. Hiding from this isn't going to fix it. That ship has sailed, sweetheart."

"The light hurt my eyes."

Emrys snorted as he brought a plate of sliced apples to the peninsula table. "We've been Other a lot longer than you, Maryam May." He stood on his toes to get plates from the cupboard. "It's going to take a lot more than that to bullshit us. Listen to your godfather and come get breakfast."

Maryam removed the sunglasses to reveal a glower. "Okay, *Mom.*"

Emrys smirked at Zackary. "Does that mean I can call you—"

Zackary jabbed at him with the spatula. "Say it, and you're sleeping downstairs."

His words drew a faint smile from Maryam as she took off the glasses and crawled onto a bar stool. She pulled a plate over and helped herself to the stack of chocolate chip pancakes and the tub of cream cheese—maple and chocolate were too sweet together. "Did you two sleep?"

Zackary turned off the oven, removed his apron, and turned with the frying pan to deposit the last pancake on the stack. "A bit."

When he turned back around, Emrys amended, "He slept for about an hour."

Maryam frowned.

Zackary got himself a plate. "I went to bed around four after I re-enforced the protective wards around the building, then the Order called and woke me up. It took some wrangling, but I convinced them to schedule our appointments for later today so you could rest."

Maryam's food went dry in her mouth. "What do you mean, 'appointments?'"

Zackary helped himself to breakfast as casually as if he was discussing the weather. "You see a doctor at noon and I have a professional inquiry at twelve-thirty."

Maryam's stomach clenched, destroying her appetite.

Zackary paused as he lifted a bite to his lips. "It's just a check-up, Maryam. Every possession victim undergoes them."

"And your professional inquiry?"

Zackary lowered his fork and sighed. "They just want to make a big show of disciplining me because I'm a demon. All I have to do is explain what happened, how *someone* didn't do what they were told," he gave Maryam a pointed look, "and they'll leave it alone. Nothing will come of it. I promise."

Maryam pushed her pancakes around her plate. "I'm sorry. This is my fault."

Emrys helped himself to an apple slice. "True enough. Stop moping."

Maryam winced. Zackary glowered as the pixie poured a cup of coffee and passed it to Maryam, then leaned on the peninsula across from her.

"This isn't over yet, so you need to stay out of your own head." He reached across and tapped her forehead. "The worst thing you can do is cage yourself in your own mind. Did you disobey Zackary and end up drawing a target on both your backs? Definitely." Emrys shrugged. "But they haven't shot you yet. Keep going. You can feel like shit about it later."

Zackary went back to his breakfast, muttering, "Thank you, Dr. Hemlock."

Emrys scowled. "I don't see *you* dispelling any words of wisdom."

Maryam internally groaned. She didn't have the energy for this. Not yet. "I think I got taller," she interjected to distract the two from a fight. "What's up with that?"

Zackary looked her over as he chewed. "I think you did, too. You look lankier." He swallowed. "As to why, it's probably just part of your bonds being cut. Most ankida-shi children were exceptionally tall, but we never bound their powers while they were growing up. This is new territory for both of us." His brow furrowed. "We hadn't factored that into the glamor." He lightly nudged Emrys. "Will you give it to her? Make sure it still works?"

Emrys dug in his pocket and pulled out the choker that Maryam had given him and Zackary the night before. "Not my finest work, but it'll do the trick."

She weighed it in her hands, shivering at the flicker of energy that nipped her fingers. "So, I just throw it on, and I go back to normal?"

"Precisely. You'll maintain your new height, but it's not so noticeable that it would give you away."

Maryam tossed her hair out of the way to tie it around her neck. "And we're sure the Order doesn't have any sort of wards that'll set it off or make me blow up?"

"The Order's magical wards are tailored for demonic and black magic," Zackary explained. "They don't deal with goodfolk magic often enough to bother warding against it. Besides, their magic is tied to the earth. It's harder to guard against that which weaves itself into the very fabric of the air." He frowned. "Did you pay attention to a single class on the paranormal growing up?"

Maryam tied the strings in a double knot. "Seeing as I never planned on being Queen of the Damned, no."

Zackary's expression became stern. "You are not Queen of the Damned."

"Certainly not," Emrys added. "Aaliyah was much hotter, no offense."

Maryam gently kicked him in the shin under the peninsula. "Fuck you, Emrys."

"Get in line, darling."

Maryam readied another smart-ass remark, but a rolling in her stomach distracted her. She squinted and grabbed the table to balance herself as the world fell off kilter. She squeezed her eyes shut and blinked a few times as the world dulled slightly, both in the colors and in detail. She lifted her hands and found normal human ears. Her tongue ran over normal human teeth. She grabbed her phone and opened the camera to find her old human face reflecting her shock back at her.

"Holy shit."

"You're welcome," Emrys replied.

Maryam turned to Zackary, who watched her with a careful, calculated look.

"How does it feel?" he asked.

"Weird." Maryam shifted and stretched. The phantom sensation followed her movements. "Like wearing a suit made of spider webs."

Zackary shrugged. "You'll get used to it." He checked his phone. "Finish your breakfast. We need to go."

Maryam scarfed down her pancakes and chugged her coffee as Zackary excused himself. By the time she finished, he reemerged in a crisp white collared shirt and slacks.

Emrys choked on an apple slice.

Maryam fought the temptation to take a picture, because Hell would probably freeze over before she saw Zackary dressed up again, and slapped Emrys in the back. "Since when do you own a tie? And a long-sleeved shirt?"

"Since last year, I think?" Zackary straightened his belt. Emrys continued to cough. "Are you going to live?"

"I think so," Emrys rasped, massaging his throat. "Just caught me off guard." He looked Zackary up and down. "You wouldn't happen to need a secretary, would you?"

Zackary responded with a dirty look. "Are you ready, Maryam?"

She sighed, hopped off her stool, and darted into her room. "Hold on. Let me at least try to not look like I know I'm the anti-Christ."

"Keep talking about yourself like that and I'm kicking you off the roof."

Maryam hunted through her closet and pulled out a lightweight black silk blazer and a pair of slacks. "You'll lose godfather points for that."

Zackary scoffed. "You have wings now, remember? You'll live."

Maryam tried to check her phone with one hand as she wrestled her new body into the clothes. Four phone calls and six text messages from her aunt and uncle greeted her. She swiped them all away as she slipped into a pair of ballet flats in an attempt to hide her height—she'd see them soon enough at headquarters.

She left her room to find Zackary with his jacket on and both helmets in his hands. He passed her the spare, tucking his under his arm as he headed for the door.

His hand touched the front door and Emrys piped up, "Wait."

They both turned, Zackary preemptively annoyed and Maryam curious.

Emrys bit his bottom lip. "Just..." His eyes darted across the floor, then lifted his gaze to the two, his brow knitted, arms folded. "Just come home safe, okay? Alex and I would fight over who gets to run the bar. We would go to court, but diplomacy would fail. It would turn to war. There would be widows and orphans. No one will win."

Zackary failed to keep a smirk off his face as he shook his head. "Bold of you to assume Alex wouldn't just slit your throat to get to the throne."

Maryam laughed. "Since when was Ectoplasm a kingdom?" Judging by the worry still etched into Emrys' face, he was so concerned that his own joke couldn't even help him. Her heart broke a little bit. She closed the distance between them, pulling him close and squeezing him tight. He tensed, then squeezed her back as tight as he could, which wasn't much. Had he always been this small?

"We're gonna come home, Em," Maryam muttered. "I promise."

"You had better," Emrys said into her shirt. "I'll burn that church down, build my own bar, and take back Ectoplasm from Alex. I'll turn it into a chain restaurant."

Maryam laughed again. "I would pay to watch that, actually."

Zackary cleared his throat. Maryam turned to find him studying his helmet far too intently.

"I was thinking, Emrys..." He fiddled with the visor. "After work, you should call around and make a dinner reservation for the three of us." Finally, he looked up, almost sheepishly—an expression Maryam couldn't ever recall seeing on his face before. "If we survive, we deserve to celebrate, I think."

Emrys blinked, otherwise frozen like deer in headlights. "O-Okay. How do you feel about Thai food?"

Zackary nodded. "I haven't had Thai in a while. Maryam?"

She looked from Zackary, to Emrys, and back, struggling to keep a giant grin off her face. "Sounds good."

"Thai food for three, then." Emrys looked around the apartment, seeming unsure of himself.

Zackary reached for the door, scrambling to get out. "It's a date." He stopped with one foot out the door, then turned back, nearly tripping over Maryam as she slipped past him. "Not *that* kind of date. A roommate outing if you will." Zackary pulled the door shut before he could risk making any more of a fool of himself. "Bye."

Maryam watched him from the landing, losing the battle to keep her face neutral.

Zackary did a double take her way and glowered. "What?"

His flustered expression broke Maryam and she laughed. "What do you mean *what?*" She imitated Zackary's deep, gruff voice on the last word. "What did I miss at that reverie?"

Zackary started down the stairs, avoiding Maryam's eyes. "Nothing. Watching Emrys care about you just made me realize that he's not that bad. Annoying, but not bad."

Maryam blew a raspberry as she followed. "Bullshit. You *like* him."

"Don't be juvenile." Zackary pulled out his keys as they walked across the bar, studying them far more intently than necessary, seeing as there were only three. "I'm nearly as old as time itself. I don't *like* people as if I were some sort of green, inexperienced adolescent."

"Fine, you *fancy* him," Maryam replied, adding a bad British accent for emphasis. "Is that better, old man?"

"Now that you know the truth, you should also know I currently outrank you in our hierarchy." Zackary raised an eyebrow. "Keep giving me attitude and you'll be running laps around the Detroit city limits from dawn till dusk."

"That doesn't sound very 'protect this child at all costs,' of you. I think my mom would be disappointed."

"You're half demon. You can handle it."

"Should you be saying things like that out lo—Peter?"

Maryam stopped cold at the sight of him as he walked through the door. He was slumped and ashen, with dark circles under his eyes as if he hadn't slept in days. Still, he smiled as Maryam caught his attention with his name. Even that looked exhausted.

"Maryam. Hey." He gave a weak wave and slipped his hand back into his pocket.

Maryam placed a plastic grin on her face. "Is everything okay? You look..." She looked him over again. "You look rough, Peter." The smell of earth-tinged smoke hit her like a wall, making her eyes water.

Peter shrugged. "I'm fine. Just slept like shit."

Zackary sneezed.

Peter looked to Zackary. "Bless you." He turned back to Maryam. "Anyway, I think I took care of whatever it was that freaked you out the other night." Peter motioned to his store. "I essentially drowned my entire apartment with sage."

Zackary sneezed again and sniffed. "I can tell."

Maryam turned to find Zackary reaching for a napkin from a nearby table, his eyes tinted red and his nose crinkled. "You good, Zack Attack?"

"Just my allergies acting up."

"Oops." Peter widened his berth. "Sorry. Didn't realize it was still that strong on me."

"Since when were you allergic to sage?" Maryam sneezed. She looked at Zackary, bewildered. Since when was *she* allergic to sage?

Petter took another step in retreat. "Wow, I am so, sorry." He held his hands up as if in surrender, like the sage smoke had been some kind of accidental assault. "I had no idea it was that strong. On a high note, though, nothing else freaky has been happening at the apartment, so if you wanted to come back over sometime, you're welcome too."

Maryam froze at the offer. She studied the human man in front of her, now safe and secure in the world of the mundane—a world she'd ripped herself from and would likely never get back. She didn't think she could bring herself to risk taking him from that—from the safety.

Zackary blew his nose, breaking her train of thought.

Peter winced. "Once I air the place out, obviously."

Maryam forced herself to smile again. "Some family stuff just popped off, so it might be a while. I'll let you know, okay?"

Peter blinked. "Okay. Sounds good." He pointed over his shoulder to the bar. "I'm gonna go get a coffee and leave y'all alone before your brother has an asthma attack."

"I appreciate your concern," Zackary said with a sniff.

Maryam watched him go, her chest tightening as the distance between them grew from a few strides to hundreds of miles in an instant.

Zackary nudged her. "You okay?"

Maryam sighed. "Yeah. Let's go."

"Your life isn't over just because you know the truth, you know."

"No, but it *is* way more complicated and dangerous." She rubbed at her eyes as the sage smoke followed them all the way out the door. "And what the hell is this about? I've never had allergies in my life. And I don't think I've ever seen you with so much as a sniffle."

"The seal on your powers essentially made you fully human, so nothing sacred or holy ever impacted you. Now that the seal's off, you've got all the sensitivities that come with your heritage."

"Is that why you never went to mass with us when I was growing up?"

"That was some of it. All the holy water and incense would have made the whole ordeal extremely uncomfortable." Zackary threw his leg over his bike. He turned to Maryam with a smirk. "Also, I just didn't want to go to mass. My desire for redemption has its limits."

Maryam climbed on behind him. "You do enough. I think God understands."

Zackary muttered, "Let's hope so," and revved the bike to life.

Usually, riding with Zackary was a reprieve for Maryam's brain. She didn't have to think or process a single thing. She could just feel the wind and rush, but today, the Order weighed on her mind every moment it grew closer.

Zackary had to peel her arms from around him once they came to a stop in St. Mary's General Hospital parking lot. "It's gonna be okay." He placed a kiss on her knuckles. "I promise."

Maryam got off the bike with a groan and removed her helmet.

"Do you need me to go with you?"

"Nah, I'm a big girl. I got it."

"At the front desk, ask for Dr. Paul Cosmas."

"Cosmas. Got it."

"And Maryam?"

She turned, hoping Zackary might reveal that it was all a test and that they could go home to pretend none of this had happened.

Instead, he gave her a tired smile and said, "Don't forget to breathe."

"Breathe. Got it." She gave him a lazy salute, turned on her heel, and marched towards wheat felt like certain death.

A blonde nurse in pink scrubs took Maryam's blood pressure, shone a light in her eyes, looked her over in her underwear, and asked her a list of medical questions longer than a pharmacy receipt. The nurse never once screamed in terror through the entire process, so Maryam allowed herself a sliver of hope. Maybe Zackary was right. Maybe they really could pull this off. By the time the doctor knocked on the door she was feeling down right...optimistic? Was that a thing she was physically capable of feeling? Apparently, she had more surprises up her sleeve than her fucked up genealogy.

A middle-aged man entered the room, wearing a lab coat and neutral, dark clothes underneath. He made up for the lack of color with glasses framed in bright translucent blue that matched the shade of his hearing aids. "Maryam Bishop?" The doctor checked the chart in his hand and gave her a gentle smile that crinkled the corners of his eyes. He held out his hand. "Dr. Cosmas."

"Nice to meet you."

Dr. Comas' face shifted into sympathy. "I heard you had a pretty nasty run in with a demon. How are you feeling?"

Maryam shrugged. "Sore. Tired. Like a particularly nasty hangover. Nothing some extra sleep and water won't fix."

The doctor raised an eyebrow. "You seem pretty unbothered. Most folks would be a lot more shaken up after what you went through."

Maryam went rigid. "I'm not different, if that's what you mean. I'm not still possessed."

Dr. Comas raised his hand in surrender. "I didn't mean it like that, I just mean what you went through was traumatic." He studied Maryam with careful, calculating brown eyes. "You hardly seem shaken up at all."

Maryam huffed. "Trust me, it's not the first time something supernatural has kicked my teeth in. Given the course of my life, it won't be the last."

"What do you mean by that?"

Maryam shrugged again and absently rubbed her sword tattoos. "Things have just been...rough, is all."

Dr. Cosmas dropped his eyes to her arms, his brow knitting together. "Do you mind if I take a look at those scars?"

Maryam froze.

"Just gotta double check. I won't touch you if you're not comfortable."

Maryam weighed her options, which were slim. The scars beneath the tattoos always led to questions and, medical practitioner or not, she didn't care to answer any.

Then again, not letting him look could make her look more suspicious.

"Go ahead." Maryam stretched out her arms, tattoos up.

Dr. Cosmas traced the scars beneath the tattoos with feather-light touches. "The work on these tattoos is immaculate. How long have you had them?"

"The one on my left was a birthday present when I turned nineteen and the other was when I turned twenty."

"Where did you get them?"

"*Tattoo, Tattoo, Lights Out.* It's over by the Eastern Market."

Dr. Cosmas beamed. "That's where my wife did her apprenticeship."

Maryam's mouth fell open. "Shut up. Your wife is a tattoo artist?"

"She sure is. My first appointment was how we met." Dr. Cosmas rolled his sleeve up to reveal a small Celtic cross just above his wrist. "She didn't tell me that it was only her second time tattooing a real person until afterwards."

"I'd say she still did an awesome job. My second attempt at anything usually sucks."

Dr. Cosmas chuckled. "Well, to be fair, she couldn't exactly just try again if she messed up." He rolled his sleeve back down. "Can I ask how you got those scars, Maryam?"

Maryam clicked her tongue. "Clever," she said. "Very clever, Dr. Cosmas."

He shrugged. "How do you think I got that first date?"

Maryam shook her head. After a moment, she lowered her eyes and traced the scars. "I was seventeen." She swallowed hard. "It was the five year anniversary of my cousin's death." Maryam's fingers fell still and her grip tightened across the swords. "I had stolen a bottle of communion wine after church the Sunday before and chugged it before our family dinner. I didn't think I could face the evening sober."

Maryam wrung her hands as they started to sweat. "Showing up to dinner shit-faced was not the great coping mechanism I thought it was, obviously. My guardians flipped out. My uncle had a friend of the family escort me to bed while he tried to calm my aunt down and some of the things that friend said were..." Her heart raced as she played back those words.

This is what unholy things do...

Maryam's body went cold. Distant, like she was somewhere outside it. She felt the long, searing bite of the blade and the smell of her own blood against the floral bathroom cleaner. She squeezed her eyes shut and forced down a deep breath.

"Can we not talk about this anymore?" Maryam opened her eyes and faced the doctor, expecting the same sympathetic pity that people always gave her on the rare occasion she told them even a small part of the truth.

She indeed saw concern, but it was calculated. Steady. Knowing. "What did your recovery process look like?"

Maryam shrugged. "I was in the hospital for a while, then I was in therapy for about a year. Everyone treated me like glass the whole time, but everything's been pretty normal since."

"How do you feel about going back to therapy?"

"The possession won't make me relapse if that's what you're worried about. I'm fine."

Dr. Cosmas' eyebrows pulled together. "Maryam, I highly recommend people who *haven't* struggled with depression and suicide talk to someone after a demonic possession."

Maryam snorted. "Why? They'll just tell me it's my fault somehow. That's what happened when I went to therapy when I was eight."

Dr. Cosmas grabbed his clipboard and flipped through the papers. "Wait, what happened when you were eight?"

Maryam frowned. "You mean it's not in there?" The doctor flipped through once more and shook his head. Maryam snorted. "Figures."

The calculation came back to Dr. Cosmas' eyes. "When you went to therapy before, was that within the Order?"

Maryam gave a tight-lipped smile. "Sure was."

Dr. Cosmas took a pen from his coat and began scribbling on a sticky pad. "There are a handful of clinics that Order members can go to that have no religious affiliation. If I give you the list, will you at least think about going to see someone?"

Maryam looked the doctor up and down. "You're not going to force me to see someone here?"

"My job is to make sure you're alright and that you're safe, not prop up the worst parts of the Order."

Maryam raised an eyebrow. "And you still have a job?"

A sly smirk slipped on the doctor's face. "They can't fire me. I know too much." He scribbled a few more notes. "All your vitals looked good, and the nurse didn't notice anything that indicated the demon might still have a hold on you. Does anything have you worried that it might still be hanging around?"

"Nope."

"No trouble sleeping last night? Troubling dreams? Change in diet? Irrational discomfort around religious imagery or artifacts?"

"No, sir."

"Okay..." Dr. Cosmas studied Maryam, his expression calculating, but also gentle and sincere. Somehow, that made Maryam squirm more than if he was being a jerks. "Let me go get you that list and get you on your way."

Dr. Cosmas excused himself, leaving Maryam alone in the silence with her thoughts, which was her least favorite place to be. She studied the tattoos, tracing the swirling designs within the hilts and the soft blue glow from the blade.

Zackary had designed them for her. She'd saved up for them and offered to pay half both times, but he'd refused.

"You stayed," he had said. "You picked yourself and kept going. That's enough payment."

Maryam's hands closed into fists

There was another knock at the door and Dr. Cosmas let himself in. "Here's that list." He handed her a sheet of paper with a pointed look. "If you ever need anything, don't hesitate to reach out and make an appointment."

"Thanks." Maryam folded the paper and slipped it in her pocket before hopping off the table. "Now, if you'll excuse me, I have to go save my godfather from the bowels of Hell."

17

Zackary made sure Maryam walked through the hospital doors before making his way around the corner to the church, shoulders heavy and chest tight. His reminder to Maryam to breathe was as much for himself as it had been for her. Mentally, he knew they could pull this off. Emotionally, he couldn't shake the feeling that an invisible anvil was hanging over his head.

Ellie McDonald waved as he entered the lobby.

"Is Sarah in her office?" he asked.

"Yep. She told me to be on the lookout." Her expression shifted to worry and she glanced around the lobby before leaning over her desk. "Is Maryam okay? People are saying she got possessed. I don't like to listen to gossip, but the Bishops and a lot of higher-ups seem really tense."

Zackary did his best to smile. "She'll be alright. Everyone's just on edge. It's not every day an exorcist's family member gets caught in the crossfire like this."

"Okay." Ellie eased back in her chair, not looking convinced. "She knows she can talk to me if she needs someone, right? I mean, I know she has you, but if she wants to talk to another human girl, no offense."

Zackary's heart melted around the edges. God bless this child.

"I'll relay the message. Thank you, Ellie. Truly." Zackary gave her another smile then made his way down the hall towards Sarah's office. The door had been left open for him, which somehow felt more daunting than if he'd have to knock. Zackary took a deep breath, braced himself, and walked in. Sarah sat at her desk, hands folded in front of her. Hiro stood against the desk, hands in his pockets, body language tense. Zackary couldn't remember the last time he'd seen his summoner so serious.

Sarah's eyes narrowed as the demon darkened the doorway. "Close the door."

Zackary fought the urge to roll his eyes as he did so. This was going to be fun.

"There's talk about sending you back to Hell and locking Maryam up."

Zackary folded his arms with a snort. "Well, that's more generous than I expected."

"You told us you could handle her."

"I told you I could keep her safe, but I can't do that if she doesn't listen to me."

Sarah gave a dry, bitter laugh. "You can command armies against God, but a twenty-one-year-old is too much for you to handle?"

Rage flared in Zackary's chest. Before he realized it, he had marched across the office and slammed one palm on the desk, jabbing the index finger of the other hand down at Sarah. "One, don't you fucking *ever* throw the rebellion in my face. Two, when's the last time *you* got Maryam to listen? Because I seem to recall the drunk memorial dinner fiasco happening under *your* roof. Things haven't been ideal, but at least I haven't had to rush her to the hospital as she was bleeding out since we've been on our own."

Anger flashed in Sarah's eyes. "How dare you."

"Knock it off, both of you." Hiro wriggled between Zackary and the desk, pushing the demon back before more temper-flaring words could be exchanged. "Throwing barbs isn't going to help."

Zackary lowered his eyes to Hiro. "Do you have any alternatives?"

"Well, obviously you need to go in there and spin a story for the board," Hiro answered.

"And they're going to believe me...why, exactly?"

"Because, I'm going to give you an order *to tell them what they need to know.*" Hiro locked eyes with Zackary over the rim of his glasses.

Zackary studied Hiro's pointed expression; brow furrowed as his gaze darted down to the band and the scar that tied them together, trying to work out the hidden meaning laced between the words.

"What would you say they need to know, Zack?"

The wheels in Zackary's head turned and the pieces fell into place. "I'd say they need to know that Maryam's not a threat. That I handled the possession. Anzuri is back in Hell, and Maryam's none the wiser about what she is."

"Perfect." Hiro readjusted his glasses. "We shouldn't have any issues then."

A knock came at the door. Zackary craned his neck to find a tall slender woman walking in, a clipboard against her pencil-skirt clad hip.

Her dark eyes fell on Zackary, neutral and unphased. "Oh, good. I was just coming to request Brother Bishop summon you."

Hiro was, in fact, Zackary's Summoner, but something about the way the woman said it, like Zackary was some sort of minion, made the demon bristle.

She stood to the side and held out her arm. "If you three will follow me please."

Zackary squared his shoulders, took a deep breath, and followed her out the door, praying to God for a small sliver of mercy for Maryam's sake. He may not deserve it, but she did.

He was doubtful that the prayer would work, but it didn't hurt to try.

Father Claude was the only familiar face on the board. Whether that was a point in Zackary's favor, or went towards his damnation, remained to be seen. Claude opened the meeting with the standard intro for the recording: date and time, persons present, nature of the issue to be discussed—"The Events of October 13th"—which struck Zackary as the most diplomatic way to put what was really going on here. As he droned on, Zackary took in the two other priests, one who sat center and the other who sat on the left.

The man on the left was Father Thomas Wright, a man in his mid-fifties (sixties? Zackary wasn't sure) with dark umber skin, no hair, and a full mouth that seemed permanently pursed. Zackary recognized him as the head of Demonology, but had never met him before. The man in the center with faint wisps of straw-blonde hair and cheeks that seem to be hallowing with age, was Father Jean Wilhelm—a liaison for the Order's headquarters in Boston. As far as Zackary knew, he oversaw correspondence between the Detroit office and headquarters, the coming and going of members between the two, and was the final say on whether a potential case of malpractice was severe enough for headquarters to address. If he was the third member of the board...

Zackary swallowed hard, wringing his hands behind his back.

Father Wright sighed and lazily flipped through a stack of papers in front of him. "Now that we have all that out of the way, why don't you explain the course of events that brought us here today, Mr. Bishop?"

Father Wilhelm checked his watch and frowned. Zackary perked up a bit. If the representative of headquarters wasn't all that interested, then maybe he wasn't as fucked as he thought.

Father Wright gestured to the chair beside Zackary. "And take a seat. You're making me nervous."

"Of course, Father." Zackary sat and wiped his damp palms on his slacks. "Friday night, my goddaughter, Maryam Bishop, came home after spending time with a friend and warned me and our roommate that the friend was being haunted."

"Wait. Goddaughter?" Father Wilhelm's mouth turned down, threatening to take the rest of his face with it. "And how is it you have a roommate that's aware of the paranormal?"

"I was given the title of Maryam's godfather when she was two. And our roommate is a member of the goodfolk."

All three sets of eyebrows shot up.

"How is it that one of our exorcists comes to have a faerie roommate without our knowing?" Father Claude demanded.

"Since when was an exorcist required to give that sort of detail about their personal life?" Zackary fired back.

Claude narrowed his eyes. "You are no ordinary exorcist, Zackary."

"The Order assigned me to remove him from Mr. John Porter's land, leaving him homeless." Zackary gave Claude a pointed look. "I was just doing my job, and the right thing."

The three old priests didn't look convinced.

"He proved himself useful on the night of October thirteenth, if that eases your mind and allows us to get back on topic." Zackary tensed, expecting some sort of reprimand for his sass, but Wilhelm and Wright only seemed to silently weigh Zackary's words while Claude glared down at him.

"Fair enough." Wright leaned back in his chair with a wave of his hand. "Continue, Mr. Bishop."

It took effort on Zackary's part to peel his gaze away from Claude's seething expression, but he managed. "As I said, our roommate proved useful. He gave us an in to a faerie circle that the demon apparently used to frequent before his summoner died, giving us a name." He met the eyes of each priest in turn. "Anzuri, Duke of the Western Hell-Lands."

The three priests tensed.

Wright folded his hands in front of him. "Are you sure?"

"I'd know that bastard anywhere, pardon my language."

"Was Miss Bishop with you?"

"I ordered Maryam to stay home and stay out of this."

"So, how did she end up possessed?" Claude demanded.

Zackary scowled. "She's grown enough to call a cab, not grown enough to listen. That's how." He glanced around the room. "Seriously.

When was the last anyone in here dealt with a twenty-one-year-old? Better yet, how many of you have dealt with *Maryam*?"

As expected, the room was silent.

Zackary dropped his eyes to his wringing hands. "She just wanted to help. Truly, she did. She didn't know what she was getting into until Anzuri got his claws in her. She saw her cousin die at the hands of a demon and couldn't stomach the thought of her friend facing the same fate."

Zackary raised his gaze. "In our line of work, it's tempting to place blame: sin, the Devil, a faltering follower, but sometimes people just make the best choice they can with what they know and bad things happen anyway."

Father Wilhelm looked from Claude to Thomas. "Is the girl facing an inquiry or is Zackary?"

"With all due respect, Father, we all know that we're both on trial here." He tilted his head slightly. "Unless you don't know...?"

"Oh, I do." Father Wilhelm's brow furrowed. "And I happen to be of the mind that one should not be held accountable for the nature of their birth."

Claude interjected. "That does not change the fact that Maryam being possessed by a demonic entity puts the entire Order, if not the world, at risk." He locked eyes with Zackary. "Does she know what she is?"

"Finally, some honesty." Zackary smirked. "You couldn't have just called and asked, Father? You had to go and drag poor Father Wilhelm all the way from Boston?"

Claude leaned over the table. "Watch yourself, Zackary." His eyes narrowed. "I'll ask you again: As a result of her possession, does Maryam know what she is?"

From the sideline, Hiro chimed in, "I order you to answer the question, Zaphriel the Treacherous. Truthfully."

Zackary shivered as the order pinched at the base of his spine like a shock, his brain scrambling for a way to wiggle out. Hiro had told him this was coming, but he hadn't had proper time to prepare. What did Maryam still not know? How could Zackary twist this?

Her father had been a Seraph before the fall, an angel among the highest ranks.

The angel most enthusiastic to break the rules and see what Earth had to offer when the idea was first whispered. The first to befriend humanity, to give them knowledge, to teach them the workings of metal and magic, to fall in love with them. She didn't know the role her father had risen to in Hell and what that gave her as a birthright.

Maryam didn't know Zackary had been a Throne—a guard of inner sanctum that was God's seat in Heaven—and that when she came fully into her power, she would rule over him along with the rest of Hell.

"No. Maryam doesn't know."

Claude's eyes narrowed. "She doesn't know what, Zackary?"

Fuck. He knew how to play this game.

"What she is."

"And what exactly is she, Zackary?"

The door of the chamber burst open. Zackary whirled to find Maryam standing in the doorway with three rosaries around her neck, a Bible in her right hand, and a vial of holy water in her left.

Before Zackary's mouth could properly fall open, Ellie McDonald poked her head around the corner with a sheepish smile. "I'm sorry, Fathers. I tried to stop her but, well..."

Father Wright held up his hand. "It's quite alright." He shifted his gaze to Maryam. "Ms. Bishop, I presume?" He looked her up and down, a glint of amusement in his eyes. "If you could kindly wait outside—"

"No." Maryam squared her shoulders. She locked eyes with the priests, uncorked the holy water, and swallowed its contents in a single gulp.

Zackary felt all the blood rush from his face.

Maryam wiped her mouth and shoved the vial in her pocket. "I'm not possessed. Zackary did his job. Let him go." She lifted the Bible, eyes still on the priests. "Unless you've got time and want me to read the entire Book of John to see if my ears burn."

Father Wright and Father Wilhelm exchanged looks while Father Claude clenched his jaw and seethed.

"Maryam Bishop, would it kill you to—"

"To what?" Maryam glared up at him. "To fall in line? To pretend you're up there because you're concerned about Zack's job performance instead of some stupid vendetta?"

Claude's face tinted red as his fist came down on the table. "SILENCE!"

Maryam planted her feet and pointed up at him as though she was speaking a curse onto his entire family line. "NO. NOT FOR YOU. NEVER AGAIN."

The words reverberated off the pillars and the high ceiling, leaving everyone in the room, and Ellie McDonald in the hallway, slack jawed.

Everyone except Father Claude, whose teeth ground together, his knuckles whitening as they grasped the edge of the podium.

Maryam fought to slow her heavy breath, her hands shaking. Despite keeping her gaze locked on Claude, she addressed the other two priests. "Father Wright, how long have you served at the Detroit branch of the Order?"

Father Wright wrung his hands as he thought it over. "About three years? Before that I was a part of the Charleston branch."

Maryam flicked her eyes to Father Wilhelm. "And you, Father? What's the last major thing to have reached headquarters in Boston concerning our branch?"

The priest scrunched up his face as he thought. "That poltergeist at the Detroit Symphony Orchestra back in '89, I think. I had just finished school."

A devilish grin spread across Maryam's face. "Interesting, because you would think that a headmaster putting his hands on a student would have made waves." She turned to Father Claude. "Wouldn't you think so, Father?"

Claude froze as the others turned to him.

"Johnathan," Father Thomas said slowly. "What is she talking about?"

An unhinged laugh escaped Maryam's lips. "Oh, don't worry. I would *love* to explain."

Zackary looked at Sarah and Hiro. Sarah looked like she might faint while Hiro looked like he might ask Maryam to pause so he could drag Claude down and beat the man himself. Zackary didn't know what to say or think. In a blink of an eye, he'd gone from trying to save Maryam to her saving him.

And what did she mean about Claude putting his hands on her?

Zackary's stomach rolled.

Maryam stilled, her eyes sharp and unblinking as she spoke. "When I was eight years old, I got it in my head that I'd try to summon a demon. I thought Zackary could use a friend." She glanced his way with a sad smile. "He was alone." She faced the priests. "So, I took one of my uncle's books to school and tried one of its rituals at lunch. It shouldn't have worked, but it did. Maybe it was a fluke, maybe I'm a prodigy. The point is, I messed up and it worked, but then the headmaster showed up." Maryam narrowed her eyes at Claude. "He didn't stop at banishing the demon, though. He hit me for what I did. He *backhanded* me."

Blood roared in Zackary's ears as red tinted his vision. In his mind's eye he saw Maryam at that age—frizzy hair, missing teeth, always underfoot, never far away thanks to the shyness that had began to creep into her personality as she realized the other kids found her odd. She had been Zackary's little shadow. His baby girl.

And Claude had *hit* her.

Zackary clenched his jaw so tight that the it popped. When this was over, he was going to put that priest on the fucking rack.

Maryam continued. "I hit a stack of chairs and then he grabbed me hard enough to leave bruises and shook me. He told me my uncle had power over demons because he was an agent of God. I, on the hand, was an abomination. Unholy."

Zackary heard a small, terrified gasp somewhere behind him—either Sarah or Ellie—as his hands clenched into fists. Rage and power crackled underneath his skin as he watched Claude squirm in his seat under everyone's scrutiny.

That wasn't enough. He needed to fucking writhe and burn for what he'd done.

"Those bruises lasted days," Maryam said. "The nightmares for longer. It didn't help that I couldn't shake him—he was everywhere. Confirmation Class? There was Father Claude, ignoring my every attempt at answering questions and finding the most eloquent ways to call me stupid. Communion? There he was again, glaring me down as he handed me the body of Christ, making sure I knew that I didn't deserve it. Maryam wants to join the choir? Sorry, we have too many altos as it is. Even in my darkest hour, he found a way to make it worse."

Maryam gave a mocking tilt of her head up at the podium. "What was it you said to me at Matthew's funeral?"

"Enough," Claude growled.

"But it was practically poetry, Father." Maryam sneered. "*'This is what unholy things do,'* you said. *'They destroy and they destroy until all goodness is dead.'*" She put her fingers together in a mock chef's kiss. "See? Poetry."

Claude snarled. "I was talking about the demon that slaughtered your cousin, you impudent—"

"Were you talking about that demon when Uncle Hiro asked you to put my drunk ass to bed at Matthew's memorial dinner?"

Did that mean...

Zackary's heart raced so fast that he was nearly light headed. All these years they had wondered what had pushed her over the edge that hight, desperate to figure out what they had done wrong—what signs they had missed that Maryam was ready to slice herself open and end it.

It had been Claude. All this time.

And Maryam had never breathed a word.

Zackary swallowed down the bile as best he could. "Maryam, what did he say to you?"

Claude sank in his seat as the two other priests stared him down. "She has completely derailed these proceedings! This has nothing to do with why we are here."

"I think this has everything to do with why we are here," Father Wilhelm replied. His icy blue eyes bore into Claude like lasers. "Answer Zackary's question, Ms. Bishop."

Maryam stared up at Claude, unblinking, her eyes as piercing and all seeing as the eyes of angels. "*How long do you plan on staining your cousin's memory, Maryam? This family? The Order? You could make it end. It would be selfish not to.*"

A weight settled over the room as dark and smothering as the ocean floor.

Sarah began to sob.

Zackary's rage turn white-hot molten. He turned and glowered at Claude, heedless of how much brimstone and unholy power seeped through his human skin. Let them throw him back to Hell. He'd make sure to take Father Claude back with him, tearing him apart every mile they fell. He wouldn't start limb from limb. He'd rip the old priest apart joint by joint, starting at his fingers.

Claude's mouth flapped open and shut, his already pale skin nearly as white as the marble floor. "I didn't...That's not what I...I merely meant she needed to think about the choices she made and—"

Zackary snarled. "Stop talking."

Claude shrank away from the deep, ethereal echo in Zackary's voice. Zackary suddenly wondered if Moses had looked this small and frail when God had spoken from the burning bush.

Maryam turned back to the board. "I don't expect justice for anything that's happened to me. Hell, at this point, I don't even expect accountability. What I do expect is that it would go very poorly for the Order if anyone found out that this church had covered up the abuse of an eight-year-old by moving the abuser to another department *in a higher position* and then continued to allow the abuser to get access to that child over the years."

Zackary didn't think the potential for scandal was at the forefront of Wright and Wilhelm's minds. They both looked ready to beat Claude themselves. Claude glared daggers so sharp at Maryam that Zackary thought she might have to dodge them. She didn't flinch, though. She didn't even blink. She stared him down with square shoulders and her gaze filled with the judgement of Hellfire.

For the first time in her life, Zackary caught a glimpse of her father in her.

"So, unless we all want to see St. Mary's all over the news, I suggest we put this whole inquiry thing behind us, yeah?" A smirk tugged at Maryam's lips. "Not gonna lie, though, the memes would be fire."

"You think you're the first person to go up against this institution?" Claude hissed. "The first to try and hold us for ransom? Where do you think those people are now?"

Maryam pointed to Claude with a snarl. "Threaten me again, Johnathan Claude. I dare you."

"Enough!" Father Wilhelm shot to his feet, his chair screeching against the polished marble. "All of you, out." He surveyed the room. "Now."

Maryam opened her mouth to argue. Zackary grabbed her by the back of her collar and pulled her towards the door, avoiding any of the priests' gaze.

The door slammed behind them.

Maryam wriggled against Zackary's grip. "Hey, easy on the silk."

Zackary released her shirt and pulled her into a tight embrace, praying the pressure would tell her how sorry he was for never knowing, for not stopping it and for failing her.

Maryam wheezed against his chest. "Zack, I can't breathe."

"Breathe in a minute." Zackary shifted one hand to stroke her hair. "None of that was ever yours to carry, Maryam. I'm so sorry none of us saw it. We never even tried."

Maryam slapped weakly against his back. "*You're* gonna be carrying a dead body if you don't let me go."

He released her and she gasped for air. Zackary watched her avoid his eyes as she straightened her shirt, her gaze focused and calculating. Her eyes had been like that for so long—serious. Worn. Tired. Even with all the jokes she cracked. Zackary had always thought it had just been Matthew's death that had caused it, but it had been this smothering, stabbing pain that never should have come to her.

And it had nearly taken her from him.

Zackary's heart wept, threatening to bring him to his knees with its weight. Twenty one years of trying to protect her, trying to do better, and she'd met the fate of all the ankida'shi before her—broken and rebuilt into an adult before her time thanks to cruelty and ignorant maliace.

"He's right, Maryam."

The two turned to find Sarah with her gaze down turned, hands shaking as they clenched her knees. "That man was supposed to be our friend. He was my *mentor* and he attacked you where a *child*." Her breath shook. "I should have seen it. I should have known. You were so quiet when we picked you up after the demon incident. And you never seemed at ease around Father Claude after that." She lifted her gaze just enough for Zackary to see the blend of rage and tears building inside "You were *eight* and he struck you." Her eyes shifted to the large wooden door, sharp and bloodthirsty. "If they don't take care of him for this, I will."

Maryam tensed, worry etching into her face. Zackary couldn't blame her—he couldn't remember Sarah ever looking so violent. So threatening.

"Jesus, Auntie, chill—"

"I will not chill, damn it!" Sarah barked. "*You tried to kill yourself!*" Her voice cracked on the last word. She brought a hand to her eyes so she could stop the tears before they fell.

Zackary recoiled from the words as if they stung. They'd never been said out loud before. None of them had ever been brave enough.

Maryam opened her mouth to reply, but then paused as her face turned green. She cradled her stomach and held up a finger in a "wait" gesture. Before anyone could ask what was wrong, she shoved the Bible in Sarah's hands and sprinted down the hall. Zackary heard the *thump* of a heavy bathroom door swing open, then close.

Sarah's rage and tears dissipated. "Should...Should I go after her?"

"Maybe give her some space," Zackary said. "This is a lot." Not only that, but Zackary was willing to bet money that the holy water had made her sick.

He looked to Hiro, who stood looking dazed and forlorn, like he'd stopped processing the world after Maryam's revelation. "Are you okay, Summoner?"

Hiro blinked as if he was just waking up. "I...I don't know." He wrapped his arms around himself.

"You didn't stop me from nearly going after Claude," Zackary said. "Why?"

Hiro's gaze turned to a steely glare. "Because I was about to ask you to hold him while I beat the shit out of him myself."

Sarah nudged her husband with a sharp look. Before he could argue, she motioned to the chamber door as it opened. Father Wilhelm called Ellie over, who had all but blended into the walls.

She scurried over and leaned in to listen as they muttered in her ear, then nodded and stepped away as the door shut again. "When Maryam comes back, could you all please wait in Sarah's office? The board will call for you when they've reached their decision."

Zackary raised an eyebrow. "That's it?"

Ellie shrugged. "I'm just the messenger." She shifted from foot to foot, wringing her hands. "I need to get back to the desk. Will Maryam be okay?'

Zackary's chest warmed slightly and he smiled. "She's tough. She'll be okay."

"Okay." Ellie nodded, not seeming convinced. "I'm here if she ever needs anything."

Sarah pulled her in for a hug. "Thank you, Ellie. I'll have her reach out."

Ellie squeezed her, then took her leave.

Maryam rejoined the group, eyes red and skin pale, as the elevator door shut to take Ellie back to the lobby.

Sarah rushed to her, hands on her arms as she looked her niece over. "Are you alright? What happened?"

Maryam shrugged. "Must have been something I ate."

Zackary bit back a snort.

Maryam dug in her pocket and pulled out the rosaries she'd worn during her stunt, handing them to Sarah.

Sarah looked them over with a click of her tongue. "Honestly, Maryam. You couldn't have grabbed my work rosary?"

Maryam shrugged. "These were flashier."

Sarah frowned. "These were blessed by Pope John Paul II."

Hiro slipped an arm around her shoulders, coaxing her towards the elevators. "Perhaps we should finish this conversation in your office."

Maryam glanced around at the others. "That's it? It's over?"

"Not quite," Zackary answered. "We were told to wait in Sarah's office."

Zackary turned Maryam around and marched her towards the elevators before she could protest. He kept his head on a swivel as they went, braced for Claude's threats to rear their ugly head in the form of the elevator suddenly malfunctioning, or a less than savory escort to one of the Order's darker corners.

A bit of tension melted from his shoulders as they reached the office without incident. The relief was short lived, because as soon as Zackary shut the door and leaned against it, he said, "She knows what she is."

Maryam whirled on him with a glare. "Zack, what the hell?"

Sarah collapsed in her chair. Hiro looked like he might be the next one to throw up.

"Oh, my God." Maryam ran her hands over her hair. "You two are acting like it's a cancer diagnosis or something."

Sarah threw up her hands in exasperation. "Maryam! If the Order finds out—"

"They won't," Zackary interjected. "I'm going to train her. Teach her how to mask her powers. The Order will be none the wiser."

Hiro folded his arms, worry etching its way into his face. "You said they'd be none the wiser when you bound her powers the first time."

Maryam stepped between her uncle and her godfather. "You don't get to pull that card," she snapped. "Not when you've *defended* the Order every chance you had."

Hiro flinched. Sarah lowered her eyes.

Zackary gently pulled Maryam out of the way. "Maryam, you're not being fair."

"Oh, *I'm* not being fair?" A bitter chuckle slipped from Maryam's mouth.

Zackary's jaw clenched. "They did their best with what they had."

"Bullshit." Maryam glared up at him, jabbing a finger against his chest. "They've been icing you out and making you a pariah like everyone else for the last twenty-one years. Why are you defending them?"

"I'm being *reasonable*—"

"Don't you dare—"

Sarah interjected, "She's right, Zack."

Maryam dropped her hand and whirled faster than if Sarah had said the room was on fire. "Come again?"

Sarah swallowed hard, then sighed. "You're right, Maryam." She massaged her temple, her other arm limp against the armrest as she fell deeper into her chair, defeated. "We tried. Really, we did, but we failed. We didn't protect you. Zackary did." Her gaze slid to him, a sad smile tugging at her lips. "He always has."

Hiro hugged his arms to his body, eyes downcast and expression pained. "We thought keeping our distance, making the Order think we were detached, would protect you—keep their eyes off you, especially after a demon possessed Matthew. We were so wrong." His gaze darted to Maryam's tattoos. "We realized too late, and then you were gone. And you've stayed gone because you're right—we've never been able to protect you from this place. We haven't taken good care of either of you."

A palpable quiet settled over the room. Zackary could practically taste it.

Maryam deflated. Her expression melted to hurt confusion. The fire flickered out in her eyes as they pooled with tears and her mouth tightened to a thin line.

Sarah stood and rounded her desk, opening her arms for her niece.

"No." Maryam stepped away. "No, just..." she wiped her eyes. "Just give me a second, okay?"

Sarah's hands curled and she dropped her arms. "Okay. Take as long as you need."

The shrill ring of Sarah's desk phone rang, making everyone jump. Even Zackary.

Hiro grabbed the receiver before Sarah could. "Hiro Bishop speaking...." His expression shifted from concern to bewilderment.

"Y...Yes, Father." His gaze darted to the others. A smile broke over his face. "Of course. I'm sure they'll all be ecstatic."

Sarah clutched at her heart and whispered, "Thank God," while Zackary let himself collapse against the door, hands running over his face. He didn't realize how afraid he'd been of getting sent back to Hell until the threat had been removed, resulting in his stomach unwinding its knots and his legs going weak.

Maryam crashed into him with a tight hug, keeping him standing.

"Thank you again, Father." Hiro hung up and turned to the others, beaming. "You're a free man, Zack. And all it took was Maryam threatening the entire institution and getting sick on holy water."

Zackary laughed. "I've won more with less."

Maryam released him so she could punch in the arm. "Oh, fuck off. That's the last time I save your sorry ass."

"Language!" Sarah snapped.

Maryam faced Hiro. "Did they say anything about what they're going to do with Claude?"

Hiro shook his head, his joy melting into concern. "No, but that's no surprise." He watched his niece's relief shift into calculation. "Make no mistake, Maryam—you might have had an ace in your back pocket, but it's only the one. Best not to overplay your hand."

Maryam sucked on her teeth. "That's an awfully fancy way to tell me to keep my head down and let Claude keep getting away with sh—being terrible."

Hiro sighed. "I'm only saying to fight your battles wisely." He hooked his thumbs into the belt loops of his pants. "Though, if you want to expose him, we'll back you. Abuse is abuse. They can't use your identity against us in that. It's your story. Your call."

Maryam winced at the words and Zachary's chest tightened.

Abuse. His goddaughter had been abused and he'd never even known it. Zackary thought he might either sick or hyperventilate if he didn't get the fuck out of this church.

Sarah chimed in, that vengeful fire back in her eyes. "But if you don't want to do anything, *I* can think of a few things."

Maryam gave an awkward chuckle, unsure what to make of that statement. Zackary didn't know what to make of it either, but he was grateful not to be on the end of it.

Maryam toed at a fraying thread of carpet. "Can I have some time? I'll call you when I'm ready to talk about it."

Sarah's shoulders eased. "Of course."

"Take as long as you need," Hiro added.

Maryam nodded, then began fiddling with the hem of her shirt as an awkward silence settled over the room. Zackary couldn't blame her—this was the longest tough conversation he'd seen the Bishop family have in the twenty-one years he'd been with them.

He decided to have mercy on Maryam and nudged her. "We should go. Emrys will want to know how it went."

Sarah perked up. "Who?"

Zackary answered, "Our roommate," before Maryam could give her own answer. When the shit-eating grin didn't leave her face, he told her, "Another word out of you and you're walking home."

"Here." Sarah reached over her desk, dug in a drawer and took out a small brightly painted tin. "At least take some mints with you. And be sure to brush your teeth when you get home." She closed the space between herself and Maryam. "Stomach acid wears at your enamel."

Maryam snorted and held out her hand. "Thanks, Auntie."

Sarah opened the tin, paused with it over Maryam's hand, then shut it and placed the tin in her niece's palm, wrapping Maryam's fingers around it and holding her hand tight. "We love you, Maryam." She had to crane her neck to meet Maryam's eyes. Zackary couldn't remember ever seeing them quite that bright. "We love you so very much."

Maryam gave Sarah a tired smile and placed a free hand on top of hers. "I love you both too."

She placed the mints in her pocket, and followed Zackary out the door, sighing as she hit the "Up" elevator button. "One hell of a day, huh?" She popped a mint in her mouth.

Zackary snorted. "Quite the choice of words."

"Maryam!" The two turned to find Ellie jogging their way. Before either of them could ask if something was wrong, she threw her arms around Maryam and squeezed.

Maryam gave Zackary a bewildered look, her arms frozen at her sides as if the gesture was foreign to her. Zackary rolled his eyes and gestures for Maryam to hug Ellie back.

She did, but still looked confused, like she might be doing it wrong.

Ellie pulled away and handed Maryam a cream-colored business card. "I wrote my personal number on the back. Text me later so that I have your number. We'll get coffee next weekend or something."

Maryam looked at the card as if Ellie had written her number in hieroglyphs. "Uh...thanks. Yeah. I'll text you. Platonically."

Zackary pinched the bridge of his nose.

Ellie laughed. "Sounds good. I look forward to your platonic text." She waved and headed back towards her desk.

Maryam turned back towards Zackary. "What?"

The elevator door opened. Zackary held it for Maryam. "You're hopeless."

"What do you mean? I nailed it."

Zackary sighed and leaned against the back wall, eyes closed, too tired to argue. They walked to his bike in heavy silence. As Zackary handed Maryam her helmet, he studied her beyond her glamor—beyond the eyes she wanted to hide and the powers that scared her. The only other person that had ever stood up for him like Maryam had was her father. Azazel had stood up for everyone before it all went wrong. First, for humanity when he watched them suffer on earth, then for the heavenly beings that Heaven had wanted to obliterate. Despite the abuse, despite not knowing him, Maryam had turned out to be her father's daughter.

The thought made Zackary smile.

Maryam fidgeted under his lingering gaze. "What?"

"Your father would be proud of what you did today."

Maryam froze, then started twirling the helmet in her hands. "Like I care."

Zackary chuckled and threw his leg over his bike. "I knew you'd say that." He turned the key. The motorcycle revved to life. "We're going to take a little detour before going home. It's still rather early in the day."

Maryam hopped on the bike and put on her helmet. "Where are we going?"

Zackary flashed her a wicked smile over his shoulder as the bike roared to life. "Somewhere I can welcome you into the family properly."

The sage didn't work. Not really. Peter got ten minutes of peace after walking back to the store before it started again. Books fell off shelves. Pens rolled across the table of their own accord. Customers called, "What?" at the sound of mutters they believed belonged to Peter. At lunch he locked up and went looking for help.

"Looking for help" just meant Googling the nearest metaphysical spirituality shop, but it felt more proactive than dousing himself in essential oil again.

Peter kept his head on a swivel as he walked into *The Dragon's Cauldron.* He'd never heard of a demon taking someone out Final Destination style in broad daylight, but he also hadn't believed in demons until recently. A part of him wished he hadn't decided to keep Wendy away. She'd no doubt mock the idea of a demon taking him out with a logging truck, but he had to keep his sister safe. That meant keeping her away.

Don't want to see anyone else hurt on your account, do you? What would your dad think?

He never thought of you as his son and this is why.

Peter wasn't sure if the voices were in his head or whispered in his ear. He had slept so little the night before that he didn't even care.

Rich, earthy incense and lofty music took the edge off his mind as he walked into the store. He meandered the isles, studying various shades of stones, introductory witchcraft books, and candles. It seemed rude to go up to the counter, guns blazing, demanding to know how to get rid of a demon without looking around the store first. And something about tracing the patterns on leather-bound journals and reading the names of old gods on statues\ made him feel a little less insane. A little less alone.

"Can I help you find anything?"

The sweet, unassuming voice startled Peter so bad that he dropped the book he'd been browsing. The old woman reached to pick it up, but Peter was faster. She apologized all the same.

"I'm so sorry. I didn't mean to startle you." She placed a wrinkled hand, studded with swirling silver rings and stones, on his shoulder. She jangled as she moved, thanks to her plethora of necklaces, and smelled of lavender. White curls framed her face like wisps of clouds around her dark umber face.

Peter smiled and put the book back. "It's fine. I'm just a little jumpy. Too much caffeine." He tried to laugh off the jitters, but the sound was hollow, tired and maybe just a little bit crazed.

Judging by the way the woman's thin gray eyebrows pulled together, she heard it too. "No point in hiding the truth here, dear. You look nearly as worn out as me and I could probably be your mother three times over."

Peter rubbed the coin in his pocket and nervously glanced around the store. The teenagers giggling over erotic candles and the perusing stranger with bubblegum pink hair was too far to hear him.

Except, upon a closer look, Peter realized it wasn't a stranger. It was Alex. Peter stepped in line with a rack of holiday cards to keep te bartender from spotting him. He didn't need anyone he knew asking too many questions.

When Alex had turned their back, Peter asked under his breath, "You've seen stuff you can't explain, right?"

The woman chuckled. "Young man, I wouldn't have opened this store if I hadn't."

Peter took out the coin. "Then maybe you can explain this." When the woman reached for it, he pulled away. "Sorry. I don't want you to catch whatever this thing's carrying."

The woman's smile reminded Peter of his maternal grandmother. "It's not chicken pox, child."

She held out her hand. Peter handed it over and watched as she weighed it in her palm, then squinted to study the engravings. Her mouth turned down and the wrinkles of her forehead grew more pronounced the longer she stared.

"Where did you get this?" she muttered.

"My sister found it." Peter didn't bother to mention where.

The woman studied the symbol. "I know this sign." She raised her eyes to Peter's, sharp and dark. "Judging by the fear in your eyes, I don't need to explain what this is or what it's for."

Peter swallowed hard. "Yeah. Safe to say that."

"Tell me everything."

Peter did. All the while, he could have sworn the air grew heavier and stale while unseen angry eyes bore into the back of his head. His gut told him to shut up, to take the coin and retreat to the apartment and never speak of any of this again, but the growing worry and concern on the woman's face told him he was right to speak, no matter how pissed Anzuri was going to be.

Prickling pain leaked down Peter's back. He rolled his shoulders and ignored it.

The woman ran the coin between her fingers in silence. "Wait here." She disappeared into a room behind a beaded tapestry, leaving Peter standing empty handed and doing his best to dodge Alex.

It didn't work. They did a double take through a gap in a book shelf, spotted him, and rounded the shelf with a smile.. "Hey, stranger. I didn't know you hung out here." They grinned, slipping their hands into their pockets.

Peter massaged the back of his neck. "Yeah...I don't know that much about this kind of stuff. I just...uh..." His hand brushed his collar. He hissed at a sting of pain as his thumb brushed something wet. He pulled his hand back to find blood.

Alex tensed. "Dude, are you okay?"

"I don't know." Peter reached behind himself again to find that the cut, gash, or whatever it was, seemed to go down the length of his back.

Alex gently pulled his arm. "Let me see?"

Peter turned and heard Alex gasp.

"You're bleeding through your shirt."

"I'm *what?*"

Alex's fingers brushed the hem of his shirt. "Do you want me to take a look?"

Peter glanced around the store. The teenagers were walking out the door, leaving just the two of them. "Yeah, real quick." He slid up the back of his shirt. Alex sucked in air through their teeth.

"Bad?"

"I don't think you'll die, but you went and fucked with some bad energy, friend."

Peter heard the shutter sound effect of a picture being taken. He dropped his shirt as Alex handed him their phone.

Peter's stomach dropped. Angry red scratches ran from the nape of his neck to his hips. Alex was right that they weren't serious, but they were bad enough to cause smears and streaks of blood.

The store owner emerged from the bead curtain and frowned at Alex and Peter. "Did something happen?"

"Something scratched him," Alex blurted. "Bad."

The woman took Peter's hand, placed the coin in his palm, and wrapped his fingers around it. "Get rid of this. Now. It probably lashed out because I bought you time with a protection spell. You've got to move fast because the spell won't hold for long against him. You're fighting a power no human should ever face alone."

Alex's eyebrows shot up. Peter avoided their eyes.

The woman handed him a plastic bag with a bushel of herbs wrapped in twine. One end was already black and worn. "Normally I don't give out my personal cleansing bunch, but this is a special case. It's a unique protective blend. Bring it back so I can know you're okay?"

Peter put it in the pocket of his jacket and nodded. "It's that serious, huh?"

The woman nodded, her face somber. "This is the darkest power I've felt in a long, long time. If you don't get rid of it soon..." She shook her head, then squeezed Peter's hand. "Go now. Get rid of it somewhere no one else will ever find it."

Peter nodded, slipped his hand out of her grip, and shoved it in his pocket. "Can do. I'll make sure to actually buy something next time, too." He gave her a sheepish smile. "I hate to ask all this of you for no payment."

The woman shook her head. "Don't you worry about that. I want you safe."

"Do you want company?" Alex offered. "This doesn't sound like the kind of thing you should do alone."

"Thanks, but I got it." Peter took a step back towards the door, forcing his shoulders down. "I think I can handle throwing this thing in the Detroit River."

"Peter—"

He let the door shut on Alex's words. Nobody else needed to get involved in this. He just had to get rid of the coin, burn the herbs, come back and buy a few books on meditation or something. Easy day.

In the car, it became his mantra against the darkness that continued to press in on him. He focused on his breathing and the radio, trying to convince himself that the hint of sulfur in the air was from something coming in through the air vents and the occasional static was from the age of his car.

The southernmost point of Belle Isle was mercifully empty. Peter parked along the road, then walked as far as the land would allow, stopping at the point where the grass became jagged dark rocks before dropping into the water that separated Detroit from Windsor, Canada.

This was where Eliza and Adam had told Peter that, after nine years of trying, he would finally have a sister. This was where Eliza had told them she'd gotten into medical school. It was where Peter had come out. Where Adam had told his children he had cancer. Where Peter had burned his grad school acceptance letter after agreeing to run the bookstore.

Despite the cold, his jacket felt too hot, like he housed a furnace inside. He lowered his hood and looked out at the line that divided water, sky, and land, breathing deep, willing the air and sunlight to wash the darkness away. The coin felt strangely hot in his hand, like a red-hot ember in the breeze.

Peter studied it one final time, pulled back, and hurled it as far as he could, savoring the way it arched through the air and disappeared into the Detroit River with a satisfying *plunk*. He waited for a moment, half expecting it to fling itself back towards him, but nothing came towards the island except the tiny clap of minuscule waves.

Once Peter was convinced the world wouldn't erupt in flames, the muscles of his shoulders unwound and the bricks on his chest fell away. He made his way back to the car, then home. For the first time in a while, he didn't feel the need to check the rearview mirror for dark figures. The only thing he felt was the AC, rather than breath on the back of his neck. With a smile and a small crank of the radio volume, he began to think maybe the old woman had solved his problem. At home, he dug in the junk drawer for a lighter, took the cleaning bundle stick from its bag and slowly, ever so slowly, eased the flame to the used end of the bushel.

The lighter flickered out.

Odd. Maybe it was running out of fuel.

He lit it again. Again, it went out. He lit it directly under the sage. Only sparks.

Peter pressed the tab with more force than necessary in his growing frustration.

Click.

Click.

Click.

A pillar of flame erupted. Peter screamed and dropped both the stick and the lighter, his fingers throbbing red where the fire had grazed him. Despite the way his hands trembled, he picked them both up. He shook the lighter.

Empty.

Maybe Maryam or Zackary would have a lighter he could borrow. He snatched his keys and wallet. Pain flashed across his forearm as if an invisible beast had sunk its claws into him. He watched as long red welts formed across his harm.

"*No.*"

Peter whirled. The whisper had come from behind, low and masculine.

His mouth turned to ash and his blood froze.

The silence of the room felt like a tidal wave ready to drop. Peter jumped as his father's old Bible launched itself off the TV stand hard enough to hit the opposite wall. It landed on the sofa with a *thump* as two pages fluttered to the floor. Peter's heart twisted, despite his fear.

He didn't care about the book itself, but it has been a family heirloom. Now it was one more thing he'd managed to destroy.

He crossed the living room to collect the pages, stepping gingerly as if he could avoid angering the demon any further. He picked them up and looked them over. One was a passage of Genesis. Looking closer, Peter realized it was the introduction of Enoch. The other was the first page of the Song of Solomon.

Peter didn't remember much from his church days, but he knew that the two weren't connected. Enoch had lived before the Great Flood, being taken up to Heaven by God Himself rather than dying. The Song of Solomon was a collection of love poetry. The one thing they had in common was that it made no sense that a demon would want anything to do with either of them.

Peter pulled out his phone and plugged the two books into the search bar. The first handful of links gave him results for each individual book, but the final link of the page, the link for a small religious newspaper article dated in 2010, caught his eye.

St. Mary's Interdenominational Congregation Celebrates Receiving Apocryphal Text, The Song of Enoch.

An icy chill washed over Peter's skin. He turned and locked the door, hand lingering on the doorknob as he leaned his forehead against the wood and took a deep, shaking breath.

He winced as another rake of pain shot down his back.

This was it, then. This was what Anzuri really wanted.

Meaning it was the last thing on Earth that Peter was letting him get.

"This is it? Freezing our asses off on Lake Huron?" Maryam shivered as she stared out over the mild waves and crisp autumn blue of the water. "I thought welcoming me into the family meant buying me a beer or something. Or maybe some light hazing."

"I wouldn't drive two hours just to buy you something we sell daily. There will be hazing, though." Zackary dropped his helmet beside Maryam's in the sand and stripped off his jacket. "Take off your glamor."

Maryam glanced around the empty beach, then gave her godfather a skeptical look.

Zackary rolled his shoulders and unfurled his wings. "You can't fly in it and there's no one around. Take it off."

Maryam sighed and untied the choker from around her neck.

The world immediately shifted—the mingling scent of earth, leaves, and water was sharper. She could make out the flickering, shifting shades of orange, red, and yellow in the trees, like pieces of wind chimes that sang a quiet, hushed song on the breeze.

If she could stay out here, alone, with no people to hide from and no Order members trying to kill her, maybe being an ankida'shi wouldn't be so bad.

"Keep your head up."

Maryam looked up to find Zackary's face somber, his chest out. She hadn't even noticed that she'd dropped her gaze.

"What you are is nothing to be ashamed of," Zackary continued. "If someone can't meet your eyes, they're not worth your time. You're a daughter of earth and stardust, celestial infinity and mortality in one." Zackary held out his hand. "It's time you own that."

Maryam stared at his hand for a moment before she gingerly took it. Zackary pulled her close, then leapt into the air, making Maryam squeal.

"Is this the hazing you talked about?"

Zackary laughed. "You haven't seen hazing yet. Open your eyes."

Maryam snuck a peek, then slowly opened both eyes, her fear replaced with awe as the clouds grew closer and the earth and water fell away.

Beautiful or not, the only thing between a long drop back to the ground and Maryam was Zackary's grip.

She squeezed him a bit tighter. "You really expect me to *fly*? I've had wings for less than twenty-four hours."

"Luckily for you, our flight doesn't lean too heavily into the laws of physics." Zackary brought them to a stop. "We rely on our will.

Our intent. Our sense of self. Should you wish to rise, you rise. The manifestation of wings is a..." His brow furrowed as he thought it over. "It's a fluke, you could say. The physical plane can only hold so much celestial energy. Some had to leak out and, somehow, that translated into wings."

"So, we're like biscuit canisters in a hot car."

Zackary sighed. Maryam got the feeling he'd massage his temple if he had his hands free.

"That has to be the least eloquent way I've ever heard it put, but yes. If that helps our existence make sense to you, sure. We're biscuit canisters."

Maryam was still for a moment, and then blurted, "You know, the more I think about it...I feel like everyone on Earth is a biscuit canister in *God's* car."

Zackary closed his eyes and let out a slow breath, no doubt fighting against a heart palpitation. "The closest thing I ever get to the aging process is listening to you talk sometimes."

Maryam snickered. "Sorry." She kissed Zackary on the cheek. "Too bad you're stuck with me." She started in on the *Godfather* impressions. "You know there's nothing more important than family."

Zackary raised an eyebrow with a hint of a wicked smile. "Keep it up. See what happens."

"Whaddya mean? This is comedy gold right here" Maryam continued. "Whassa matta wit—"

Zackary dropped his arms.

Maryam plummeted. She screamed for Zackary, but her voice was lost in the wind. No sooner did she find him against the dusty blue of the sky did he disappear again as she spiraled towards the ground.

We rely on our will.

When had Maryam ever exercised her will in anything other than running away? What else was there for her to do? What did she *want* to do?

Our intent.

Maryam glimpsed her tattoos as her arms spread wide. That was not her anymore. That girl had died on the bloody bathroom floor but a new one hadn't taken her place yet. A ghost had walked away instead.

Our sense of self.

Maryam closed her eyes and took the deepest breath the roaring wind would allow.

It was the deepest breath she'd taken in years.

Should you wish to rise, you rise.

The deep dark below had tried to take her once. Maryam would be damned if she let it take her again.

She snapped her wings open and shot upwards, slicing the air like an arrow. The wind roared in her ears and her blood tingled with the rush. When the momentum abandoned her, she flapped her wings to steady herself, the unused muscles sharp and burning, but steady.

Maryam blinked her eyes open against the blinding sunlight. The world through these eyes made her gasp. The beach and the shallows winded along the surface of the earth, the planet swirling with color below as crisp white clouds bloomed above and below her. She could faintly make out Detroit to the south while Lake Michigan gradually swallowed the horizon to the north. There was so much to take in that Maryam felt removed from her body. From her senses. It was as if she were the sky, with all eternity to savor it all.

No wonder Zackary and the others had left Heaven for this. How were stagnant golden streets and white temples supposed to compete with all these ever-shifting colors and shapes?

Zackary.

Maryam searched for him above, then below. She finally spotted him a few hundred feet down with that same stupid smirk on his face, now with a splash of satisfaction.

Anger flared in her chest as she snarled and yelled, "You think that was funny, you bastard?"

Zackary laughed up at her, the sound bright and joyful. "I *told* you there'd be hazing. Welcome to the family, flightling."

Maryam grit her teeth and plummeted after Zackary, struggling against awkward, uneven wing beats to get to her godfather so she could drown him.

Zackary's smirk grew into a grin as he took off. Despite the wind, Maryam could hear him laughing as she chased him.

He didn't aim for the beach, though. Zackary pulled up just above the trees, shooting north along the coast. Maryam nearly crashed into the pines, but managed to course-correct and stay on him at the last second.

She could never catch him, though. She would brush the hem of Zackary's pants and he would veer right. When she felt the rubber of his sole, he'd drop like a stone and glide over the water.

Maryam nearly took a dip when she tried the same move, but found her anger replaced with bubbles of laughter as she let her fingers brush the cresting waves below.

Zackary led them back to the stretch of beach where they had started just as the sun touched the tree line, though Maryam hadn't given up. Her outstretched hand scraped his ankle as he pulled up to avoid the beach. With a chain of profanities, Maryam did her best to stop. Her bare feet burned as they skidded across the sand before she tumbled to the ground. She could hear the flap of wings as she wiped the grit from her face.

"Your landing needs work," Zackary called. He landed with the grace of Christ walking on water. He crossed his arms over his puffed-out chest as he looked her over. "Not bad for your first time, though."

Maryam scrubbed the sand from her jeans. "Yeah, considering you *dropped me from a mile above the earth.*"

Zackary shrugged. "It was three-fourths of a mile, at best."

"Still. I will have my revenge."

"Good luck." Zackary snorted. "My kids said the same thing and never managed to..." His face fell, his joy retreating back into his usual somberness. He turned away, grabbing his helmet from the ground. "We should go. It's getting late."

"Don't do this." Maryam said.

He stopped, his back still turned.

"Don't shut me out anymore You're so lonely and your kids are my family. They're my heritage. They've been kept from me my whole life and I won't let them be shoved down anymore to keep the Order comfortable."

Zackary dropped his head, fingers tracing the visor of his helmet. "Lonely, am I?"

Maryam closed the space between them, wrapping her arms around Zackary's waist and squeezing tight, smushing her cheek against the cool leather of his jacket. "Carrying this alone all these years? You must be."

"Sarah and Hiro knew about them. Matthew, too."

"We both know that's not the same as talking about them."

Zackary paused, then placed his free hand over Maryam's. He squeezed and Maryam swore she felt a hitch in his breath as he tried to keep back a sob.

"In the beginning, I had a life."

Maryam almost mistook Zackary's voice for a wave crashing on the sand.

"Three children. One born of a lover some years before and two born in wedlock, but that didn't matter. Not to anyone. We loved and raised whatever child was before us, because we saw them as promise and wonder—children born of Heaven and Earth." Zackary squeezed his goddaughter's hand. "You had so many cousins, Maryam. *Siblings.* A vast, eclectic, beautiful family that would have absolutely adored you."

Zackary let out a laugh muted by a sob. "You and my daughters would have run me absolutely ragged with all the trouble you'd get into. I know it. And my wife would have defended you lot with every breath. She always did."

Zackary shifted out of Maryam's grip to turn and hold her face in his hands. The sight of the strongest, most stoic person she knew fighting back tears closed Maryam's throat and blurred her vision.

"That is why I *refuse* to let you bow your head to hide these eyes. Glamor yourself to stay safe, to fight another day, but never out of shame. Your ankida'shi brothers and sister had nothing to be ashamed of ten thousand years ago and you have nothing to be ashamed of now. Understand?"

Maryam nodded. She didn't trust herself to try and speak without the dam breaking.

"Good." Zackary kissed her on the forehead and let her go. "Speaking of glamors, I should teach you how to weave your own before we go home. Close your eyes."

Maryam eyed him wearily. "You're not going to draw on my face with a sharpie or something are you?"

Zackary snorted. "No. Just close your eyes."

Maryam obeyed, then peeked to make sure this wasn't another trick.

Zackary scoffed. "I promise I'm not going to do anything to you. The hazing's over." Maryam shut her eyes properly. "Breathe deep. Let everything go. No expectations, no pressure, nothing. How do you see yourself? Who do you want to see when you look in the mirror?"

Maryam tensed. Pep talk or no pep talk, she wanted her old face back.

A brush of energy settled over her skin like an old worn sweater—not hiding her, just protecting her. With or without the glamor she wasn't a monster. She wasn't some sort of bloodthirsty creature that the Order needed to put down. She was Maryam. Just Maryam. Human and angel, fallen or otherwise. Heaven and Earth. Human and more.

Something, someone, amazing.

She opened her eyes to find Zackary beaming.

"You look lovely."

She pulled out her phone and opened the camera, leaving herself speechless.

It was her old face, yet not. Her eyes looked human, but there was a new sharpness behind them. Were there more freckles than there used to be? She'd always loved her freckles. The set of her jaw looked stronger and there was something new and knowing in the subtle smirk across her mouth, like she knew who she was, or at the very least knew who she wasn't.

"I do. Thanks," she said, examining herself from multiple angles.

Zackary scooped up Maryam's helmet and tossed it to her. "Let's head home. You're going to be starving in about five minutes from flying and I'd rather not see you hangry before you have full control over your powers."

Maryam scowled as she caught her helmet and followed, but knew she couldn't argue. The spot where her shoulders met her wings had started to feel like noodles and would probably hurt worse than the world's worst leg day tomorrow.

Zackary took out his phone as they walked, tapped the screen a few times, then lifted it to his ear. "Emrys." He winced. "Yeah, I know. Sorry. We got tied up with some stuff. Are you good with takeout instead? We're about two hours out." Zackary scowled as he listened to the other hand. "I'm sorry, do you *want* us to go to Order Jail by flying around Detroit?" He sighed and removed the phone from his ear. "Maryam, what did you want?"

Her stomach gave a small growl. "A mountain of pad Thai with a slightly smaller mountain of tofu spring rolls."

Zackary brought his phone back. "Did you hear her?...Just order whatever for me..." He scowled again. "Try it and you're sleeping under the bar." He hung up with a sigh.

Maryam snickered. "Aw, you don't mean that."

Zackary scowled at her.

Maryam gave him a playful shove. "C'mon. We're all about honesty today, so spill. What's your issue with him?"

"He can't take a hint, for starters."

"Are you straight?"

Zackary rolled his eyes. "Sexual orientations are about as stable in the face of eternity as a beach is against the tides."

"So, what's the deal?"

"Why do you care?"

"Because you're lonely. In multiple ways. I know you are."

Zackary paused and studied his goddaughter's face before walking on without an answer.

Maryam groaned as she followed. "Zack, I swear, if it's some bullshit *Twilight*-level excuse about you potentially hurting him or breaking a bed during sex—"

"Christ, Maryam, I'm a demon," Zackary snapped. "Both sides tacked *Treacherous* on the end of my name, for fuck's sake." He ran his hand over his hair. "The Forces that Be have made it abundantly clear that I don't get to be happy. More importantly, I don't *deserve* to be happy." Zackary's shoulders drooped. "And that's for the best. Emrys is just one more potential loved one I will inevitably fail."

Maryam listened in silence and let the peace sit for a while after Zackary stopped speaking. As they neared his motorcycle, she said, "So...what I'm hearing is *Twilight* rules."

Zackary sighed and climbed on the bike. "We never should have let you watch those stupid movies."

Maryam climbed on the back. "Excuse you, I read the books first." She popped on her helmet and lifted the visor. "My point is, you've let Heaven, Hell, and the Order get in your head about yourself. How could you *not* deserve to be happy after all the good you've done? Besides..." Maryam wrapped her arms around Zackary and held him tight. "There hasn't been a single time in my life where you've failed me."

Zackary placed a hand on Maryam's arms and squeezed. "Thank you. I needed to hear that." Zackary's throat closed around the end of his sentence. He cleared his throat and rolled his shoulders. Maryam let him go and he placed his hands on the bike handles. "Breath a word of this conversation to Emrys and you'll be flying circles around the Detroit city limits from dawn 'till dusk."

Maryam gave a mock-salute. "You got it, god-daddy."

"Call me that again and you'll be flying laps around the city limits for a week."

The bike roared to life and jerked into motion before Maryam could reply, nearly knocking her off. She scrambled to grab hold of Zackary and decided to save her smart-ass remarks for another time.

The two were greeted with the sweet scent of peanut sauce and the intertwined smell of multiple fried foods, making Maryam's mouth water and her stomach threaten to devour itself. Zackary had definitely been onto something in curbing her hanger. She nearly ran Emrys over as he greeted them in her beeline for the food.

"Congrats on not going to Order Jail!" He squeezed Maryam in a hug. "I went a little overboard with the food. And ordered an ice cream cake. I don't know how to stop myself when it comes to celebrations."

Zackary hung up his jacket and helmet. "Do you know how to stop yourself *ever*?"

Emrys shrugged, then lifted up the brightly decorated cake to show the words, *Congrats on Not Going to Order Jail*. "The poor teenager at the store was very confused, but she humored me."

Maryam laughed. "Thank you, Emrys. This is all very sweet." She rounded the peninsula counter and opened the plate cupboard. "And the surplus of food won't be an issue, I promise."

A knock came at the door. Maryam, mouth already full of spring roll, called for the guest to come in.

Alex popped their head in the door, eyes bright. "Emrys said there was food?"

"Sure is." Maryam forked rice noodles into her mouth. "Help yourself."

Zackary elbowed her. "Stop talking with your mouth full."

Alex slipped off their black platform boots and joined the group in their pink striped socks. "Thank you. I got tied up at *Dragon's Cauldron* and the bus was late. Didn't get a chance to eat dinner."

Zackary paused with a piece of tofu between his chopsticks. "Is there something wrong at the Cauldron?" he asked. "Is Ms. Suzie okay?"

"She's fine," Alex answered, spooning noodles onto a paper plate. "That old lady's going to outlive all of us." They glanced from Zackary to Maryam. "You guys remember Peter? The guy Maryam fell on the night that weirdo wandered in?"

Maryam's food turned to ash in her mouth. She forced herself to finish chewing before asking, "We've hung out a little bit since then. What happened?"

Alex picked at their plate. "Something's...haunting him. Left giant scratches down his back in the middle of the store while Ms. Suzie was trying to help get rid of whatever it was." They took a drawstring pouch from underneath their top. "She made me a charm keeping whatever it was away from me, since I touched him to get a better look at the scratches."

Zackary shoved his plate away to lean forward on the counter. "Do you happen to have pictures?"

"I do, actually." Alex pulled out their phone, swiped across the screen a bit, then turned the screen towards the group.

The image turned Maryam's stomach sour. Four angry gashes glared up from Peter's pale olive skin like claw marks. Two leaked trickles of blood, making Maryam fear she might hurl.

This was their fault. They had failed and now Peter was paying for it.

Maryam shot to her feet. "We need to get to him. Now."

Zackary eased himself up. "Maryam, slow down."

"We *can't*. Peter's got about five minutes before he's in the middle of a full-blown possession."

Zackary gestured to the general direction of the book store. "We run over there, guns blazing, and Anzuri is going to skip the possession and just kill him."

"Can we back the fuck up and explain what the hell is going on?" Alex exclaimed.

Maryam and Zackary exchanged looks.

"Oh, for fuck sake." Emrys dropped his hands on the table. "Zackary works for an organization of exorcists and Maryam is their Number One Pariah. *Ectoplasm* is just a cover."

"Emrys!"

"Em, are you serious right now?"

Emrys gestured to Alex. "They're an eye witness! They're a part of this now!"

"That's not your call to make!"

A frantic knock at the door silenced the fighting. The group exchanged looks. Maryam sighed and went for the door. Because surely, whatever was on the other side couldn't make things worse.

At least, that's what she thought before she discovered Wendy standing on the other side.

Peter didn't call their mother in the middle of the night and make her cry. He didn't ignore texts and phone calls from his family, only letting them know that the store wouldn't be open today due to illness.

"I don't care about that," Wendy heard Aunt Jae tell her mother over the phone. "I care about my nephew. Something isn't right with him. I'd go, but the doctor has me on bedrest..."

"Jae, don't you even think about going over there. If the doctor says don't move, don't move. The last thing we need is you going into labor on top of whatever is going on with Peter. I'll go check on him after my shift. I'll break the damn door down if I had to." Eliza Bailey didn't swear.

Wendy waited for her mother to hang up before speaking. "I could go check on Pete if you want," she said as Eliza pulled up to the curb outside her school. "It's only a short bus ride."

Eliza sighed and unlocked the doors. "Baby, remember what happened last time—"

"Oh, my God, I got lost *one* time—"

"The answer is no. Whatever's going on with your brother, I've got a bad feeling about it."

Wendy got out of the car and shut it with more force than necessary.

"Hey!" Eliza yelled. "One, don't slam my door. Two, you are to go to your tutor's house after school like you're supposed to."

Wendy groaned and fought the urge to roll her eyes as she turned to face her mother. "Leah lives in those bougie apartments by Whole Foods, though. That's only two blocks away."

"Then we'll go as soon as I pick you up and you will wait in the car. Now go on." Eliza flicked her wrist towards her daughter. "You're gonna be late."

Wendy scowled.

"And fix your face."

Wendy glared as her mother drove away, having no other recourse for rebellion.

Alicia and David met at her locker, concern etched into both their faces.

"Any word from Peter, yet?" Alicia adjusted the books on her hip.

Wendy shook her head. "Nothing. Everyone's getting worried."

David massaged his neck. "I'm really sorry, Wen. I should have never taken you two out to that hospital."

Alicia lightly smacked him in the chest. "Will you stop? There is no demon."

Except Wendy wasn't so sure. If Peter was only moody and isolating himself, Wendy would suspect that his depression had reared its ugly head, but something had spooked Maryam the night she'd come over. The same something knocked books from their shelves in the store. And Eliza had said that Peter mentioned something lurking in the house.

But David wasn't the one who needed to apologize. This was on Wendy for bringing that coin to her brother as a bribe. Something has been attached to it and now it was eating Peter alive.

At least she had a way to fix this. If the demon, entity, or whatever it was, was tied to that stupid coin, all she had to do was find it and get rid of it. Easy day. Hopefully.

Wendy counted down each minute of her classes until she could get to her brother. Leah, her tutor, met her at their usual spot, and Wendy had never been more grateful that Leah insisted they study at her dad's Midtown apartment rather than the school library.

Twenty minutes before Eliza normally picked her up, Wendy feigned a family emergency by pretending to read an urgent text message and claiming her mom was already waiting for her. Leah helped her gather her notes and insisted she walk Wendy out, but Wendy refused to let her. She gave Leah's window a quick glance to make sure the coast was clear before taking off for the store.

She made it with seven minutes to spare—more than enough time to swipe the coin, throw it in a nearby dumpster, and let Eliza know she was with Peter, even if it guaranteed a lecture.

Except Peter's door didn't budge when Wendy unlocked it with her copy of the key.

"What the hell?" Wendy threw her weight against the door. It gave an inch. And then another. Wendy shoved and pushed until she could wriggle into the apartment, finding the sum of all Peter's furniture on the other side of the door.

The subtle stench of rot greeted her, stronger in the dark somehow. She held her breath as she flicked on the light, almost expecting something to appear. Nothing did. Just an unnervingly quiet apartment. She still felt watched.

"Pete? Are you here?"

She found him in his bedroom fast asleep, curled in on himself under a pile of blankets, despite the sweltering heat of the apartment—another sign that something was wrong. Wendy had never known Peter to turn on the heat until the middle of December.

Her big brother had never looked quite so small before. Had he been eating? Even in the sliver of light from the hall Wendy could tell he was growing gaunt and pale. She eased his door closed and began snooping around the apartment. It would be easier to steal that damn coin with him asleep, anyway.

At least, it should have been. It wasn't on any of the kitchen counters or in the junk drawer. The TV stand proved fruitless as well.

The couch held his discarded keys and wallet, so Wendy dug between the cushions. A small shock bit her fingers as she brushed something round and metallic. "Ah, ha!" She dug out the coin and held it up triumphantly. "Got you, you little—"

A shadow blotted out the light.

Wendy whirled to meet a face made of smoke and obsidian eyes. Her scream was cut short as it snatched her by the throat, dragging her to the wall and slamming her against the plaster. It grew as it lifted her towards the ceiling by her neck, consuming Wendy's vision. Its rot and brimstone stench made her gag on what little air she could steal. The beast's sharp, inky teeth, framed by a cracked, crooked smile froze her in place.

"Peter," she whimpered, tears welling in her eyes. "Peter, help me, please." Her voice hardly amounted to a squeak. Her sleeping brother couldn't hear her. The monster would devour her and then Peter would die. Dad had wanted them to take care of each other. Wendy had failed. They were going to die, and it was all her fault.

"GET YOUR GODDAMN HANDS OFF MY SISTER!"

Peter sprang from the hallway, baseball bat in hand, and a vicious snarl on his face. He swung at the figure. It jerked out of his range and swiped at his face, leaving gashes across his cheek. Peter wound to swing again.

The monster's grip tightened on Wendy's throat. Spots dotted her vision as she gagged and wheezed.

Peter froze, his eyes wide and calculating.

Finally, he dropped the bat. "You win. Let her go."

The monster's grip loosened just enough for Wendy to get a sliver of air. She used it to rasp, "Peter, no."

"Let her go and I won't fight you anymore." Peter kept his hands up, as if to prove he had nothing left to hide. He eased himself to his knees, gaze still raised. "Just let my sister go."

Through her asphyxiated haze, Wendy could have sworn the darkness chuckled, its voice a deep rumble like an earthquake within a cave. It released her, letting her drop to the floor, gasping for breath and straining to see past the stars in her vision.

Peter collapsed as the monster engulfed him, seeping into his skin until it was gone.

Peter violently convulsed on the floor.

"No!" Wendy crawled to his body and held him by the shoulders. He thrashed in her grip, muscles taut and his throat straining as if he was trying to scream, but the monster had stolen his voice as well as his body.

"How do I make it stop?" Wendy sobbed.

"Run" Peter seized her arm so tight it hurt. "Get out."

"I won't leave you."

"You have to." Peter forced a smile to his face. "It needs me alive. I'll be okay."

"Dad told us to take care of each other!"

Peter strained to look out the window. "Wendy, I can't fight him." He gasped for air. "You have to—" He screamed in pain, his back arching and hands becoming claws, then he went limp.

Terrifyingly limp.

He went so still that Wendy stopped crying, not sure whether to panic or mourn.

She shrieked as Peter's eyes flew open, now seas of bottomless inky black.

"Tell Maryam Bishop to join me at the gates of Heaven or I'll hurl her into the deepest pit of Hell." It wasn't Peter's voice. Wendy had never heard a voice so sinister and cold before. "Go!" it screamed, scaring Wendy to her feet.

She ran from the apartment as the monster cackled from her brother's mouth.

Her mother's car skidded to a stop at the store front below. Eliza shot out from the car and slammed the door as her daughter jumped down the stairs two at a time. "Wendy Lavone Bailey, I told you to wait. Where is your brother?"

"It's not Peter," Wendy panted, grabbing hold of her mother's coat. "The demon got him."

Eliza clicked her tongue and pushed past her daughter. "If you two don't stop this demon foolishness—"

"Mom, no!" Wendy scrambled to grab hold of her. "We need to get help!"

"That's what I'm doing!" Eliza yanked away, but froze at the sight of Peter watching them from the apartment landing, his eyes black pits and his face cold and soulless.

Eliza stumbled back, her face pale. "What on Earth..."

Wendy pulled her mother towards Ectoplasm. "Mom, we gotta go."

Eliza let Wendy lead her away as she dug out her phone. "I'm calling Pastor Marcus."

"Don't. He'll only make things worse." Wendy ignored the honking cars as she ran across the street with her mother in tow. "We need Maryam."

"Since when do you know a Maryam? Wendy, what is happening?"

Even if Wendy understood, she doubted she could put it into words.

She threw open the door of the bar and made a beeline for the counter, despite her mother's protests and the dirty looks of patrons trying to order. "I need to talk to Maryam," she shouted over the music.

The bartender frowned at her. "You can't be in here, kid."

Wendy felt Eliza's hand on her shoulder. "I'm sorry. We were just leaving," her mother said.

Wendy wrestled away. "Please, I need to talk to her. It's an emergency."

The bartender studied her, then gestured to a metal staircase ascending along the back brick wall. "She and Zack got home about twenty minutes ago."

Wendy took off again, bounding up the stairs and banging on the door until Maryam opened it, nearly getting Wendy's pounding fist in her face.

"Something really bad has Peter," she said. "And I think you're the only one who can stop it."

Maryam felt more nauseous than when she had chugged that holy water. "What do you mean something really bad has Peter? What happened?"

Wendy gulped down a few deep breaths before continuing. "I tried to go talk to him. No one had heard from him all day. He had this coin." She waved her hands as she tried to find the right words. "It's this...this talisman or charm or something. It had this bad thing attached to it and I didn't know and gave it to him and now it has him and it's my fault." Wendy's composure cracked and a small sob slipped out.

Maryam guided her into the apartment and wrapped her arms around her, letting Wendy cry into her chest.

A woman ascended the stairs in Wendy's wake, frazzled and looking strikingly like Wendy. "Can someone please explain what the hell is happening to my son and who you people are?"

Maryam looked towards Zackary, as did Emrys and Alex. He flashed them all a dirty look, then tried to ease his expression as he rounded the counter and approached the woman.

"Mrs. Bailey, I take it?" he asked.

The woman scowled. "It's *Doctor* Bailey, actually."

Zackary gave her a customer service smile. "My apologies, Dr. Bailey." He wrung his hands as he searched for words. "I'm afraid your son has found himself entangled with a particularly violent supernatural entity."

Dr. Bailey's brow furrowed.

"Time is of the essence to untangle the two, but the process is often considered rather..." Zackary tipped his head left, then right as he searched for words. "Archaic."

Dr. Bailey's eyebrows shot up. "You're talking about performing an exorcism on my son? A bunch of people I've never met?"

Even Wendy looked skeptical as she inched away from Maryam.

"That is what it's commonly known as, yes."

"My son is *sick*." Dr. Bailey reached for her phone. "I'm calling 911 and a pastor I actually *know*."

Zackary and Maryam moved to protest.

Emrys cut them both off. "If I may, Doctor..."

A strange, static energy slithered into the room, making the hairs on Maryam's arms stand up with a shiver. She watched as Emrys approached Dr. Bailey, slow and calculated, a strange spark in his eye she hadn't seen before. He smiled wide, almost too wide, as he placed a hand on her wrist.

"You can trust us. We're friends. Your children are in good hands."

Dr. Bailey's eyes went wide with panic, then dreamy and dull.

"You must be tired." Emrys lowered her wrist, guiding her hand to place her phone back in her pocket. "Why don't you go home?" He glanced at Wendy. "Your daughter will call you when it's all over."

Emrys let her go, flipping some sort of switch. The strange energy dissipated, and Dr. Bailey blinked. Concern still pulled at her features, but there was no panic. No hint that she was dealing with anything out of the ordinary or that she'd been touched by magic.

"And you're *sure* he'll be okay?"

Emrys placed his hand on his heart. "You have my word as a son of Hemlock."

"Okay..." Dr. Bailey dug for her keys in her purse and walked back towards the front door. Alex opened it for her. As she stepped over the threshold, she pointed to Wendy with a stern look. "Don't you be out all night. You've got school tomorrow."

Wendy blinked, looked around the room for confirmation that this was really happening. "O...kay? You feel alright, Mom?"

Dr. Bailey gave a tired smile. "Worried about your brother, but he'll be okay." She looked to the total strangers that she was suddenly trusting with her son's life and soul. She moved to speak, then paused. "When you see Peter, tell him I'm sorry. And that we love him."

Zackary gave her a sympathetic smile. "I'm sure he knows how loved he is, but we'll be sure to remind him."

Dr. Bailey nodded and pulled the door shut behind herself.

Tension sat heavy in the room until Wendy whirled on Emrys. "I'm sorry. Did you just *hex* my mother?" she demanded.

Emrys waved away her concern. "Of course not. Just a bit of magical suggestion. Think of it as a magical Trazodone."

"How is that better?!"

"We're sorry, Wendy, but it was the right call," Zackary said. "The last thing we need right now is for the mortal authorities to get involved." He wrinkled his nose. "And for a *protestant* to play exorcist."

Maryam raised an eyebrow. "What's wrong with protestants?"

Emrys clicked his tongue. "Oh, darling. If you have to ask..."

Maryam jabbed a finger at him. "Fuck off, Em. Do you even know the difference between Catholics and Protestants?"

Emrys shrugged. "One still dresses up for church and the other wears jeans."

Wendy gave him a bewildered look. "I'll hand over every cent of my college fund if you can find me a Black church with everyone in jeans. Those are the white protestants."

"Wait, which one are Presbyterians? Or is that a third thing?"

"Can someone *please* explain what is happening to the only normal person in the room?" Alex asked frantically. "I feel like I'm losing my mind over here."

The room settled and went somber. Again, all eyes fell on Zackary.

"We don't exactly have the time to explain." Zackary sighed and massaged the back of his neck. "Alex, Emrys was telling the truth. I've been an exorcist since Maryam was two, as are her aunt and uncle. We left to get some space because the organization can be toxic."

Maryam snorted. "To put it mildly."

Zackary flashed her a dirty look. "Wendy, your brother's been possessed by a powerful demon from the dark court of Hell. We tried to stop it, but it looks like we failed." His shoulders drooped. "I'm sorry. Peter came in last week wearing so much sage that there was no way I could have sensed or smelled it on him."

Wendy searched Zackary's face. "How would you *smell* a demon?" Her eyes went wide. "Unless..."

Zackary shook his head. "That's not important right now. We need to get to your brother. Take us to the apartment. We need to figure out where Anzuri is headed next."

Maryam's chest tightened. "No. She's staying here with Alex."

Alex scoffed. "Excuse you. When did you hear me volunteer to babysit?"

"I'm sixteen," Wendy snapped.

Maryam blocked Zackary's path to the door. "I mean it, Zack. I'm not letting another kid see what I saw with Matthew."

"Maryam." Zackary placed his hands on her shoulders.

"No." She shoved him off. "No one else. I mean it."

"We're going to need her to get through to Peter if he's still in there. Neither of us have a close enough relationship with him to do it."

Maryam prepared to argue, then sighed in defeat. She studied Wendy—the worry etching into her face and the way she seemed to be shrinking in on herself. How much more would she disappear if Anzuri, who she brought to Peter's doorstep, destroyed her brother for good?

How soon afterwards would she self-destruct the way Maryam had?

She turned back to Zackary. "It gets too bad and I'm getting her out."

Zackary nodded. "Fine by me. Let's go." He looked at Wendy. "C'mon. Before it gets too bad." Grabbing his keys, he added to Alex, "Can you hold down the fort?"

Alex sputtered. "I guess! Not sure what the hell else I'm good for at this point."

Maryam winked and flashed finger guns at them as the group walked out the door. "Thanks. You're a champ."

Silence and the lingering stench of Hell greeted them all as they entered the apartment. The air felt stale against Maryam's skin, as if all movement and life had gone out of it. The space itself felt uncanny with the way Peter's life had been abandoned—his keys and wallet sat on the table while clean dishes dried on the counter. The fridge hummed and the stove clock flicked to another digit. The whole thing felt unnatural. It was like it was a completely different place than the warm, welcoming, safe apartment Maryam had visited a few days ago.

"I don't understand it," Wendy looked over the pile of furniture that had been pushed against the door. "I thought demons just wanted to mess shit up. Why go anywhere? Why not keep Peter here and keep torturing him? That's what they do in the movies."

"And faeries in movies are everyone's friend and won't rip your name from your soul," Emrys interjected. "Don't believe everything you watch, love."

"I hate to admit it twice in one day, but Em is right," Zackary said, running his hand over the bookshelf, meticulously studying each title. "What exactly did Anzuri say to you when he took Peter?"

Wendy turned to Maryam. "He said for you to meet him at Heaven's gate or burn in Hell. Something like that."

Maryam rubbed at her chin. "When I was possessed, he said something about breaking down Heaven's gates. He needed sheet music for some sort of song by Enoch."

Zackary's face blanched. "The Song of Enoch. It's not a real song—it's a book."

"Wait, like in the Bible?"

"It's not in the Bible. It's a grimoire disguised as apocrypha."

Maryam blinked, her expression blank.

Zackary sighed. "Did you pay attention in a single Biblical Literature class?"

"We both know I didn't."

"Also, some of us weren't forced to endure Catholic school," Emrys added.

Zackary pinched the bridge of his nose. "Apocrypha is typically Biblical scripture outside the cannon. In the case of the Song of Enoch, it's a grimoire disguised as a collection of poetry attributed to the prophet Enoch, much like how the Keys of Solomon is a grimoire attributed to King Solomon. Biblical scholars used to think it was actually a lost section of the Book of Psalms. Once the Order caught wind of it, they snatched it up and hid it away. The academic world hasn't seen it since."

"Please tell me the Detroit branch of the Order doesn't have a copy."

Zackary switched to massaging his temple with both hands.

Maryam groaned. "Of course, they do." She turned and headed towards the front door. "Can we catch him if we fly?"

Wendy trailed behind. "Wait. *Fly?* You can't be serious."

"What am I doing, then?" Emrys asked.

Zackary turned to him with a calculating look. "Follow behind on foot. Call us if you spot him. It's a long shot, but maybe we'll be lucky for once and he hasn't made it yet."

"Hellooooo." Wendy waved her arms. "Anyone going to answer my question about flying?"

Maryam threw open the door. "Your brother is possessed by a demon, and you think we can't be serious?"

Wendy stuttered as she followed the two of them to front landing. "Okay, maybe you are serious but how?" She studied Maryam for a long moment. "You're not human either, are you?"

Maryam paused and thought about how to answer that. *Human and more*. Given that she'd only had about thirty-odd hours to process what she was, that was what she had settled on, but it didn't feel like the right answer right now.

Maybe she didn't need to give Wendy an answer right now. Maybe, though her question was understandable enough, Maryam didn't owe her that. Maybe she didn't owe anyone that.

Instead, she tensed and focused on lowering her glamor to unfurl her wings. *Only* her wings. One monster was plenty for Wendy to face at the moment.

Zackary did the same. With a flick of his wrist, a tingle of energy washed over Maryam's skin, creating what she assumed was a shield to keep them invisible from the busy street below.

Wendy gasped, eyes darting between Maryam and Zackary. "You're not demons? You're angels?"

Maryam shrugged. "Same difference."

Wendy chuckled. The sound was slightly unhinged. "Yeah, sorry. My mistake."

"You can process what this means for your worldview later," Zackary said, offering her his hand. "Let's go save your brother first."

Maryam climbed onto the railing, spread her wings, and dropped. Her feet just barely brushed the hood of Peter's car before she shot up into the air. Behind her, Wendy shrieked as Zackary took off with her in his arms. Maryam snickered.

She flew close enough to Zackary to stay cloaked in his glamor. He landed in the Order's courtyard as light as the feathers that covered his wings, Maryam landed hard, crashing to the concrete with the grace of a cinder block. She glowered at Zackary as he smirked at her. "Showoff," she grumbled, picking at a patch of torn skin.

Zackary gently set Wendy on her feet. "It's all part of the learning process. Your uncles and I took much harder falls when we were first learning to move in our quasi-mortal forms. Your father—" He froze.

Maryam sighed. "There's no point in tiptoeing around him. We're going to have to talk about him eventually."

Zackary studied her for a moment, then a sad smile came to his face. "Your father once tried a stunt too close to the ground and wound-up face-first in a marsh. He stormed out of that water so mad we thought he'd beat us all senseless for laughing. He just threw us in that disgusting bog instead."

"Sounds like something I'd do." Maryam dusted herself off. "Apple doesn't fall that far from the tree, I guess."

"No," Zackary sighed. "No, it does not."

The team rounded the corner to the front doors of the church. Maryam eased it open and waited. The sanctuary stood stoic and still, not a single candle or church pamphlet out of place, but a siren sounded from somewhere deep within.

Maryam and Zackary exchanged panicked looks and sprinted up the center aisle, Wendy in tow. Zackary veered right instead of the normal left towards the elevator and Maryam course corrected. They both skidded to a stop at the sight of a metal door busted in and the red flashing light above the staircase beyond.

Zackary herded Maryam and Wendy behind himself before descending the stairs, his steps ginger and his arms up, ready to swing. At the bottom, he peeked out the second broken door and turned to the girls.

"Let me make sure it's clear," he said.

Maryam hadn't heard him. He'd failed to shield her from the blood streaked across the lobby floor and the body that hung limp over the reception desk. Maryam's heartbeat roared in her ears as she shoved passed Zackary and stumbled towards the desk, her feet slipping in the pools of blood from scattered broken bodies.

"No, no, no, no, please, no." The words grew frantic as Maryam took in the tributaries of blood branched down the desk, pooling on the floor.

She pulled Ellie McDonald's limp body from the desk, cradling her on the floors as she pulled her hair from her face, finding glassy, blank blue eyes beneath. All that was left of her throat was a tattered mess of wet crimson and pink.

Pain bloomed beneath Maryam's shin—she'd landed on one of the pearl beads from Ellie's necklace.

"Elle, please, c'mon." Maryam couldn't breathe. There wasn't enough air and Ellie's blood was leaking onto Maryam's shirt and the girl was so heavy and cold already.

Her head lulled to the side as Maryam gently shook her.

Maryam choked on a sob. "Zackary! Zackary, help!" She searched for him frantically, finding him only a few steps behind her with Wendy at his side, her face buried in his arm. "Tell me how to save her."

Zackary wrapped an arm around Wendy, holding her tight as he met Maryam with a broken expression. "You can't."

"*You* do it, then," Maryam begged.

"She's gone, Maryam."

"THEN WHAT'S THE POINT OF US?" Maryam screamed. "WHAT WAS THE POINT OF LEAVING HEAVEN AND COMING DOWN HERE IF WE CAN'T SAVE THEM?"

Wendy flinched against her volume.

Zackary dropped his gaze to the top of Wendy's head. "We've never had power over death, Maryam. It doesn't belong to us."

Maryam took in a shaking breath. She laid Ellie down, scooped up a few of Ellie's pearl beads, and slipped them in her pocket as she stood up. "When we find Anzuri, I'm going to rip him out of Peter and tear him to shreds, starting with his throat."

"We should wait for the rest of the Order. Tell them what we know."

Maryam spat, "Fuck the rest of the Order," and sprinted down the corridor.

"Maryam, wait!" Zackary chased after her, with Wendy still clinging tight to him.

Maryam knew the archives well. On the days she had been forced to come to work with her aunt and uncle, she'd slip off and hide until it was time to go home. There was something about being that deep below ground, that removed from the world, that settled her in a way being around others never could, but now Anzuri had tainted the quiet dark of the bedrock halls and turned them ominous.

The archives sat behind carved wooden doors. One sat cracked open, revealing nothing but inky blackness mixed with overpowering incense. Maryam's mouth went dry and her palms felt damp. She walked home in the dark, stared out into it beyond bonfires on family camping trips, but there was something about the dark of the Order's archives that put her very soul on high alert.

Flipping on the amber-tinted lights didn't help. They made the rows of towering bookcases feel ancient and secretive in a way Maryam felt she had no right messing with. Even when it had been her sanctuary, she had never dreamed of touching any of the books—she had always brought her own.

"I can feel him, but he's impossible to pin down," Zackary muttered. "They burn all that incense to neutralize some of the darker energies attached to some of these books. It's throwing off my senses."

Maryam believed him. Her head had started to ache in a way it hadn't when she visited the archives with her powers sealed. "We'll split up, then. Take Wendy with you."

Wendy shifted from foot to foot, looking unsure.

Maryam patted her on the shoulder. "I've had my powers for about ten minutes," she said. "If something goes wrong, I'd rather you be with him."

Zackary nodded in agreement and slipped off with Wendy in the opposite direction.

Maryam knew it was the right move. They'd cover more ground and, hopefully, have Anzuri pinned by the time the Order arrived, but every fiber in her being told her to run back to Zackary. She rounded a corner, reaching a dead end, and swore under her breath.

Hot breath hit her neck. "It's a labyrinth in here, isn't it?"

Maryam jumped, turning with a swing of her fist. Anzuri cackled as he slipped out of the way.

Maryam's stomach churned at the sight of him. Peter's entire front was caked in blood, starting at his mouth. Even the spaces between his teeth were red as Anzuri sneered, his bottomless black eyes glistening with masochistic glee. From his right hand dangled a tattered yellowed manuscript bound in leather. Maryam couldn't properly see the cover or the spine, but she knew what it was.

"Quick little bastard aren't you?" she snarled.

Anzuri shrugged. "The boy's not much, but he's a body." Anzuri drew a knife from Peter's belt. "And I don't need him for long, so I can play a bit rough with him."

Maryam's blood boiled at the sight of the cuts and bruises on Peter's arms and face. He couldn't have been possessed for more than an hour and his body already looked to be on death's doorstep. If Anzuri held him much longer, Peter wouldn't have a body to come back to.

"You can either leave Peter of your own free will or I can cut you out and escort you to the gates of Hell myself," Maryam snarled.

"Oh, you can have his body back in a bit, but I'm afraid that will require a trade." Anzuri pointed to Maryam with the hand holding the Song of Ezekiel. "Hand over your own body and the boy goes free."

Maryam didn't dignify the offer with a response. She charged ahead, hands aimed for the throat. Anzuri dodged and swung his blade, nearly catching Maryam in the face. She dove for him and he slipped away like smoke, running the other way through the archives.

With a deep breath and a blink, Maryam stripped off the rest of her glamor. If a mortal couldn't catch him, she couldn't fight like a mortal. She took off after him, the bookshelves flying by in a blur. Anzuri took a corner too slow. Maryam tacked him to the ground.

The Song of Enoch flew across the floor.

"Zackary!" Maryam bellowed. "I got him!"

Anzuri cackled as Maryam wrestled him onto his back. He spit blood in her face with a grin. Why *did* they always resort to spitting?

Maryam recoiled with a snarl and raised a hand to strike him across the face.

"Careful, Maryam," Anzuri snickered. "Don't want to hurt your boyfriend, do you? He'll be scared enough if he ever sees that face of yours."

Maryam tightened her grip on his wrists. "Shut up. I've got bigger problems right now. Zack, hurry up!"

Anzuri raised Peter's eyebrows with a wicked sneer, turning Peter's once handsome features to a horrifying mask. "I am not your enemy, Maryam."

"Right. So sorry. How could I have made such an obvious mistake?"

Anzuri looked her up and down. "Look how much stronger you are now that you're free. Fighting you like this is like night and day."

"It's not a fair fight. My glamor's down and you're in the body of a human man."

Anzuri scoffed. "Is he a man, though?"

Red spotted Maryam's vision. She snatched Anzuri by the throat, not hard enough to hurt Peter, but plenty hard enough to make the demon choke.

"Okay, okay, touchy subject," Anzuri gasped, clawing at Maryam's hand. "My point is that you're powerful, Maryam. Maybe more powerful than me, given your seraph blood. With a bit of training, you'd be more powerful than Zaphriel and I combined."

"Stop lying."

"I'm not lying. You're the daughter of Azazel—the First Teacher, second only to the Devil himself. What little you lack in physical strength, you would more than make up for in political power." Anzuri's expression turned equal parts sinister and gleeful. "Do you know how much strength it takes for an angel to stand up to God? To organize a revolt comprised of both celestial and mortal beings? To flourish in the wastelands of Hell? Your father's blood practically makes you the anti-Christ. You could take the title if you wanted it. Lucifer has no children left to claim it. No one could stop you."

Maryam's mouth went dry, her hands trembling. Her legs would have given out if she had been standing, both from the weakness in her knees and the way the room had started to spin.

That had been why the demon that took Matthew had said her father was building her a throne. Why the Order despised her and had wanted her dead the moment she was born.

She wasn't just half-demon—she was a princess of Hell.

"He loved your mother, you know," Anzuri said softly. "He wanted to create a new world for her. For you."

Maryam's breath caught.

"Maryam!" Zackary charged down the aisle, Wendy close behind him. He grabbed the book from the floor and shoved it into Wendy's hands before pushing Maryam out of the way and hauling Anzuri against a bookcase.

"You never know when to quit, do you?" Zackary snarled.

"Can you blame me?" Anzuri huffed. "Hell's rather crowded these days." His gaze drifted to Maryam. "Imagine how much better it would be with us all here. All this space. All this freedom. We wouldn't have to possess humans to get a taste of it if we threw off the yoke of Heaven.

"Don't listen to him, Maryam." Zackary began to trace the seals needed to banish Anzuri. "*Though I may walk through the Valley of the Shadow of Death—*"

Maryam grabbed his arm to stop him. "What would actually happen if Hell were to break open? If Heaven was brought low?"

Zackary looked at her in terror.

Anzuri grinned. "We'd rebuild the world for all beings. Beings like Zaphriel and I. Beings like you. You'd never have to hide or feel shame for what you are ever again. You'd be free."

Zackary yanked his arm away from his goddaughter. "Shut *up*, Anzuri."

"Doesn't that sound nice, Maryam?"

Maryam swallowed hard. "It— "

She heard shouting from behind the archive doors. Zackary dropped Anzuri and pulled Maryam to run, but the doors burst open before they could make any distance.

Before Maryam could put her glamor back on.

Exorcists poured into the archives, crosses and holy water at the ready with weapons Maryam had only read about in her uncle's books as a child: chains and cuffs made of blessed iron.

The exorcists moved towards Maryam as quickly as they did Anzuri.

"Run! Take Wendy and get out of here!" Zackary yelled, pushing her deeper into the archives.

Panic launched Maryam into the air towards the vaulted ceiling. These people didn't know her. They had a job to do and, with her monstrous appearance, it meant they'd be attacking first and asking questions later. If she could just get to the exit—

A chain wrapped around Maryam's ankle. She crashed to the floor. Her impact against the stone tiles reverberated through her body so violently that she couldn't see straight to fight back, not that she had the strength to. The chain had sapped her dry, draining her even of her normal human strength. Through their sea of legs, she could see Zackary fighting his way towards her.

"Zackary, don't!" Maryam cried, watching helplessly as Anzuri attacked the exorcists who tried to restrain him. She heard a sickening crack as he socked one man in the chest. Another collapsed as the demon slammed his face against a bookshelf. He ran towards Wendy, who stood frozen, her eyes wide. She struggled as he tried to wrestle the book from her. He stuck her across the face, took the book as she fell, and ran. The exorcists who chased him didn't have a chance.

"Zack, please! He's getting away!" Maryam pleaded.

He didn't listen. His hand just barely brushed against the blessed iron around Maryam's wrist when a chain wrapped around his neck. He snarled and clawed at it, as the exorcists at the helm pushed him to his knees like a dog.

"Don't hurt him," Maryam begged as they dragged her up. The only response she got was a woman painfully yanking her arms behind her back. "He's not doing anything wrong! Please, you've got to listen to us! There's a demon trying to open the gates of Heaven. Stop wasting time on us!"

"I assure you," said an icy, stony voice. "Time spent bringing you two to heel is far from wasted."

Maryam's blood froze in her veins as Father Claude made his way through the remainder of the crowd. Even as a child, Maryam had never seen his eyes so full of rage and disgust as he glared down at her. His hatred for her had always been filtered. Tapered. Now, it was on full display. Every person in the room looked at her with the same level of disgust.

Except for Hiro, who trailed behind Father Claude at a jog. His eyes fell on Maryam, then went wide as her face turned ash-pale.

Of course. Of *course*, all of this had to happen the night *both* of them were here.

"You see? What did I tell you?" Claude snapped at Hiro. "They were conning you. The both of them. You and the rest of the board only saw what you wanted to see and look at what it got us. Now, we're chasing after a demon who managed to get its hands on God knows what."

Maryam snarled up at the man. "We're on the same team, you dick. We were trying to stop him before he could get the Song of Enoch or hurt anyone else."

"The dead order members we passed are a testament to how good of a job you did," Claude snapped. "Who's to say this isn't all a farce?" He glanced around the crowd, making sure he had everyone's attention. "It's rather convenient that you happened to barge in here the day your name was cleared—almost as if you knew you wouldn't be suspected, had you gotten away with your little heist."

"Father, that's enough," Hiro hissed.

Claude whirled on him with rage in his eyes. "It is *not!* It never has been! Five people would still be alive if we had handled this the way we should have twenty-one years ago! Who knows how many others will be dead by the time the night is over!"

Zackary struggled against his chains. "Maryam had nothing to do with this!"

Claude stormed up to Zackary, bent close and seized him by the jaw. "Since Maryam found out the truth, has she said a single thing that would make you question her loyalty to humanity?"

Zackary's eyes narrowed to murderous slits. "I don't take orders from you."

Claude's fingernails dug into Zackary's jaw as he bared his teeth down at the demon. "Hiro!"

"Father—"

"Tell him to answer me now or you and Sarah are *both* excommunicated."

An uneasy whisper rippled through the crowd.

Hiro's face greened as he looked from Zackary, to Claude, then back. He wouldn't look at Maryam. "Zaphriel," he said slowly. "Since Maryam found out the truth, has she said a single word, phrase, or utterance that made you doubt her loyalty to humanity? Even for a moment?"

The question stung. The way he avoided her gaze stabbed her right through the heart. Maryam felt so stupid for thinking things might get better between them, that their apology meant anything when they were still both owned by the Order.

Zackary clenched his jaw and pursed his lips tight together. He writhed and strained against his chains like he was drowning in the magic that bound him, forcing him to answer. Blood trickled from his nose and welled in his eyes like tears. With a gasp, he blurted, "She stopped me from exorcising Anzuri to ask what the world would be like if he opened the gates of Heaven. He said that he would rebuild the world for demons and people like her. She didn't get to reply before you all barged in."

Maryam's stomach rolled. That's not how she'd meant it. She hadn't had time to explain.

"But I know Maryam. *You* know Maryam, Hiro." Zackary struggled to turn to his summoner. "Even if she was tempted, the second she learned how many human lives it would cost, she never would have followed him." Zackary panted, gasping for breath, as he looked to Maryam, his face twisted in shame and streaked with blood. "I'm so sorry."

Father Claude faced the crowd of exorcists with a proud smirk on his face. "And there you have it. With all that *corrupting* power in her veins," Claude motioned to Maryam with a look of disgust, "why wouldn't she be curious? Why wouldn't she want to embrace everything her father's people stand for? The destruction. The greed."

"Get permanently bent, you hateful, petty, power-hungry fuck," Zackary snarled. "You've preyed on Maryam for her entire life because you're afraid of her and you've poisoned every person you could against her. Against a *child*. And now that the Order messed up on your watch and let an actual threat get its hands on a powerful piece of occult magic, you're looking for a scapegoat." The demon glared up at the priest with enough fire and brimstone to scorch the sun. "You're a despicable coward with an ugly, venomous soul. That's all you've ever been. That's all you'll ever be."

Zackary spit at FAther Claude's feet.

At any other time, Maryam's mouth would have fallen open, but the look in Father Claude's eyes as he turned on the demon was feral. Bloodthirsty.

He whirled on Hiro, hand outstretched. "Give me his talisman."

Maryam's entire body went numb, her throat closing in on itself.

Hiro backed away, one hand going to Zackary's talisman around his wrist. "No."

Claude motioned to a few nearby exorcists. "Take it from him."

"No!" Maryam pulled against the chains, her shoes scraping against the floor. Even with her powers drained, two additional exorcists had to help hold her back.

Hiro thrashed against the exorcists piling on him, swinging fists, and throwing his weight against anyone who made the mistake of getting in his way. Despite the fury in his eyes and the snarl on his face, he was no match against three men on each arm and the others who pinned him in place. One of them wrestled the woven purple band with Zackary's seal from Hiro's wrist and handed it to Claude.

"Leave him alone," Maryam begged, tears welling in her eyes. "This is all my fault. Punish me instead. They'll torture him if you send him back!"

Claude drew a small knife. "It's no less than he deserves."

"You heartless bastard!" Maryam screamed. "Zack's right, you're a fucking coward!"

"Maryam." Zackary's calm sent splinters across Maryam's heart. His weak smile broke it completely in two. "It's going to be okay."

"Not without you here," she sobbed. "Don't leave me."

Zackary turned to Hiro with a sad smile. "Take care of our girl."

Father Claude folded the talisman over the blade.

Zackary spared Maryam one last glance. "I love you. I'm so proud of you."

The talisman snapped like a strand of hair.

Zackary erupted into flames so blinding and hot that Maryam had to close her eyes and lean away, lest she be consumed too. There was no scream, no shriek of pain or loss, just a roar of flames and light, then silence, darkness, and numbing cold.

Maryam counted to three, then forced herself to open her eyes and stare where her best friend, her godfather, her everything had been. His chains sat in a heap. There were no scorch marks, no smoke, not a single sign to prove Zackary had ever existed at all, dissipated like a brimstone-laced mist.

Her chains had just enough give for her to place her forehead on the cold tile and scream as if her heart had been ripped out. She would rather Zackary be dead than were she knew he was, enduring torture she knew would never end. Even when the Order killed her, even if they saved Peter and Emrys moved on and life went back to normal, Zackary would still be in Hell's prison, being punished for eternity for daring to call out evil when he saw it masquerading as righteousness.

And it was all her fault.

"Finally." Father Claude sighed with relief. "I'll sleep a tad easier knowing he's back where he belongs."

Maryam's eyes snapped open.

It wasn't *all* her fault.

She launched herself at the priest. Her fury wasn't enough to break those damn chains, but it was enough to scare the other exorcists back a few steps.

He stood deathly still, eyes narrow and fixed on Maryam's.

"You are vile," she hissed. "You're evil and heartless and there isn't any glimmer of God's light or love in you."

Claude scoffed. "God doesn't spare the rod for any of His children, and you two deserve a particularly large, heavy rod." He glanced menacingly at Hiro. "It's not my fault some people never taught you that. I'm merely remedying a problem twenty-one years in the making."

Hiro glared back, his fists shaking as the exorcists still held him back.

A war cry broke though a room, making Maryam jump, as Wendy charged from a nearby isle, brandishing a broken table leg like a spear aimed at Maryam's captors. The exorcists disarmed her before Maryam could call for her to stop. She struggled only for a moment, overwhelmed by the grown men pinning her place. She looked at Maryam with desperation and defeat in her eyes, her left cheekbone shifting from red to purple from Anzuri's strike.

Maryam didn't have anything to offer except, "I'm sorry."

"Make the girl comfortable," Claude ordered without sparing Wendy a glance. "Put Hiro somewhere secure as well. I'm sure Boston will love to learn we have a demon sympathizer in our midst. The rest of you, find that demon."

Maryam imagined how satisfying it would be to break that man's neck one day.

He flashed Maryam a proud smirk, then turned his back to walk toward the door. "In the meantime, we're going to deal with *this* particular problem once and for all."

23

Anzuri ran cackling through the night. The high from leaving three exorcists dead and mangled propelled him down the abandoned streets with his stolen lungs and muscles burning. It had been too long since he felt the rush of tearing a human apart. He couldn't wait to do that to the angels.

"You should honestly be thanking me, Peter," he muttered as he slowed to catch his breath. "How many humans get to behold both the gates of Heaven and Hell the way you will?"

There was no response from the back of Anzuri's mind, only the sensation of being glared at that sent a shiver down his borrowed spine. Anzuri laughed again. His right arm twitched in a spasm, cutting his laughter short as he tensed to keep control.

"So, there's some fight left in you after all?" Anzuri rounded the corner and paused at the sight of the sprawling cemetery before him with a sneer. "Good. It's no fun if you just give up."

Go to Hell.

The voice was distant and small, but boiling with rage.

"You know, it always tickles me when humans say that." Anzuri crossed the street, turned the iron gate's padlock over in his hand, then snapped it from the chains like the tag on a Christmas present. "I've seen all of humanity's history, lived its darkest hours. Some of you are worse than us."

In a remote corner of Woodlawn Cemetery sat an old mausoleum overgrown with weeds, completely hidden by brush, the family line having either moved on or died out. Dead vines scaled the Doric columns and the stained glass had dulled under years of dirt and dust. The greened metal door gave in with a swift kick. Anzuri peaked in and surveyed the interior.

Whatever family had once called this their final resting place had most certainly had money when they were alive. At least four generations were entombed behind marble slabs that lined the walls, framing a space large enough to host a small gathering, should relatives be inclined to sit before the stone altar at the head of the mausoleum.

Anzuri approached and studied the figure of Mary, her hands framed around her immaculate heart, head downcast. He picked up the statue and gave a small huff of amusement, then pulled his arm back and flung the statue through the window above the altar. As broken glass sprinkled to the floor, he drew the Song of Enoch from under his arm and began flipping through the pages. Three-fourths of the way through he stopped and began reading, burning the shapes and symbols into his memory.

Satisfied that he had what he needed, Anzuri walked to the center of the stone room and knelt, bringing a knife to his forearm.

"So sorry, Peter," he muttered as he sliced, breathing into the burning pain. "This might sting a bit."

Anzuri smeared the blood against the dirty concrete with ancient words of summoning on his tongue. They felt like wine in his mouth—aged, familiar, and soothing. The air around him crackled. Blood and magic replaced the scent of rot and dust. Anzuri copied the patterns within the Song of Enoch over the entire floor, cutting slice after slice into Peter's skin. By the end, everything past his shoulders throbbed. There were only smears of blood and gashes where light umber skin had once been.

Anzuri stood to wait for his legions to join him. The second he got upright, pain shot through Peter's body and he doubled over, gagging and coughing.

Blood dribbled from his lips. Shaking off the ache, he wiped his mouth and gulped down air. He couldn't blame Peter this time—the physical body was doing its job and rejecting an invader, even if it was a spiritual one. He wiped the blood from his mouth and walked to the door to wait for those of his legion that had hid in the shadows of Earth all these years, waiting to be summoned.

The demons and hellions crawled out of the dark in all sorts of forms. Business professionals, stay-at-home parents, homeless wanderers, even children. More had managed to snatch bodies for his service than he could have imagined. It was plenty of blood, bile, and sinew for the task at hand. Around them hummed the energy of their unseen companions—those who had not been able to steal a body, but knew the call of their master all the same.

Peter strained against his prison, twitching a few muscles and causing a faint ache in Anzuri's temple. The demon smirked.

Let all those people go. You've already got me.

"Noble, but the magic of old requires far more than mere sacrifice." Anzuri stood from his seat on the mausoleum steps. "It calls for blood."

His soldiers and followers fell to their knees, their void-black eyes down-turned as he spoke. "Who of you remembers the days when we roamed free in this world?" Anzuri bellowed. The hellions and lesser demons bared their teeth in elated, thirsty grins. "Bodies of our own, enjoying all this world had to offer, enjoying *them*." Anzuri gestured to his stolen form. "Bathing in their awe and worship, gorging ourselves on their labors and bodies. Now we do their dirty work."

The monsters snarled.

Anzuri raised his hands. "The other royals of Hell will only enslave you down below, but I will lead you to the gates above. Finish this mission for which I have chosen you and I'll make you royalty here on Earth."

He could feel the way Peter recoiled at the bloodthirsty smiles on every face. Anzuri's borrowed heart raced from the rush of power over another.

"Heaven has grown complacent," Anzuri continued. "When we first rebelled, everything was new. All of us were wide-eyed and young. Foolish. But the world has grown quiet. It has fallen into a routine: God and his pets sit behind their gates while those who dare to build, those of us who dare to dream of *more*, are cast out and made to suffer for it."

Backing towards the mausoleum, Anzuri opened the doors for his following, his brothers—

Your cult.

Anzuri ignored Peter and beckoned the gathered forward. "Heaven never expected to hear from us again. They never anticipated that someone would shepherd you into the light. Come forward, brothers, and punish them for their negligence!"

Demons and hellions poured into the temple of the dead. Over half spilled out onto the stairs and the lawn. Each held a weapon, poised to cut flesh. Some held knives, others held shards of glass, a few had tools never meant to tear human skin, but could do so with enough painful force. Their leader took his place before them, lifted the Song of Enoch, and began to read.

Anzuri chanted as they spilled human blood. It dripped and pooled on the patterns beneath their feet. Instead of ruining the twirling crimson stains, they set them alight with an ethereal glow.

Energy crawled up Anzuri's legs, like sparks of fire sinking into his veins. The more it consumed him, the brighter the crimson pattern on the ground glowed until the mausoleum was bright and Anzuri could feel the power pouring from his hands.

With the final word, a roar erupted as if the universe was splitting in two.

Anzuri threw up his hands in victory, laughing triumphantly. "Go forth, brothers!" he bellowed.

The fallen screeched in response as their human forms tore apart. Skin and bone melted, peeling and ripping to reveal the damned creatures beneath—humanoid beings with inky black skin and ram horns, crimson and gold creatures with too many eyes, too many hooves, multiple sets of wings, or no discernible features at all. The unseen stepped into the light from their formless existence—more unholy monsters than Peter could ever hope to count.

Anzuri shielded and closed his eyes against the consuming, all-encompassing glare. The roar rattled from within his bones.

Then, it went silent.

Anzuri opened his eyes to find only white. It dulled, only slightly, as his eyes adjusted. In the distance, beyond his followers, he could make out intricate golden pillars framing golden bars woven together in intricate knots and patterns. Around the pillars spiraled the history of the universe in images and symbols as old as God and his angels.

Anzuri took a deep breath of cold, cloud-like air to steady himself, lest he fell to his knees in relief at the sight of home.

His legions roared, spoiling the silence and reminding him that the gates still had to fall. They took off across the negative space, sprinting wild through the nothing that both existed and didn't. Giddy laughter bubbled up behind Anzuri's lips as they banged, shoved, and prodded the gates. Despite their abuse, the gates remained immaculate.

They did, however, begin to slide, ever so slightly.

"Take it all!" Anzuri ordered over the racket. "Every last golden brick! Ever last—"

White-hot pain ripped through his core, drawing a shriek from him as he doubled over, falling to his knees. He caught himself on hands erupting into splitting skin and sores. Anzuri bit back a painful moan as his stolen vessel drove knives and arrows through every fiber of itself.

I'm sorry. Were you in the middle of something?

"How dare you," Anzuri snarled. "How dare you stand in the way of a new world?"

How dare you try to build it with our blood.

Anzuri writhed as another surge of pain shot down his borrowed spine and he collapsed.

His body hit bloody cement and dirt. With a haggard breath, he sank into what was left of Peter's mangled form, the gates of Heaven now an eternity away. He could feel Peter loose inside, lashing and reeling like a caged wild horse.

Anzuri sank inside his vessel. He opened his eyes to find Peter with his left arm free from the shackles that had held him chained between two pines in the center of a misty forest. His left, free hand was swollen and mangled from breaking his own thumb.

Anzuri grabbed hold of the mangled hand, twisting it and savoring Peter's scream of pain before knocking him to the ground. He savored the soft give of bone and flesh as his foot collided with Peter's ribs. He pulled Peter up by his collar, only to slam him back down to the earth with a fist to his face. Flecks of blood hit Anzuri's lips. The taste of salt and iron took the edge off his fury at being thwarted. He beat Peter until he was calm enough to see the flawed logic in obliterating him. Dead bodies were damn near useless after rigor mortis set in. He was already cutting it close.

"I was going to let you die quickly," Anzuri panted, slicking his hair from his face. "Now, I'm going to find your pretty little sister, end her while you watch, then *maybe* I'll let you die."

Peter managed a huff of laughter though his swollen, bleeding lips. "You can't beat Maryam and Zackary. Not with my body like this."

Anzuri sneered. "Those two can't protect your sister while their necks are on the chopping block."

"They'll get out of it."

"Maryam's not as strong as she likes to pretend."

A glimmer of light came to Peter's one good eye. "Then why do you look so afraid?"

Anzuri kicked him again, satisfied at the sound of something cracking, then turned his back.

With a deep breath, he came back to the physical world. It stank of gore and dust. He sat up, the human blood in his veins boiling at the pulverized mortal bodies strewn about the mausoleum floor. His followers had given up their vessels and now had nowhere to return, their ethereal forms buzzing around Anzuri like a furious swarm.

He slammed his fists into the cement with a roar of furry. Peter's attempt to regain control had broken Anzuri's concentration so severely that the bridge to Heaven has severed. He would have to start from scratch and, even if Anzuri had beaten him down for good, his body wouldn't last long enough for even a sliver of his legion to gather anew. The idea was practically laughable.

Trying with an akinda'shi body, however... Now, there was a thought. Because, as much as Anzuri loathed to admit it, Peter was right: Maryam no doubt had figured out some sort of scheme to save herself.

Unfortunately for her, he had been scheming for thousands of years longer.

24

Wendy cradled her head in her hands, afraid it might explode all over the room the exorcists had locked her in. One of the men had turned on the gas fireplace for her, but the heat did little to warm or comfort her. The cozy stillness of the study with its old yellowed books and antique desk didn't help either. Not when her brother was God knew where and possessed by a demon while her captors wanted Maryam dead. Oh, *and* she had watched a person burst into flames, apparently sent to Hell. *The* Hell.

And she was responsible for all of it. If she had been where she was supposed to be instead of sneaking out and acting a fool, none of this would have happened.

Her phone buzzed, dragging her out of her own head. It was a message from her mother: *I'm going to bed. Got an early surgery. Don't stay out too late.*

That short guy back at Maryam's apartment has done a magical number on Eliza if she was still unphased about what had happened back at the apartment.

Holy shit, magic was *real.*

Wendy texted back, *We won't. We love you.*

Wendy's throat tightened. She had no idea if Peter would ever get the chance to tell Eliza that himself.

Love you too, Eliza replied. *I'm sorry I keep canceling on you two. We'll do something fun together this weekend. Kisses.*

Tears welled in Wendy's eyes, blurring the screen. She placed her free hand over her mouth as she choked back a sob. A statue of Jesus caught her eye on the desk. With a sniffle, she reached out and traced his robes, praying for the first time in years.

It felt useless to pray that everyone would come out okay. They wouldn't. Instead, she prayed for strength.

Wendy took a deep breath and dragged herself out of the chair.

The exorcists had said someone would be there to explain what was happening and to get her home while they looked for Peter—not that she trusted them after how they had treated Maryam and Zackary. The moment they opened the door would be her chance to run, so long as she was prepared to fight. Not that she had much to work with. All she had was shelves full of books. Maybe she could break a leg from the chair? It didn't look too sturdy.

A vent near the ceiling gave a loud *THUNK*.

Wendy shrieked and snatched up the chair as a shield, but paused as a familiar voice swore and muttered from beyond the vent. The screws came loose and the vent cover fell to the carpet as a short, slender figure leapt to the floor, coughing and dusting himself off.

"The things I do for those ingrates," the man who had put a spell on Eliza grumbled. "Zackary should consider himself lucky to be pursued by someone as brave and selfless as me."

He paused and blinked at Wendy. Recognition dawned on his face a beaming grin as he launched himself across the room, wrapping Wendy in a bear hug that lifted her off her feet.

"Wednesday!" he exclaimed.

"It's Wendy," she wheezed.

The man let her go and bowed so extravagantly that she knew he had to be Other—like Maryam and Zackary, only more so. "My apologies. Emrys Hemlock, at your service. What happened? It's absolute chaos outside and I can't get a hold of anyone." He patted his pants clean. "Zackary always ignores my texts, but it's strange not to hear from Maryam."

Wendy began to pace. "The exorcists, the Order, whatever you call them, stormed in while Maryam was trying to save my brother. They don't like whatever the hell Maryam is and they're going to..." She swallowed hard. "I think they're going to kill her. They sent Zackary to Hell. *Hell*. It's a real place." Wendy wrung her hands. "Peter escaped. Or the demon escaped with Peter's body, I guess. I don't know."

Emrys' face paled, then darkened into a vicious storm. "They're going to regret that," he muttered.

Wendy took a step back.

A knock came at the door. Wendy scrambled for a weapon. Emrys slipped behind its hinges, as quick and silent as death. The exorcist who walked in hardly got out a syllable before Emrys struck him in the back of the head and he crumpled to the floor.

Wendy gave a panicked squeak.

"Don't worry. He's alive," Emrys explained before Wendy could truly panic. "Murder's probably a turn off for Zack." He peaked down the halls, then closed the door. "Do you know where they're keeping Maryam? Did you see where they took her?"

Forcing her gaze from the body on the floor, Wendy tried to remember. They'd been dragged separate ways from the archives. All she knew was that Maryam was wrestled and shoved onto an elevator going down while Wendy had been taken up two levels.

"I can probably find her," Wendy concluded. "I don't know how I'm going to do that with people running trying to clean up this mess, though."

Emrys studied the unconscious man, rubbing his chin in thought. His gaze shifted to Wendy. "Do you trust me?"

She sighed. "You're all I got for the moment, so yes."

"Good enough." He dug around in the desk until he found a pushpin, then pressed it to his left thumb with a wince. "I should warn you, this is going to be a little strange and very disgusting." He squeezed his thumb until a bead of blood bubbled up.

Before Wendy could ask what he meant, Emrys stepped forward and ran his thumb across her forehead. She cringed and fought back the urge to gag, but was distracted by the tingling sensation flooding her body. Her vision blurred and swirled. When it cleared again, she swore she was looking at the world from a higher angle. She felt long swaths of soft fabric against her skin and craned her neck against the sudden stiff collar at her throat. Flabbergasted, she pulled out her phone and opened the camera, gasping when she saw an older version of herself, dressed in a cassock, staring back.

"Emrys, what..." She trailed off, unable to pick from all the questions in her head.

When she lowered her phone, she nearly screamed. Emrys stood before her with leaf green skin and hair now dark as the midnight sky. Ram horns arched above his head, elegant and wild like the smile on his face. The only thing about him that hadn't changed were those devious blue eyes.

"Sorry, love," he chuckled. "Didn't mean to startle you."

"I honestly shouldn't be surprised anymore," Wendy replied. "Next thing I know, Peter's going to sprout a tail after all this is said and done."

Emrys weighed the thought. "Your brother's cute. He could pull it off." He poked his head out the door once more. "Find Maryam and get her free. She'll have a better idea of where to rendezvous than I do, so have her text me once she's out."

Wendy followed behind him, glancing out the empty hallway over his shoulder. "What are you going to do?"

The smile that came to Emry's face was so menacing that Wendy almost felt bad for the people it was intended for.

Almost. Their plan to execute Maryam dampened her sympathy.

"I'm just going to provide a little distraction," he answered. Then he was gone, leaving Wendy to head the other way in search of the archives.

She only dared to walk so fast, not wanting to draw attention to herself. Down the elevator two stories, a left, a right, two more lefts, and she passed the archives with two men posted outside the door. She pretended to ignore them on her way to the other elevator. Once in with the doors shut, she exhaled and clicked the "close" button. She'd have to check the floors one by one.

The first level down proved useless. Nothing but filing cabinets, computers and a security guard that eyed her as she wandered. The next floor looked like some sort of medical ward, but still no Maryam. The idea of an expansive secret demon-hunting compound would have been cool, if the demon hunters weren't about to kill her friend.

A stranger in a maroon hoodie and jeans stood on the other side of the door on the next floor, hood up and shoulders slightly slouched as if they were attempting to avoid attention.

Wendy held the door open as she studied the stranger, eyeing his familiar short dark beard. Instead of getting off, she watched the stranger board the elevator until the light bulb lit in her head.

"You're Maryam's uncle. Hiro, right?"

The stranger froze, then flashed a dagger-sharp glare as he reached for his pocket.

Wendy backed up against the wall, hands up in surrender. "Whoa, chill. I'm on your side."

Hiro paused.

"I'm Peter's sister, Wendy. Maryam's roommate, Emrys, did some magic or whatever and now I'm incognito."

Hiro faced forward and studied Wendy from the peripherals. Before she could be offended by the side eye, he said, "You're glamored?"

"If that's what you call having blood smeared on your forehead to create an optical illusion, then yes. Personally, I would just call it nasty." She lowered her hands. "How could you tell?"

Hiro lowered his hood. "You can see through a faerie glamor if you look from the corner of your eye."

The elevator dinged. Hiro slammed the "Closed" button before the doors could fully open. "Here's how we're going to play this: You're coming to ask Maryam if she would like a performance of last rites tomorrow. I'm a new exchange student from the *Athenaeum Pontificium Regina Apostolorum* in Rome. I'm here to shadow you."

Wendy's brow pulled together. "Ain't no way I'm remembering that."

"Then say I'm from the Vatican. I just arrived today and the airline lost my luggage, so I'm still in my traveling clothes. Should be good enough." Hiro studied Wendy for a moment. "If you can't do this—"

"I can." Wendy squared her shoulders. "I have to if I'm going to make this right."

Hiro met her gaze for a moment longer, then hit the button to open the doors. "Let's do this, then."

The hall beyond was made of dull stone and fluorescent light, as if the people who had spent years of craft and care on the building had given up once they reached this place. Hiro and Wendy passed storage room after storage room until they rounded the corner and found a desk outside a door of bars with a sleep-deprived young woman fixated on her phone. She sat up straight at the sight of the two, folding her hands and sitting forward.

"Yes, can I help you?" She gave Wendy a plastic smile.

"I was sent to ask Maryam Bishop whether she wanted her last rites before tomorrow," Wendy replied, squaring her shoulders and wringing her hands behind her back to keep them from shaking.

The woman blinked. "They've already decided to kill her?"

Wendy gave a dramatic sigh. "I don't know. I'm just following orders."

The woman fiddled with a pen on the desk. "That just seems...fast. I heard they didn't even see her actually do anything wrong." She shook her head and put her fake smile back on. "I'm sorry, Sister. It's not my place." Her gaze shifted to Hiro. "Who's your friend?"

"Antonio Ferrari. Exchange student from Italy. Please excuse his dress—the airline lost his luggage."

The woman's smile turned genuine as she launched into rapid Italian.

Wendy's heart hammered in her chest. "Sorry, I should have mentioned that he's taken a vow of silence until God shows him how he's meant to serve."

"Oh, I'm sorry. It's just been a while since I was able to practice." The woman took the cap off her pen. "Can I get your name, Sister?"

"Emrys Wednesday."

The woman jotted down the names and the time, then pressed a button. The barred door clicked open. "There you are, Sister." She said something else to Hiro, who merely nodded, and they were on their way.

Hiro took the lead as they descended a small set of stairs down into a stark chamber. "Nice job," he said. "My Italian's rusty. It would have given us away for sure."

"Don't be too impressed," Wendy replied. "Antonio Ferrari was an actual exchange student at my school last year. If I hadn't remembered him, you would have been Espresso Vespa."

Hiro choked back a laugh.

The spark of joy dissipated as the two walked among the cells. Wendy kept close, keeping her eyes down to avoid the people who lashed at them through the bars, gnashing their teeth and spitting profanity. Others muttered to themselves, paced, cried, and scratched at the walls, engraving strange markings with rubble. Somehow, those were the ones that disturbed Wendy the most.

"What's wrong with them?" Wendy whispered.

"They're possessed. Some of them for years, despite our best efforts...Either we can't name the spirit, can't find the holy text to combat it, or the person they were is too far gone to fight with us."

Wendy shivered. To be trapped down here, both physically and mentally. To imagine her brother trapped like this... She couldn't stomach it.

Hiro stopped so short that Wendy ran into him. He grabbed a hold of the bars of a cell with worry and desperation etched into his face. "Maryam! Maryam, are you okay?"

Wendy's stomach sank at the sight of her, bound in chains from her shoulders to her waist, latched to the cement floor. Her wings looked like they might snap; they were so tight against her back, her feathers droopy, and her downcast face hidden by her wild, wind-blown curls.

"Maryam, talk to me," Hiro pleaded.

She lifted her gaze. Wendy recoiled at the sight of her eyes, flinching at how alien they were against her otherwise familiar face. The thought that she'd worn a disguise because she knew Wendy would react this way, that everyone would react this way, despite how she fought to save Peter, weighed Wendy's chest down with shame.

The reaction didn't seem to bother Maryam, though. She smiled. It was sad and tired, but despite the sharp teeth behind her chapped lips and those strange inhuman eyes, it still held a spark of life.

"What do you want talk about, Uncle Hiro?" Her dry voice cracked like a smoldering, dying fire. "The accommodations or the staff?"

25

Maryam had never seen Hiro Bishop look so incredibly unsure of himself. His hands trembled as he gripped the bars of her cell, his expression anguished and terribly uncertain. Any other time, it would be unnerving. Now, with certain death on her door, Maryam found herself indifferent.

"Does Aunt Sarah know what's going on?" Her voice caught on the name and she blamed her dry throat. If she broke now, she couldn't face the morning with her head held high.

Hiro shook his head. "No idea. I heard someone mention getting a hold of her, but she's not answering my calls or texts. They won't make a move to..." He trailed off. "To do anything to you until they know she knows, though."

Maryam did her best to shrug, despite the weight of the chains. "They're going to execute me. Just say it. I'm a big girl."

"I won't accept that," Hiro snapped, kneeling and tinkering with the padlock. "We're getting you out."

Maryam's heart pounded against her ribs. He couldn't. He was already in so much trouble for standing up for her and Zackary. She couldn't let him face a cell like hers.

"Hiro, stop," Maryam ordered. "Don't you dare."

"Shush, Maryam, I'm trying to concentrate," Hiro grumbled.

"I can't let you give up everything." Maryam tugged and strained at the chains, but all she did was tire herself out. The blessed iron had sucked away all her strength. "Hiro Bishop, listen to me!"

"It's still *Uncle* Hiro, Maryam Grace. This situation doesn't change that," Hiro barked. "And if I can't save you, if I can't *love* you, what is the damn point of professing to serve a God who will hold me accountable for what I've done for the least among us? If I can't stand up for you, what is it all for?" He went back to the lock. "This institution is broken. The Rosary Order's tie to the Lord I vowed to serve has frayed and it's about to snap. I'm done pretending not to see that."

Maryam sat dumbfounded. Hiro had never sworn in front of her before. Never. And hearing him speak against the Order felt downright unnatural.

The lock popped open. Hiro rushed in and got to work on Maryam's chains. "I'm not walking away from being your uncle just because it suddenly got harder." The lock clicked. "You're the only kid we have left, Maryam." Hiro began stripping the chains from Maryam's body. "I love you, kiddo. And I'm so sorry we stood by and let this place, these people, hurt you. We failed you."

The world came to a screeching halt.

I'm sorry.

I'm so sorry.

The words seeped into every corner of Maryam's insides, like a hand kneading a muscle she'd held tight all her life. The words were too blunt for all the hairline fractures in her heart and too small for the canyons in her soul, yet perfect and beautiful enough to draw a sob from her tired, worn lungs as the chains fell away.

Maryam threw herself into Hiro's arms as the last link of iron hit the ground. She couldn't remember the last time she'd buried her face into his shirt to savor the familiar pine cologne she and Matthew had bought him every Father's Day. His stubble scraped her forehead, and for a moment, she was small again and her uncle, her guardian, was holding her after a particularly terrible dream. For a moment, things were okay.

Maryam breathed deep as strength poured over her like a tidal wave now that the chains were gone. She had to remind herself to be careful with Hiro so she wouldn't crush him as she held him close. She stretched her wings, the stinging strain feeling like heaven. Hiro adjusted his arms to make room for them and squeezed her tight until she pulled away, wiping her eyes.

Maryam got to her feet and stretched. "You okay, Wendy?"

The teenager folded her arms. "It's Peter we should worry about. I don't think he's got a lot of time. Also, pray that Emrys' magic holds out on my mom. If I get sent to military school or something for this craziness, I'm gonna be pissed."

A punch of laughter escaped Maryam. "I respect your priorities."

Maryam heard rushed footsteps and pulled Wendy and Hiro behind her. As she curled her hands into fists, Emrys skidded to a stop. He held onto the frame of the door as he panted and slicked his hair away from his sweaty face.

"Oh, good. You found her," he panted. "No missing limbs? Only emotional trauma? Good." He grabbed Maryam's wrist and dragged her towards the door.

Maryam dug her heels into the cement. "Wait, whoa, do you know where you're going?"

Emrys gestured to Hiro. "That's what he's for. Let's go already. This isn't going to be a place we want to be shortly."

Maryam narrowed her eyes. "What did you do?"

"I created a distraction."

"By doing what, exactly?"

Emrys chewed on his bottom lip. "You're not going to like it."

Maryam towered over him. "Emrys Hemlock—"

He waved his hands in surrender. "Okay, fine. A bunch of people were in the middle of a meeting about how best to kill you and I didn't appreciate that at all." He glanced around nervously. "I slipped away and stumbled upon the level below this one. The people inside those cells are a bit more..." He winced and waved his hand and from side to side. "Temperamental. Turns out these locks aren't charmed whatsoever and none of them were too fond of any of the people in the meeting, so..."

Hiro pushed Maryam aside and snatched Emrys by the shoulders. "Are you crazy? Do you have any idea what could happen if those people manage to get out of this church?"

A smile came to Emrys' face that unnerved Maryam. "They seem preoccupied with your co-workers upstairs. I wouldn't worry too much."

"That too! You just released the Order's most violent possession cases on a group of unprepared exorcists!" He gestured wildly to the drab hall around them. "These poor souls are only possessed by hellions. The people you unleashed were possessed by *actual demons*."

Emrys let loose a crazed giggle and leaned in, holding Hiro's gaze with an unhinged grin on his face. "They're trying to destroy my people. My *home*. They're lucky a bunch of vengeful demons in half-starved bodies are all I let loose on their self-righteous, hateful carcasses."

Hiro's grip tightened his grip on his Emrys. "That isn't the way to handle this, you insane bastard."

Maryam pried the two apart, holding up a hand to keep Emrys at bay. He hadn't moved to hurt Hiro, but Maryam didn't trust the wave of strangeness that had claimed him. "Stop it, both of you." Their glares were sharp enough to stab an unsuspecting passerby, but they listened all the same.

Maryam massaged her temple with a sigh. Hiro wouldn't leave the exorcists and she couldn't leave Hiro, but Emrys certainly wasn't about to voluntarily fix his mess.

She needed Zackary. He would have known what to do.

She squeezed her eyes shut to shove down the pain and loss. "Fuck. Okay, Uncle Hiro, get Wendy out while everyone is preoccupied and find a place to bunker down. Wendy, start brainstorming. We need a list of places your brother could be."

Emrys tip-toed back towards the door.

Maryam snatched him by the back of his shirt. "You're helping me clean up your mess."

Emrys folded his arms like an indignant child. "Never. They deserve to be the ones terrorized for a change."

"What would Zack want you to do?"

Emrys pursed his lips as he thought about it, taking entirely too long to reach the right answer, then threw his head back with an angsty groan. "That's cheating, Maryam May."

"Tough shit, pixie boy."

"Maryam." Hiro caught her arm as she followed Emrys towards the door. His brow furrowed as he studied her, his gaze as soft and concerned as it had ever been when he watched her walk into a world not made for the likes of her, as if this day changed nothing, despite the way it changed everything.

Maryam squeezed his hand with a smile. "Don't worry. I love you too." She pulled from his grip and gently, but firmly, shoved Emrys in front of herself. "March."

Emrys grumbled as they weaved through stone corridors until the halls turned stark white and tiled. The screams gave Maryam the rest of her directions, along with the man who came tripping out of a large chamber. He paused long enough to flash a malicious, bloody grin, then sprinted towards them, only to come up short and crumple to the ground when Maryam's fist met his jaw.

Emrys threw himself out of her range. "Gods above, Maryam! What the hell?" he exclaimed.

"You got any other ideas?" she yelled back.

A possessed woman charged, foam dripping from her mouth. Before Maryam could throw another punch, Emrys stepped forward, tripping the woman off balance and twisting her outstretched arm behind her back before swiping his hand over her eyes. She crumpled to the ground, sleeping as if a creature of Hell hadn't taken control of her body.

"You have powers now, you brute," Emrys chided, motioning to the woman.

"Oh, shove off." Maryam rolled her eyes. "You've got about 150 years on me. C'mon." She made her way to the chamber, keeping an eye on Emrys as she went.

The sight inside turned her stomach.

For every exorcist in the room there were two or three possessed victims clawing, biting, and throwing Order members like rag dolls.

The possessed swarmed her before she could get a lay of the room. One man thought twice about trying to bite her after her fist collided with his teeth. She went easy on the twelve-year-old girl that latched onto her leg—at least, throwing her off instead of slamming her into the marble seemed easier. Weight on her wings nearly pulled her off-balance. She pried a woman off her back and hurled her into a shrieking teenager aiming for her jugular.

For every blow Maryam landed, a set of teeth ripped into her skin. Arms wrapped around her limbs faster than she could pry them off. Ragged fingernails clawed at her face. Sparks of pain shot into her spine as feathers were ripped out of her wings. Another wave overtook her balance and she went down. Even on the cold marble floor, she fought, now frantic and fearful.

Hands pinned her arms and legs to the floor. Her wings twisted painfully against her back. Panic began to overtake her, sending her heart racing and her breath rushed and ragged.

Her power wasn't there. That power that had launched her into the sky had abandoned her.

She couldn't breathe. She couldn't save Peter. Zackary would be trapped in Hell forever.

Through the forest of legs, she saw Emrys go down. His head hit the tile with a painful *thud* as a man twice his size pinned him by his throat. Terror entered his eyes as he clawed at the man's face. Another came and pinned Emrys' arms to the ground, cackling as he gaped for air.

They're trying to hurt my people. My family.

Emrys had found a home just in time to die.

Maryam screamed his name. The sound of her own voice rattled her bones and shook loose something deep and slumbering in her soul. It felt like sunlight—bright, warm, and endless, scaring away the nightmare monster that held her down. The victims screeched and scurried away. Maryam scrambled to her feet, swinging and out for blood.

With a wave of her hand, Emrys' assailants flew through the air and crashed into the pillars on the other side of the room. Maryam could feel their weight, as if the air had become an extension of her, but in her fear and rage, they hadn't weighed much.

Emrys gasped, coughing as he rolled over and watched Maryam with awe.

Those demons were the only example Maryam needed. The rest of them cowered, shielding their eyes from the faint golden light Maryam emitted. Their whispers made her too uneasy to marvel at the light and the power shooting through her blood like lightning.

"I know that light."

"One child survives."

"Azazel's daughter—"

"*Shut up!*" Maryam's voice echoed off the towering walls. The demons shrunk back. "I'm not Azazel's anything."

A few dared to peek past their hands at her.

"But, as you bastards can tell, I inherited a handful of cool tricks." She lifted her hands and the demons recoiled. Some of them begged for her to stop.

Maryam smirked. "So, unless you want to see how much I'm not on your side, you're going to fuck off back to Hell and take the rest of your friends a little message." She stood up taller, straightening her shoulders and meeting the eyes of the exorcists watching in confusion and fear. "There are forces here that will fight for the light and goodness of Earth. I am one of them. If I were any of you, I wouldn't mess with us."

She caught the proud, mischievous grin on Emrys' face.

A disgruntled murmur rippled through the crowd of demons. A few glared at Maryam while others snarled. Some hissed their dissent. She had said the wrong thing and made the wrong enemies, but what else was new?

The demons screeched and cried as she waved her right hand in the form of a cross, channeling the memories of Zackary and Hiro as best she could. "*In the name of the Father, the Son, and the Holy Spirit, I condemn all of you back to the depths of Hell!*"

Maryam's ears rang as the demons screeched, begging for any punishment but this, but she held her gaze as their victims fell to the ground. The silence that fell over the sea of limp bodies hit Maryam like a wave, overwhelming and disorienting.

Emrys caught her as her legs began to give out. "Are you alright?"

"I'm fine," she muttered, draping an arm over his shoulder. "You?"

"I'll survive. Not the first time I've been choked out. Probably won't be the last."

Maryam sighed. "Why are you like this?"

"It wasn't sexual! Well, it *started* sexual. You see, there was this kelpie with an exceptionally large—"

"Later. We gotta go." Maryam scooped Emrys up, despite his protest, and considered their exits. The halls were too narrow for flight and there were too many exorcists that probably still wanted her dead. There was only the cross-shaped skylight above.

Perfect. She had always thought those things were tacky.

The exorcists either watched, frozen with apprehension, or helped the injured. Not a single one moved to approach. Across the room, she spotted Father Wilhelm from the hearing. His face was scratched up and his cassock disheveled, but his eyes were steady and bright as he watched Maryam. His smile was so small she almost missed it.

She smiled back, then launched into the air. With a wave of her hand, the glass shattered, the pieces blown outward. Maryam shielded Emrys through the broken glass, then cold wind and darkness swallowed them. Stars shimmered above, silent and indifferent to what she was the night she'd had. The icy breeze was as renewing for her soul as it was for her body.

Judging by Emrys' grip around Maryam's neck, he didn't share the rejuvenating sentiment. "Are you sure you're good to fly right now?"

"I'll be fine," she replied over the wind. Her phone buzzed. "Get that for me?"

Emrys craned his arm around to dig the device from her pocket and light up the screen. "One message from your uncle. *Sarah snagged the keys to the retreat center up near New Haven. Meet us there.*"

"Tell them we'll be there in maybe forty-five minutes," Maryam said. "I haven't quite figured out the drive-to-flight ratio yet."

Emrys typed the message and slipped the phone in his own pocket. "You don't know any tricks to get there faster?"

Maryam shook her head. "Zackary didn't get around to teaching me."

Emrys' face sobered. "Is he really..."

Maryam's heart sank. "Yeah, but don't worry." She held Emrys a little tighter. "We're getting him back."

St. Mary's Blessed Rosary Retreat and Camping Grounds sat roughly fifty miles north of Detroit, maybe fifteen minutes off of I-94. The main retreat center was the only point of light for miles, so Maryam felt confident that no one saw her drop to the building's front lawn.

She set Emrys on the ground before collapsing into the cold wet grass. The smell sent her back to being a child, catching fireflies alone while the rest of her cabin made s'mores and sang about Jesus. Or maybe that was a dream. She was so exhausted that she wasn't sure anymore.

A warm hand gently patted her face. "Maryam, c'mon. You'll get sick out here in the chill," Emrys encouraged.

"I'm fine." Maryam heard a sliding glass door and rushing footsteps.

"Maryam!" Hiro kneeled beside her, holding her face in his hands. "Did they hurt you?"

"I'm *fine.* Just need coffee. A few Red Bulls. Maybe coffee made with Red Bull."

Hiro pulled her to her feet with a grunt. "You need rest."

Maryam's eyes fell on Wendy as she hovered in the doorway, wringing her hands. "We sort of found Peter."

Maryam stood a bit straighter. "Where?"

"Nowhere good," Hiro answered.

Maryam watched the TV above the fireplace as her uncle eased her onto a hard, threadbare sofa. The screen showed a mausoleum roped off with caution tape and lit up with flood lights. It has been put on mute, but Maryam didn't need to hear a thing. The headline below the news anchor woke Maryam up with ice in her blood.

Mysterious Massacre at Historic Detroit Cemetery. Law Enforcement Says "No Leads."

Maryam scrambled for the remote and turned on the audio. Her mouth went dry as she listened.

The grounds keeper had called the cops when he heard screaming in the oldest part of the cemetery. They found no less than twenty mangled bodies scattered across the stone floor of a mausoleum that had been broken into. The victims had yet to be identified. Officials were even further from issuing a cause of death or the possibility of a suspect. It looked like the people had been torn apart from the inside.

Maryam's terror turned to rage. "That bastard's going to pay."

"When his attempt to open the gates of Heaven failed, he disappeared," Hiro said, pacing and massaging the back of his neck. "He could be anywhere in the city."

"Then we lure him out and end him." Maryam got to her feet, worried the old worn sofa would put her to sleep, even with the springs stabbing her back. "Zack and I did it once. We can do it again."

"He wasn't this strong before."

"I wasn't an ankida'shi before."

"That little mass-exorcism stunt might do the trick," Emrys chimed in. The three looked through a window in the wall to find him tinkering with a coffee maker in the community kitchen.

Hiro opened his mouth to address him, but then shook his head and turned to Maryam. "What little mass-exorcism stunt?"

Maryam flashed Emrys a dirty look before answering. "I somehow managed to send all the demons Emrys set free back to Hell." She sighed and ran her hands over her tangled hair. "Don't ask me how. If Zack was still here, I bet he'd know." Her chest tightened.

Hiro squeezed her shoulder. "We're going to get him back when you get your strength back."

Maryam placed her hand on her uncle's. "No. We do it now. I'm not leaving him there."

Emrys froze, the measuring cup in his hand stopped in mid air, filled with coffee grounds.

Hiro shook his head. "You've hardly had a chance to rest since your powers were unlocked."

"I won't be able to rest knowing they're torturing him."

A voice on the staircase brought Maryam's mind to a screeching halt.

"Maryam? Is that you?"

Maryam froze, then looked up to find Sarah staring down at her from the open winding staircase. She couldn't tell if the terror on

Sarah's face was *of* her or *for* her, so she snapped her glamor back on before peeling her tongue from the roof of her mouth.

"Hi, Auntie."

Sarah's gaze darted to Hiro. "Did they see her?"

"They did." His expression turned grim. "They didn't take too kindly to it."

Sarah descended the stairs. "Did they hurt you?"

Maryam sighed. "No, but they definitely were planning on it, in no small part due to Claude's fear mongering."

Sarah stopped in her tracks and paled. "He didn't."

Maryam scoffed. "Have you met the man?"

Sarah looked to Hiro, then to Maryam as she stuttered. "I just hoped that..."

"What?" Maryam scoffed. "That he'd change? He's a holier-than-thou religious nut and I'm literally the spawn of Satan. Why would he ever show me mercy?"

"You are not anyone's *spawn,*" Sarah snapped. "You are our niece. You are my sister's daughter."

"I'm also half demon. I think it's time we stop ignoring the fact that he takes that personally."

Sarah bit her bottom lip, brow furrowed as she thought.

"Fuck, Aunt Sarah. Why do you keep defending him? You were ready to rip him apart back at the hearing."

"Language." She studied her niece for a moment, then closed the space between them, eyes locked with Maryam's, and reached up to hold her face in her hands. "Let me see you."

"You're looking right at me."

"Let. Me. See. You."

Maryam sighed. With a blink, her glamor was gone. It took a conscious effort not to avoid Sarah's eyes, but Maryam managed. She knew both of them deserved that much.

Sarah refused to blink. "Everything we ever did was to keep you safe from this."

Maryam smiled sadly. "This was never the problem, Auntie. The Order was."

Sarah only stared into her niece's strange, inhuman eyes.

"Now that I'm here, what are you going to do?"

Sarah's lips pursed into a thin line, then she placed her hands on her hips, staying silent far longer than Maryam was comfortable with. "For starters, I brought a frozen pan of lasagna up here with me. It's got Italian sausage and pepperoni, your favorite." Sarah said. "I imagine flying burns a lot of calories. While you all get settled, I'll make some phone calls to keep the Order off your trail."

Maryam stared, wide-eyed and shocked. "Th...thanks. I appreciate it."

Sarah gave a tense, thin-lipped smile and excused herself to one of the smaller conference rooms.

Wendy looked from Maryam to the now-empty staircase. "And I thought my family was messy."

Maryam scoffed and walked into the kitchen. "That actually went better than I thought it would." She sat at the flimsy plastic table and pulled a nearby notepad towards her, and massaged her temple. "So, it looks like Anzuri tried to get to Heaven and failed. Uncle Hiro, how much of that was due to the fact that Peter's human and how much of it was Anzuri's own incompetence?"

Hiro joined her and Emrys in the kitchen. "Hard to tell. The spells in the Song of Enoch are designed to be performed by a single practitioner, if I remember right. Who knows what could have been thrown out of whack by having a demon in a human body perform it."

"Do you think he could try again with Peter?"

"Not if he has any sense. He'll be looking for a new vessel. Peter won't last much longer."

"What about my body?" Maryam asked. "Would he have a better chance with me?"

"It's possible." Hiro frowned. "Don't tell me you're thinking of setting yourself up as bait."

"It would be faster than searching every dark corner of Detroit. It's no New York, but it's big."

Emrys sat beside her, setting one of two mugs by her paper. He handed the other to Wendy, who sat down across from him. "What if we searched St. Damian's?"

Maryam shook her head and took a gulp of coffee. "Zack cleansed the place. Anzuri can't get back in." She scowled at the overwhelming smokey taste. "Did you fill the entire filter with grounds?"

Emrys' brows pulled together. "Was I not supposed to?"

"Drip coffee and espresso aren't the same, Em."

Wendy took a long sip on the jet fuel Emrys tried to pass off as coffee, then froze. "What about Belle Isle?"

"What about it?" Maryam asked.

"What if we set a trap for Anzuri there? Peter always disappears off to Belle Isle when he's got something on his mind. Anzuri has to know that. He'll know we're looking for him."

"Hiro's brow scrunched. "It's usually pretty populated, isn't it?"

Wendy shook her head. "Not so much now that it's getting cold. And the east side has hiking trails and woods. A few beaches. Plenty of cover."

Emrys stroked his chin. "How often does Easy Breezy perform outside Ectoplasm?"

"Never. It's not a real band. It's just a way to blow off steam."

"Not anymore. Now, it's also bait."

"Okay, slow down," Hiro waved a hand to get everyone's attention. "You want to throw a *concert* to lure out a member of Hell's dark court, and then perform an *exorcism* ten feet away from the crowd?"

"It would preferably be five hundred yards or more, but essentially."

Hiro blinked in bewilderment, then leaned back in his chair, slicking back his hair as he let out a long breath. "It's not impossible, but we'd need to set up some powerful wards. Exorcisms aren't exactly peaceful and, even if we didn't have to worry about bystanders overhearing and getting curious, Anzuri could hurt more people."

"I can cast a few illusions. A few suggestion spells to bounce people off the area." Emrys faced Maryam. "We need Zackary for the heavy lifting."

Maryam turned to Hiro. "How do we get him back?"

Hiro opened his mouth to argue, then sighed. "Come on."

Maryam and the others waited at the base at the stairs while Hiro gathered his things. When he joined them again, he had a leather satchel slung across his shoulder, a tattered yellowed book in one hand, and a gnarled homemade broom in the other. He led the group out the back, holding the door for them as they passed.

Maryam shivered in the October cold. "We can't do this inside?"

"You want to clean blood out of the carpets when we're done?" Hiro thrust the broom into Maryam's hands. "Sweep the basketball court, if you please." He gave the book to Emrys. "Find Zackary's seal. It would be under Zaphriel the Treacherous." He pulled a few lighters and candles from his bag and handed half of them to Wendy. "Help me get these lit."

Hiro looked over the work once it was nearly done and took a long dagger encrusted with quartz and moldavite from his bag. "When you're finished with your candles, Wendy, you might want to wait inside.

She set down the last of her candles and folded her arms with a huff. "Zack doesn't scare me."

"It's not fear I'm worried about." Hiro took off the satchel and tossed it aside. "The contract only gives him a mortal form."

Wendy blinked.

"So, he won't be wearing clothes."

She headed towards the retreat center "Say less."

Maryam held her hand out for the knife. "I should do it."

An uneasy quiet settled over the night.

"You've done good by him, Uncle Hiro," Maryam said, "But after what Father Claude did, I want him as far from the Order as possible. I'll make the contract, as long as you can walk me through it."

Hiro studied her for a moment with a wary, calculating gaze that slowly turned warm and proud. Under any other circumstance, it would have put tears in Maryam's eyes, but the prospect of blood sacrifice and opening a portal to Hell dampened the warm fuzziness.

Her uncle turned the knife over to her. "You've got to follow my instructions exactly."

Maryam studied the blade as it caught a flicker of candle light. "For Zack, I think I can handle that."

The slice of the knife burned. Staying steady to trace the circle Hiro had drawn years ago proved to be a bitch. Maryam silently vowed to never stop harassing Zack for how many small details filled his seal when so many of his brothers' were relatively simple. Instead of a woven bracelet, Hiro gave Maryam a locket at the end of a silver chain—harder to break and close to her heart.

Energy coursed up Maryam's arm as Hiro handed her the worn, handwritten book. That energy turned to fire in her bones, threatening to consume her the longer she gazed down at the seal painted in ink on the open page. The air crackled with power as she spoke the long-dead words, some in Latin, others in Aramaic, others still in fractures of Akkadian. The air turned hot and sharp, like winds carrying lightning. The wind picked up and howled, forcing Maryam to raise her voice, powerful and desperate in equal measure.

An inferno erupted within the seal, so bright and hot that Maryam had to shield her eyes and step back. She looked over her arm and met a thousand eyes, sparkling like gemstone as they whirled on rims of liquid topaz. Opal-like wings curved upwards, encasing Maryam with the flames. As her eyes adjusted she swore she could make out a small curled form in the center made of molten gold, like a faceless child.

"Zack?" she called. "Zackary, are you okay?"

The demon inched closer. "I know not such a name." The voice was like a distant rumble of thunder.

Maryam's heart tightened. "Don't you remember me? It's Maryam."

He came closer, reeking of brimstone. "Mistress Maryam, what is it you want from me for the price of your blood?"

Her throat closed at the sound of his distance and formality, scared that she couldn't reach what she truly wanted. "I want you back."

The demon who had once been Zackary continued to whirl its many-eyed rings in silences for a moment. "Your payment has been in vain, for this is a command I do not understand."

"I want my godfather back," Maryam blurted. "I want my best friend back. I want *Zackary Bishop* back. We *need* him right now."

Hiro squeezed Maryam's shoulder. "Easy. His mind doesn't work like ours right now. He's something outside of time and space as we know it. You need to give him clear instructions that he can easily follow."

Maryam swallowed hard and took a deep breath of hot, stinking air. "I wish for your companionship, Zaphriel the Treacherous. I wish for you to be at my side so long as I walk this Earth and for you to guide me when I don't know what to do."

The eyes surveyed their surroundings. They hardly seemed to register Hiro's presence before they locked onto Emrys, who didn't recoil. Instead, he stood taller, refusing to blink against the blinding flames. Maryam swore a small, unafraid smile came to the faerie's face.

The eyes returned to Maryam, the golden child within uncurling and turning it's featureless face towards her. "Such odd requests from a child of Earth and Heaven. You are...strange."

"Says Tim Burton's Christmas tree topper," Maryam snapped. "Are you taking a deal or not?"

The wheels froze. The golden child stretched out its hand. "We have a deal."

Maryam offered him her injured arm, blood still dripping on the asphalt. He took it and sank black razor teeth into her skin, sending fire and needles through her entire body. She bit down on her bottom lip to keep from screaming as the pain blinded her. She shook her head for Hiro to stay away.

The demon released her and brought his teeth to his own wrist. A small pool of ruby-read crimson formed against gold. Maryam lifted the locket. He pressed his bloody skin against the printed insignia inside and she shut the locket.

The temperature plummeted and the wind died. The heat from Hell melting away, the firelight snuffing out as quickly as flipping a switch. Maryam exhaled as the wheels and eyes flaked away like ash, leaving only the golden form, wings tucked in to shield the morphing body.

Zackary collapsed to the pavement in a heap of wings and limbs.

"Zack!" Maryam ran to him and knelt, gingerly turning him over and brushing hair from his face.

For a moment, she panicked. Zackary's hair had been platinum, tinted gray, and pin-straight. The being in her arms had strawberry-blonde hair with a bit of wave. When his eyes fluttered open, they had Maryam's horizontal pupils, framed in alien bright green.

"Maryam?"

Maryam's tension eased. That was Zackary's voice, if a bit raspy and tired. He lowered his eyes to the locket around her neck. "You...You're the one who made the contract?"

Maryam's throat threatened to close. "That's right. You're mine now, asshole." She sniffed. "Do you remember any of that? Do you remember anything at all?"

Zackary studied the still-bleeding cut on her arm, then looked to Hiro and Emrys, crouched over Maryam's shoulder, recognition coming to his eyes alongside tears. Choking back a sob, he pulled her into a tight embrace, burying his face against her shoulder.

"You fucking scared me. I thought I *lost you* lost you." She squeezed him as hard as possible, trying to breathe through her own oncoming wave of tears. "We've been a mess without you."

Emrys scoffed. "Give us some credit. We did pretty well."

Maryam pulled away, helping Zack to his feet, noting the way he trembled, despite the way he kept his wings wrapped around himself against the cold. "Says the one who freed a bunch of violent demon-possessed people," she pointed out.

Emrys threw up his hands in exasperation. "It helped! You're welcome."

Zack blinked in alarm. "You did what?" He shook his head. "Later. First, clothes. Hiro, if you'd be so kind?"

Emrys clicked his tongue. "Fair enough. I won't be very useful with you walking around in all your glory."

Maryam looked to Zackary for his reaction. There was a small smirk where there should have been a glare as he gingerly took a few steps into the grass.

Maryam wondered if she'd brought back the right demon after all—normally, Zackary would have replied with a barbarous retort.

Emrys bandaged Maryam's arm as they sat on the sofa while Hiro led Zackary upstairs, gently shaking her when he noticed the way her head bobbed. "I know it's not about me," he muttered. "But, thank you for bringing him back."

"Heh. You *liiiiike* him," Maryam teased through a yawn.

Emrys clicked his tongue. "You're such a child." He eased Maryam to her feet. "You should get some rest. I saw Sarah taking pillows and blankets to the dorm rooms upstairs."

"I'm fine."

"Liar. You look like the undead, you're so tired. " He led her up the stairs, and picked one of the made-up rooms at random to tuck her in beneath cheap sheets and a worn fleece blanket. "Let that strong heart rest," he whispered, placing a kiss on her forehead.

Exhaustion stopped Maryam from arguing. Sleep finally took her as Zackary poked his head in the room wearing clothes too small for his towering frame. Emrys muttered a smart comment that Maryam couldn't hear and Zackary snapped in return. Maryam had just enough strength left to smile as she finally went under.

If she could save her godfather maybe she could make everything else right, too.

27

Zackary hadn't returned from Hell yet. Not really. Emrys could tell by the way his knee bounced and his eyes darted around the room as Hiro got him up to speed. He winced when Emrys set his mug in the sink, as if the sound was too loud, and tensed when Hiro said they should try to get some sleep, as if the idea of being alone terrified him. Still, he smiled that neutral, polite smile of his and excused himself to one of the rooms for the night.

So did Emrys, but his mind refused to settle. He laid on top of the blankets, staring at the ceiling, playing back every nervous tick and glance that had given away that Zackary wasn't okay. Not really. How hadn't Hiro seen that? Were things different between them now that Maryam held the contract instead? Did Hiro just respect Zackary's unwillingness to talk?

Why the hell did Emrys even care? It wasn't his problem.

He turned over, punched his pillow a few times, then dropped face-first into the lumpy down that smelled of age. Minutes passed. Every single muscle in Emrys' body stayed tense, his mind alert.

He turned over, keeping the pillow over his face, and groaned. "Son of a witch's cursed tit." He threw the pillow on the ground, jumped out of bed, and marched down to the room Zackary had claimed.

He knocked softly. "Zack?"

No answer.

Emrys knocked a tad louder. "Zackary, it's me." Still nothing. Emrys rolled his eyes and toed at the carpet. "Zackary, c'mon. We need to talk about your...*feelings*, or whatever."

The only response was silence.

"Zack?" Emrys slowly turned the handle and poked his head in to find the room empty, except for the made, untouched, bed.

Through the window, Emrys spotted a fair-haired figure making its way towards the tree line. He crossed the room and peered into the dark, recognizing Zackary just as he disappeared out of sight. Emrys sighed and left the room. If Zackary wanted to take a midnight stroll to shake off the shock of being back on Earth, who was Emrys to stop him? He was a full-grown demon. He didn't need a babysitter.

Except when Emrys went back to his room, he still couldn't fucking fall asleep.

He swore into his pillow again, threw on his shoes, and slipped into the night.

Zackary had taken a trail, thank the gods. The last thing Emrys wanted to do was track him through the woods at night. It was doable, but annoying in the dark. He called for Zackary at a speaking volume, not wanting to spook him in his current state, or anything else who might call these woods home. The only things that responded were frogs and crickets.

Emrys came to a clearing that led to the property's lake. It had been outfitted with benches and three towering crosses to serve as an outdoor chapel. Regardless of the respectful attitude Emrys kept towards the Organized Folk, something about the field felt wrong. Inverted. Unholy, even. The open air and dark skies of night belonged to his kind. The daylight was easy enough to share, but the night held secrets. Unknowingness. Mystery. All those things that the people of order feared, leading them to write everything down so the world could be simple and known.

Maybe that was why Zackary had come here. This place was like him.

He sat at the base of the center cross, looking out over the water, curled in on himself as he pulled at the petals of a dandelion, his eyes distant and not really seeing the undoing he caused. He stopped plucking as Emrys neared.

He leaned back against the cross and closed his eyes. "Go away, Emrys. I'm not in the mood."

"You're never in the mood." Emrys sat down in front of the cross on the left. "That's kind of my whole problem."

Zackary opened his eyes and stared out at the water, twirling the dandelion. "What do you want?"

Emrys leaned against the wood. "I just want to talk."

Zackary sighed. "What's there to talk about? I was in Hell, now I'm not."

Emrys stretched out his legs, nudging Zackary with a shoe. "That's more than enough to talk about. That must have been terrifying. And going from a celestial body to a mortal one? Isn't that jarring?"

Zackary scoffed, then finally looked at Emrys, his eyes calculating. "Seriously, what do you want, Em?"

"I want to make sure you're okay."

Zackary gave a tired, bitter laugh. "I'm not." He dropped the flower and ran his hand over his hair. "I'm absolutely not. Thanks for checking, though." He got to his feet and began to pace.

Emrys wasn't sure whether to follow him or not. "Zackary—"

"Stop it, Em," Zackary snapped. "Just stop."

Emrys got to his feet. "No. You just said you're not okay."

Zackary whirled on him with a snarl. "And how do you plan on making it okay?" he barked. "How are *any of us* supposed to make *anything* in this wretched, sinful, fallen world okay? Why the *fuck* should any of us even bother if none of it matters in the end?"

Emrys felt his heart crack a little. "Zackary, what you do matters."

Zackary gave that bitter laugh again. "You have no idea just how much it doesn't." He wrung his hands. "Every act of kindness, every time I turned the other cheek, every time I told Maryam to choose the higher ground, it all just..."

Zackary shook his head, then buried his face in his hands. "Jesus Christ, Em, I didn't know where my skin started and the blood ended. And it all heals over so they can start again. They must have blinded me a hundred times. Ripped my wings off a thousand. I have no way of knowing. They did it all because I *dared* to say we were wrong. To say we should have tried to work towards peace with the angels instead of war."

Zackary's voice broke as he fell to his knees. "I cried to God, Emrys. And the God who claims to be merciful, the God who claims to be forgiving stood by and did absolutely nothing *AGAIN*, despite all my penance." Zackary's arms fell to his sides as tears streaming down his face. "If God doesn't change, if my brothers don't change, *then what is the goddamn point in trying?*"

Emrys stood in silence, feeling as small and useless as the stars above. He could hardly navigate normal feelings. This...he didn't even have the vocabulary to process this, let alone the vocabulary to voice an answer. Instead, Emrys knelt down, gently took Zackary by the arm, and pulled him against himself.

Zackary held tight and began to sob.

Emrys wasn't sure how long Zackary clung to him. He didn't care. He kept one arm around the demon and the other holding Zackary's head to the crook of his neck until his sobs eased to trembling breaths. When the breaths eased into stillness, Emrys decided to try to speak.

"Zackary..." He wet his lips, looking for words. "Let's say you're right. Let's say nothing you've done to prove demons can be redeemed matters."

Zackary scoffed and pulled away, wiping his eyes and avoiding Emrys' gaze. "Nice pep talk."

Emrys caught his chin so that their eyes met. "I'm not done." His heart skipped a beat at the shock that registered on Zackary's face. "Just because the good you do doesn't matter to the world or God, or whatever, doesn't mean it doesn't matter at all."

Zackary frowned, apparently not following.

Emrys pressed on, despite feeling foolish. "What you've done matters a great deal to the Bishop family. Maryam's mother wanted her to live. To be human. You're the reason that happened. They might not have always seen it, but you protected their little family from the Order's wrath. You protected *Maryam*."

"Not always," Zackary grumbled, his chin dropping slightly. "The scars beneath her tattoos prove that easily enough."

"No one can protect us from ourselves, Zack." Emrys kept him up, refusing to let him fall. "You've done everything for that girl. You were home to her when the rest of the world turned its back. You were home to *me* when the world was trying to swallow me whole. I'd say that means a great deal. And if God and your brothers don't value that, then I say to Hell with their opinion. Pun intended."

Emrys held his breath as he watched the wheels turn in Zackary's mind, his newly strawberry-blonde eyebrows pulled together and his green eyes calculating. Emrys' heart began to pound. Had he said the wrong thing? Had it been so bad that Zackary would try to send him away again? Emrys' eyes dropped to Zackary's lips. How had the two of them wound up so close?

"Emrys?"

"Y-Yes?"

"I think I'd like to kiss you, now."

Emrys' brain stopped functioning. He hadn't known what to expect, but those words hadn't even been on the list. So, he did what he always did when words and thoughts failed him—he took what he wanted, pulling Zackary in with a hungry kiss.

Zackary melted against Emrys, gently pushing him back until the cold grass tickled the nape of his neck and the warmth of Zackary's body blanketed him. Emrys tangled one hand in Zackary's hair, pulling the demon's lips harder against his. The other hand found its way underneath Zackary's shirt and traced its way up his stomach.

Zackary shivered and traced a line of kisses from Emrys' mouth, to his jaw, and came to rest against his neck. Emrys drew a hiss of breath as Zackary's teeth found his skin and let it out as a moan. Heat pooled low in Emrys' stomach as Zackary's hands slipped under his shirt and his fingers glided along his ribs to hike up his shirt.

Those fingers still trembled.

Emrys' eyes snapped open. "Zack, stop."

Zackary's lips lowered to Emrys' clavicle.

"I said *stop.*" Emrys pushed him away.

"What? What's wrong?' Zackary pulled back, brow furrowed as he studied Emrys' face.

Emrys propped himself up on his elbows. "You're still shaking."

"So?"

"So, you're not alright yet."

Zackary lifted an eyebrow. "And you care...why?"

Good question—one Emrys wasn't about to answer willingly, even to himself.

He lowered his gaze to Zackary's chest and walked his fingers up the front of his shirt. "You'll be distracted, so I'll be distracted. It'll take all the fun out of it." He looked back at Zackary's face through his lashes, a smirk on his face. "I'm greedy and want all of you."

Zackary caught Emrys' hand with a smug smirk of his own. "Emrys Hemlock, I do believe you're starting to genuinely care about me."

Emrys' heart raced as heat rose in his face.

Zackary choked back a chuckle. "Are you *blushing*?"

Emrys stared up in stunned embarrassment.

Zackary broke into genuine laughter, the kind that shook his shoulders and brought wrinkles to the corners of his eyes that Emrys had never noticed before.

Emrys realized that, to his horror, he found those small wrinkles...cute.

No. No, no, no. Emrys's targets were not cute. They were gorgeous, bangable, and a million other adjectives, but under no circumstances where they ever *cute*. Cute meant he was comfortable. Comfortable meant there were feelings, and Emrys Hemlock abso*lutely* did not catch feelings.

He shoved Zackary away and worked to wriggle out from under him. "Get off me, you old gargoyle."

"Wait." Zackary grabbed Emrys by the waist and pulled him back to the grass as he rolled onto his back. "I'll stop teasing you if you stay and stargaze with me for a while. Having you here."

Emrys let himself be tucked into the crook of Zackary's arm, his head resting on the demon's chest. "Just for a little bit. I don't need you thinking I *care*."

Zackary snorted and held Emrys tighter. "You absolutely do care."

"Oh, shut up." Emrys turned so he could see the hazy glow of the Milky Way spilling across the sky. "What did you call the constellations? Back when you first came to Earth."

Zackary stilled, his breath easing into a deep, comfortable rhythm. "We came to Earth far from here. What would one day be known as Mesopotamia, then a dozen other names. The sky was different."

"What was it like?"

"So very bright."

"Tell me about it?"

Zackary told Emrys about the first named constellations and all the faint stars people could no longer see. He told him about the fresh clean water of the Euphrates and the way his children and the others like them would splash and swim in the heat of the dry, dusty afternoon. He told Emrys about his wife. The way she smiled. The way her tongue stuck out when she was focusing on the magic he'd teach her. He told him how jealousy didn't work the way it did now, so his wife and his first love were good friends who would tease him about the way he ate pomegranate seeds. They wrote spells together and treated each other's children like their own.

The syncopation of Zackary's voice and heart beat lulled Emrys' eyes closed, relaxing him until he wasn't sure if he was still lying in the grass, floating in the stars, or drifting down the Euphrates. All he really knew was that, for the first time since his mother died, he was safe.

Maryam wished she could take a twelve-hour nap and wake up with a performance completely planned more often. The dream seemed more like a nightmare, however, as Hiro explained that the quick planning was mostly the result of Order-related connections.

"Don't they all want my head on a pike?" she asked over cereal Sarah had bought from the nearest gas station. "Why are any of them helping you?"

"I told them it's a benefit concert," Hiro explained. "But they're also not asking many questions. Plausible deniability and whatnot."

"So, you're saying that a bunch of exorcists do, in fact, want to help an unholy child of the damned?"

Hiro snapped his newspaper and took a sip of coffee that had turned out only a fraction better than the pot the night before. "I don't know who this child of the damned is you speak of, but there are plenty of people who want to help *you*."

Wendy took a bite of her own cereal as she leaned against the corner. "Is there a band called Children of the Damned yet?" She washed it down with a plastic cup of apple juice. "If not, you should take it."

Maryam pointed to her with her spoon. "I think you're onto something, but let's put a pin in that for now." She flicked the spoon in her uncle's direction. "Whatever they want to call me, I'm the enemy, so why help?"

Hiro raised an eyebrow. "Are you really the enemy, though? You entered the Order to stop Anzuri from getting the Song of Enoch, knowing full well what might happen to you if anyone saw you. Then, Father Claude, one of their own, showed up and practically sentenced you to death while you were in the middle of risking your life. Order members are devoted, but they're not mindless, Maryam."

Maryam hid her doubtful look behind her Styrofoam bowl as she drank her cereal milk.

"Well, not all of them, anyway."

Maryam pursed her lips, still doubtful. Her twenty-one years of life seemed to fly in the face of everything Hiro said, but if there were enough folks in the Order to help them pull off this exorcism, she supposed she could wait and voice her complaints another time.

Hiro folded the newspaper, set it aside, and finished off his breakfast. "Have you seen the boys this morning? I was hoping to have this place cleaned up and get on the road by ten."

Maryam raised her eyebrows. "They aren't out doing exorcism-prep stuff?"

"I don't think so," Hiro replied. "Zackary would have told me. And I stopped to check on him this morning and his room was empty. Emrys' too." His phone rang. He looked at the screen. "It's your aunt."

Maryam's stomach knotted. Sarah had gotten up and driven back to Detroit before anyone else had woken up and Maryam couldn't tell if her aunt had wanted to get a jump on the day or avoid seeing her full-ankida'shi niece.

"Is she upset with me?"

Hiro gave her a sympathetic look. "No, sweetheart. She's just got a lot to process." He stood and kissed her hair on his way out of the kitchen. "Find Zack and Emrys for me?" He answered the call as he stepped out the sliding door.

Maryam sighed and pulled out her phone. She didn't believe Hiro about her aunt either, but she agreed that finding their missing supernaturals was more pressing.

Zackary's phone rang four times before he answered with a groggy, "Hey. Sorry. Be there in a minute."

"Be there in a mi—Zack, where are you?" Maryam demanded.

"Went for a walk last night. Sat down and fell asleep."

"Is Emrys with you?"

Maryam didn't get an answer.

"Zackary. Is Emrys with you."

"We're both on our way. See you in a second."

Zackary hung up before Maryam could ask any more questions and, holy shit, did she have questions.

Maryam was halfway thought a second bowl of cereal by the time the two of them came in through the sliding glass door, both disheveled and sporting leaves and twigs in their hair. Zackary plucked dead grass from his hair as he entered the kitchen behind Emrys.

Maryam tipped back in her chair and swirled her coffee in its cup as she watched them. "Morning, sunshines. Sleep well out beneath the stars?"

Zackary glowered in response as he poured himself a Styrofoam cup full of coffee.

Wendy slid over to allow Emrys to help himself to an apple from the bag on the counter.

He took a bit and asked, "How are you feeling?"

"I'm fine, but that's not important."

Zackary snorted as he sat down and pulled over the box of cereal. "You performed a large-scale exorcism with a flick of your wrist *and* your first demon summoning in the same day, but that's not important?"

"I said I'm fine. What happened with you two last night?"

Zackary and Emrys exchanged looks that held an entire conversation. The only sound was Wendy taking an extra large sip of juice as she watched the impending drama.

"Like I said, I went for a walk last night." Zackary poured milk into his bowl. "Emrys came to check on me. We started talking and wound up falling asleep."

"Outside? *In October?*"

"It's not as if we feel cold like mortals," Emrys said around a mouthful of apple. "And the nearby lake is quite relaxing."

Maryam narrowed her eyes as she studied him, looking for some sort of tell. It came when he got to his feet mumbling something about needing coffee and asking if anyone else needed some. As he turned towards the counter, Maryam caught sight of a circular bruise against his neck. She almost fell out of her chair when she connected the dots.

"Zackary Bishop, you lying slut!"

Zackary broke into a fit of coughs as he choked on his breakfast. "Excuse you?" he rasped.

"Excuse *me*?" Maryam shot back. "You're the one fooling around in the woods with the audacity to lie about it!"

Zackary dabbed at the milk spilled on his shirt. "I don't know what you're talking about."

"Are you telling me a squirrel gave Emrys that hickey?"

"Wouldn't be that surprised, honestly."

Emrys sat back down with the smug smirk of a cat that had stolen a bowl of cream. "Really, Zackary? After all that crooning and pining, you want to hide our relationship?" He took a sip of coffee. "Never figured you for a scoundrel."

Zackary motioned to Maryam. "'Our 'relationship' is none of her business! And there is no relationship until you say, 'Yes.'"

Emrys raised an eyebrow. "One date constitutes a relationship, now?"

"More than just sleeping together would, and you're the one who used the 'r' word."

Wendy snorted. "'Relationship' the 'r'-word, y'all."

Maryam cut in. "Hello, excuse me. Can we go back to the part where you said you're not my business? You are absolutely my business."

"No, *you* are *my* business. It's different. I'm your godfather."

Maryam scoffed. "Nice try. That excuse doesn't cut it anymore."

"How about the fact that I'm still training you, which means I can make your life *very* difficult," Zackary shot back. "How does *that* excuse work, flightling?"

Maryam glared down the table. "You don't fucking scare me." Zackary glared back.

Emrys finished his apple in three giant bites, chugged his coffee, and ran a hand over the bruise. He leaned towards Maryam to show her the cleared skin. "Better?"

"Yes, you harlot."

"Good. I'm going to leave you to this family spat and start collecting the sheets. Wendy, come along."

Wendy blinked. "What? Why?"

Emrys nudged her out of her seat and marched her towards the door as she tsked.

Zackary watched them go, then turned to find Maryam still glaring at him. He sighed and ran his hand over his heart. "Why do you care what I was up to with Emrys?"

Maryam studied Zackary for a moment, then stabbed at her bowl with her plastic spoon, leaving crescent divots. "I thought we were each other's ride-or-die is all."

"That doesn't mean I'm telling you every graphic detail of my life."

"Zack. You don't tell me *anything* about your life. You never have. It took you a week to tell me your favorite color."

"My favorite color bore no real impact on the school supplies you picked."

"That wasn't the point, dude. Fuck." Maryam pinched the bridge of her nose. "I just..." She dropped her arm. "Neither of us really have any adult friends outside of one another. At least, not until recently. I keep hoping that, now that I'm grown, you would let me in, even just a little bit."

Zackary's gaze darted across Maryam's face, serious and calculating. His expression softened to a tired smile as he shook his head. "It's hard to remember that you're an adult sometimes. And talking about intimate matters doesn't come naturally to me." He leaned back in his chair and dragged his hand down his face. When it reached his chin, he said, "I'll talk, but you call me a slut again and you're flying laps around Detroit until your wings fall off. Got it?"

Maryam crossed her heart. "Scout's honor."

Zackary raised his eyebrows as he raised his coffee to his lips, clearly doubting Maryam's claim. He took a sip, keeping his eyes down. "I didn't lie. Jumping from Hell to a mortal body on Earth can be jarring on the best of days. Add Hell's prison to the mix and the fact that the back and forth was so fast and..." Zackary shrugged. "I wasn't feeling myself. I went for a walk and Emrys followed to check on me. Things got physical. Emrys noticed that I still wasn't feeling great and told me to stop. We went back to talking and fell asleep. That's it."

Maryam tried to keep the goofy, gleeful smile of her face as he spoke, but failed.

Zackary scowled at her. "What?"

"That's precious."

Zackary dug at his cereal forcefully. "Oh, fuck off."

"I'm serious!"

Zackary scoffed.

"Zack, I'm not kidding. I like the idea of you and Emrys. You actually act like you feel things like a normal person with Emrys around and you're safe for him. He can put down roots with you. With us." Maryam propped her head on her hands and leaned across the table, batting her eyelashes. "So...when's this date you mentioned?"

Zackary gathered his Styrofoam dishes. "There is no date until Emrys agrees." He dumped it all in the trash, a hint of sharpness coming to his gaze. "I care for him...But I need to be sure we're really what we're after."

Maryam opened her mouth to ask for clarification as Hiro joined them in the kitchen.

"I've got good news." He slipped his phone into his pocket. "Sarah has Claude convinced you're hiding up on Mackinac Island with Father Ivan. Remember that camping trip we took with his church?"

Maryam frowned. "I haven't talked to him since I was twelve."

"No, but he always doted on you, and Claude would like nothing more than an excuse to harass him for it. That'll give us time to find Anzuri."

"Let's go, then. Peter doesn't have much time."

There were details to finalize, the set-up at Bell Isle Beach to check on, and a succinct plan of action to form. Hiro had even managed to schedule a quick interview on a local radio station to plug the concert. While Zack and Maryam saw to that, Emrys glamored a nearby patch of woods for the exorcism—anyone who got too close would suddenly feel the need to return to their car and leave after hearing nothing but the wind and the occasional lap of water from the Detroit River. Lord knew there would be enough screaming and yelled prayers to attract unwanted attention otherwise. Maryam tried her best not to think about it as they sat over lunch at a diner across from the island.

"There's one more thing we need for this to work," she said. "You have to let me go up on stage alone."

Stillness settled over the table, then everyone argued at once.

"Maryam, are you out of your mind?" Hiro demanded.

"And give Anzuri a clear shot at you?" Zackary argued.

Emrys shook his head. "Absolutely not."

"Listen. Seeing me up there by myself is bound to give Anzuri a false sense of confidence, even if he knows it's a trap. He doesn't know Zackary's not tied up at the Order. He doesn't know about Emrys. He doesn't know about you, Uncle Hiro. We need that edge. If you haven't noticed, our past interactions have both ended with us getting our collective asses kicked. Our stats are not great."

"We got rid of him at the hospital," Zackary huffed indignantly.

"Yeah, after he ripped my soul wide open and nearly stole my body to bust through the gates of Heaven."

Zackary glowered in response.

"Fine," Hiro sighed. "Under one condition."

Maryam's stomach churned in anticipation.

"Give Sarah and I a chance to make things up to you." Hiro turned to Zackary. "To both of you."

Maryam blinked at her human uncle, then at her demon godfather. Zackary stared just as blankly back.

"It's not a condition. Not really. You're right about Anzuri, as much as I hate it." Hiro said. He gave a sheepish smile. "I just didn't know how else to bring up the fact that Sarah and I want to do better." Sadness touched his eyes. "We really let you down, cupcake. Will you give us another chance?"

Maryam's throat tightened around every feeling and answer that came to her. Anger felt petty, but any sense of forgiveness felt dammed up by distrust. There was the airy lightness of relief, but doubt dropped through it like a boulder.

She fiddled with her straw wrapper, eyes downcast. "There's a new Vietnamese place down the street that we've wanted to try. Family dinner next weekend?"

Hiro beamed. "We would love that."

Maryam could only take his smile for a moment—it just brought up even more feelings she didn't have time for. She downed the rest of her soda, slammed the plastic cup on the table, and picked up the check as she slid out of the booth. "Then let's go perform an unsanctioned exorcism."

Even with Zackary and Emrys helping her set up, the notion of playing alone felt strange. Maryam had only ever played by herself in the privacy of her room and as much as she knew they needed the element of surprise, a better time to start going solo felt like never.

Emrys climbed off the stage and began to wade through the thin crowd, using a bit of magical persuasion to help it grow, and keep an eye out for Anzuri. Zackary placed a hand on Maryam's shoulder. He opened his mouth to speak, but then just sighed.

Maryam gave him a tired smile and placed a hand on his. "I get it. It's hard to watch your favorite goddaughter grow up."

Zaph gave her a playful shove. "Bold of you to assume you're my favorite."

Maryam shoved him back.

After a lingering, gentle stare, Zackary ruffled her hair. "You've been the biggest pain in the ass out of all of them, if that counts for anything. And I'm proud of you."

The words knotted in her chest. For the first time in years, she couldn't think of a smart-mouth reply. Instead, she settled on, "Thank you."

He smiled and joined Emrys in the crowd.

Folks passed by and trickled in. Maryam spotted familiar faces from Ectoplasm in the crowd and waved awkwardly when they cheered, making her realize how much she really did need Alex and Emrys with her. She didn't feel like much without them.

She looked out over the park to make sure Wendy was where they had told her to be: up at the nearby covered picnic area, looking like a regular kid doing homework in a hoodie. The second she saw Anzuri approach, she was to blink her phone flashlight on and off towards the stage.

Maryam didn't think Anzuri's approach would be nearly that obvious, but it made Wendy feel useful and would hopefully keep her out of trouble.

When the clock hit six o'clock, she tapped the mic and addressed the crowd. "Good evening, Detroit. How are we doing tonight?"

The crowd hooted and hollered.

Maryam smiled as her nerves eased a bit. "I'm Maryam Bishop. To those who don't know me, hi, thanks for coming out. For those who know me from Ectoplasm—" A few of the regulars cheered and waved water bottles that definitely contained alcohol. "You're probably wondering where my partners in crime are. Well, we're mixing it up a bit tonight." Maryam took a deep breath. "I'm going to be performing some of my original work for you today."

Zackary froze towards the back of the crowd. Any attempt he had made to listen to her music while she was growing up resulted in shoes being thrown at him or her bedroom door slamming in his face.

Maryam nodded to him, then began playing out the first notes of her song. The finger-plucked riffs made her feel naked and vulnerable after years of hiding behind the raucous vibrato of rock and roll, like she was stumbling through a foreign language in an attempt to speak to a sea of strangers.

"*The girl on the altar made of water and sand, she's speaking in tongues. It's part of God's plan.*"

Maryam raised her eyes and found Zackary staring at her, standing still in a sea of swaying people, his expression unreadable through the distance between them.

"*The angel cried, 'Free her and now stay your hand.' Your dagger still dropped. You're no Abraham.*"

The notion that others could understand her, despite never knowing what she came from, what she was, floored her. Then again, she thought, alienation wasn't uncommon, especially in a world tearing itself apart as one half made peace with itself and the other half resisted.

She hoped one day it would get better, but she'd never been an optimist.

The awed silence, punctuated by the breeze off the river, followed by roaring applause, began to change her mind just the tiniest little bit.

"Holy shit—eh, I mean wow. Thanks, guys."

A few people laughed.

"Look, fair warning, I don't know how to behave in public. I usually have Zackary nearby to keep me on a leash."

More chuckles and even a few hoots from Ectoplasm patrons.

Maryam tweaked the tuning of her guitar. "Oh, yeah. Duh. I totally forgot to mention that one's called..."

The title died on Maryam's tongue when she looked down into the crowd and spotted Wendy, one arm twisted behind her back and her face a flimsy mask of fury over terror. Behind her, Anzuri grinning up at Maryam with Peter's bleeding, mangled mouth. With his bloodshot eyes, graying skin, and oozing wounds, it looked like he had even less time than Maryam and the others had thought.

Whatever weapon he had to Wendy's back, judging the way she arched away from him, she might not have a lot either.

And the clock was speeding up.

Maryam felt Emrys' hand on her shoulder. It was the only thing she could sense beyond the roar of her rushing blood.

"We're fine. This is fine," he whispered. "You've got this. I'll cover for you."

He nudged her away from the mic and took the guitar from her hands, disarming the audience with a smile. "Evening, everyone. My name is Emrys Hemlock. Some family stuff has come up suddenly, so I will be taking over for Maryam, but fear not. I am just as entertaining and twice as pretty."

Nervous chuckles rippled through the crowd as Maryam eased herself off the stage and made her way towards the woods. She could feel Anzuri following, lingering just out of sight, pressing in on her brain like the ringing in her ears.

The muted sounds of the concert told Maryam she'd passed into the glamored area. Anzuri's smell of rot and brimstone hit her before she even faced him.

"Clever little act. Did you honestly think I wouldn't grab a little insurance, though? I'm hurt. It's like you don't know me at all."

Maryam slipped her hands in her pockets, praying that made her look more confident than she felt. "I'm still new to this bullshit," she replied. "So, yeah, my bad." Her gaze darted to Wendy.

Wendy gingerly struggled against her captor. "Save my brother and we'll call it even."

Anzuri cackled and muttered in Wendy's ear, "Your little friend is nothing without her pet demon." He sneered at Maryam. "Where is the treacherous one, anyway?"

Maryam glared. "The Order sent him back to Hell, no thanks to you. Say hi for me after I kick your ass."

"Fine, but I'll take the girl with me."

Wendy winced and whimpered against the sharp point at her back.

Maryam lifted her hands in surrender. "Easy, Anzuri. Hurting her won't help you. Hell, it doesn't look like Peter can help you anymore either."

Anzuri scowled. "Oh, I tried my best with him, but it didn't end well. Very messy." His dark, soulless eyes lit up as he pulled the Song of Enoch from his jacket. "With you, however, things would go quite differently."

"You'd have to give up both Peter and Wendy," Maryam ordered. "I won't make any bargain that keeps them in danger."

Anzuri clicked his tongue. "Fine, but you're getting the shit end of the deal." He shrugged. "A teenage girl and a husk? I'm practically robbing you."

Maryam's blood ran cold. "What do you mean?"

"I mean it's been very quiet in here ever since I taught Peter a little lesson about talking back." The smile on Anzuri's face was nasty enough to turn milk sour.

Maryam's breath hitched. She focused on her heartbeat. Anzuri could be lying. He was probably lying. He *had* to be lying. Peter couldn't be gone.

"Here's my offer, then," Maryam said, taking a few steps forward. "Hand over Wendy, leave Peter, and you get me."

Anzuri scoffed. "As if I'd be so stupid as to believe you."

Maryam scoffed back. "What do I have to lose? Zack's gone, the Order wants me dead, and my aunt and uncle are afraid of me. The least I can do is make sure my friends are safe." She refused to blink as she added, "And your world actually sounds like it might have space for me."

Anzuri studied Maryam with a glare.

She inched closer. "Here's the plan: I pull Wendy out of danger, then you grab me. Easy as that."

"You'd turn against our family in Heaven so easily?" Anzuri asked with a sneer.

Maryam held out her hand. "My family's gone."

Anzuri sneered as he released Wendy. She lunged for Maryam.

Maryam pulled her into her arms. Anzuri's broken fingernails snatched her sleeve as she yelled, "Now!"

Hiro and Zackary burst from the brush, knocking Anzuri to the ground. He shrieked as he crashed into the dirt. Zackary pinned him with his arms outstretched. Anzuri spat in his face and howled as Hiro splashed him with holy water, thrashing as if they were torturing him. Maryam could hardly hear her uncle's prayers over the screams. Wendy cowered in her arms, covering her ears against the cries ripping from her brother's throat. Maryam held her tight, whispering that it would be alright, that Hiro was one of the best and that Peter would be fine.

"You've killed him, you bitch!" Anzuri shrieked. "You think you can win like this? By *lying*? We invented lies. We knew of deceit before humans ever laid eyes on the Tree!"

"Maryam, don't listen to him," Zackary ordered.

She hadn't heard a word past, "You've killed him."

You've killed him. You've killed him. You've killed him.

She knelt beside Peter's body as his eyes rolled back and a violent spasm wracked his body. "No! Fuck! Zack, go in and get him."

"A human body can't handle two demons as strong as us, especially one this wrecked." Zackary grunted as he struggled to hold Peter still. "We'd tear him apart."

"What about someone half-demon?"

Hiro and Zackary froze.

"He could still die."

"He'll die anyway at this rate."

Hiro met Maryam's eyes. "Do it. Bring him home."

Maryam squeezed his hand, then turned to Peter's terrifyingly still body. With a twinge of nausea, she traced the way Anzuri had possessed her in her memory and placed her forehead to Peter's, willing her energy against his soul.

Inhale, she was surrounded by oak and ash trees.

Exhale, she was surrounded by dense trees, mist, and twilight.

The fog chilled her skin and the scent of the shadowy forest sharpened her mind as she listened for Peter. She called his name. On the wind came a raspy sigh, like the final exhale before death. Beyond that, a soft cry. Maryam sprinted towards the sound, still calling for Peter.

She saw them through the trees—Peter chained to a trunk by one wrist, his other hand purple, misshapen, and limp as he hung from Anzuri's clawed hand. Anzuri now looked every inch the demon he was.

Two could play at that game.

Her wings caught the wind as she wound up a punch. "Hey, fuck-face!"

Her hand collided with Anzuri's jaw as he turned, sending him sprawling. Peter crumbled to the ground. Maryam knelt just long enough to confirm he was still breathing.

Anzuri wiped the blood from his mouth. "You little wench. You should have given yourself to me. If you're going to whore yourself out, it might as well be to someone who wants to build a better world."

"It sounds so appealing when you say it that way."

With a wave of his hand and a roar of flames, a sword of fire erupted in Anzuri's grip. "I'm going to incinerate you both. Then, when your body is mine and mine alone, I'm going to shred apart every member of your freakish little family. The road to my victory will be smeared with their blood."

Maryam took a deep breath to slow her raging heart.

She was light. She was energy. She was power older than the Earth and she was as resilient as the rock beneath her, no matter what anyone said. Anzuri just hadn't realized yet.

Maryam summoned her light as a blade as bright as Anzuri's. With a hint of smugness, she willed the hue to match her hair.

Anzuri's victorious expression drooped. With a growl, he swung. His sword embedded itself in a tree as Maryam ducked. He sprang into the overcast sky as Maryam charged and swore. Zackary hadn't taught her to fight like this yet.

Voices on the winds distracted her.

"Behold, I give you the authority to trample on serpents and scorpions, and over all the powers of the enemy..."

"Peter...Please, please, please, come back. I'll help you with the store. I'll never sneak out again. I'll be perfect."

"C'mon, Maryam. Hurry."

Maryam shook off the nerves. She could do this. She *had* to do this.

Maryam launched herself into the air, barely clearing the treetops before Anzuri nearly took her head off. She parried and jabbed, slicing his bicep and nicking his wing.

"Do not rejoice that the spirits submit to you," she said, *"But rejoice that your names are written in heaven."*

"Shut up!" Anzuri screeched, plunging his sword towards Maryam's gut.

She hissed as it grazed her ribs.

"They don't want you! Don't you get it? No matter how many of them you save, no matter how hard you work, humanity will always reject you. The Order will always reject you."

Maryam snatched a handful of Anzuri's feathers and slammed her forehead into his face. Her head pounded at the impact more than she expected, making her wonder how the Hell he'd pulled the move off back at St. Damien's. Three spinning visions of Anzuri held his face and groaned in pain.

"I'm not doing this for humanity," she panted, squinting to see straight. "I'm doing this for Peter."

Anzuri swung again, nearly impaling Maryam's right shoulder. She brought her sword down on his arm. He thrusted his blade past her body, slicing apart the tendon of her wing. Her cry of pain grew to a scream as he pulled the sword through joint below. She dropped from the sky like a boulder. A branch cut her screams short as it knocked the wind out of her on her way down.

The forest spun in her vision as she used a tree to pull herself up. The white-hot pain in her wings and a throbbing sprained ankle made it impossible to think. If only she could rest. Or breathe. She needed help.

She needed Peter. With Zackary and Hiro working on the outside, Peter rejecting Anzuri might be enough to end things, but with how badly he'd been beaten down, both physically and mentally...

Maryam froze at the flapping of wings and willed her sword away, doing her best to blend into the shadows of a fallen tree.

"Where are you, little monster?"

She held her breath to listen for Anzuri's footfalls. She dared to close her eyes and focus. She exhaled, feeling the energy of the world, the landscape of Peter's mind, ripple like a radar signal. He was still alive.

And Anzuri was right behind her.

Maryam dropped and tumbled. Her hair tugged at her scalp as it caught beneath Anzuri's blade.

A flash of light. Her sword in her hand, plunged upward, straight between Anzuri's ribs.

His sharp inhale was short. Too quiet a response for so much damage.

Maryam froze, her eyes locked with the demon's until the trickle of his blood on her hands made her recoil. Anzuri collapsed against the fallen tree, grasping for balance, his voice a choked whisper around the bubble of blood on his lips.

"...How?"

Speaking felt like melding clay in Maryam's mouth. "I guess we both underestimated me."

Anzuri sneered. "It seems so. Congrats on completing your journey of self-discovery. Too bad it came too late to save anyone."

"I'm getting Peter out of here."

"He won't want to leave this place." Anzuri slid to the forest floor, his grin still triumphant. "Not after what we've been through together."

Maryam's stomach churned. Anzuri was lying. To prove she knew it, she glared and turned her back on him, making her way back towards Peter on woozy legs.

She found him motionless on the forest floor. Maryam wanted to run to him, to cradle him in her arms until everything was right again, but her limbs felt more and more like lead by the second. She eased herself down beside him just as he opened his eyes.

His expression went from disorientation to terror in a fraction of a second.

Maryam inched away from him. "Easy, Peter. It's me, Maryam."

"I'm possessed, not crazy," he laughed, the sound high and unhinged.

"You're trans, your main on Mario Kart is Luigi, for some weird reason, and you almost named yourself Apollo like some sort of mega nerd."

"Okay, it's you." Peter winced and eased himself to his knees, leaning against the tree for support. His face scrunched as he cradled his mangled hand to his chest. The pained expression made the circles under his eyes darker and the lines of his face even deeper. "God. Any more of this fuckery and my head's going to explode." His voice sounded brittle, like glass under a steel-toed boot in the dirt.

Maryam took him by the shoulder. "I know, but I need your help, Peter. This is your body, so you've got to be the one to end this. Declare that you renounce Anzuri and take your body back. I'm not strong enough to fight him for you anymore."

Peter raised an eyebrow. "That sounds way too easy."

"Trust me, that bastard won't make it easy. It's all a mind game. I'd rather beat his ass into oblivion but..." She gestured to her mangled wing.

Peter licked his split lips. "Will I remember anything?"

"I don't know. Most folks remember most of their experience."

Peter's face paled. "Maryam, I can't."

Maryam's stomach dropped. "What do you mean you *can't?* Peter, if we don't end this, you'll *die.*"

He grabbed Maryam by her torn, dirty shirt. "Maryam, people are *dead* because of me. I don't even know how many. I tried to play the hero and deal with this on my own and it backfired. Now there are a ton of families who may never know what happened to their loved ones because Anzuri tore them apart. What do I say to Wendy? To our mother?"

Maryam held Peter's face in her hands. "That wasn't your fault."

"It was. I should have stopped him. I should have gone to someone, *anyone*." He hung his head. "I wanted to prove I could protect my family—that I was worth all my dad lost. I'm not."

"What do you mean? Of course you are."

Peter shook his head, avoiding Maryam's eyes. "My dad's family stopped talking to us when I came out. He and mom supported me wholeheartedly, but my grandmother was too religious to forgive him for it." Tears welled in his eyes. "The church his family had attended for three generations cut us off. That place was a cornerstone of his life and when I came out, he threw it away without a second thought. No one would answer our calls while he was dying. Not the church, not our family, and he just wanted to spend his last days around people he loved." Peter choked on a sob as he brought his good hand up to hide his face. "I did that. I cost my dad his family and community and I wasn't even worth it."

"Oh, Peter." Maryam pulled his hand away and wiped his tears with her thumbs. "You were his *child*. And if his so-called community and family couldn't see that, then that's on them. They have no idea what they're missing out on because you are incredible."

Maryam gently pressed her forehead against Peter's. "You can't save everyone, Pete. Believe me, I wish we could. But you can save yourself, right here, right now." A tired smile came to her face. "You already broke your own hand to save both Heaven and Earth from a demon. I'd say that the hard part is over."

Peter sighed. "I'm so tired, Maryam."

"I know." Maryam lifted his face, her heart racing with relief as she realized his hazel eyes still held light. "Just a little further and you're home free. That's all you have to tell yourself."

Peter looked too tired to be convinced.

Having run out of ideas, Maryam kissed him.

His lips were rough. Maryam tasted a hint of blood as he kissed her back, but she savored the press of his mouth and the heat of his breath, grateful that she was already kneeling or her legs would have buckled, both at the relief of feeling him still so alive and the unfamiliar joy of being kissed—of being treasured.

As Peter pulled away, Maryam muttered, "Please tell me that cheesy action movie stunt wasn't what convinced you to stay alive."

Peter gave a small huff laced with amusement. "Call it the cherry on top of your beautiful, thoughtful monologue."

Maryam gave him the softest shove possible. "Get bent, Bailey."

"I'd say it's a little late for that." Peter grabbed hold of the tree trunk, his face scrunched in pain as he hauled himself to his feet. "Walk me through exactly what I need to do."

Maryam grabbed hold of his good hand as she crawled to her feet, doing her best not to sway as the forest tilted around her. Thinking past the pounding in her head felt nearly impossible. "You have to dig down in your very soul and claim yourself—all of you. Nothing Anzuri hurls at you can hurt unless you let it."

Peter sighed. "Easy day. That's definitely not something that usually takes people years of therapy to accomplish."

"Well, I ran him through with a flaming sword. That should make it easier."

Peter blinked. "Yeah, I suppose that would knock him down a few pegs."

"First, allow me to deal with this." Maryam braced herself beside the anchor of Peter's chain. Nausea and weakness be damned, she pulled, gritting her teeth until a link gave out and the broken pieces fell to the ground.

She turned to find Peter staring up at her wide eyed in awe. "Drool over the muscles later."

Peter shook off the expression, grabbing hold of Maryam to steady himself, nearly knocking her over with the sudden weight. "Right. Let's go kill a demon."

Maryam slipped an arm around his waist, grateful for the support and warmth of him. "Sounds good."

They walked with heavy, uneasy steps, listening carefully to the wind in the leaves. Beyond the breeze, Maryam could still hear the others, pleading and praying.

A blade whizzed through the air, centimeters from Maryam's nose. She whirled, then regretted it with the way it made the world spin.

"Damn it," Anzuri hissed, one hand against his side, soaked in blood. The other held an identical knife. She left him wounded enough that the sword sapped away too much energy. "It seems I can't catch a break."

"No." Maryam pulled away from Peter. "No, you can't."

Maryam lunged for him, then choked as the demon's dagger slipped between her ribs. Anzuri gave a weak cackle of triumph with blood on his lips. Maryam hooked his leg. He crumpled to the ground, Maryam not far behind.

"Reject him, Peter. Forsake him." Maryam ordered, struggling to hold Anzuri as black dots blurred her vision. For the first time, she wondered if she'd make it back.

Anzuri had enough strength left to scream. "No, no, no, please! Peter, don't do this!'

Peter covered his ears. "Anzuri, I cast you from my body. Return to the depths from which you came."

"But, you'll see them, Peter! Every person you were too weak to save, you'll see them in the dark for the rest of your life. I can let you hide. I can keep you safe. I'll let you stay in this nice little forest. I'll fix it up and I'll never touch you again. You love it here, don't you? You've loved it since you were a boy, when you were scared to be a boy."

Peter shouted louder, "I said I rebuke you, Anzuri! Get out of my mind and get out of my body!"

Maryam's grip tightened. "You heard the man. Time to go."

"Please, no," Anzuri whispered as Peter continued to shout. "Please, Maryam. I just wanted them to know how they hurt me. Hurt *us*. I just wanted to go home."

"So did Ellie McDonald, you son of a bitch," Maryam hissed.

His whimpering turned to a snarl. "I would have been merciful." Hiro and Zackary's prayers grew louder, drowning out Anzuri's voice. "When your father hears of this betrayal, he will not be."

Maryam smirked as her grip tightened. "What's he gonna do? Ground me?"

The sun came out from behind the clouds, growing brighter until blinding light swallowed the forest. The warmth swallowed Maryam like a blanket. The breath in her lungs turned thin and light, yet warm, like life itself danced and weaved around her soul.

Then, nothing.

Darkness.

Then a splitting migraine, cool autumn grass, and a baited silence. Someone—Wendy—burst into a sob as someone else sighed.

Someone shuffled in the dirt beside her.

"Maryam?" Peter sounded as if he hadn't had water in weeks, but his voice was gentle. It was him. No sign of Anzuri's sharp darkness in a single syllable.

"Here," Maryam whispered back. Her hand bumped into his and Peter interlaced his fingers with hers. Maryam squinted into the twilight sun to find everyone crowded over her and Peter. When the light added to the pain in her head, she closed her eyes.

"I thought I was gonna lose you both," Wendy sobbed, throwing her arms around her brother.

"Did you really banish him?" Zackary asked. "Is he gone?"

"Seems like it," Peter wheezed, smothered by Wendy's embrace. "Head's really quiet. And hurts."

"We'll get you help," Hiro said. "Just hold on."

Maryam felt Zackary's familiar warmth as he knelt beside. "You did well." She could hear the smile in his voice. "Have you considered a career as an exorcist?"

She laughed, though the movement grated against her joints like sandpaper. With a painful swallow, she answered, "Maybe when Hell freezes over."

Life settled into a slow, sleepy pace. Every spare moment seemed to be spent curled up somewhere. Maryam slept the hardest, sometimes needing Zackary or Emrys to shout when they woke her up.

A whole week after the exorcism, she still managed to sleep until noon. With nothing on the agenda, she lounged for a bit, then threw on the closest clean clothes she could find and slipped out of her room to make coffee.

Zackary slept sprawling on the couch with Emrys' feet in his lap as he napped at the opposite end. No great confessions of love had been made, much to Maryam's disappointment, but Emrys could get through one or two whole conversations without flirting and Zackary no longer threw quite so many barbs.

They talked quite a bit, much to Maryam's surprise, often late into the night.

She nudged Zackary awake. He jolted, his eyes unfocused. "Is everything alright?" he whispered, brows pulling together.

"Yeah. I'm gonna go see Peter. Do we need anything while I'm out?"

Zackary tapped Emrys awake. The pixie shifted and stretched as he yawned, "We need honey."

Zackary gave him a bewildered look. "We just bought some. How much do you eat?"

Emrys pulled a blanket from the back of the sofa and snuggled into it. "I wouldn't have to eat any if you gave me some sugar, Sweetness."

Zackary smirked. "You're sweet enough for the both of us, when you want to be."

Emrys poked his head out of the blanket to scowl at him

Maryam laughed. "I'll pick some up."

As she slipped out the door, Emrys waved over the back of the sofa. "Tell Peter we say hi."

"I will." Maryam nearly collided with a person on their entryway. "Father Wilhelm?"

The priest had nearly knocked her in the face as Maryam opened the door. He blinked, eyes wide, as if he hadn't expected her to look human. He composed himself with a clearing of his throat and reached in his coat pocket.

"Ms. Bishop, how are you?" The old man gave a thin, fragile smile.

Maryam shrugged. "Pretty okay, all things considered." She frowned. "You didn't fly all the way back to Boston just to turn around and come back did you?"

"I actually hadn't left yet," the priest said. "A tiny bit of grace in all this, I suppose." He handed her a white envelope held closed by a crimson wax seal with her name on the front in immaculate cursive. There was no address, as if the only way it could have been delivered was face-to-face.

Maryam accepted it gingerly. "What's this?"

"A formal written apology on behalf of the entire Rosary Order. And a job offer."

Maryam froze.

"Everyone's heard what happened by now. Hiro hasn't been able to stop talking about you. In the ever-changing world of spiritual warfare, we could use an ally like you."

Maryam didn't mean to laugh. Honest. Father Wilhelm seemed kind enough, but Maryam couldn't help herself. "Let me get this straight: the Order spends twenty-one years punching down on me, starts planning to kill me, and then offers a piece of paper to patch things up so you guys can use me?"

Father Wilhelm sighed. "I told them you would say that. I apologize for their audacity."

Maryam looked over the envelope, then slipped it into an inner pocket of her jacket. "For that, I won't return it to its sender in shreds." She looked over Father Wilhelm, gauging how sincere he might be. "I'll think about accepting the apology, but the job's not gonna happen."

The priest stepped in her way as she tried to descend the stairs. "Father Claude's been placed on sabbatical."

Maryam raised an eyebrow. "Wow. You guys are almost genuinely sorry, huh?"

Father Wilhelm furrowed his brow, mouth pursed, as if he didn't quite get what she meant.

"Essentially putting the bastard on a paid vacation isn't the act of goodwill you all think it is. The answer's still no. I'm not working for the Order."

Maryam slipped past Father Wilhelm and practically skipped down the stairs through the bar. Her wings were neatly tucked away and cloaked in glamor, but it felt like she was flying. At the front door, she turned and added, "If you could, though, please let Claude know I said 'fuck you', if he hasn't left yet."

Maryam strode out the door and down the street without a final glance at Father Wilhelm, but she could have sworn she heard a sudden burst of laughter from the priest as the door swung shut.

For the first time in forever, Maryam boarded the bus without her earphones in. Her mind was quiet enough that the silence didn't result in a deafening roar. Her phone rang with Hiro's picture on the screen.

"What's up?"

"Hey, cupcake. Which Vietnamese place are we meeting at tonight? There's Pho-Ever on Woodward and Pho-Real on Cass. Both are pretty close to your place."

Maryam shifted in her seat. "Pho-Ever. Ironically enough, Pho-Real is some sort of weird fusion place nobody asked for. Super overpriced."

"Got it. Is Emrys coming?"

Maryam's eyebrows shot up. "Do you want him to come?"

Hiro sighed. "I feel like we got off on the wrong foot. If he's going to be a part of your and Zackary's lives, I figure I should make an effort."

Maryam let out an impressed whistle. "Wow. Claude-free Uncle Hiro is getting wild."

"You heard about that?"

"Sure did, and I'm toasting to it tonight at dinner."

"Please don't," Hiro groaned.

"I'm teasing. I won't. Maybe. We'll see where the night takes us." Maryam nervously bounced her foot. "Is Aunt Sarah...okay?"

The line went silent.

Hiro had called Maryam two days after they'd gotten Peter to the hospital. The Order had been in an uproar ever since Maryam—an ankida'shi—took down a member of Hell's dark court. Father Claude's efforts to kill her in the midst of the crisis clearly hadn't done him any favors. Sarah's position between both Claude and Maryam had made work hell. She still hadn't reached out to talk to Maryam besides a few "I love you" text messages, which made Maryam think Hiro's request for an apology dinner was a ploy to get his wife and his niece in the same room. Maryam couldn't bring herself to deny her uncle that.

"She will be," Hiro replied finally. "Just give her time.'

"Time. Got it. I'm at my stop, so I'll talk to you later. Love you."

"Love you too, angel girl."

Maryam struggled to keep the goofy grin off her face. "You're embarrassing, you know that?"

"Just doing my job." Hiro chuckled and hung up.

Maryam had prayed that they would take Peter to any other hospital other than the one run by the Order, but it was the only one in Detroit where he could be treated with no questions asked. They had told his mother that he'd been hit by a car. Maryam had suggested they say he was hit by a semi. Peter had laughed at the idea. Hiro, Zackary and the doctors had not.

She showed her ID to the nurse at the desk and rounded the corner to Peter's room. Inside, she could hear laughter.

"Man, you always cheat," Wendy whined. Maryam entered in time to see her throw down her Uno cards.

Peter threw his hands up. It was the first time Maryam had seen him move in all week without flinching. "How do you cheat at Uno?"

"I don't know. Being possessed gives you magic powers or some shit."

"Stop swearing. And no, it didn't. You're just a sore loser."

Wendy flicked a card at her brother. As he blocked it, he spotted Maryam and his grin grew wider, practically glowing. The sight made Maryam's stomach flip.

"I was starting to think you were getting bored of me," he said.

"Nah." Maryam fiddled with the petal of one of his "get well soon" flowers. "When you're a healthy member of society again, then you'll be boring."

Wendy groaned as she got to her feet. "I'll be back in a second with your Skittles, cheater."

"Get those berry ones if they have them," Peter called.

"You're so bougie."

"Rather be bougie than bad at Uno."

Wendy's hand popped into the room and flipped Peter the bird.

Maryam chuckled and shook her head. "Glad she's okay. I don't think most people would be."

Peter leaned back against the pillow. "She's annoying, but she's tough."

Maryam nodded in agreement and sat down on the edge of the bed. "How are you feeling?"

Peter shrugged and studied the bandages that still covered most of him. "Pretty okay. I slept without nightmares for the first time last night. The nurse said I might be able to get out Monday. The doctor recommended therapy for a while."

Maryam snorted. "No joke. That was..." She didn't know the right words for what had happened any more than she knew them for her feelings toward Peter. Terrifying didn't seem big enough.

Peter took her hand, distracting her attempts to finish that sentence. "Thank you, for the hundredth time."

"For the hundredth time, you don't need to thank me," Maryam replied, shifting closer. "You would have done the same."

"Yeah, but you've got wings—it looked way cooler than if I had saved you."

Maryam shook her head. "Your priorities are a bit skewed. Did you know that?"

Peter smirked. "Part of my charm." He ran his bandaged thumb over the back of Maryam's hand. "Speaking of charm, did mine work well enough at Mario Kart night to get me a second date?"

"You mean the night I figured out that you were haunted by a demon and had to plan how to save your immortal soul?"

"Obviously. We've only had one Mario Kart night."

Maryam studied the anticipation on Peter's face, wishing he was kidding but glad that he wasn't. "I don't think that qualified as a first date, Pete."

"Okay, well, have I charmed you enough to get a re-do on the first date?"

Maryam couldn't help but laugh at the insanity of the implication. "I'm an ankida'shi, Peter."

"And in what language does that mean, 'Super hot Amazon warrior?' I only ever took Spanish, but that's the only obvious translation."

"It means I'm half-demon. Not human."

"And I'm an Aquarius. We all have our flaws."

"Demons are going to come after me to either use my power or kill me."

"The Department of Education wants money I don't have for a degree I'm not using. We can go on the run together."

Maryam gave Peter an exasperated look. "You're exhausting."

"And you're amazing." Peter brought Maryam's hand to his lips. "One date? Please?"

Maryam opened her mouth to answer, only to sigh. "Pete..."

Peter's eyebrows raised.

Maryam's shoulders slumped. "I can't. Not right now." She gently pulled her hand away. "There's so much going on right now that I don't understand and that scares me. I can't add anything else to my plate right now." She wrung her hands. "I'm sorry. I shouldn't have kissed you before. "

Peter shrugged. "Heat of the moment and all that." He smirked. "All things considered? It was a good kiss. Let me know when you want a great one." He gave a goofy, over the top wink.

Maryam rolled her eyes to avoid thinking about the way her heart sped up. "Like I said, you're exhausting."

"And yet we both know you're going to keep me around."

Footsteps in the hall drew Maryam's attention

"I'm coming back in," Wendy called. "Y'all better be acting right."

Maryam flushed and straightened her coat. "Peter's right—you're the worst."

Wendy threw the bag of candy at her brother and dropped into the chair beside his bed. "He's been talking shit, I see." She glanced around the room, bounced on her toes, then picked at her ripped jeans. "So...what's next?"

Maryam frowned. "What do you mean? Like, today?"

"I meant in general. What do we do after...*this*? Do we, like, change or something?"

Maryam ran a hand through her hair. She'd been wondering the same things lately. "We just live, I guess," she finally answered, playing with a stray thread in her sweater. "There's nothing else you can really do." She looked at both siblings. "Just promise me, if you need to talk about anything that happened, you won't keep it to yourselves." She mindlessly traced her tattoos. "Zackary likes to tell me that the truth can prick a finger or slice an artery, depending on when you face it. I couldn't stand it if either of you wound up in the latter situation.

Peter eased back against his pillow, arms folded. "Smart man. Demon. Whatever. Wish I'd been that smart three weeks ago."

"Was it really that long ago?" Wendy massaged her temple. "I feel like I aged a decade in that time." She glanced at her brother. "That makes you ancient, huh?"

Peter swung a spare pillow at Wendy despite the way he winced. "Girl, shut your ass up."

Wendy caught it. "I thought we weren't supposed to swear."

Maryam got to her feet to get out of the crossfire. As she took a step back, her phone buzzed.

Below Zackary's name the screen read, *Just got a weird case. Call?*

Maryam scowled at the screen and typed back, *No.*

Zackary fired back almost immediately, *I'm not asking you to help the Order, I'm asking you to help me.* Ellipses appeared, then vanished, then reappeared. *Unless the whole Anzuri thing scared you for life. I would understand.*

Maryam sighed. "Give me a second, guys. I gotta make a call." She stepped into the hall and dialed Zackary's number. He didn't get the chance to greet her before she said, "Those bastards better not be expecting me to work for free."

"So glad you have a servant's heart." Zackary huffed. "Yes, you will be compensated once you help me get a hoard of hellions out of a house. Apparently, a kid brought home a spirit board that wasn't properly cleansed. The mom's losing her mind."

"Give me her number. I'll see what I can do."

"You still sound like exorcist material," Zackary teased.

"Oh, shut up." Maryam paused, watching Peter and Wendy, safe and whole, through the doorway. "Maybe. One day. I don't know. For now, just let me learn how to live."

"Shouldn't be too much trouble," Zackary replied, pages flipping in the background. "You already know how to fly."

After

THE LAST THING FOR Claude to clean out was the bottom right door of his desk. It had the least amount of clutter, but proved to be the hardest to open. The pictures inside hadn't aged a day, though seeing them in their drug store envelopes and white Polaroid outlines made Claude feel ancient.

He'd managed to go through five entire rolls of film at Sarah and Hiro's wedding. The only image he'd been captured in was the ceremony. He'd officiated, stayed for the entire reception, then stayed to help clean up afterwards. Every glossy version of Sarah beamed with joy. She was the same in the pictures he'd taken in the hours after Matthew's birth, despite her exhaustion.

She stopped smiling like that the day Mary showed up on their doorstep half-frozen, half-crazed, and starving. It had been a miracle she survived long enough to bring Maryam into the world.

Well, *miracle* wasn't quite the word Claude would use.

Another paper envelope held a collection of pictures of Matthew Bishop. He was a different age in every picture, but his smile remained the same—bright, open, and warm. Not a day went by that Claude didn't wish he had asked to be in just one of these instead of always volunteering to take them. Just like real life, Maryam was underfoot in all of them once she had come along, only a few steps away from Matthew at any time. The last picture featured Matthew beside his over-stuffed Civic, on his way to his new apartment in Ann Arbor with Maryam sitting on the hood. He only lived in that apartment a month before he died.

He placed those in the shoe box as well and went further back in time.

These pictures, featuring Sarah and Mary in their school days, were grainier. Sarah was always so pressed and pristine when she was growing up, not a single blonde hair out of place in her flower clips and high ponytails. Mary was always scraped knees, dirt, and grins with missing baby teeth. As a teenager, she was wild with tall, stiff red hair and heavy make-up. Angry. Challenging. She had turned out a lot like her mother, Grace, that way.

Maryam had turned out a lot like them both.

Claude hated how much of them he saw in that she-demon. How much they both haunted him. From the moment he saw that fiery red hair above her evil little eyes, he knew he'd never again have a moment's rest.

Because if the ghosts didn't torment him, his guilt certainly would.

The last picture had earned a frame to starve off age. It was older than the others with its sepia tone and hazy finish.

It was the only one Claude had been in voluntarily. He stood on the stairs of the Rosary Order's headquarters in Boston, some fifty years younger, just after teaching his first year at the Academy of Exorcism. Grace, one of his most promising students who had just finished her first year, had insisted they take a picture together, just the two of them. Before Claude had realized what had happened, she had jumped on his back and the photographer had snapped the photo, capturing Grace laughing in triumph and Claude scrambling to catch her before she fell and broke her neck on the steps.

Grace had refused to listen to Claude's rants about how compromising it looked.

Grace, Mary, and Maryam could be triplets. Same hair. Same bright, open smile. Even if he couldn't see them clearly in the old photo, Claude knew they all had the same bright green eyes. He could never forget those eyes.

Sarah had taken after her father, both in appearance and temperament, it seemed.

Claude did the math in his head. Wherever she was, Gracie was seventy-four, about to turn seventy-five, provided she was still alive.

Who was he kidding? She was alive. She had to be. She was just living a different life, maybe with a different name, maybe with children and grandchildren. Maybe with a husband. Wherever she was, Claude prayed she wasn't alone and that she'd found a way to forgive him.

A knock on the door frame made him scramble to shove the picture into the shoe box with the others. "Your cab is here."

Claude gave the priest in the doorway a plastic smile. "Eager to move into your new office, I see."

Father Wright frowned. "This isn't about the office and you know it. We're trying to help you. You need a break from this place. You've been with the Order your entire life and you've never taken a sabbatical before. It'll be good for you."

Claude scoffed as he delicately placed the shoe box of pictures in his suitcase. He knew Wright meant *good for the Order* and he couldn't disagree more. Things had been going downhill since he was overruled all those years ago and Zaphriel the Treacherous had been allowed to perform exorcisms under a human guise and a human name.

Order members siding with those two hell-beasts, like they were a pair of pariahs, showed that it was getting so much worse. Maryam's shrieking and blubbering had gotten to all of them

Maryam. It was always Maryam.

Deep down, Claude knew he deserved this. Maybe they all did for their weakness, but that didn't mean it was over. He could still save the Order, maybe the world if it came to that. He had friends where he was going. Powerful friends.

Claude pulled the handle from the top of his suitcase and rolled it out of his office without looking back. The Order had made it perfectly clear that, for now, there was nothing for him here. He comforted himself as he stepped out into the sunlight with the fact that things would not always be this way. Maybe Wright was right. Maybe he did need time away from the problem to get a better idea of how to solve it.

Wright leaned down to give his friend one final worried look through the open window. "You'll be missed. Call when you arrive in Rome?"

Claude continued to wear a fake smile. Wright really did mean well. He just didn't know any better. "Of course, but I don't want to hear any complaints when I wake you up in the middle of the night."

"Oh, you know I wouldn't." Wright slapped the hood of the cab with a grin, apparently convinced there was no bad blood between him and one of his oldest friends. "Take care."

"You as well." Claude rolled up his window and turned to the driver. "To the airport, if you'd please."

Detroit flew by in a familiar, bitter-sweet blur. It was a good city filled with good people, despite what people said and the darkness it harbored.

Flowers, candles, garlands, and pictures overflowing outside Woodlawn Cemetery weighed heavily on Claude's shoulders, reminding him how close that darkness had come to rearing its ugly head. He'd give Maryam this much: she'd ensured it would lie dormant for a little while longer.

But it really would be only a little while. Now that she'd tasted it, he doubted she could keep away.

It wasn't her fault. It was her nature.

Then again, maybe that was Claude's fault too. All the more reason he had to fix this.

Once on the highway, he dug his reading for the journey out of his carry-on. Out of the corner of his eye, he saw the taxi driver give the book a double-take. Claude didn't blame him. His paperback copy of the second volume of *The Three Books of Occult Philosophy* was hefty, to say the least.

Reading eased his nerves, despite the weight of the book. It would be worth it when he found the answers and his friends in the Vatican shared what they had as well—it was the only way to gather allies strong enough to defeat this evil before it swallowed the Order and the world around it.

Angels had beaten back bands of demons in the First Age. Claude was sure the right ones would come alongside the right believers, true believers, and gladly do it again.

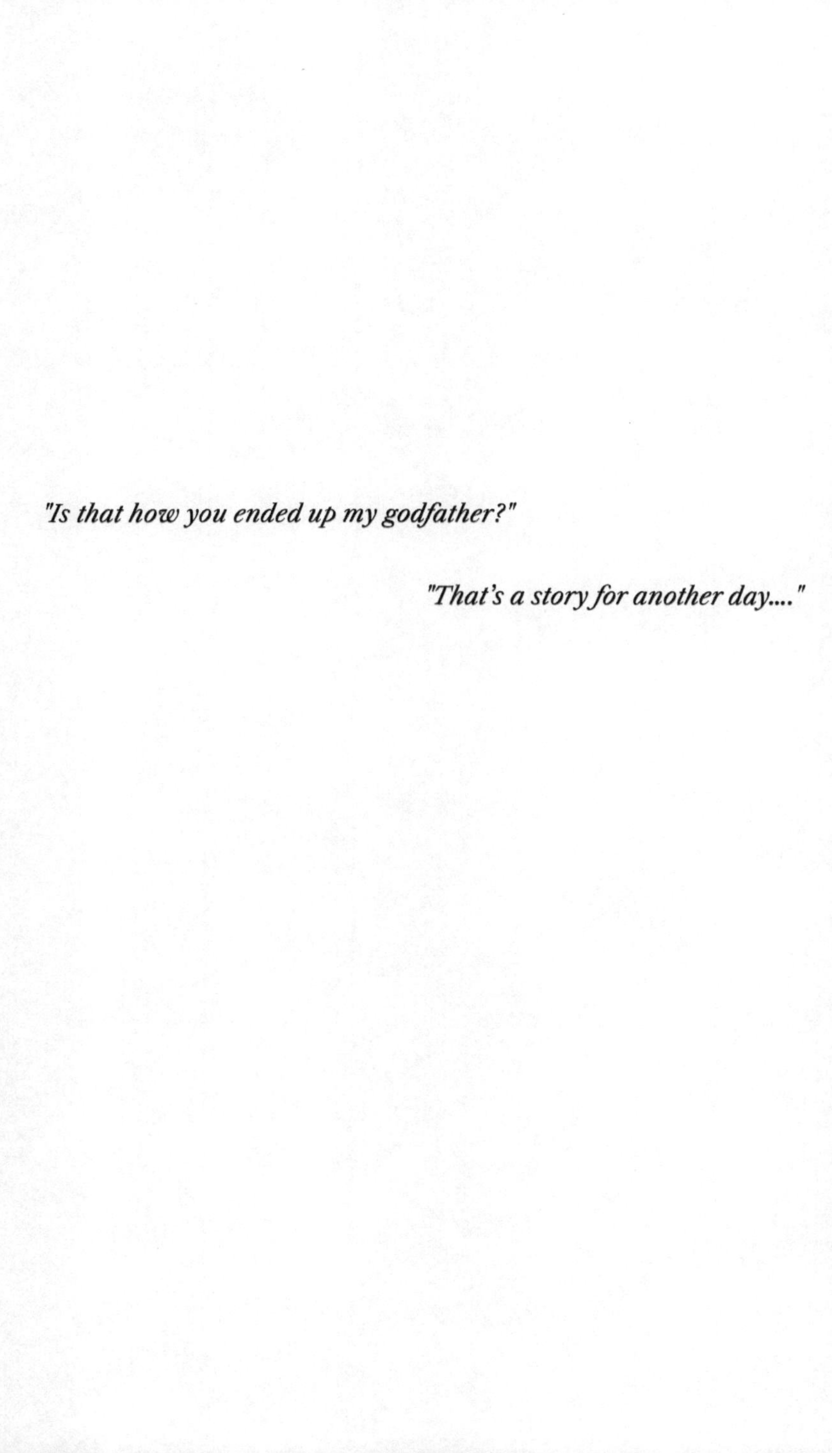

"Is that how you ended up my godfather?"

"That's a story for another day...."

DEMONS & MUSEUMS
A ROSARY'S REJECTS NOVELETTE

The book in Zaphriel's hands housed knowledge older than fallen empires. Older than the language it was written in and older than a thousand languages before it. It predated the very *idea* of books and the trees that had been cut down to make this one. Zaphriel flipped through the pages, amazed that humanity had managed to take even slivers of deep, unknowable secrets and boil them down into printed words and pictures. For the first time in a long time, Zaphriel was reminded that there was nothing "mere" about humans.

"I have a question," said one human in particular, breaking Zaphriel's concentration.

Zaphriel closed his eyes, breathed deep, and turned to face the human with a plastic smile. "Yes, Summoner? What is your question?"

Hiro Bishop kicked his feet up onto his desk and snapped the papers in his hand upright. "Have you ever researched what people have written about you? Like how some people look themselves up on the internet?" A smirk crept onto his face, revealing the man's hunt for a reaction rather than an answer.

Zaphriel allowed his pleasant expression to melt into exasperation. "No, Summoner. I have never looked into what is written about me." He shut the book and placed it back on Hiro's shelf.

Hiro's expression turned calculating as he watched Zaphriel's movements. "Are you alright? You sound tired."

"I'm fine." Zaphriel straightened his shirt, as if attempting to remove the wrinkles in the fabric could remove the dark circles under his eyes. "Maryam didn't want to sleep last night is all."

Hiro frowned. "You could have called Sarah or I."

"It's really alright." Zaphriel began to study the rest of Hiro's shelves to keep himself busy. Truth be told, he was always tired, even when the two-year-old Hiro had summoned Zaphriel to protect slept through the night. As a celestial being burdened with eternity, he was always tired, even if existing in the current mortal coil meant that the most mind-melting aspects of eternity were somewhat dulled.

Hiro looked back to his papers for a moment, then back to Zaphriel. "You're not the least bit curious about what people have said about the notorious Zaphriel the Treacherous through the centuries?"

"I'm sure whatever they have to say pales in comparison to what I was called in the depths of Hell, Summoner." Zaphriel tried to keep his rising annoyance locked away. Demons weren't meant to show any malcontent with their masters. They'd lost the right when they had rebelled against Heaven.

Zaphriel's gaze darted up to the ornate clock above Hiro's desk. "You should finish reviewing the report, Summoner," he said, softening his tone as much as he could. "It's nearly three and Father Bob has to leave early today."

Hiro craned his neck to look at the clock. "So it is." He settled into his chair and looked back at the papers and his eyebrows pulled together as if he meant to finally finish reading the chronicle of Zaphriel's weekly activities. "No worries. I'm almost done." No sooner did Zaphriel drop his gaze back to the shelf, did Hiro say, "You forgot to mention that I sent you to pick up the mail yesterday morning at approximately seven a.m." Zaphriel looked up to find that damn smirk again. "You were out of my sight for an entire three minutes. You could have gotten up to all kinds of dark mischief."

Zaphriel inhaled deeply with his jaw clenched. "My apologies for the mistake." He crossed the study and reached for the papers. "I'll annotate it at once."

Hiro yanked the papers out of his reach and readjusted his sleek round glasses. "I'm only joking, Zaphriel."

Zaphriel knew that and he hated it. The jokes and the questions were Hiro's attempt to pry beyond Zaphriel's human façade. Past the multi-eyed, multi-winged creature that he had summoned in his rundown Boston apartment two years ago, searching for something Zaphriel had lost eons ago.

Hiro set the papers on his desk, pulled up his chair, and reached for a pen. "If it makes you feel any better, I don't like this whole process any more than you do." He tested the pen on a notepad and then scribbled his signature at the bottom of the last page. "It's a waste of everyone's time."

Not liking the process was an understatement for Zaphriel. *Despise* was more accurate. He hated recalling every minute of every day of his life, hated turning it in for Hiro to review, and hated turning it in to Hiro's employer, the Rosary Order, upon Hiro's signature. It was embarrassing. Distrusting a demon was one thing. It was prudent. Natural, even. Expecting him to report his every move to anyone other than the human who had summoned him was downright insulting. There was punishment for rebelling against his Father and the angels, then there was...this.

Hiro got to his feet, tapped the stack of papers against the desk, and slipped them into a blank cream folder. "Looks like you had a rather quiet week."

Zaphriel fought the urge to roll his eyes. Hiro had summoned him to babysit an actual baby—most weeks were quiet. Not that Zaphriel was complaining. He was happy to change all the diapers, do all the laundry, and watch all the mind-numbing cartoons in the world without complaint since it meant he was free from the tortures of Hell.

"We'll drop this by Father Bob's office and be on our way." A glint of mischief touched Hiro's dark eyes. "It's pretty quiet around here. Might as well leave a bit early, too, right?"

Zaphriel didn't reply. Demons were the last creatures anyone should ask about bending the rules.

The two stepped out of the office and into the stark white corridors of the Rosary Order—a secret society of spiritual professionals from various traditions fighting against the supernatural forces of darkness. Most major cities had a branch office, some in nondescript churches, some below the city streets, like the Detroit office where Hiro and

Zaphriel found themselves. Despite the Order's diversity, its name and the number of people in cassocks gave away its ancient, Catholic roots.

Zaphriel felt those roots tangle around his neck as he walked down the corridor with dozens of pairs of eyes on him. Agreeing to Hiro's contract meant that Zaphriel had a human body all his own, but everyone still knew what he was. In such a small, close-knit world, people talked. Hiro liked to tease Zaphriel that it was because his human façade was exceptionally handsome—dark, deep-set eyes, a strong jaw, a muscular build, and thick platinum gray-tinted hair that he preferred to wear long—but Zaphriel knew better. He'd dwelled on Earth enough through the centuries to know the differences between lust, hatred, and fear in another's gaze. One came when the Powers that Be designed your body to tempt humanity. The others came when you were the first demon to be contacted by an exorcist in an organization's history.

Father Bob's office was tucked away in a far corner, which kept a good number of prying eyes off Zaphriel, for which he was grateful. Unfortunately, this meant dealing with Father Bob in person, which had yet to be a pleasant experience. Hiro knocked and received a gruff, "Come in," in return. The exorcist gave Zaphriel a wry look as he opened the door.

The old priest's office smelled faintly of dust and mildew, no matter how pristine he kept it. Zaphriel had long suspected it came from the ancient man himself, but he wasn't about to ask. Father Bob looked up from an enormous tome and eyed the two over a pair of slender reading glasses that made the rest of his features appear too small for his face.

"Ah, Hiro." Father Bob removed the glasses, only slightly improving his appearance. Zaphriel wondered if the real issue was the near-permanent look of disappointment on the man's face rather than his features. "That time again, already?"

Hiro gave a tight-lipped smile as he handed over the report. "Funny how Thursday comes around the same day each week."

Father Bob pointed his glasses at Hiro with a dirty look as he opened the folder. "Mind yourself. Time doesn't move the same way when you're old."

Hiro chuckled. "I'll remember that." He craned his neck to study the open book. "We didn't interrupt your devotional time, did we?"

"A new translation of the Sinai Bible, actually," said Father Bob as he removed the pages of the report. "Complete with Father James Calvin's commentary."

"You'll have to let me borrow it when you're finished."

Father Bob scoffed. "Heretical rubbish. Every word. How a man like that rose to authority in the San Franciscan branch of the Order will forever be a mystery. Between him and the research department going off the rails, I don't know what this organization is coming to."

Hiro raised an eyebrow. "What's the research department up to?"

"Bah!" Father waved his glasses dismissively. "Some of the young ones have gotten it into their heads that we might be able to enlist certain demons to help with exorcisms." He pointed the glasses up at Hiro. "I told them to look at you and what a tight hold you have on *that* one for proof that they were wasting their time." He pointed the glasses at Zaphriel. "All they would be doing is doubling their work."

Hiro blinked. "And you didn't think to send them my way?"

Zaphriel watched his master's hands, clasped behind his back, clenched into entangled fists.

Father Bob snorted and put the glasses back on his face. "Of course not. You're a busy man. No need to bother yourself with such nonsense."

Zaphriel caught the way Hiro's jaw twitched with tension as Father Bob scanned the report. A tense silence hung in the air as the priest read. Judging by the way the old man leaned back in his chair and hummed to himself, he was none the wiser about it.

"The little girl had a birthday, did she?" Father Bob asked.

Hiro nodded. "Indeed, she did. Doesn't feel possible that she's two already."

"Hm." Father Bob continued to scan the report. "And she hasn't manifested anything...strange?"

Zaphriel tensed and held his breath.

"Not at all," Hiro stood a little taller, his shoulders back. "She's a perfectly normal little girl." He motioned to the stack of paper. "If she were anything different, we would have reported as much, both in Zaphriel's weekly report and in a separate message sent to headquarters in Boston."

Zaphriel released the air from his lungs, feeling silly for his reaction. Hiro had been truthful enough. Zaphriel's charge, Maryam, was turning out to be perfectly normal, but questions about her always made the walls close in on Zaphirel a bit. He'd had children of his own, once. The fear that Maryam might one day end up like them threatened to make him hyperventilate. It didn't matter how irrational the fear was. Sometimes he wondered if that fear, born of an unhealed heart, was meant to be a part of his eternal punishment.

Intentional or not, Zaphriel knew he deserved it.

Father Bob stroked his first of three chins as he continued to read. Eventually satisfied, he clacked the stack of papers on the desk and slipped them back into their folder. "Looks good enough, from first glance. I'll give it a more thorough read-through later and make sure it gets on Father Samuel's desk." He pulled out a pocket watch. "I hate to rush you out, Hiro, but I have a doctor's appointment."

Hiro's eyebrows rose as he began toward the door. "It won't be going to Father Claude anymore?"

Father Bob stood and took his coat from the back of his chair. "Didn't you hear? Claude's headmaster over at St. Mary's now."

"Hm. That's a..." Hiro took a few steps to think about his response. "That's a...choice, I suppose."

Father Bob snorted. "That's the most diplomatic way I've heard it put, but I can't say he didn't need the change. The man's been in the field too long. He's never taken a single sabbatical."

"And being in charge of *children* is supposed to serve as a sabbatical?"

"You know what? I said the same thing."

Zaphriel fought to keep a smile off his face. He didn't like Father Jonathan Claude any more than he liked Father Bob, but Hiro was right. Even to Zaphriel, demons made more sense than children. A demon's method of causing terror and mischief was rather routine—possession of a victim, the movement of objects from one place to another, various bumps in the night. With children, it was anyone's guess what they'd do from one moment to the next. His oldest had reached twenty-two, and even then, he had been unpredictable.

Zaphriel shoved the thought away, annoyed with himself for letting so many thoughts of his kids bubble up.

"We'll get out of your hair, Father," Hiro said, moving to open the door. "Thank you for taking time to speak to us."

"Of course. And Hiro?"

Hiro paused.

Father Bob eyed Zaphriel over the rim of his glasses, then looked back to Hiro. "Stay vigilant. Don't fall for his docile veneer like those fools down in research."

One of Zaphriel's eyebrows ticked up before he could stop himself. If Father Bob was faced with the constant threat of hellfire, he'd probably end up pretty docile himself.

Hiro gave a tight-lipped smile that didn't reach his eyes. "I appreciate the reminder, Father." He departed, nearly leaving Zaphriel behind with his angry pace.

Zaphriel followed out the door and again pretended not to notice the stares that tracked him. He even did his best to avoid glancing up at the security camera in the elevator that took them up to the church above the Order, St. Mary's Liturgical Church, an interdenominational fellowship nestled inside what had once been the grandest Catholic cathedral in Detroit. The building was still grand, thanks to the Order's care for the towering pillars and stained glass, but it was no longer Catholic. Christians from an eclectic array of traditions gathered on any given Sunday. Additional services had been incorporated in recent years to accommodate Order members of newer, arguably more eccentric, denominations, much to the scandal of the old guard.

Tension melted from Zaphriel's shoulders as he stepped out into the mid-spring sunshine. He closed his eyes and breathed in the anonymity that came with walking down a city street, feeling lighter, even if that anonymity happened to smell faintly of car exhaust.

Hiro marched across the parking lot as if he were on a mission. "The audacity of that man," he grumbled. "Talking about you like a dog on a leash."

Zaphriel shrugged, slipping his hands into his pockets. "I've endured worse."

"That doesn't make it right." Hiro snapped, digging out his keys and punching the unlock button. "And to discourage the research department's efforts without even asking me if I wanted to talk to them. The absolute *gall*!"

A faint smile tugged at Zaphriel's lips as he slipped into the car, hitting his knees on the glove compartment thanks to his towering height and the size of the Civic. Hiro started the car and pulled out of the parking spot in stormy silence. Zaphriel propped his elbow on the windowsill and watched as the Detroit skyline came into view alongside the highway, absently listening to the radio. The station insisted that they only played the best music of the 80's, 90's, and today, reminding Zaphriel, with just a bit of awe, that it hadn't just been a different century the last time he was on Earth; it had been an entirely different millennium. Two years and he wasn't used to that yet.

He stole a glimpse at Hiro as they settled into the flow of traffic, wondering what the man was thinking. Zaphriel had wondered that about Hiro more than any other human he had worked for. Then again, most humans summoned demons to serve them out of greed, whether that be greed for money, sex, power, or knowledge. Hiro had summoned Zaphriel for none of that.

"I want you to protect this child," Hiro had said, unblinking against the hellfire that had encased Zaphriel in the binding circle, shielding the squalling infant in his arms from the heat. *"Bind her and keep her safe."*

"And what do you demand for yourself?" Zaphriel had asked, his voice rumbling and ethereal.

"Be this child's guardian. Be her friend and her guide. Do this for me and you escape the tortures of Hell."

Zaphriel had crouched down and tasted the human blood pooling in Hiro's sliced skin, which bound him in a mortal body that stretched and wrapped around his unknowable soul. No sooner had his new, unsteady human feet touched the floor was a baby with cloud-white wings and bright green eyes with pupils like a goat's thrown into his arms. An ankida'shi baby. Half mortal, half angel—fallen, no doubt. The first of her kind since the dawn of human history.

"Her name is Maryam," Hiro had said. *"She's my niece."*

Hiro's voice broke through Zaphriel's thoughts. "Do you think it's possible? For a demon to exorcise another demon from a human body?"

Zaphriel blinked as he mind caught up to the present. "I've never thought about it, but so long as the demon performing the exorcism outranks the one inhabiting the victim, I don't see why not. Your biggest challenge would be summoning a demon who was high enough in Heaven's hierarchy to have authority over the demon you're facing, and then designing a deal in a way that they can't turn on you. Exorcisms are chaotic. Who knows what a high-ranking demon might try to use that situation for."

Hiro was quiet for a moment. "What indeed," he mused.

Zaphriel tensed, uncomfortable with the calculating tone of Hiro's voice.

"What were you before you fell, again?"

Zaphriel swallowed. "A Throne, Summoner."

Hiro's eyebrows shot up and gave an impressed whistle. "One of the top three? Impressive."

It had been impressive, standing guard between the Creator's inner heavenly sanctum and the rest of creation; Zaphriel's thousands of eyes always watching, six wings beating in time with the breath of the universe. Then, for reasons only known to the Creator above, Zaphriel had been selected to be a Watcher—an agent from Heaven sent to Earth to keep tabs on humanity as it grew and developed. His rank hadn't meant much to the humans he had befriended, then loved, then fought beside in the rebellion. It had meant even less to his jailers in the depths of Hell.

Hiro's phone rang, rooting Zaphriel in the now. He wrestled the clunky Nokia brick from his pocket and placed it against his ear.

"Hello?...Yeah, I know the case...." Hiro's brow scrunched as he listened. "No, I—Andre, no." His voice sharpened. "Andre. We have two whole children at home. We can't...I mean neither of them are old enough to stay home alone for an entire weekend. Maryam just turned two, for goodness' sake. What did you think I mean?"

A laugh caught in Zaphriel's throat before he could stop it. He hadn't the slightest idea what Hiro had meant by "two whole children" either.

The sound drew Hiro's attention. Zaphriel froze as Hiro's gaze slid to him and locked on, filling the demon with instant dread.

"If Sarah and I both have to come, then Zaphriel is watching the children."

Zaphriel heard Andre exclaim, "What!?" at the same time as himself.

"If the Order wants to drag a pair of parents out to the field at the same time, then so be it, but do you have any idea how hard it is to find someone in the parish to take both a twelve and a two year old with this short notice?" Hiro rolled his eyes. "He's a demon, Andre, not a damn coyote."

Zaphriel's mouth dried with panic. "Summoner, you can't seriously be considering—"

Hiro held the phone to his chest. "Zaphriel, I'm on the phone." He brought it back to his ear and listened. "Fine. You tell them that, then." The phone gave a shrill beep, making Hiro wince. "I only have a minute left on my phone. I'll call you back from home." He hung up in the middle of whatever Andre was saying and wrestled the phone back into his slacks, muttering, "Could have sworn I just put an hour's worth of minutes on this thing."

"Summoner, don't do this," Zaphriel pleaded. "Call the parish. St. Mary's has to have someone who can take Matthew and Maryam for the weekend. The Order knows you have children."

Hiro scoffed. "And what are we supposed to do with you? Stick you in a closet? It's been two damn years. I'm sick of them treating you like a grenade without a pin."

Zaphriel massaged his temple. "This is about Father Bob, isn't it?"

"I have the capacity to be angry about more than one thing at a time, don't you worry."

"Drawing attention to me isn't going to help anything. It's not going to help *Maryam*."

"Zaphriel the Treacherous."

Zaphriel stiffened with the harsh authority in Hiro's voice.

"You're to stop arguing with me on this matter until I open it back up for discussion. That's an order."

Heat slithered down Zaphriel's spine as the magic of their contract took hold, making him shiver and stretch as if he had to make room under his skin for the invisible binds Hiro had placed on him. His jaw clenched and his throat tightened, his own body threatening to lash out against him if he so much as thought too hard about disobeying. At best, the magic would choke him until he fell in line. At worst, his body would begin to tear itself apart from the inside out, no doubt starting with Zaphriel's lungs.

Drowning in one's own blood sounded like quite the damper to put on a day, so Zaphriel shut his mouth and turned back to the window, hand cupped over his mouth as he watched the buildings glide by.

Hiro pulled the car off the highway two exits early. Zaphriel turned and watched him silently as the exorcist took one unfamiliar turn after another until they pulled into a parking spot outside a storefront framed by a fenced-off patio. The warm green sign above the business read *The Stout* in faded gold lettering.

Zaphriel thought long and hard before he spoke. "What are we doing, Summoner?"

"What does it look like we're doing?" Hiro turned the car off, then turned to Zaphriel with a smirk, any annoyance from their argument left behind on the highway. "We're getting a drink."

Zaphriel held back his reply until he could figure out how to call Hiro's idea stupid without getting smacked with another command. "It's hardly four, Summoner."

Hiro shrugged as he got out of the car. "You know what they say: It's five o'clock somewhere."

"No one *actually* says—"

Hiro shut the door and rounded the car.

"...that." Zaphriel massaged his temple with a groan and followed Hiro into the restaurant.

Between the low lighting, rich dark wooden walls, and the lively bagpipe music, *The Stout* proved to be a comfortable little place. The hostess at the door beamed at Hiro and greeted him by name. After routine pleasantries, she led the two to a small booth in the far back corner. When she moved to set menus on the table, Hiro waved them away.

"Just the regular, if you please, Jan. Both for me and my colleague here."

Jan nodded and made her way towards the bar.

Zaphriel snorted as he slid into the booth. "We're colleagues now?"

Hiro smirked as he folded his hands on the table. "Would you rather me tell the truth?"

"You wouldn't."

Hiro ticked up an eyebrow and Zaphriel's stomach plummeted to the floor.

A blonde waitress came by with two pints of dark beer and a smile aimed at Zaphriel, curiosity in her eyes. "It's been a while, Hiro. Who's your friend?"

"Hi, Jan. This is Zaphriel the Treacherous." Hiro slid a pint towards himself. "He's an ancient demon from the dawn of time who fought against God and His angels to preserve humanity's freedom to explore the occult sciences, but his side lost and he was damned to Hell." Hiro sipped a bit of foam from his beer. "He goes by Zack for short."

The blood drained from Zaphriel's face as he stared at Hiro in horror.

Jan tossed her head back as she laughed. "This is why you're my favorite, Hiro. I never know what you're going to say."

Hiro flashed her an innocent grin. "That's why Hollywood pays me the big bucks."

Jan went back to smiling at Zaphriel, looking him up and down. "Is Zaphriel the Treasonous a part in Hiro's next movie?"

"It's Treacherous," Zaphriel corrected, which felt stupid. He caught the mischievous light in Hiro's eyes as the exorcist sat there, letting his demon flounder. "And yes."

Jan giggled, her smile showing all of her teeth. "Acting sounds so fun. I couldn't do the crazy schedule, though."

"It's...rigorous, to be sure."

Jan giggled yet again. "You look tough enough to handle it."

Zaphriel blinked. What was happening?

An awkward silence set in. Jan dropped her hand from her hip and began back towards the bar. "Well, I'll leave you two alone and check on you in a bit."

"Thank you, miss." Zaphriel waited for Jan to be out of earshot before whirling on Hiro. "What the hell was that?"

Hiro wiped foam from his top lip. "I believe the kids call it 'flirting'. Are you interested? I can probably drop hints and get you her number, if you want."

Zaphriel narrowed his eyes.

"The hostess, maybe? Her name's Jackie. Real sweet. Smart, too. She's about to move to start her hospital residency, though. so it might have to be long distance. Wants to be a brain surgeon."

"I meant spilling my whole identity and the part about Hollywood."

Hiro chuckled. "Oh, that." He took another sip of beer. "Turns out, if you tell people you're a creative type, they excuse all sorts of eccentric things. As far as anyone here knows, I'm a freelance screenwriter." He shrugged. "*Drag Me to Hell, Paranormal Activity*—you know, small productions like that." Hiro smirked at his own joke, an amusement lost on Zackary, who continued to scowl. "Pretty sure one of the cooks here is gay, if it's men you like. No judgment here, and he makes a shepherd's pie that is to *die* for."

Zaphriel's frayed nerves snapped. He didn't have time for Hiro's stupid attempts to build camaraderie. Not when he had apparently lost his mind and blatantly rocked the Order's boat.. "Why the hell are we here, Summoner?"

Hiro's chipper demeanor mellowed as his gaze darted across Zaphriel's sour expression. "I thought this would be a safe place to talk. No Order. No distractions. You and me. Man to man."

Zaphriel scowled and reached for his beer. "Technically, I'm not a man." He lifted the pint to his lips, hoping the alcohol might calm him a bit. "I'm a demon."

"Is that why you're being so fucking difficult?"

Zaphriel inhaled his beer, choking and sending a stream dribbling down his front as he coughed. Hiro didn't swear. Not like this. Not at Zaphriel. Not at anyone.

"About watching the kids?" Zaphriel yanked a handful of napkins from the dispenser and dabbed at his shirt. "I'm not being difficult, I'm being sensible."

"Liar." Hiro folded his arms. "You've been scared to put yourself on the Order's radar since I summoned you. You're trying to make yourself as small as possible, like a dog afraid to be beaten."

Anger pricked Zaphriel's chest. That's exactly what he was, wasn't it? A dog that had been beaten down when it dared to disobey. He thought Hiro understood that. The rest of the Order certainly did.

If Hiro knew how below the belt his words were, he didn't seem to care. He kept talking. "When they see that we can trust you, doors are going to open up, like the one to the research department. That could change things radically, both for you and for Maryam."

Zaphriel hardly heard him. He was remembering a different door opening up. One that flew open just as he was telling his youngest to hide, because she had stayed home sick while his wife had walked her sister to school and that was the last day he would see any of them alive. Why hadn't he held them all tighter that morning? Why hadn't he taken them all and run for the mountains when his brothers had warned that the angels were coming?

"Imagine what she'll be able to do if—"

"No."

Hiro's brow furrowed. "What do you mean 'no'?"

Maryam was two years old. Fucking *two*. Angels had dashed babies younger than that against rocks as they raided every Watcher village along the Euphrates, not just Zaphriel's. The blood of babies had streaked that river red. "It's just...I said no, Summoner."

"Why are you being such a coward? If you keep acting like this, I'm just going to order you to—"

Zaphriel slammed a hand on the table, rattling the pints. "*You're going to get Maryam killed, you naive dipshit!*"

He froze in his seat, the roaring memories in his head cut short by the tense silence of the restaurant. Why was it quiet? Why wasn't anyone talking? He stole a glance towards the rest of the restaurant to find everyone staring at him and Hiro with nervous expressions. Jan smiled down at her current pair of customers, muttered something, and headed towards Hiro and Zaphriel.

"Is everything alright?" She leaned in with a grin that gave away her own unease.

"Y-Yes," Zaphriel answered. "I apologize, I...um..." He curled his hand to a fist and rapped it against the table. He'd never liked lying. Never been good at it.

"We're sorry, Jan." Hiro leaned in and lowered his voice. "Zack left the service about six months ago. His last tour in Iraq was..." Hiro paused, deciding how to finish his lie, "...dicey. He still has trouble sometimes."

Zaphriel sank back in his seat, wishing he could fold himself into the pleather. "Sum—Hiro, don't—"

Hiro held up a hand to stop him. "It's okay. You don't have to be embarrassed."

"I'm so sorry." Jan gently put a hand on Zaphriel's shoulder. "Can I get you anything?"

Zaphriel forced a smile. "No, I should be okay now. Sorry to cause a scene."

"It's okay. Trust me, we've had worse." Jan squeezed his shoulder. "Let me know if there's anything I can do."

"Thank you, Jan," Hiro said. He watched her walk away, his expression calculating as he watched the rest of the restaurant. Once she was out of earshot and chatter had resumed, Hiro turned to Zaphriel. "She forgot to thank you for your service."

"Stolen valor?" Zaphriel hissed. "Seriously?"

"I was working with what I was given." Hiro's eyes locked onto Zaphriel, unblinking and calculating. "I knew that look on your face. Our more senior exorcists get it if they're made to talk about their worst cases for too long." His gaze eased into worry. "I'm sorry. I shouldn't have said I was going to force you into something you so strongly opposed for Maryam's sake. I didn't mean to bring back painful memories."

Zaphriel clenched his jaw to keep his mouth from falling open. Millennia upon millennia of existence and damnation and not once had he ever gotten an apology for...*anything.* Not from other demons. Not from his summoners. No one. He didn't even know what he was supposed to do with one now that he had it.

Hiro spared him from having to figure it out. "I need you to explain it to me, though," he said. "Why don't you want to stay with the kids? What has you so spooked? It's just two days and we'll only be a phone call away."

Zaphriel swallowed, his mouth working again now that his heart had slowed. He balled up a napkin in one hand, watching himself wrinkle and fold the cheap paper to keep himself rooted in the present. "No one was safe when the angels came." He traced the condensation on his pint with his free hand, studying his warped reflection in the dark beer. "It didn't matter how small the village, how human the half-angel children looked, how mundane our lives. We had betrayed our Creator, we had led humans into sin, our children were a sin, and for that we had to be punished. Our families and homes were obliterated."

Zaphriel took a long, reflective sip of his beer, focusing on the brightness of the hops and the bite of the bitterness to keep him grounded. "The community where I lived was particularly small—just a handful of families. When the angels began cleansing the earth of us, our leaders, a triad of former Seraphim, told us to lay low. If we appeared normal and human, maybe we would be overlooked." Zaphriel flinched against the echo of that door in his mind flying open.

His daughter screaming, then silent forever on the end of an angelic spear. "It didn't work."

He tightened his grip on the napkin until his nails dug into his palm. "I lost my two girls and my wife. My son was away, conducting military training up in the mountains. He was about fifteen years older than the girls." Zaphriel took another gulp of beer, wishing for the first time in a long time that he could get drunk as easily as humans. "I lost him about a year later in one of the final battles. I don't remember which—they all blend together in my head and, if the battles were ever named, those names were lost to time."

Zaphriel's mind went quiet then. It always followed that pattern—the violently loud memories and then an exhausted, icy stillness like the heat death of a universe. A warm hand on his drew him out. He looked up to see Hiro's face, broken and pained.

"I'm so, so very sorry, Zaphriel." Hiro squeezed Zaphriel's hand. "I didn't know. I didn't even stop to wonder."

Zaphriel gingerly pulled his hand away, using both to frame his drink. "It's...well, I won't say it's okay, but I understand. There's no way you could have known, but that's why we *can't* bring attention to myself or Maryam." Zaphriel shuttered at the thought. "Bad things happen when entities like us draw attention from those in power. Those who are afraid."

"You're not 'entities,'" Hiro hissed. "You're people."

"We're demons."

"You're *souls*, just like us." Hiro ran a hand over his hair. "I understand your fears. Truly, I do, but hiding isn't going to help Maryam." His gaze sharpened. "I know what it's like to be different in this organization. It makes you a target." Hiro removed his glasses and began to polish them with the hem of his shirt. "I wasn't raised in this world like so many of the others. My parents hid their work from me. As far as I knew, they were helping St. Mary's establish a normal church in Japan. I didn't know they were forming networks and alliances with Shinto and Buddhist institutions all over the country until they were shipped back in boxes after facing a demon their scriptures were useless against. I was tossed into St. Bishop's orphanage at fifteen years old with no idea that demons and monsters were real. Let me tell you, that was not fun." Hiro slipped his glasses back on, his gaze sharp and focused. "Maryam needs to know how to hold her own. She needs to see *you* hold your own. This is how change starts."

Zaphriel shook his head. "If something goes wrong—"

"Then I will be the one to blame." A wry smile came to Hiro's place. "I'm your summoner, remember? I risked excommunication to bring you here and I'll risk it again if it means getting you and Maryam a shot at a better life."

Zaphriel frowned. It was good to remember that he wasn't in charge—after leading his own legion of lesser demons, it was still easy to forget—but so many things could go wrong.

Hiro propped his elbow on the table to use his fingers to count. "I'll write out a full itinerary for the weekend and we'll get you a cellphone that's only to be used to check in with me and for emergencies. The Order will have a copy of both the itinerary and your number so they can do a spot check if they feel the need. After this weekend, if you still feel horribly uncomfortable, nothing changes. Deal?" He extended his hand across the table.

Zaphriel only blinked at it. "You're not ordering me?"

"No. I'm asking as your friend and Maryam's uncle."

Zaphriel's heart eased in his chest. He hadn't had a friend in centuries. With friendship came trust—trust that Zaphriel could handle this. Trust that Hiro truly wanted to make things better for Maryam. Trust that they'd both die for her if they had to.

"Okay." Zaphriel took Hiro's hand and gently squeezed. A faint smirk tugged at his face. "You know, most people would say being friends with a demon makes you a heretic."

Hiro snorted as he leaned back in his seat. "Please. Everyone already calls me a heretic. They just don't know that I know." His phone chirped from his pocket and Hiro wrestled it out. "And there goes my last credit," he grumbled. "Sarah wants us home. Now."

Zaphriel chuckled at the nervous notes in Hiro's voice. "But I thought we were talking man to man. That calls for at least another round." He waved to flag down Jan.

"Very funny," Hiro said. He drummed his fingers nervously as Jan approached and Zaphriel's smile grew. "Zaphriel, don't you dare."

"Could we get the bill please, Jan?" Zaphriel asked.

Jan grinned and headed towards the bar. "Sure thing."

Hiro glared at the smirking demon, then chugged the rest of his drink. "You know, I think I liked you better as my minion."

"Too late. We made a deal. You're stuck."

Hiro paid, apologizing again for Zaphriel's military-induced outburst—at which Zaphriel cringed internally and hurried out of the bar from embarrassment—and joined Zaphriel outside. As they headed towards the car, he tossed Zaphriel the keys. "Congrats. You get to drive."

Zaphriel gave him a bewildered look. "Don't tell me you're inebriated after one drink."

"I don't know. I drank it pretty fast." Hiro opened the passenger door and slid in.

Zaphriel looked down at the keys in his hand, then at Hiro. "You can't be serious."

"Why not? I've let you drive before."

"Because a demon-possessed man broke your arm."

Hiro clicked his seatbelt. "Well, now we get to see how you do when you're *not* in a stressful situation. Think of it as a sort of, 'Welcome to being treated like a real person' initiation."

Zaphriel knew well and good that there was no such thing, but he got in the driver's seat anyway, adjusted the seat and mirror, and turned on the car. Once he got back on the highway, he dared to fiddle with the radio dial, changing to a rock 'n roll station, much to Hiro's surprise. He drummed on the steering wheel, savoring the hum of the road beneath him and the glide of the wheels. The sense of freedom it gave him made him feel like maybe good things could happen to him on Earth.

Almost.

Zaphriel pulled the car up to the quaint little house in the quaint little cul-de-sac primarily owned by the Order. Many of the houses had been gifted to the organization at the passing of retired members, so while they ran on the outdated, the neighborhood was safe and the neighbors knew how to keep a secret. It wasn't home—nowhere was home when you were damned—but it was shelter in every way that Zaphriel needed.

Inside, the usual smell of lilac had been overpowered by the warm scent of tomato sauce, bread, and garlic. Zaphriel could see into the kitchen from the doorway where Matthew, Hiro's son, sat in a dining table chair pulled in front of the stove with a gaming device in his hand. On his lap lounged a red-haired toddler, bare feet dangling and her red hair a bird's nest of curls and displaced clips as she munched on an apple slice.

She pointed to the screen with one chubby baby finger. "Up!" she instructed. "Matty, up!"

"I know!" Matthew shook his shaggy brown hair from his dark eyes and mashed the buttons feverously. "No, no, no!" A crashing sound came from the game. Matthew threw his head back with a groan. Maryam mimicked the sound and thrust her head back against his chest with a smile, happy to be included.

"What are you two clowns up to?" Hiro called as he hung his jacket.

Maryam whirled at the sound of his voice. Her normal, human green eyes lit up at the sight of the two as she gave a squeal of joy and crawled from Matthew's lap.

The boy put his game on the counter so he could help her down. "Making sure dinner doesn't boil over." He shook his shaggy hair from his eyes again. "Mom's mad at you."

Hiro sighed. "I know." He beamed as Maryam ran his way with her arms outstretched. "Hey there, cupcake!" He groaned lightheartedly as he leaned down to scoop her up, wincing as his knees popped. He ignored the ache and tossed the toddler in the air, making her giggle.

That sound sparked a candle in Zaphriel's chest he thought had burned down to nothing. He smiled as he watched the two, despite himself. He couldn't help it whenever it struck him how alive Maryam was—her wild hair, her alight eyes, perpetually stained cheeks, and babbling words and laughter.

She was *alive*. The first ankida'shi in thousands upon thousands of years, alive.

Sarah's voice broke through the moment. "Hiro? Can you come up here please?"

Zaphriel lifted his gaze to find the petite blonde woman standing atop the short staircase, surveying her domain with a frigid look and the air of a displeased queen.

Hiro's smile faltered. "Coming, my love." He handed Maryam to Zaphriel and muttered, "Pray for me."

Zaphriel snorted as he placed Maryam on his hip.

The toddler offered the demon her apple slice. "Zack, appo?" They'd tried their best to get her to say, "Zaph." She didn't struggle with any other words that included an *f* sound in it, yet he'd been "Zack" for months now. The family had ultimately given up and let it be.

"No, thank you," he said. "You eat it."

She shoved it towards his face and Zaphriel dodged, not trusting where those hands or the apple had been.

"You eat it," he said. "Go *nom, nom, nom*." Zaphriel made exaggerated chewing motions, making the little girl giggle. She put the apple in her mouth, chewing it the animated way Zaphriel had showed her.

"There you go." Zaphriel kissed Maryam's forehead and stroked her hair, taking a moment to reach beyond the physical world to check the spell he had woven around her tiny soul. There were no frays. No weak links in the magic that glinted like a mesh of golden silk, cloaking

Maryam's true nature from the world that would hate her for it. Kill her for it.

"Are you really going to babysit Maryam this weekend?" Matthew asked, beginning to play his game again.

"I believe I'm babysitting the both of you," Zaphriel answered.

"You can't really *baby* sit me," Matthew argued, eyes locked again on the screen. "I'm twelve."

"Then I'll twelve-year-old sit you then."

"Can we go to the museum? Mom and Dad were going to take me to the Power Man exhibit since this is the last weekend it's here, but they can't go now."

"I'll talk to your father about it."

Matthew's eyes lit up. "Oh, hell yeah."

Zaphriel frowned. "Language, Matt."

"Hell's in the Bible," Matthew reminded the demon.

Zaphriel raised an eyebrow. "You weren't quoting the Bible, were you?"

Matthew pursed his lips, but didn't argue. The last time he had insisted on using a bad word from the Bible, "ass," he'd wound up with a grounding that hadn't ended until he had completed an entire exegesis on the word. Zaphriel had been impressed by the boy's research skills. Matthew seemed to have a grasp on ancient Greek, Latin, and Aramaic that could put some adults in the Order to shame.

A pot on the stove hissed as it boiled over.

"Matt!" Zaphriel set Maryam down to dash across the kitchen and remove the pot from the red-hot burner. "I thought you said you were watching dinner."

"Sorry!" Matthew scrambled from his chair, flitting around Zaphriel in a panic. "I'm sorry."

Zaphriel turned off the stovetop before looking at the boy, doing his best to keep what he knew was a "dad look" from his face. The efforts didn't seem to matter—Matthew's face scrunched into worry, his mouth in a severe frown as if a boiled-over pot was likely to get him kicked out of the house. Zaphriel knew it wouldn't end with anything that severe, but Sarah's lectures could be...a lot.

Zaphriel release the tension from his shoulders. He knew what it was like to live under the shadow of high standards. "It's fine. Let's just be more mindful next time, okay?" He fought the urge to ruffle Matthew's hair. They might be civil with each other, friendly even, but placing a hand on the human boy was a line Zaphriel wasn't brave enough to cross, as if he might corrupt him just from a comforting touch. "Let's get dinner set up so it's ready for your parents."

Matthew's expression eased into something close to a smile. "Okay."

The two worked together to set the table and serve up the food, taking turns placating Maryam, who insisted on helping in her own two-year-old way. The table looked fit for a Norman Rockwell painting by the time Hiro and Sarah joined the rest of their household, Hiro looking content, though a bit worn, and Sarah fiercely scowling.

She strode through the kitchen, eyes locked on the back door. "Zaphriel. Outside. We need to talk."

"Oh...okay." Zaphriel looked to Hiro as he finished putting Maryam in her highchair. Hiro shooed him away and took over toddler duty, stripping Maryam of her shirt.

Zaphriel followed Sarah out into the small square yard. He stood by the door, stiff as a guard on duty, as his summoner's wife paced the length of the concrete patio. She halted at the far corner, massaged her temple, and dug in her pocket. Zaphriel watched, eyes bulging, as the demonologist took out a pack of cigarettes, lit one, and took a long drag of it with her eyes closed.

She tilted her head back and let the smoke out in a quick, slender stream like steam from a kettle. "I thought I'd beat this habit, you know?" She brought the cigarette back to her lips. "It was the only bad habit from my sister that stuck with me." She took another drag, then dropped her eyes to the cement as she flicked away the ashes. "These aren't even really mine. I got a new office at work, and they were in the desk. I should have thrown them away, but something told me today was going to be a *day*."

Zaphriel wasn't sure whether Sarah was even really talking to him. He swallowed against his dry throat as he tried to figure out what to say. "I'm sorry. I know my presence causes you a great deal of stress."

Sarah shook her head. "It shouldn't. You're the reason Maryam's still alive. You're the reason I still have a part of my sister." She let out a sour chuckle and gestured to her cigarette. "Other than this, of course."

Zaphriel hadn't known Mary Bishop. After Hiro had thrust Maryam into his arms, he'd bound her powers, rendering the baby mortal, and then walked with her back and forth in the cramped living room, both still naked and new. He'd listened to Hiro and Sarah's worried mutters as Maryam's mother continued to lose blood. After what Zaphriel had figured was about an hour, Hiro had whisked Mary away. Sarah had come into the living room and nearly jumped out of her skin, as if she had forgotten that her husband had conducted an unsanctioned demonic summoning fifty feet from where her sister had just given birth. She'd hurried into her and Hiro's bedroom and returned with clothes that she shoved in Zaphriel's arms as she whisked Maryam away.

Their relationship hadn't improved much in the two years since that night, but Zaphriel didn't begrudge Sarah her coldness. He knew what it was like to be constantly reminded of what you'd lost. He saw it in every stained-glass window at St. Mary's, every cross and statue Hell, he saw it in Maryam.

"What do you think about Hiro's plan?" Sarah asked, scratching along her forehead with her cigarette hand. "Can you handle it?"

Zaphriel's eyebrows shot up in surprise at being asked. "I believe so, yes. Matthew's well behaved and I'm good with Maryam. I'm more worried about what the Order will say if they get so much as a papercut."

"That was my concern, too."

Zaphriel thought he might faint from shock. Sarah was asking his opinion *and* thought he just might be safe on his own with the kids? She was right; it was a *day*.

"Everyone signed off on Hiro putting his name on the line for this little experiment, so I guess it's a go, then."

Zaphriel's expression shifted to concern. "Did you sign off on it as well?"

Sarah sighed. "Unfortunately, I think my husband's right. The Order is going to see Maryam as a threat when she grows up, even if they don't have a good reason. People are going to have to learn to trust you eventually if we want her to be safe. If this can convince the Order that a full demon isn't dangerous, then maybe they can be convinced that a half-demon won't be dangerous either."

Zaphriel's jaw clenched as the weight of Sarah's words settled on his shoulders. "I won't let either of you, or Maryam, down."

Sarah took a long drag on her cigarette as Zaphriel spoke, her blue eyes sharp as jagged ice as she weighed the words. "You had better not." She crouched to put out the cigarette. "Because bad things are going to happen to you if you do."

"I know. I go back to Hell."

"Wrong." Sarah looked up at Zaphriel through her eyelashes, still curled in on herself, balancing on the balls of her feet. "If you do anything to make the Order come for Maryam or allow harm to come to my children, I am going to make sure I get my hands on you first so I can make you *beg* for the horrors that await you. *Then* you go back to Hell, Zaphriel."

Zaphriel swallowed hard. He shouldn't have been afraid. Intellectually, he knew that. Sarah was five-foot-three and one day might blow away in a strong wind with her slender build, yet the way she crouched on the ground, spine curled and perched like a wild thing, made Zaphriel fight the urge to back up.

"I've seen a lot of exorcisms," Sarah said in a low, level voice.. "I know just how much a body can take and yours isn't even mortal. Not really."

"I get it," Zaphriel snapped. He folded his arms, as if it could hide the way his heart hammered in his chest. "And, honestly, if I got either of those kids hurt, I would likely ask you to torture me for it anyway. I'd deserve it."

Sarah stopped tapping the end of the cigarette against the concrete.

Zaphriel bounced his eyes away, desperate to look anywhere but at her. "I've always deserved it." His grip on his upper arms tightened. "I know that."

Sarah stayed still, watching Zaphriel, "I don't think that's true, actually."

Zaphriel whirled in shock at the words.

Sarah stood and slipped the half-smoked cigarette into its pack, her gaze on the ground. "Don't get me wrong, you hurt my kids, I hurt you. And I hate how much of Maryam's life depends on you since you cower behind Hiro every chance you get."

Zaphriel flinched, but didn't argue.

"But I don't think you deserve to keep hating yourself. Not after all you've been through and all this time." Sarah lifted her gaze, her sharp blue eyes drilling into Zaphriel's. "Even if my husband's crazy plan works, you're always going to be the bad guy in someone else's story, Zaphriel."

Zaphriel blinked, every word he knew failing him.

"You don't have to process that right now. It's just something to think about over the weekend." Sarah shrugged. "But we're clear about what's going to happen if you mess this up, yes?"

Zaphriel nodded. "As crystal."

"Good." Sarah began towards the door. "Then let's eat. Arguing with Hiro always leaves me drained and hungry."

Zaphriel let a small chuckle slip. "Because he's so erratic?"

"There is that." Something close to a smile came to Sarah's lips—the first Zaphriel could remember being aimed at him. "And the fact that he's usually right."

By the time Hiro and Sarah left town, Zaphriel the Treacherous had been erased and Zackary Bishop had taken his place, complete with a driver's license, car insurance and registration, a bank account, and a Social Security number. The Order fabricated it all.

For some reason, that made Zaphriel all the more nervous. He triple checked Maryam's diaper bag before he and the kids left the house on Saturday and quadruple checked the car's mirrors. Once on the road, he didn't dare go a mile over the speed limit. His left hand drummed on his thigh as he drove, itching to use the turn signal at a moment's notice.

Matthew gave a disappointed sigh and began flipping through radio stations. "You don't drive like a demon."

"How are demons supposed to drive?" Zaphriel's face didn't even twitch in response to the comment. He kept his eyes locked onto the freeway, especially on the red Ford pickup that couldn't seem able to choose a lane.

Matthew shrugged. "I don't know. Fast? Fun? You drive like a grandma."

"I have two children in the car."

"Isn't Maryam technically a demon?"

Zaphriel whirled towards Matthew. "Of course not. She's only demon kissed." He put his gaze back on the road. "What makes you think she's a full-fledged demon?"

Matthew settled on a classic rock station and sat back in his seat as casually as if he'd made an observation about the traffic. "When a mom's possessed, doesn't the baby turn into one?"

"Absolutely not. The child may tend to attract dark spiritual forces, but they are still mortal." He glanced at Maryam in the rearview mirror. She babbled away to the stuffed raccoon in her lap.

The "demon-kissed" story had been Hiro's idea. As far as anyone without a need to know was concerned, Maryam's mother had been possessed by a demon while she was pregnant. The exorcism had stressed her body into labor. Zaphriel was there to ensure that the demon that had possessed her mother, or any other dark forces, never came for Maryam. If Maryam never knew what she was, then the Order couldn't conjure insane theories about her selling the Earth to her demon father, or whatever other craziness they whispered when the Bishops weren't around.

"What made you think demon-kissed children become demons?" Zaphriel asked.

"Adam McDonald at school said so. He said Maryam's the Anti-Christ."

A flicker of rage ignited in Zaphriel's chest. "You can tell Adam McDonald to…" Zaphriel trailed off. Telling Matthew that Adam McDonald could shove his opinion up his ass probably wouldn't get him sent back to Hell, but it wouldn't earn him any points with Hiro and Sarah. *Especially* not with Sarah. Zaphriel shivered at thought. "Tell Adam McDonald that it's dangerous to speak on things he's not educated about."

Matthew's eyes lit up. "Does that mean I can ask you a bunch of questions? So I can be properly educated?"

Zaphriel weighed the question. He put his blinker on, pulled off onto his exit, and waited to come to a halt at the stop sign before running a hand over his hair. "You can ask questions, but I reserve the right not to answer them." He glanced at Matthew before making a left turn. "Why have you never tried to ask me questions before?

"I thought Mom would get upset." Matthew fiddled with the drawstring of his hoodie. "She acts like you'll turn into a little cartoon demon and tell me to do bad stuff if we talk too much."

Zaphriel fought back a smirk. "I have nothing but deep respect for your mother." He pulled the car into a burger chain restaurant. "But I understand her hesitation. It's only because she loves you, though."

Matthew unbuckled his belt with a roll of his eyes. "Doesn't mean she has to baby me."

"She's not babying you. She's trying to protect you." Zaphriel got out of the car and opened the back door to get Maryam. "Parents look at situations through lenses that kids don't have. Sometimes, those lenses help them see things clearer, sometimes they cloud them.

The problem is that it's nearly impossible to tell which is happening in the moment." Zaphriel unbuckled Maryam, placed her on his hip, and grabbed the diaper bag, handing it to Matthew. "So, even if she frustrates you, be sure to give her plenty of grace, okay?"

"You sound like my dad." Matthew slung the bag over his shoulder. "Were *you* a dad?"

Zaphriel stopped in his tracks. He gave Maryam a small squeeze to steady himself, then kept walking. "Let's save the questions for after we get our food."

Matthew followed into the restaurant quietly, ordered promptly, helped settle Maryam in a highchair, and politely thanked the server that brought their food. When Zaphriel caught the curious glint in the boy's eye, he began to suspect Matthew's manners had been motivated more by the fear that he might get his question privilege revoked rather than genuine politeness. Zaphriel still counted it as a tally in his favor, seeing as he could report back to Hiro and Sarah that Matthew had been exceptionally well behaved—Zaphriel needed all the wins he could get.

"I can start with an easy questions if you want." Matthew slathered a fry in ketchup. "Where were you born?"

Zaphriel couldn't help but snort at the idea that his celestial origin was in any way "easy."

He carefully dumped Maryam's chicken nuggets onto her tray as he thought about his answer. "I don't know if I was actually born, honestly. I remember a bright light, a chorus of voices...darkness and stars. I think I saw the ring of dust and rock that would eventually become this solar system. It might have been a different solar system, actually. I can't be sure."

Matthew's mouth fell open as Zaphriel spoke, his eyes going wide. "Woah." He beamed. "What else?"

"It's hard to say." Zaphriel strained his memory as he wiped ketchup from Maryam's hand. "That was eons ago. It's fuzzy and I don't even know if there are words for everything that existed at the beginning." He remembered wings and eyes, fire and halos. Music that would make a mortal spontaneously combust from the raw cosmic power within it. Being confined to a mortal body limited his comprehension of celestial things, though. It was like trying to remember a language he had once spoken fluently but had forgotten over time.

"So, when you came into the universe, were you a baby? Did you get to be a kid?"

Zaphriel tried to recall any self-awareness of a physical self. His brow creased with the faint headache that was forming from the effort. "I don't think so, no."

"Oh." Matthew frowned. "I'm sorry. Being a kid is fun most of the time."

Zaphriel chuckled. "Being one of the first creatures on Earth was fun."

Matthew sat up a little straighter and leaned over the table "Where did you go when you came to Earth the first time?"

"It's an area historians call the Fertile Crescent." In his mind's eye, Zaphriel saw the tall grass on the banks of the Euphrates. He saw humans for the first time in the distance—nervous, suspicious, and fragile, but also lithe and beautiful things. He heard the chatter of children gathering water and smelled the smoke of cook fires and baking bricks.

"I know where that is." Matthew propped his elbows on the table, leaning in closer. "We learned about it at school. It's called Mesopotamia now."

Zaphriel smiled. "I believe it's changed names quite a few times since it was called that."

"Can you show me on a map at the museum? I wanna see where you lived."

Zaphriel found himself caught off guard, his chest swelling with an unfamiliar warmth.

Joy. For the first time in centuries, Zaphriel the Treacherous felt real, uninhibited joy.

"Matthew," he said. "I would love nothing more." He gestured to Matthew's tray. "But first, you need to eat your lunch."

Matthew took a giant bite of his burger. "Can I still ask questions, though?" he asked around it.

Zaphriel sighed. "Only if you don't talk with your mouth full."

Matthew struggled to swallow, having not sufficiently chewed. "I can do that."

By the time they left the restaurant, Matthew had a full profile on Zaphriel: His favorite color was green, his favorite song was Samuel Barber's *Adagio for Strings*, though thanks to Hiro's influence, rock music was growing on him. His favorite places were Athens and Venice, though he imagined they had changed a lot since he'd been summoned there, and his least favorite was Paris, hands down. It was dirty, overrated and its occultists were stuck up.

"I know your mother is rather partial to France, though," Zaphriel said as they walked back in the car. "So, maybe leave that part between us."

Mathew smirked. "Okay, but that secret will cost you."

Zaphriel smirked back as he held up his keys. "How about you keep it because I'm the only one who can drive?"

Matthew opened his mouth to argue, then thought better of it. "Okay, you win there."

"I know I do." Zaphriel chuckled and turned on the car. "Plus, twelve's too young to be making deals with demons."

"What about thirteen?"

"Absolutely not."

"Sixteen?"

Zaphriel paused. "We'll see."

The museum was free to all Detroit residents, which now included "Zackary Bishop." Free admission included the special traveling exhibit they had come to see—Power Man: The Comic, the Art, the Legend.

The smile it put on Mathew's face convinced Zaphriel that he'd pay thousands if he had the money.

Matthew's eyes lit up at the sight of his favorite superhero's origins splayed out from start to finish. The second they approached the first sketch of Power Man, dated 1938, he launched into the lore, both the character's as well as the creator's. Between wrangling Maryam and keeping an eye on their surroundings, Zaphriel only caught maybe every third word, but he made sure to mutter the appropriate, "is that so?" and "really?" at the right intervals.

Having apparently figured out Zaphriel's plan to keep her contained, Maryam took off running across the gallery with a squeal. Zaphriel swooped down and scooped up the toddler just before she could run in front of an elderly couple, both walking with canes.

"I'm so sorry," Zaphriel said to the pair, setting Maryam on his shoulders. Up there she would be entertained *and* out of the way for the moment.

The old woman studied the little girl with a soft, wistful smile. "It's quite alright." Maryam drummed a little rhythm against Zaphriel's forehead and laughed when he winced. The woman chuckled. "She's a lively one."

Zaphriel caught Maryam's wrist. "You have no idea."

The man adjusted his glasses. "That hair of hers is gorgeous. Does she get it from her mother?"

Zaphriel paused. "She does."

"Not to worry." The old woman pointed to Zaphriel with a glint in her eye. "Girls always grow up to look like their fathers in the end."

"I'm actually..." Zaphriel stopped himself short, not because the truth didn't hurt (it did), but because two strangers didn't need it. Besides, odds were it would only bring out more questions. "I've actually heard that before." He forced a smile. "But all my other kids look like their mother, so we'll see with this one." He slowly turned to rejoin Matthew. "You two have a nice day."

With his back turned on the couple, Zaphriel's shoulders slumped slightly. He shook his head, cursing himself a fool. So what if he wasn't Maryam's father? He hadn't been summoned to be. He just needed to do his job. He'd always understood that well enough.

So, why did it suddenly hurt a bit to remember that she wasn't his?

Maryam patted the top of Zaphriel's head. "Zack, down?"

"Are you going to stop running?"

"Ya."

Zaphriel doubted it, but he let her down anyway. Sure enough, he wound up chasing her back to Matthew, who was studying a Power Man costume, looking far gloomier than he had when they had first come to the exhibit.

"Something wrong?" Zaphriel asked.

Matthew shrugged.

Zaphriel scooped Maryam up, one arm supporting her bottom, the other around her waist. "C'mon, tell me what's up."

Matthew gave him a skeptical look, like the demon might laugh at him.

"Talk to me and I'll buy you ice cream at the museum café when we're done here."

Matthew continued to calculate. "I thought you said I'm too young to make deals with demons."

Zaphriel resisted the urge to call Matthew a smart-ass. "I'm offering as your friend." He readjusted Maryam. "Now, what's bothering you?"

Matthew's brow pulled together. "We're friends?"

Zaphriel found himself slightly caught off guard by both the realization that actually having a friend might be nice and the surprise that Matthew didn't know if he was serious or not. "If that's okay with you."

Matthew looked back to the costume, wringing his exhibit pamphlet into a tube. "Is it stupid to be into kid stuff like Power Man?"

Zaphriel gave Matthew a bewildered look. "Of course not. What makes you say that?"

"I don't know. I just..." Matthew shrugged. "Mom and Dad are busy with work all the time or they're worrying over Maryam. I know their work's important and hard, and I know Maryam's different but..." Matthew swallowed hard as he wrung his hands. "I get lonely sometimes. Dad was supposed to bring me to this since Power Man is *his* favorite too." He blinked away the faint shine of his eyes and wiped at his nose. "Sometimes I think Mom and Dad would want to spend more time with me if I was into more adult stuff like demons and cursed artifacts.."

A laugh escaped before Zaphriel could stop himself. Matthew flashed him a dirty look.

"I'm sorry," Zaphriel said. "I'm not laughing at you. When I think 'mortal adult stuff' I think things like mortgages and taxes, not the occult."

Matthew folded his arms. "It's not my fault my family's weird."

"You're right, it's not. And it's very understandable why you feel lonely."

Matthew kicked at a speck of dirt on the floor.

Zaphriel put Maryam, who had started to squirm, on the ground and held tight to her collar as he bent forward to meet Matthew's eye level. "Matt, look at me."

He did, eyebrows pulled together and brown eyes worried, ready for a lecture.

"You are twelve. Things like Power Man and video games, and whatever else twelve-year-olds like are exactly the kinds of interests you should have." Zaphriel paused, remembering the sort of mischief his own kids had started getting into at twelve. "So long as those interests don't get you into trouble." Matthew perked up a bit at that, so Zaphriel kept going. "And as for your parents…" He ran his free hand over his hair. "It's okay to be sad that they work a lot, but it's not something you should feel guilty about. Remember what I said about parents having special lenses?"

Matthew nodded.

"The same thing applies here. You've seen what a bad demon can do. That's why Maryam doesn't have a mother. Your parents have a special gift. They're using it to make the world safer for everyone."

Maryam plopped down on the floor and began playing with the Velcro on her shoes. Confident her preoccupation would give him two minutes of peace, Zaphriel released her shirt.

"And I'm proud of you for sharing your feelings with me. That's very hard to do."

Matthew nodded, then took a steadying breath. "You know, I bet you were a really good dad."

Zaphriel froze, a knot forming in his throat as his chest tightened.

Before he could say anything, Maryam stood and made a mad dash for a family with a service dog, forcing Zaphriel to jump into action. He snatched her up, swung her over his shoulder, and steadied himself as he walked back to Matthew. "Now tell me," he said, all of his feelings locked back away where they belonged, "if one was to start getting into Power Man, where would they start?"

Matthew's face lit up, chipping away a bit at the permafrost in Zaphriel's chest. As Matthew launched into where to start the comic series (different than if one were to want to start the TV series), Zaphriel begrudgingly admitted that maybe Sarah had been right. Maybe he wasn't the bad guy. Not in his own story.

The museum cafe proved to be quite charming. Late spring sun streamed down from a ceiling of skylights and lit an airy, comfortable courtyard decorated with archways and ivory. Ornate windows and round stone towers jutted out from the high walls, giving Zaphriel the surreal feeling of being in an impossibly clean Old World city street. Matthew opted for a mango smoothie once they reached the counter while Zaphriel ordered a small serving of chocolate ice cream for himself and Maryam to share. They found a quiet booth in the corner. Matthew drank his smoothie while Zaphriel spooned bites of ice cream into Maryam's wide baby-bird mouth.

"What's it like having a body?" Matthew asked between sips. "Like, as a demon. My dad didn't have to steal that body from someone else, did he?"

Zaphriel paused at the question, giving Maryam the opportunity to stick her hand in the ice-cream and shove a fistful in her mouth.

Zaphriel took her hand and did his best to clean it with a napkin. "No, this body is my own." He slid the cup of ice cream further onto the table and dug in the diaper bag for a wipe. "When a human makes a deal with a demon, the demon samples the human's blood. I don't understand the mechanics of it, but the pact and the sacrifice causes the construction of a mortal body."

"So, what do you actually look like?"

Zaphriel smirked at Matthew as he cleaned Maryam's hands. "Horrors beyond your mortal comprehension."

Matthew's eyes widened as his mouth fell open. "That's so cool," he muttered in awe. "Can I see?"

Zaphriel laughed. "I'm not going to take on my celestial form in the middle of a human restaurant."

"Will you do it when we get home?"

"Absolutely not. I'm not setting the living room on fire for your amusement, Matthew."

Matthew's mouth fell open. "You catch *fire*?" He put his smoothie down and placed his hands together to beg. "I promise I won't tell my parents. I *super* promise."

Zaphriel flashed the boy a stern look. "I said no." His tone took him by surprise. He hadn't used that tone since his children were alive.

Matthew pouted for a moment, then went back to his smoothie. Zaphriel did his best to bite back a sigh as he helped Maryam feed herself ice cream. The awkwardness of the silence crawled over his skin. He hadn't meant to snap. Hadn't meant to make a display of authority and he sure as hell hadn't meant to actually *mean* to have any sort of authority.

He had been able to lock away the fact that he had once been a father for millennia, but now he couldn't escape the memory for more than a few minutes.

Desperate to rid himself of the discomfort, Zaphriel glanced around the courtyard for a distraction. Near the exit, he spied a sign pointing towards the Ancient Near East gallery.

"Did you still want me to show you where I used to live?" he asked Matthew.

The boy's disappointment eased. "Do they have a map?"

Zaphriel smiled in relief. "We can certainly find out."

With desserts eaten and trash disposed of, the three made their way to the gallery.

A brush of heavy, dark energy lifted the hair on Zaphriel's arms the second they entered.

He grabbed Matthew by the shoulder and pulled him back. "Don't."

"What's wrong?"

Zaphriel swallowed against his drying mouth as he scanned the gallery. Nothing looked amiss. Patrons perused the variety of clay and metal artifacts, speaking quietly amongst themselves, oblivious to the thin mist of dark energy engulfing them like a cloud. Nothing in the brightly lit display cases looked particularly powerful or malicious, but something was amiss; the faintest hint of sulfur laced the air and Zaphriel felt as if he couldn't get enough air in his lungs, like a menacing weight had settled on his sternum.

Zaphriel passed Maryam to Matthew, eyes still scanning the gallery. "Take your cousin and go stand at the courtyard exit," he said. "Be ready to leave the second I come get you."

"But what—"

"Matthew." Authority seeped back into Zaphriel's voice. "I'll explain in the car. Right now, I need you to do what I say."

Matthew shifted Maryam on his hip, took her bag from Zaphriel's shoulder, and hurried away. When his footsteps completely faded, Zaphriel entered the gallery.

The cloud of dark energy was thin, thankfully. Whatever lingered couldn't be that strong. Zaphriel meticulously studied every coin, seal, and scrap of pottery, both the English description and what little of the cuneiform he could still read. Nothing felt wrong or out of place until he reached a small, sealed clay pot that, otherwise, would have been completely overlooked.

Darkness radiated off the artifact, pressing against Zaphriel's skin. The chatter around him in the gallery changed into soft, rapid whispers that dug into his ears. He leaned in and squinted to study the pot, finding only a small winged figure pressed into its surface. Any sort of inscription had been worn away with time. Beneath, its description only read, "*Clay talisman thought to ward against unknown evil spirits, 6th Century BCE. Donated anonymously.*"

Hiro needed to know about this. The Order needed to know. How long had a demon been sitting in the middle of the Order's back yard? Zaphriel's racing mind paused as he studied the gallery in the reflection of the display case. What had once been a busy gallery was now empty. Zaphriel stood and looked around the silent room, dread freezing in his lungs.

Matthew. Maryam.

Zaphriel rushed to the gallery entrance to find the courtyard exit empty. This entire corner of the museum had apparently emptied. Horror knotted in his stomach and felt like it might fall out through his feet. Before he could shout for Matthew, movement flashed in his peripherals. Zaphriel turned. A blunt, blinding pain collided with the back of his head and the world went black before Zaphriel's body fell.

Voices murmured in the dark, sharp and malicious like a prowling snake through the underbrush. The voices slithered through Zaphriel's mind as he awoke and his head throbbed in time with his sluggish heart as he opened his eyes to soft light and gentle shades of blue and gray. His gaze focused to reveal an empty event hall decorated with evenly spaced marble-like pillars and landscape photography on the walls.

Maryam and Matthew were nowhere to be seen.

Adrenaline shot through Zaphriel as he tried to jump to his feet, only to be held in place by ropes securing him to one of the pillars. Straining revealed that his wrists had been tied behind his back in an extra attempt to restrain him. Panic sent his heart racing faster the harder he strained. He couldn't breathe with these damn ropes pressing in on him.

"Matthew!" he called, silently begging for the boy to appear out of thin air. "Matt!"

"Shhh. You'll wake him."

Zaphriel jerked his head up to find a man standing over him with a sneer, one hand against the pillar, the other at his hip and his ankles crossed. He was young—mid-twenties, maybe—with sandy blonde hair and an athletic build within a black security uniform. Zaphriel couldn't tell what color the man's eyes might be—they were inked out from corner to corner with the putrid black of demon possession.

Zaphriel glared up at the man. "What do you want?" he demanded. "Where are my kids?"

The demon in stolen skin gave a condescending scoff. "*Your* kids?" He stood away from the pillar and folded his arms, studying Zaphriel with a raised eyebrow. "The girl I can believe, but since when do demons go around claiming mortal children as their own?"

Zaphriel's entire body went taunt. "None of your goddamn business," he snapped. "Now, where are they?"

The demon sneered. "The boy's tied up to your right."

Zaphriel craned his neck to look around the corner of the pillar. In his peripherals, he could faintly see a limp shape leaning against the marble. He turned back to the demon with a glare. "Where's Maryam? If you've hurt her, I'll—"

The opening of a door and the click of heels cut him off. "Calm down, handsome." A woman clad in a black pencil skirt and a white blouse came into Zaphriel's line of sight. "Just had to go change her diaper." She shifted Maryam higher on her hip. "Didn't want this little angel to start screaming and give us away, now did we?" She tapped the tip of Maryam's nose, making the little girl giggle and grab for the woman's hand. Her stuffed raccoon dangled from her other hand. The woman must have dug it out of the diaper bag.

Maryam looked at Zaphriel and waved. "Zack, hi."

Zaphriel forced a smile, despite the way his heart felt like it might shatter his ribs from the inside. "Hi, sweetheart. You being good?"

Maryam nodded, nearly knocking herself off balance. "Ya."

The woman flashed Zaphriel a smug smirk that lit up her dark, soulless eyes. "See, this is why I told my friend here that knocking you and the boy out was going too far." She gently cradled Maryam's head with her free hand and kissed her red curls. "I knew you'd be reasonable with the right motivation."

Zaphriel's blood boiled and his teeth ground together until his jaw popped. "Who are you? What do you want?"

"I am Uria." The woman gestured to her companion. "This is Emush." Uria stepped closer and knelt down, perfectly balancing Maryam on her lap as her black demon eyes bore into Zaphriel's. "You, on the other hand, need no introduction, Zaphriel the Treacherous."

Zaphriel only sharpened his glare in response.

"Imagine our surprise when another demon, and not just any demon, but the Throne that betrayed both God and the Fallen, showed up in our gallery." A smile spread across Uria's lips that looked unnervingly too big for her human vessel's face. "We haven't been that excited since the old man who owned our vase finally offed himself."

To Zaphriel's right, Matthew groaned as he began to wake. Zaphriel listened as he struggled against the bindings and whimpered as the situation caught up with him.

"Zaphriel?"

"I'm right here, Matthew," Zaphriel said as calmly as he could. "It's okay." He turned back to Uria. "Let the children go. They have nothing to do with this."

Uria hiked Maryam up higher on her hip. "True, but they're also the easiest way to keep you in check." She smirked. "I wonder how much faster you would have sold out your brothers if Heaven had captured your little half-breed family instead of slaughtering them."

Red tinted Zaphriel's vision as he lunged at the woman, ropes or no, and snarled, "Go fuck yourself."

Uria gave a mocking click of her tongue and cover's Maryam's ears. "Language, Zaphriel."

Emush snickered.

Zaphriel forced himself to breathe deep. Panicking was going to make things worse. Matthew and Maryam couldn't afford him making things worse. "If you two can possess humans, why bother with me? Why not stay under the radar?" He glanced around the room. "And this doesn't look like a particularly secure location."

"Unfortunately, unlike a big strong Throne like yourself, our influence is limited. Some of us were only created for the dregs of Heaven's Infantry." Uria stood back up. "We may have enough power to charm this space so no one enters, but that's only because we're so close to our vase. And once people get too far out of our reach, we lose our grip." She took a few steps forward to tower over Zaphriel. "You, however, can go wherever you please. We want to know how and you're going to help us do the same."

Zaphriel snorted. "Why? Because you asked so nicely?"

Uria nodded towards Emush. "Take one of the boy's fingers."

Zaphriel's blood froze. A nasty smile spread over Emush's face as he drew a long, curved blade from the back of his belt and Zaphriel was back in the village, his daughter's broken body in his arms as he ran through the bloody streets, angelic swords and spears glinting in the sun as they cut down everything in their path.

"No." He struggled against the ropes. "No, no, no, please."

Matthew grunted as he struggled harder against the ropes. "Don't touch me, you bastard!"

"See, Zaphriel? You're a bad influence," Uria said.

Spit slicked Zaphriel's mouth, his body threatening to vomit. "It was a contract!" he blurted.

Emush left his line of vision.

"IT WAS A CONTRACT! IT WAS A FUCKING CONTRACT!"

The room stilled. Emush came back where Zaphriel could see him. Zaphriel leaned back against the pillar, his breath labored and a cold sweat dewing his skin. He swallowed against the swelling nausea in his gut. "I was contracted by Matthew's father to protect Maryam. If it's part of your contract, a human summoner can grant you a body of your own."

Maryam's bottom lip jutted out and she began to whimper in response to all the shouting. Uria gently shushed her and rubbed her back, studying the child with a furrowed brow. "Why does she need protection?"

Zaphriel's jaw clenched shut.

Uria looked to Emush.

"Her mother was possessed by a demon," Zaphriel lied. "I was contracted to make sure she doesn't manifest any sort of powers or draw the attention of any other demons."

Uria glowered down at Zaphriel, her hand still slowly skimming up and down Maryam's back. "He's lying. Take an ear, Emush."

"I'm not!" Zaphriel strained against the ropes as Emush rounded the pillar. His wife's blank eyes flashed in his mind, her throat bright and slick with blood, his oldest strewn across her mother's body with a knife in her back.

Not again, not again, not again.

Zaphriel thought he might suffocate. There wasn't enough air. "I swear I'm not lying. You can feel it on her, can't you?"

"I feel a *binding spell* on her, you idiot," Uria hissed. "That's how I know you're bullshitting us."

Matthew grunted and whimpered as he strained against the rope. "No, no, no! Stay away from me! ZAPHRIEL, HELP!"

"SHE'S ANKIDA'SHI!"

The words echoed off the walls, leaving an awestruck silence in their wave.

"She's ankida'shi," Zaphriel repeated after a few deep breaths, his voice and body shaking. "Her mother was a part of a cult trying to bring fallen angels back to Earth. They thought ankida'shi children could be a bridge between the mortal and celestial realms. Maryam's mother ran when she realized a new world order would mean a war. Her sister and brother-in-law, Matthew's parents, were exorcists. They delivered Maryam, then summoned me to hide her powers."

"She's not yours, then?"

Zaphriel leaned back against the pillar, his eyes closed and his heart sinking in defeat, because he wouldn't let his stubbornness get another child killed. Never again. He'd take Hell again before he would let that happen. Hiro and Sarah were smart and capable—they'd figure out another way to protect Maryam.

"She's Azazel's," he finally said. The name tangled on his tongue. He hadn't said since that night two years ago.

Uria blinked, the name of the rebellion's leader nearly knocking her over. "You're lying."

Zaphriel let out a small, bitter laugh. "I told this much of the truth. Why start lying now?"

Uria blinked at him again, and then began to pace. She ignored Maryam's whining as the child attempted to get down, staying frightfully quiet in thought until Emush spoke.

"What are you plotting now?" he asked.

A dark smile crept onto her face as she continued to pace. "Something I never even dared to dream about." She stopped and looked at Emush. "Why settle for mortal bodies when we could ask for status in the dark court?"

"You mean Hell?"

"Of course." Uria stroked Maryam's hair. "Seeing as we've found ourselves in possession of its princess."

Zaphriel's stomach knotted.

Uria looked down at Zaphriel with newly ignited malicious glee. "Originally, we were going to force you to fetch our vase and help us get bodies of our own, seeing as we can't touch the thing ourselves. Now, you're going to fetch our vase, and then the three of us are going to find somewhere nice and private where we can use these shells to summon the Devil's General."

Zaphriel felt the blood drain from his face. Not only had he dragged Matthew and Maryam into danger, but now Uria was discussing handing Maryam over to her father and sacrificing the two humans they had possessed to do it.

Uria gestured to Zaphriel. "Emush, untie them both. Put the boy in this chair here." She maneuvered a nearby seat next to her with her foot. "Take Zaphriel to get our vase. You know where the tools are." Her eyes fell on Zaphriel as she sat herself down at the table, drawing a knife of her own from her waistband. Judging by the ornate design along the blade and the gems encrusting the hilt, it also had been taken from the museum. "The boy loses a body part for every thirty minutes you take."

Zaphriel stayed still as the ropes came loose. His heart nearly jumped out of his throat as Matthew tried to make a run at Uria, his hands still bound. Emush snatched him by the collar of his shirt, knife drawn.

"Matt, stop!" Zaphriel yelled. "Stop."

Matthew looked Zaphriel's way, not afraid, but wounded, and gave up the struggle, allowing Emush to shove him into the chair. The boy glared up at the demon, looking like he might lunge again the second either Uria or Emush's backs were turned.

"Matthew, no," Zaphriel said, voice forceful. "I will fix this."

Uria tittered. "Like you fixed things for your first family?" She held up the knife for Maryam to see, keeping it just out of her reach and letting it catch the light. "That's cute."

"Leave him alone, you bitch," Matthew snarled.

"Matthew Bishop!" Zaphriel snapped. "Enough!"

Uria laughed again and pointed the knife at Matthew. "Better listen to your babysitter, little boy."

"Sure you can handle him?" Emush asked as he jerked Zaphriel to his feet "He's quite the little pistol."

Uria scoffed. "As if I'm afraid of a *child.*" She jerked the knife towards the door. "Go. We need to get our vase and get out of here before the museum closes. I don't want to deal with alarms if we don't have to."

Emush yanked Zaphriel towards the door. When Zaphriel tripped over his own feet in an attempt to keep the children in his line of sight, Emush shoved him forward. "Move."

Zaphriel obliged, letting himself be led through the doors and down the corridor once again filled with regular people who didn't seem to see anything out of the ordinary about a bound man being led down the hall "This much power and you two still need someone else to do your dirty work?" he muttered.

Emush gripped Zaphriel's wrists harder. "We could be as powerful as you and we would still need assistance," he grumbled. "The old priest that sealed us in that damn vase cursed it so that we can't touch it, even while possessing a mortal body. It has to be someone else."

"Who was the priest?"

Emush snorted. "Hell if I know. I never got the man's name, and it was nearly seven thousand years ago."

"So, you were there in the Beginning?"

"When you high-ranking bastards spat in Heaven's face so bad that they came down and kicked our asses? Sure was. Thanks for that." Emush led Zaphriel around a corner and brought him to a halt. "We've really loved running from damnation and hiding in the shadows all this time. Been a real treat."

"For what it's worth, I'm sorry," Zaphriel said. "We were the only ones who were supposed to get hurt."

"Yeah, well..." Emush worked at untying Zaphriel's bonds. "I've heard humans exchange a saying over the years: shit rolls downhill."

"I'm familiar." The bonds fell away and Zaphriel massaged his wrists, giving Emush a quizzical look.

"Don't get clever." Emush's hand drifted to the knife on his belt. "You can't work with your hands tied and the second you try something, all I have to do is find another vessel and go tell Uria to cut that boy's throat."

Zaphriel began calculating, despite the warning. His eyes fell on a sign for the nearby bathrooms. "Understood. Any chance we have time for a restroom break, though?"

Emush scoffed. "You can't be serious."

"The thing about having a mortal body of your own is that they do, indeed, function like mortal bodies. And I had to go *before* you knocked me unconscious, so this is overdue."

Emush rolled his eyes and gestured towards the men's room with an exasperated sigh. "Fine. For that boy's sake, though, you better make it quick."

In all his incarnations on Earth, Zaphriel never imagined he might actually be grateful that his body was, in fact, mortal. He eyed the counter for potential weapons as he crossed the room to the urinals and played through every potential advantage he might have as he unzipped his pants.

Emush could jump bodies, so a real fight was out of the question. All it would take was a few moments of clear concentration and he'd find another vessel and tell Uria what had happened. Even if he did want to make a physical assault work, he might have to hurt the human host. Maybe even kill him.

But what if he attacked on both a physical *and* spiritual front? Zaphriel might not have carried much real influence as a Throne, but he still outranked Emush and Uria. What was he supposed to do with that, though? Demons weren't summoned to fight other demons. That wasn't their purpose.

That didn't mean it wasn't possible.

He'd told Hiro that a summoner would need a demon of a higher rank than the one inhabiting the human body and a way to control said high-ranking demon. Check and check—Zaphriel outranked both Emush and Uria and he was kept plenty in check by the fact that both children in his charge were in danger. The idea was so off the walls that it just might work.

Zaphriel didn't have a choice but to make it work. Matthew and Maryam *needed* him to make it work.

He glanced around the restroom as he finished and zipped his pants. The only thing not bolted down was an industrial roll of cheap, dense brown paper towels that had been placed beneath a busted dispenser. There had to be something else, though. He desperately needed there to be.

Zaphriel walked over to the counter, careful to keep his hands where Emush could see them as he turned on the water.

"Seriously? You're washing your hands?" Emush chided.

Zaphriel pumped a handful of soap. "I know a lot of you missed the memo, but being a demon doesn't mean you have to be uncivilized." He ripped a stretch of paper towel from the heavy roll as he took one final look around the counter. No other weapons.

Zaphriel stifled an internal sigh as he threw away the damp paper. Good thing he was well beyond caring about his dignity

Zaphriel snatched the roll and slammed it against Emush's head in a single swing, knocking the demon into the wall of a stall before he crumpled to the ground. He'd hardly even groaned before Zaphriel was on top of him, using his legs to pin Emush' arms at his side. He clamped a hand over Emush's mouth, the other hand drawing a cross against his forehead. Emush howled behind Zaphriel's hand.

Zaphriel clamped down tighter and scrambled to remember a verse. Any verse. "*In him we have redemption through his blood, the forgiveness of sins, in accordance with the riches of God's grace that he lavishes on us.*"

Emush thrashed, pulling free enough to bite down on Zaphriel's hand.

Zaphriel fought back a cry of pain and traced a symbol of banishment he'd seen in Hiro's books against Emush's chest. "*He made known to us the mystery of his will according to his good pleasure, which he proposed in Christ.*". The scent of sulfur laced the air. Zaphriel dug deep, remembering what it was like to believe in something greater than himself.

Blood trickled down his wrist. He winced as Emush bit harder. "Emush," he hissed passed the pain. "In the name of the Three that may yet redeem me, I order you to come up out of this man and descend to Hell!"

Emush let out a final anguish cry, then the bathroom went quiet. Zaphriel held his breath, terrified by how still the purely human man lay beneath him. When the man groaned and blinked, revealing ordinary brown human eyes, Zaphriel sighed and scrambled off of him just as the door burst open with patrons.

Zaphriel scrambled to his feet, cradling his injured hand. "I-I don't know what happened. He just started raving about demons and then he collapsed. I made sure he was breathing, but I don't know if he's all there. I think maybe he had a seizure?"

The crowd paid him little mind. They were too busy trying to get the man to respond, trying to decide what do and who would call 911.

Zaphriel slipped away in the confusion, sprinting for the cafe. He skidded to a stop before the door, then cracked it open ever so slightly. He listened for a sign of disturbance, a sign that Uria had begun to rethink her plan and, if Zaphriel was lucky, make a run for it. "Uria?" No reply. "I've taken care of Emush. Let the kids go before I have to do the same thing to you."

"Zaphriel, she's gone!" Matthew called. "She took Maryam and ran through the kitchen!"

Zaphriel's heart threatened to jump through his throat as he burst through the door to find Matthew alone, bound to his chair. He sprinted across the distance and dove for Matthew's ropes. As soon as they fell away, Zaphriel shoved his phone into Matthew's hand. "Call your parents and then call the Order. Both numbers are in there."

He took off for the empty service counter, clearing it in a leap and winding through the empty maze of chrome counters and shelves. He searched the coolers and freezers, just to be sure, but they were empty. Zaphriel fought the rising panic tightening his gut as he hunted for the back door. Uria couldn't have gone far. Not without a new vessel. He found the door and burst through. She said she couldn't control a body if it got too far from her vessel. She—

Movement flashed across Zaphriel's vision as sharp burning pain ripped through his gut. He froze, registering the blood-thirsty grin on

Uria's face just before she jerked her hand up, slicing through more of Zaphriel's abdomen.

He choked on a pained cry as he grabbed her wrist with one hand, the other snatching a hold of her neck. Her eyes bulged, then she snarled, struggling to twist the knife. Zaphriel winced with a hiss, fighting to shove Uria against the far wall, propelled by trembling legs.

The taste of copper bloomed on his tongue as he squeezed Uria's throat. "Where's Maryam?"

Uria bared her teeth. "Worry about yourself, Watcher."

Zaphriel tightened his grip on her wrist as best he could with his failing strength. "Tell me or I send you to Hell." A smirk twitched at the corner of his lips. "They don't take kindly to newcomers, especially angels who've been dodging their eternal punishment for millennia."

Uria's face paled. "You're bluffing."

"When you meet Emush down there, ask if I bluff."

Uria glared. "She's in the utility's closet down the hall to the right. Asleep. I couldn't have her screaming the entire time I made a run for it."

Zaphriel's grip tightened further, even as his vision started to blur.

Uria wheezed against Zaphriel's grip. "Do I look like I'm in a position to lie?"

"No." Zaphriel dipped a finger into his own blood. "But I am."

Uria shrieked as he drew a cross against her forehead with his own blood.

"For God did not send his Son into the world to condemn the world, but in order that the world might be saved through him."

Uria withdrew the knife and drove it into Zaphriel's side.

He bit back a scream as the pain blinded him. "*Whoever believes...*" He coughed. Blood dripped from his lips. "*Whoever believes in him is not condemned, but whoever does not believe is condemned already...because he has not believed in the name of the only Son of God.*"

"Why won't you just die?" Uria shrieked.

Zaphriel's knees buckled. "I'm not losing my children." Black spots dotted his vision. "Not ever again." Zaphriel weakly traced the banishing seal against Uria's chest. "Uria, by the power of the Three that hold my redemption, I condemn you to Hell."

Uria screamed one final time, and then her host went limp. The weight of the woman dragged Zaphriel to the floor. He sprawled out beneath a ceiling that had started to spin and grow dim. Footsteps raced towards him but never seeming to get closer.

"Zaphriel!" Matthew's face appeared before Zaphriel, distant and blurry. "Zaph!" It sounded like he was speaking through water.

Zaphriel tried to point to the utility closet, but he only managed to drop his hand in the general direction. "Get your cousin. Did you call everyone?" Working his jaw felt like using a rusted hinge and his mouth had begun to tangle.

"They're on their way. Mom and Dad too."

"Good." Zaphriel's eyelids felt like concrete. "Don't tell them I used the f-word in front of you."

Matthew replied, but cold darkness pulled Zaphriel under, turning the boy's words into a muted hush.

Warmth.

Light refracted off the swift river like a million stars and the tall grass hissed as a cool breeze wafted down from the distant mountains in the north, providing a rhythm for the harmony of his daughter's chatter and shrieks of joy.

A name reached him on the wind. The one he'd taken for the sake of cumbersome mortal tongues and limited mortal minds. The one that named a man who had descended from heaven to love and live like a mortal. A man who crafted magic and miracles to help them starve off age, death and limits like a tourniquet.

That name again.

He turned to find the speaker walking his way on a dirt path, a baby on her hip. The breeze tossed her long dark hair about and ruffled the feathers of the baby's speckled wings. She beamed with a smile brighter than the nova that had birthed him.

She cupped her mouth with her free hand and called, "Paging Doctor Anderson."

Zaphriel jolted awake to a throbbing pain and dull florescent light. Instead of the sunny riverbanks of home, he lay stiff and sore on sheets that smelled of bleach. He tried to unstick his cottony tongue from the roof of his dry mouth. Fuck, it felt like he'd woken up from death itself. What the hell had happened?

Images flashed, sending Zaphriel's heart racing. The demons. The exorcisms. The museum. The kids.

Zaphriel shot up in bed, propelled by his racing heart, and threw off the sheets. A pair of hands steadied him as his bare feet hit the icy floor.

"Easy!" Hiro's hands tightened on Zaphriel's shoulders. "Easy. You've got an IV in."

Zaphriel reached for the needle taped to the back of his hand, but Hiro was faster, snatching his wrist.

"Rip that out, and I swear to God, I'll tell them to tie your ass down."

"The kids are in danger." Zaphriel struggled against his summoner. "They could be—" He trailed off as the room began to spin, then slumped against Hiro as his damaged mortal form gave out. He let out a hiss as the pain in his core flared up.

The knife. He'd been stabbed. And *bitten*, now that everything was coming back to him. The hand without an IV was wrapped in a bandage.

Hiro lifted Zaphriel upright. "The kids are fine, Zaph. They're at home with Sarah. Lay back down before you rip your stitches."

Zaphriel slowed his breath, allowing himself to be gently pushed back down onto the bed. He lay back and took in the room around him as Hiro pressed a button to bring the bed into a sitting position. A generic oil painting of Jesus hung on the opposite wall below a ceiling trimmed in faded purple and gold. The Order's colors. He was in the hospital attached to St. Mary's. Another flash of pain sliced through Zaphriel's middle and he winced.

Hiro's brow pulled together. "Do you need more pain meds?"

"I don't know. I've never been in this sort of situation before." Zaphriel traced the puckered line of stitches that ran from his belly button to just below his diaphragm. "Jesus. It's a wonder nothing fell out."

Concern etched itself into Hiro's face. "The doctors said you'd be dead if you were mortal."

"Thank God for little miracles, I guess." Zaphriel grimaced at the stale taste in his mouth and motioned to the full pitcher someone had left on his bedside table. "Can I get something to drink?"

Hiro nodded and poured water into a flimsy plastic cup. "Matt said you exorcised a demon."

Zaphriel sipped the water, trying to decide how to answer. "Technically, I exorcised two demons."

Hiro froze, making Zaphriel tense. How badly had he fucked up? How much time did he have before the Order made Hiro send Zaphriel back to Hell? Would he at least be allowed to say good-bye to the kids?

Zaphriel sat up straighter in bed, setting down his cup with a shaking hand. "I'm sorry, Summoner. I should have done better. I should have—"

"Zaphriel." Hiro lifted a hand to silence the demon. "You almost died protecting my son and my niece and went above and beyond what the research department thought was possible. What the hell are you apologizing for?"

"Everything you just said," Zaphriel answered. "They wouldn't have been in danger in the first place if it wasn't for me."

"Matt said the demons knew there was something different about Maryam from the start," Hiro argued. "She would have been in danger anyway and you protected her. That's been your job all along, hasn't it?"

"Yeah, but..." Zaphriel shook his head and sighed, leaning back against the bed.

"No buts. You absolutely kicked ass, Zaphriel." Hiro took a seat and dug into a backpack he'd stashed beneath it. "Even the Order thinks so."

"What do you mean?"

Hiro pulled out a cream-colored folder and handed it to Zaphriel. "See for yourself."

Zaphriel frowned as he took the folder, opened it, and began to read. His breath caught in his chest as he read the words *Contract of Employment.* He rubbed his eyes and read it again. Clearly his brain had been damaged when he'd lost all that blood at the museum, because there was no way that was what it said. When the words didn't shift into anything else, Zaphriel looked up at his summoner in bewilderment.

Hiro beamed. "The Order wants to make you an exorcist, Zaph."

Zaphriel let out a shaky laugh. "This is...This can't be real."

"It is. I promise."

Zaphriel laughed again, setting the folder on his lap to slick back his hair. His touch felt distant, as if his celestial soul didn't sit quite right in his mortal body. "Is my IV drugged? What is *happening* right now?"

Hiro leaned in. "You can *exorcise other demons*, Zaphriel. Do you understand what a big deal that is? Nothing new ever happens in the Order. *Ever.*"

"I don't know if I can do it again. It could have been a fluke. What about the demons that outrank me?"

"What about all the demons that *don't*, Zaph? You were a Throne, for Christ's sake." Hiro opened the folder again and held up the contract. "Zaphriel. They are offering you *freedom*. You wouldn't have to be under my thumb all the time. You wouldn't have to submit those stupid reports."

"I know, but..." Zaphriel dropped his gaze. "Summoner, what if I fail?"

"What if you succeed?"

Zaphriel opened his mouth to argue, then shut it again upon realizing he didn't actually have a sound argument. Of *course* he thought he would fail. That's what villains did.

But was Zaphriel a villain? Had he ever been? Or was he merely a soul who had wanted more than to stand guard outside an inner sanctum he could never enter? Had he truly turned his back on his Creator, or had he just wanted to understand everything else that had been created?

You're always going to be the bad guy in someone else's story, Zaphriel. Don't be the bad guy in your own story, too.

Hiro handed back the folder. "If you want more proof that I'm right, take a look behind the contract."

Zaphriel gave him a look, then flipped through the pages until he found a sheet of stiff cardstock. He removed it and studied the words framed in gold foil and handwritten in precise calligraphy:

Certificate of Godparenthood

<u>*Zaphriel the Treacherous*</u> *is hereby named godfather of* <u>*Maryam Grace Bishop*</u> *before the parish of St. Mary's Interdenominational Congregation.*

As the Holy Spirit completes the Trinity, the above named completes the parental trinity of the above child, ensuring they grow in God's ways until they rejoin Him in His kingdom, or He returns in glory.

Amen.

Zaphriel's throat closed as his vision blurred. He lifted his gaze to Hiro, his mouth slack and his brain unable to process the gift he had been given.

Hiro gave a shy, sheepish smile. "I'm sorry. Did I overstep?"

Every word Zaphriel tried to form got stuck behind the lump in his throat.

"I can rescind it if you want," Hiro continued. "I just had no idea how to repay you for what you did and I know nothing can replace the family you've lost but I thought..." He ran a hand through his hair. "I'm sorry. I'm rambling. You don't have to be her godfather."

"No!" Zaphriel pulled the certificate out of Hiro's range as he reached for it. "No. I love it." He sniffed and wiped his eyes. "I just didn't know how to respond. This is..." He studied the certificate. "This is the most beautiful thing anyone's ever done for me, Hiro, truly. Thank you."

The exorcist beamed. "You used my name." He raised a hand before Zaphriel could stutter an apology. "No take backs!" His phone rang, drawing his attention. He dug it out, read the name and answered. "Hi, love." He glanced at Zaphriel. "No, he's awake...No, I'll come down and meet you. I want to grab coffee anyway." Hiro got to his feet as he hung up. "Sarah and the kids are here to see you. Apparently, Matthew has been bouncing off the walls with worry." Zaphriel's still-panicked heart stilled and melted a bit. "He was worried about me?"

"He saw you take a knife to the gut." Hiro grabbed his jacket from the lounge chair as he gave Zaphriel a flabbergasted look. "Yes, he was worried."

"Mind grabbing me a coffee, too, if it's not too much trouble?"

Hiro scoffed. "No caffeine. You're still injured."

Zaphriel scoffed back. "I'm a demon."

"Yeah, an *injured* demon."

Hiro was gone and down the hall before Zaphriel could argue. To distract himself from the pressing silence, he opened the folder again and began to read the contract. By the end, his mouth had fallen open again and he had rubbed his eyes more than once to believe them.

He would be free. No more weekly check-ins or reports. He wouldn't have to darken the Order's doorstep at all outside of picking up assignments and they would pay him. Not a huge salary, of course—no one in this line of work made much—but enough that he'd have a pretty penny saved once Maryam was old enough to decide whether she wanted to stay within the Order or not.

He could build a life for her. He could build a life for his goddaughter.

"Zaphriel!"

He looked up just in time for Matthew to launch himself into Zaphriel's arms. The demon caught the boy and held him tight, ignoring the pangs of pain in his core as he felt across Matthew's back and his head.

"Matthew, be careful!" Sarah snapped, trying to pull the boy away.

"He's alright." Zaphriel gently loosened Sarah's grip. He released Matthew and held him out at arm's length to study him "You're alright? You're not hurt?"

"No." Matthew's face scrunched up around teary brown eyes and he sniffed. "But this was all my fault. I got you hurt because I wanted to go to that stupid exhibit." His bottom lip quivered as he choked back a sob.

"Oh, Matt. It's not." Zaphriel pulled him close and opened one arm for Maryam, who had started to whine to be let onto the bed. Sarah let her go to him, the apprehensive look still fixed on her face. "I had an amazing day with you and Maryam. One of the best I've had yet.

It wasn't your fault that there were entities there that wanted to hurt people. You couldn't have known."

Matthew sniffed and wiped his nose. "I didn't tell anyone about Maryam."

Zaphriel gave him the biggest, proudest smile he could muster. "See? You did amazing." He awkwardly waved the folder in his hand. "Plus, it's not all bad. I got a job out of it."

Hiro stood a little taller, a paper cup of coffee in his hand. "You decided to take it?"

Zaphriel looked down at Maryam, who had started to play with the bedsheets, trying to pull them over her head. When it wouldn't reach her red curls, she turned to inform Zaphriel, using words of her own making. Zaphriel grinned, savoring those green eyes that he would make sure would see a world outside the Order. A world where she would know she would be good enough.

He pulled her close and kissed her forehead. "What sort of godfather would I be if I didn't?"

Hiro grinned.

"Um, Zaph?" Matthew wrung his hands, his gaze shifting from the demons to his parents, then back. "I sort of told my parents about the swearing. Including the f-word."

Zaphriel turned to Sarah, one eyebrow arched. "Does this mean I'm never allowed to babysit again?"

Her husband and son also watched her, waiting for her final judgement.

Sarah shrugged. "It was an exceptional circumstance. Emotions were running high. I think a bit of grace would be acceptable in this case." A playful smirk tugged at her mouth. "Even for a demon."

***

Zaphriel spent entirely too long putzing around on the stairs in front of St. Mary's. It had been well established that he wasn't going to be struck down with lightning when he walked through those doors and, according to Hiro, the fact that he was now a recognized exorcist within the Order was all anyone could talk about, so everyone would know why he was alone, but it still felt unnatural walking in without Hiro as a buffer. He looked at his watch and massaged the back of his neck. Matthew got out of school in thirty minutes, which gave him more than enough time to pick up the cases—his *first* cases—then drive around the block to St. Mary's Interdenominational Academy. It wasn't anything he couldn't handle. In fact, he had *insisted* that he could handle it, but now that he was here...

"Zack, in? In?"

Zaphriel turned in time to see Maryam getting ready to slip her head between the bars of the rail along the stairs. He swooped down and scooped her up before she could follow through with her intention and undoubtedly get stuck. "No in," he said. Maryam whined and reached for the rail. Zaphriel blew a raspberry against her exposed stomach, making her squeal as he brought her upright. He watched her face light up, revealing more baby teeth than he remembered seeing the last time he had checked. The observation made him pause. He looked at the towering doors, then back at the few steps left for him to scale.

One day she was going to have to walk through them herself too, and Zaphriel would be damned (well, damned again) if anyone beyond them made her feel this unwelcome.

He took a deep breath, kissed Maryam on the forehead, and marched up the stairs and through the doors. Hiro had hastily scribbled directions to the proper office on the back of a shopping receipt, but the closer Zaphriel got, the more he knew the way.

He schooled his face into a polite, neutral expression, then knocked on Father Bob's door. The old man grumbled for him to come in. He didn't look particularly surprised to see Zaphriel, but he didn't look particularly pleased, either, as he stood with a weathered old briefcase and rounded his desk.

"Hiro told me you were coming," he said, handing the case to Zaphriel. "Dug this out of its resting place and dusted it off for you. It was mine when I first became an exorcist."

Zaphriel blinked and slowly took the case from him. "Th...Thank you—"

Father Bob waved the words away. "Can't have you carrying case files all willy-nilly." He gave Maryam a quick, calculated glance. "She looks well. Healthy. Human."

Zaphriel adjusted her on his hip. "She is."

Father Bob glanced from Maryam, to Zaphriel, then back several times before speaking. "Hiro told me what you did for her and his boy. That was very brave. Very selfless."

Zaphriel shrugged. "I did what anyone would do."

Father Bob gave an indignant snort. "You've already disarmed a good number of people in this institution with your heroics. No need to be humble, too." His expression grew shrewd. "You're a colleague now, so I'll speak to you as one." Father Bob narrowed his eyes. "I don't know what to make of you, Zaphriel the Treacherous."

"It's Zackary."

"What?"

"I'm going by Zackary now," Zaphriel explained. "Or Zack. Wanted to try something more human sounding for a while. Thought it might help put clients at ease. Maryam already calls me Zack, anyway."

Father Bob blinked; his feathers ruffled. "That just proves my point. What do I *do* with a demon like you?" He deflated a bit. "But you've proven to me that this universe isn't all it's been written to be and, as a learned man, I have a responsibility to change my view based on this new information." He looked away, as if embarrassed. "And I respect you enough to tell you so."

Zaphriel allowed a small smile to creep onto his face. "Thank you, Father. I appreciate that."

Father Bob waved Zaphriel's words away again. "Now, off with you." He headed back towards his desk. "You won't get any extensions on your assignments just because you're new."

"Of course. Have a good day, Father."

The old priest gave a grumble of acknowledgement as Zaphriel took his leave.

Back in the car, waiting for Matthew, Zaphriel send Hiro a text message, struggling with which button would give him which letter. "*I kno wat u did. Bob dosnt handl assignments.*"

A reply came back moments later. "*Prove it. :-)*"

Zaphriel chuckled, then turned to watch as kids began to pour out of the school. His phone buzzed and he looked down to find a message from Sarah. "*How r things?*"

Zaphriel answered, "*Fine. Alls well.*"

He turned to find Matthew walking towards the car and waved with a smile. His phone buzzed again with a message from Sarah.

"*Good. Youre a good godfather. Id hate to have to replace you.*"

Zaphriel chuckled nervously, not sure how serious she was. He looked up at Maryam in the rearview mirror and tugged gently on her cloaking spell. He peeled it back, ever so slightly. When the little girl looked up from her toy, a pair of long, horizontal goat-like pupils looked back at him.

She beamed, waved, and said, "Hi."

Zaphriel smiled back. "Hi, babygirl."

The opening of the passenger door broke Zaphriel's focus.

"Are Mom and Dad working?" Matthew asked, sliding into the car.

"No, they're at home. I actually asked if it would be okay if we went and got ice cream, since our last outing got a little botched."

Matthew's eyes lit up. "Seriously?"

Zaphriel started the car with a proud smirk. "Seriously."

As he pulled onto the road, he checked on Maryam. Her green eyes were human again. Normal. Safe. So long as they stayed that way, his words to Sarah would stay true.

Because this was his story, and this chapter was going to be a good one.

Acknowledgements

To my brilliant wife, Rozzie—thank you doing life with me, even the chaotic and unexpected parts like your husband deciding that he's going to self-publish a novel. You're best life partner I could have asked for and the cutest editor in the industry.

To Tulip—Neither *Angels & Exorcists* nor *Demons & Museums* would be as good as they are without your brilliant insights. You are a gift. The world gets a fuller glimpse of the infinite kaleidoscope that is God and Their love thanks to your and Sarah's presence in the Body of Christ.

To Kari (Look! You're the first listed fan!), Bellz, and Autumn — Thank you for rooting for this group of rejects since 2019 and all my random quips and brainstorms in your inboxes. You keep me going.

To Douglas Pratt and Amber D. Lewis — Thank you for emboldening me to take the leap to publish and thank you for dealing with my endless stream of questions. I couldn't have done it without you two! And thank you to everyone in the writing groups of Memphis for all your support, suggestions and encouragement!

To Mandy and Karin of *The Incoherent Fangirl Podcast* — Thank you, thank you, THANK YOU for having me on the show. It was an honor. You both are AMAZING and I can't wait to see you continue to do amazing things and read your books!

To those of you who took a chance on this zany little book because it showed up on your feed out of the blue, I can't thank you enough. We all know how many books are out there. From the bottom of my heart, thank you for coming along on this journey with my merry band of rejects.

And to those who have been hurt by those who tried to save your soul at the cost of your unique, beautiful light, I see you. You are loved and you are not alone.

Coming in February 2025

For the first time in his 150 years of life, Emrys Hemlock is enjoying a sense of routine. He has a stable job (a first for him), a reliable roof over his head, and his demon roommate, Zackary, is about to give into Emrys seductive wiles—it's only a matter of time.

But something fae and strange is killing young men on the frozen shores of Lake Superior, and the Rosary Order needs Emrys' and Zackary's help in stopping it.

The dangers Emrys and Zackary face will mean they have to trust each other, and Emrys has learned the hard way that trust can come with deadly consequences. Can Emrys' icy internal walls be strong enough to withstand the genuine sparks of affection he's beginning to feel for Zackary? Or will the walls melt, setting both Emrys' heart, and the investigation, alight with unholy fire?

Turn the page for a glimpse in the next book in the Rosary's Rejects saga:

Sirens & Snow: The Rosary Reject Novellas I

Emrys had never liked routine before. There was something unnerving about a string of days, weeks, and months where nothing went wrong. However, within the walls of Ectoplasm: Coffee and Spirits, the routine felt less like a house of cards ready to fall and more like a safe warm den that smelled of coffee, caramel, and hops.

He was four months into his most recent living arrangement and, with the exception of holidays, very little changed between one day and another: wake up, eat breakfast with Maryam, flirt with Zackary, work, squabble with Zackary, work again in the evening, most days—because, honestly, what else did he have to do?—make a few more passes at Zackary, then call it a night. And then, he'd get up and do it all over again. Much to his own surprise, he liked it that way.

"Em, do you have that chai?" Maryam asked from down the bar.

"It's on your left," Emrys replied, eyes locked on the foam he was meticulously pouring in the shape of a heart. It hardly mattered on to-go orders, given the lids, but he was determined to master it. He silently wondered if he should be horrified at what he had become as he placed a cardboard sleeve and a lid on the coffee, then decided it didn't matter as the cute Wayne State sophomore smiled at him.

Bright purple movement outside the front windows caught his eye. He watched as Alex, a fellow employee of Ectoplasm, sped-walked into the building, bundled from head to toe. Emrys shivered in the sudden sharp bite of February chill from the open door and longed for the millionth time for spring.

"Fuck, it's like *The Day After Tomorrow* out there," Alex said as they peeled off their garments and shook off the flecks of melted snow and ice.

"Nah, not enough people dying in the streets," Maryam chimed in.

Zackary flashed her a dirty look over his laptop as he typed away at the bar. "There are customers, Maryam Grace."

Maryam folded her arms. "That movie's almost as old as you are. Saying people die in it doesn't count as a spoiler."

"It's macabre and inappropriate," Zackary explained. Before Maryam could say anything even more macabre and inappropriate, Zackary turned his attention to Alex. "Is something wrong? You're not on the schedule until tomorrow."

"I wanted to talk to you about that, actually," Alex said, brushing melted droplets from their deep purple hair. "Would you be okay if I switch with someone on Valentine's Day?"

Maryam smirked as she leaned on the counter. "And why, pray tell, would *you* need Valentine's day off?"

Alex bristled. "Did I indicate that it was any of your business?"

Maryam's smirk grew with the realization that she'd struck a nerve. "If you want *me* to take it, I want deets."

Alex turned to Emrys. "What about you?"

"Don't know yet," Emrys leaned on the counter across from Zackary. "*Someone* hasn't told me what our plans are."

Zackary began typing again, eyes on the screen. "That's because *someone* will be will be busy with a bar full of awkward first dates and lonely people looking to score thanks to this gaudy, insufferable holiday. The emergency escape rideshares aren't going to call themselves. Besides, that's your night to close, remember?"

"Fine by me." Emrys tipped Zackary's screen forward so that the demon couldn't see the contents. "What are we doing afterwards?"

"Going to bed."

"Together?"

Zackary gave Emrys a sickly sweet smile as he gently pried Emrys' fingers off his computer and opened the screen again. "I'll treat you to a nice cup of tea and you can tell me all about your day. How about that?"

Emrys scrunched his face in disgust. Months ago, when Zackary said that he was going to flirt sweetly whenever Emrys flirt dirty, he had expected him to give up after a day or two, but he was still at it, meeting Emrys' passes with sugar more often that barbs, throwing Emrys off kilter with his heart racing.

Emrys scoffed. "Gods. Why are you such an old man?"

"I'm not. Why won't you let me take you out to dinner?"

Emrys glared, decided to not give Zackary the satisfaction of a reply, then turned to Alex. "Sorry, love. Looks like I'm on the schedule already."

"Now, this is going to sound crazy," Maryam interjected, "But you could try talking to an employee who *isn't* me or Emrys. Pretty sure the rest of the staff thinks you're mute."

Alex groaned, then shoved their hands in their pockets. "Fine. Take my shift, Maryam, and I'll text you tonight."

"Hell yeah." Maryam pumped a fist. "A glimpse into Alex's mysterious personal life."

Alex checked their phone and headed back for the door. "Tell anyone what I tell you and I'm hexing the shit out of you and your first born."

"Joke's on you—I'm not having kids."

"Tell that to the hex." Alex held the door for a pair of customers and slid into a parked beat-up old car. Maryam welcomed the newcomers with a smile and asked if they'd been to Ectoplasm before, leaving Emrys to watch Zackary as he continued to work.

The demon had grown less reclusive in the months since Maryam's celestial powers had been unleashed. He had slowly begun to work on miscellaneous administrative work at the bar rather than his office, provided the place wasn't nearing max capacity. He and Emrys even got along, provided Emrys wasn't on his bullshit, but that wasn't about to stop in earnest any time soon. Not really. It wasn't his fault he wanted what he wanted—and what Emrys wanted was those green eyes locked on him, those strawberry blonde waves tangled in Emrys hands, as Zackary did all sorts of unholy things to him with that chiseled body.

"Keep staring at me and I'm writing you up for harassment," Zackary said without missing a key stroke.

Emrys snorted. "I wasn't staring at you."

Zackary gave him a doubtful look.

"I was gazing forlornly. There's a difference."

A ghost of a grin crept onto Zackary's face as he continued to work.

That was the first genuine smile Emrys had seen from him all day. Something about being the one to draw it from the broody demon sent butterflies fluttering though Emrys' stomach, making him giddy and nauseous in equal measure, which meant he needed a distraction. He took a rag from the bucket of sudsy water below the counter and began wiping the spot beside Zackary, though no one had sat there in over an hour. "Do you really think Valentine's Day is gaudy and insufferable?" he asked.

"I suppose not." Zackary sat back, arms crossed, as he studied the screen and ran his thumb back and forth across his chin. "I guess I've always known love to be a quiet thing," he said. "While I suppose there's nothing wrong with loud, exuberant displays of affection, I feel like it cheapens it a bit." He shrugged and went back to typing. "That's just me, though."

Emrys smirked. "Okay, but what if there was a *good* reason for Valentine's Day to get loud?"

Zackary flashed him a dirty look. His gaze slipped passed Emrys and locked on the front door, his expression shifting to confusion. "Father Wilhelm?"

Emrys turned. He didn't know a Wilhelm, but anyone that went by Father was bound to be from the Rosary Order, meaning the visit was work related, meaning it made no sense that this Father Wilhelm would show up at Ectoplasm. Emrys was stunned that anyone at the Order even knew where the place was.

The classic black cassock gave Father Wilhelm away. He was an older white man, pushing his mid-fifties if Emrys was to wager a guess, with peppery hair that still held a hint of its original deep brown hue along his strong hairline. His smile was soft and genuine, betraying that he was as comfortable walking into the bar as if he had walked through the doors of a church. If his expression and loose body language didn't say as much, his eyes would have. There was a sparkle within their hazel hue that Emrys liked instantly, along with the rest of the priest.

Father Wilhelm was a bit old in mortal years for Emrys' taste, but there was a first time for everything, he supposed.

"Afternoon, Zackary." The priest removed his scarf with a hint of a chuckle. "Don't look so excited to see me."

Zackary shut his laptop, along with his slightly gaped mouth, and stepped off the bar stool. "Sorry. It's always a pleasure, but I don't think anyone from the Order has ever paid us a visit before."

"Oh, I did several months ago," Father Wilhelm said. "When I delivered a letter to Maryam apologizing for the Order's mistreatment and offering her a job in our ranks."

Zackary scowled towards his goddaughter, who was busy wiping a table at the other end of the bar. "Funny. She's never mentioned that before."

The priest chuckled. "Oh, no. I didn't mean to get her in trouble."

"Well, if you didn't, she'd find a way into it on her own." Zaphriel sighed. "What can I do for you, Father?"

"A rather unique case came in this morning," Father Wilhelm said. "One I think you two would be uniquely capable of handling."

Zaphriel's eyebrows raised. "You mean me and Maryam?" He folded his arms. "Between the fact that she's only ever helped me begrudgingly and the fact that she turned down your job, it might be a hard sell, Father."

"Oh, I'm not done trying to convince Maryam yet, but she's not who I'm talking about." Father Wilhelm's gaze fell on Emrys with a curiously mischievous glint. "I'm talking about Mr. Hemlock here."

FOLLOW ME ON SOCIAL MEDIA!

FINNELY.RAY   FINNELYRAY

FINNELYRAY
@GMAILCOM

KOFI.COM/
FINNELYRAY

AUTHOR_FINNELY.RAY

SUMMON UPDATES, CONTENT AND MORE!

But Wait! There's More!

Want access to a swoon-worthy bonus scene?
Use the QR code below to download Chapter 27.5 from my Kofi Shop.
While you're there, check out some sweet merch. Some of it's hand made!

Want to be first in line for beta reads, ARC Calls, and free books from other awesome authors? Sign up for my email newsletter! All it costs is your immortal soul!

(I'm kidding.)
(About the free books things. Not the soul thing.)